STRANGER AT THE GATE

ALSO BY JOHN HEARNE

Voices Under the Window
Stranger at the Gate
The Faces of Love
The Autumn Equinox
Land of the Living
The Sure Salvation

JOHN HEARNE

STRANGER AT THE GATE

THE CAYUNA QUARTET: I

INTRODUCTION BY
F.S.J. Ledgister

PEEPAL TREE

First published in Great Britain in 1956
by Faber and Faber Ltd
Republished in 2020 by
Peepal Tree Press Ltd
17 King's Avenue
Leeds LS6 1QS
England

Copyright © 1956, 2020 Shivaun Hearne
Introduction F.J.S. Legister © 2020

ISBN13: 9781845234546

All rights reserved
No part of this publication may be
reproduced or transmitted in any form
without permission

For none of us liveth to himself,
and no man dieth to himself.
Romans xiv, 7.

For
F. R. AUGIER

INTRODUCTION

F.J.S. LEDGISTER

I

I was a thirteen-year-old schoolboy when I opened my first West Indian novels (excluding novels for children, of which I had read a few). These were *The Obeah Man* (1964) by Ismith Khan, and *Land of the Living* (1961) by John Hearne. Khan's urban Trinidad did not speak to the rural Jamaica I'd been living in and observing over the previous year, but Hearne's fictive Cayuna did. It helped, of course, that, like his narrator, Stefan Mahler, I was an immigrant and seeing Jamaica with immigrant eyes. Quite how Hearne was able to pull off the trick of seeing his homeland through the eyes of an outsider and keeping it plausible throughout the novel, I was not sure. He did it, however, with great elegance of style.

I was drawn to Hearne's novels, and read those available to me – including the thrillers he wrote together with his friend Morris Cargill about a fictional Jamaican secret service whose dashing agents, Robin Blackmore and Jassy Vane, managed to carry off major capers – as soon as I could lay hands on them. His mastery of style, his ability to move the reader along whether with a piece of sophisticated description or with a dirty joke is fully developed in those three novels.[1] Indeed, we can see an arc of stylistic development between his first novel, *Voices Under the Window* (1955), and his last published novel, the magnificently written *The Sure Salvation* (1985). *Voices* is his only mainstream novel set in a real Caribbean country, Jamaica. His thrillers certainly are, but the last of them, *The Checkerboard Caper*, is partly set in a fictional state, Abari, on the South American coast.

Abari appears again for a brief moment at the end of *The Sure Salvation*. For me this raises a question: Did the fictive Caribbean of John Hearne's imagination exist alongside, or under, the actual islands and continental adjuncts? Certainly, in the novels, ships sail from Jamaica to Cayuna at a speed that suggests that in another day they'd make landfall in Trinidad, in Barbados, St Lucia, or another eastern Caribbean isle. Cayuna is no great distance from Navidad, St Pierre and Nuevo Aragón, all three, like Cayuna, products of Hearne's mind. It's also not so far from Cuba, two hundred miles southeast of it, in fact, which, like Jamaica, is a real place, unless, perhaps, it is a product of some larger fiction in which all of us are taking part.

In reality, all of these fictive places are calques of actual locations. Abari of Guyana, where Hearne worked in the late 1950s, and where there is an Abari River. Navidad of Cuba, St Pierre of Haiti, Nuevo Aragón – a bare mention in *Stranger at the Gate* – of the Dominican Republic. Cayuna, of course, is Jamaica with the serial numbers rather roughly filed off. When I read *Land of the Living* for the first time, I could not help but notice that I was located, according to the map inside the cover, in the parish of Arcadia. *Et in Arcadia ego*.

Why did Hearne have to create a fake Jamaica, when the real Jamaica was there in front of him? Couldn't he just have invented fake neighbourhoods or fake parishes, in the style of a Victorian novelist imagining English counties into existence, rather than a whole imaginary country? I don't think he could have. Every novel that deals with questions of change and development in a small country, and Jamaica, for all that it is the most tentacular of nations, is a small country, can too easily become a *roman à clef*. Is Roy McKenzie in *Stranger at the Gate* based on Richard Hart, an actual figure in Jamaica's political life at the time, who was, like McKenzie, a solicitor and deeply interested in history? There are obvious differences: Hart's father was also a solicitor, and not the owner of a furniture store, for one, and McKenzie's service in the RAF, alongside his boyhood friend Carl Brandt, during the Second World War, is another. Hart did not leave Jamaica during the war, but spent some time in detention there as a political prisoner. There's also the dedication of the book to the historian

Roy Augier, now Sir Roy, who served alongside Hearne during the war, although he did not go to school with him, and who played a role in Jamaican public life in the 1950s as an advocate of the West Indies Federation. Was McKenzie Augier? I doubt it very much, just as I doubt that he was altogether Hart. Again, Hearne awards Cayuna its own microscopic Communist Party a couple of decades before Jamaica actually acquired one. Actually, in what might be termed a magnificently West Indian fashion, in the 1970s two orthodox communist parties arose at once, both owing allegiance to Moscow. Earlier, the People's Freedom Movement, led by Hart and Ferdinand Smith, the latter previously a leading figure in the US Communist Party and labour movement in the 1930s and 1940s, was neither the only political organisation on the radical left in 1950s Jamaica, nor was it quite a full-fledged communist party.

There is another issue, one that does not come up in this the first novel of the quartet, but does in the latter three. Jamaica is a real place with real people, just a couple of million of them at independence in 1962, many of them prickly. To write about the real Jamaica might invite someone to claim that they were being libelled. This might go doubly hard if the person claiming to be libelled was a politician. And Hearne was not an apolitical writer. He was a man who had serious commitments within Jamaica's politics, and to have suggested that public figures in Jamaica were guilty of the sort of peculation that Cayuna's Thomas Littleford (in *Land of the Living*) gets up to could have had most unfortunate results for Hearne, though his lawyers might have prospered.

Even so, the artifice of creating a fictive version of Jamaica cannot but make the reader wonder what, beyond the avoidance of litigation, is being pointed at. One of the important elements in *Stranger* is the way that Hearne brings to the fore one of the most important political tensions in modern Jamaican history: that between those who think that conflict between socioeconomic classes is determinative and those who believe that struggle between the races will determine the outcomes of history. We see this in the way that Tiger Johnson responds to the efforts of Cayuna's communists, and how he is willing to betray them when he believes it is to his advantage, because his primary ideological concern is with the condition of black people and with their historic ethnic identity as Africans. People of mixed race like McKenzie, regardless of their political pretensions, are not to be trusted by the Tiger Johnsons of this world.

Rachel Ascom in *The Faces of Love* (1957) illustrates the precarity of being mixed race in a completely different way. Ascom, the daughter of a black police officer and a white peasant (a combination entirely possible both in Hearne's fictional Cayuna and in the real Jamaica), is a woman on her way up in the newly prosperous 1950s, and like all newly arrived members of the upper-middle classes, she finds herself both admired and regarded with contempt. It is interesting to see her through the eyes of the narrator, Andrew Fabricus, a member of a former plantation family, who observes her manoeuvrings with sympathetic pity. Underlying Ascom's view of the world we find the '72 Riots (an analogue for the Jamaican Morant Bay Rebellion of 1865), and a father tortured by the colonial authorities while her white grandmother looked on in silence.

The meanings of race and power in the colonial West Indies were not opaque to Hearne, and he did not turn away from them. A social and economic climber, of mixed race like so many of Hearne's central characters, Rachel carries inside her both anger and resentment against the horror of racial and colonial oppression, and a real capacity for love that crosses racial boundaries. We see this in her triangular relationship with the Englishman, Lovelace, and the Cayunan, Jojo Rygin (whose surname, alluding as it does to a famous bandit of the 1940s, is a Jamaican in-joke).[2] But it is also pertinent to see that Hearne recognises that Ascom's status is precarious not only because she looks to rise to positions of wealth and influence previously monopolised by people much paler than herself, but also because she is trying to do it in a society in the process of decolonisation, in which African Jamaicans are also actively seeking racial and social justice. Here, Hearne did not hide from the fact that racial mixture in Jamaica primarily meant an African majority that had been subordinate in economic, social and cultural terms to minority white and mixed-race groups and was demanding change. Not least, Hearne recognised that Rachel has to struggle because she is a woman. As such, her road to success is still based on her ability to manipulate more powerful men with the tools available to her. This leads both to her success and to her downfall, and to that of her sometime lover, Jojo Rygin, himself a person of mixed race and social precarity, a man of great ability, whose potential for greatness, it turns out, is limited by a tragic flaw.

Hearne writes with an acute awareness that his novels are set in a decade of rapid change. Revolution is a theme that surfaces again and again in his work, though it generally takes place off-stage in the real world setting of Cuba through the real agency of Fidel Castro and his comrades in the Sierra Maestra. Nicholas Stacey (in *An Autumn Equinox*), a veteran of Latin American political struggles, believes revolution to be ultimately futile, a casting off of old chains and their replacement with new. Young Jim Diver, in the same novel, does not; with all of the enthusiasm of the young, Diver sees only the progressive vision. He fails to see the hard political calculation that goes alongside it. Diver's effort to run an underground press fails, and he is warned off. Hearne himself seems to be suggesting the futility of revolution through the image of Pierre-Auguste, the Haitian pensionary constantly plotting a return to his homeland. In *Stranger at the Gate*, the whole impetus for the novel derives from a failed revolution and the need to rescue the revolutionary leader, Etienne, from the fictitious St Pierre where his life is threatened by a counter-revolutionary invasion – an allusion, no doubt to the USA's support for the anti-communist dictatorship of Francois Duvalier in Haiti.

The relationship of race and class, the precarity of mixed-race status, emerge in *The Autumn Equinox* as they do in its precursors. Eleanor Stacey's concern regarding their servant Sonny's apparently feckless behaviour, and his cruelty to Pierre-Auguste; Sonny's resentment of Cayuna's power structure; Nicholas Stacey's relationship with his brother, Lionel, and mother, Judith, are all part of a complex web of race and class. Nicholas and Eleanor may be, both racially and socially, at the top of society, but their position there, as people of white appearance but mixed race, is uncertain. Nicholas Stacey has, after a lifetime, made peace with his past. His daughter, Eleanor Stacey, for all that she is in so many respects a worldly young woman, retains a degree of innocence.

As well as a character such as the American Jim Diver in *The Autumn Equinox*, who is one of the narrative voices in this multi-voiced novel, Hearne essays another, and more alien, outsider as the narrator in *Land of the Living*. Stefan Mahler is established immediately as European, a Jewish escapee from the Holocaust that has swallowed up all the rest of his family. He is also, unlike any of Hearne's other protagonists, a scientist, a zoologist at Cayuna University. All of this is relevant to the direct clash between Europe and Africa that occurs when a member of the Afrocentric Sons of Sheba movement (Rastafari, not at all disguised) destroys a fish tank containing specimens Mahler and some of his students have collected for study. We are exposed directly to the mystical language of rebuke and aspiration of the Sons of Sheba. Mahler dismisses it, to a student, as the effects of ganja; he fails to see that we have hit a moment of true seriousness in the novel: Western science, and its dominant, all-seeing eye, has encountered an African rejection of its gaze.

Mahler, indeed, does not take Cayuna entirely seriously. While he recoils from his English colleague's description of the place, and all other such colonies, as "Surbiton in the sun" – albeit with a rather longer commute into central London – he looks at end-days colonial Cayuna with a degree of detachment and distance that comes from a lens shaped by other ways of seeing: by the cultures of Germany and England; by the facts of his whiteness and Jewishness; and by the scientific discipline to which he is committed. At the same time, Cayuna catches him in its arms, or rather her arms, those first of Bernice Heneky, the black bar owner who becomes his lover, and then those of Joan Culpepper, the white flight attendant who becomes his wife. Further, his relationship with Oliver Hyde, editor of one of the two local newspapers, is crucial in integrating Mahler as a curious observer of Cayuna's middle-class society and, as a newly arrived outsider, someone who is motivated to find out about Cayuna's politics and its recent past. One can see this as Hearne's way of making connections to the earlier novels.

We can see most clearly in *Land of the Living*, the last published of the quartet, how Hearne places threads, or, more accurately, thick ropes of connection to the other Cayuna novels. There's the mention of Rachel Ascom; the fact that Oliver and Sybil Hyde live in what was Jojo Rygin's house; the reference to Isaac Azoud (patterned on Abraham Issa, a Jamaican entrepreneur of Levantine Arab origin) in all four of the Cayuna books, though he does not appear in any of them. As such, *Land of the Living* creates the kind of network of reference that strengthens the fictive illusion that Cayuna has an existence beyond the pages of the novels. By this stage in the quartet, the reader is embedded there. Given what we know about the Afrocentric gangster Tiger Johnson (last seen in *Stranger at the Gate* attempting to see what he can get for betraying the communist Roy McKenzie), we can predict that the Afrocentric preacher, Marcus Heneky, Bernice's father, will join with the Sons of Sheba and, together with Tiger Johnson, join in a revolutionary uprising designed to bring power to the black (as opposed to mixed-race) people of Cayuna. It is a revolt ripped from the recent headlines in Jamaica, being loosely based on an attempted uprising centred on the congregation of an Afrocentric preacher, Claudius Henry and members of his family in 1960. Henry called himself "the Repairer of the Breach" (Isaiah 58 xii), while Heneky, in imitation, is made to appropriate the style of "Healer of the Wound" – for which, alas, there does not appear to be a Biblical citation. Henry's revolt failed and he was sent to prison, but he went on to play an important role in the election of the radical government of Michael Manley in 1972. In 1960, activist Afrocentric struggle still only appealed to a minority of African Jamaicans, but it is clear that Hearne saw this element as a threat to the kind of Jamaica he loved and wished could be preserved.

The story of the Cayuna quartet comes to an end with the deaths of Bernice and Marcus Heneky, cut down by a Son of Sheba with rapid cutlass strokes, just at the moment Marcus Heneky's revolt has been brought to a peaceful end by his daughter. Stefan Mahler may be left to live happily ever after, but Hearne leaves us to feel that Cayuna's fate might not be so happy.

Across the four novels (plus three short stories set in Cayuna[3]) there are key themes that echo again and again. One of these is race, in particular the relationship between black and white. But also the relationship between black and not-so-black. Here,

Cayuna is shown as approaching a point of change in its history. Hitherto, its life, public and private, has been dominated by Eurocentric people of pallor. Hearne could see, clearly, though perhaps not unemotionally, that the future of Cayuna (and, for that matter, of Jamaica) did not belong to them. It was the majority people of unashamed African heritage who owned the future. The only question was how they would own it and shape it.

The voices of the subordinate race are heard throughout the quartet. There is Tiger Johnson admonishing the communists that he will go along with their class struggle only as long as it marches with his understanding of racial struggle; there's Sonny in *The Autumn Equinox* who sees himself as destined to be exalted in a future in which black men *like himself* (but not like the pathetic Pierre-Auguste) are in charge; or Jojo Rygin and Rachel Ascom confidently treating white men as equals; or members of the Sons of Sheba speaking as if the white man, Mahler, did not even exist. Hearne has not the least trouble providing us with examples of black self-assertion that cover a range from the self-confident to the self-interested.

Furthermore, he puts into the mouth of a white man, a policeman at that, Superintendant Barraclough in *Land of the Living*, something of an understanding of the crisis faced by intelligent black and mixed-race youth in an overwhelmingly black, just beginning to decolonise, Caribbean territory in the middle decades of the twentieth century. This is a society that has lived through several centuries of a colonialism whose racist, Eurocentric assumptions have remained part of its education system and dominant ideology. As Barraclough tells Mahler:

> "Oh, I know what you mean," he said. "Othello."
> "What?"
> "Othello."
> The massive, nearly animal face, florid as a freshly cut steak, was oddly shy, like that of a man admitting a risible vice. " It's an idea I've thought of occasionally. Did you ever imagine you were a Walter Scott knight, Mahler? Or Robinson Crusoe? Or, later on, one of the real men, like a great general or a politician? Figures like that from stories or life?"

"Yes. Of course. Plus a few like the Maccabees that you wouldn't have heard of."

"Now, take the case here," he said. "You're black, and as a child you'll imagine yourself being all those people. Part of a story or real history. But then you grow up and if you're sensitive at all you find that you can't. You're not part of it. Stories and history that are part of a big pattern don't belong to you. You joined the pattern as a slave. Very late in the day. Although you're now part of it and can't ever escape. You don't have any legends or history that's your own to build on. Except Othello. The only black face that everybody accepts that has any dignity. I think it's a hell of a fix to be in. It's why you get somebody like Heneky. Even 'Tiger' Johnson, although he'd be a crook anywhere he was born. I mean, they're both trying to find a state where they can be Robinson Crusoe instead of always being Man Friday." (*Land of the Living*, p. 260)

It doesn't matter who or what you are, you have no heroes in the white man's world, except the tragic figure who kills himself after he has been misled into distrusting his wife by his seemingly most faithful officer. Of course, this is a white man's view, presented by a white man, and it misses the fact that the young black man might have other heroes than Iago's tragic victim, that, in fact, there might be heroes springing up from the ranks of the previously ignored, or that the young black man knows that Africa has a past of cultural richness and intellectual complexity. Again, we may note how in *Stranger at the Gate*, the conversations between the wealthy, white landowner, Carl Brandt, and Henri Etienne, the black communist on the run from a counter-coup, whom Brandt is temporarily and reluctantly sheltering, are some of the most nakedly human and moving interactions in the novel.

What is intriguing is that Hearne manages to get race as right as he did. He was not black, did not share in the experiences of poor black Jamaicans, yet managed, in the Cayuna novels, to get the voice and sensibility of black Jamaicans onto the page.

The reverse side, of course, is that he is undoubtedly more knowledgeable and inward in his presentation of the attitudes and sensibility of the paler part of Cayuna's population, though he is careful, from the beginning, to make most of his protagonists people of mixed race. It is noteworthy that when the narrator is unambiguously white, that narrator – Jim Diver, Stefan Mahler – is not Cayunan, and is being constructed by Hearne out of his reading, his experience of the outside world, and his imagination. The characters he is most inward with are those like the plantation owner, Carl Brandt, a man who has a dash of African in his ancestry who does not seek to suppress the fact. Brandt also gets along with Jojo Rygin, once introduced to him, and is clearly impressed with Rygin's endurance and possession of what people like Brandt regarded as the manly virtues, as is the near-white narrator, Andrew Fabricus. Rygin's acceptance by Brandt is one sign of the value of manliness, and masculine conceptions of virtue, as ways in which, we may suppose, Hearne hoped the barrier of race could be overcome at the end of the colonial epoch. In the eyes of the white or near-white upper class and upper-middle-class men who go hunting with Rygin, and who ride out the hurricane on the mountain with him, both his skill at bird hunting – a quintessentially masculine activity in late colonial and early post-colonial Jamaica, and thus in Cayuna – and his courage and hardihood during the storm, mark him as worthy of their respect and admiration. It is, fundamentally, a rurally-rooted and patriarchal vision of society.

But whilst there are aspects of the colonial world that Hearne clearly loved – as seen in his sensuous delight in the domestic interiors of the Brandt estate and its traditions of hospitality – I don't believe Hearne's attitude to the end of the colonial West Indian world is hostile or his acceptance of the inevitability of its end is grudging. There is none of the resentment, hostility, and not-so-veiled contempt that is on display in the white Barbadian novelist J.B. Emtage's *Brown Sugar* (1966). At the time of writing the novels of this period, at least, Hearne appears to have welcomed change, recognising that people who resemble himself are no longer going to be at the centre of life in the new, post-colonial West Indies. His characters are finding ways to adapt to a changing age, either by moving the changes along faster, as Roy McKenzie or Jim Diver seek to do, or by working within the system to ameliorate matters, as Andrew Fabricus eventually does. (However, as noted below, by the late 1970s,

Hearne had almost wholly fallen out with the direction that Jamaica was taking under the radical decolonising politics of Michael Manley.)

Another central element in the four novels is the value Hearne places on liberal democracy. Cayuna is approaching independence – an unspoken but essential element in the overall thrust of the narrative – and is doing so as a democracy. This is particularly the case in the novels in which Andrew Fabricus and Oliver Hyde appear as significant characters – *The Faces of Love* and *Land of the Living*. It is also a key element in the short story "The Wind in this Corner", a story that illuminates both those novels without affecting either. (The story is about the internal affairs of a political party and in the process it suggests that Cayuna and Jamaica are not exactly parallel, no matter how similar they may seem). Hearne knew that democracy was not possible in a country such as Cayuna/Jamaica unless the majority, formerly a subject race, is brought to power, and this knowledge both underlies and flows through his entire body of work. Hearne was not, and could not have pretended to be, a working-class black Jamaican, but his sympathies were with them as his fellow citizens.

What he wanted, there can be no doubt, was a country where black Jamaicans could flourish without either being oppressed by a greedy white or near-white upper class, or being taken for a ride by black confidence tricksters in the guise of nationalist politicians; nor did he want a country where the formerly oppressed black majority sought to turn the tables on the white and pale brown minority. It is not evident, though, that Hearne felt confident that what he hoped for would come to pass. Jojo Rygin, in *The Faces of Love* (1957), manages to show men of the upper class that he, too, is a man, but he ends up as an Othello figure whose Iago is also his Desdemona. Yet, there is no evidence to think that Hearne saw the fictive fate of this avatar of black freedom and creativity as the inevitable future of people like Jojo in Jamaican reality. I don't think that Hearne saw himself as a prophet. Nonetheless, the figure of Jojo Rygin, stabbed in the back, metaphorically, by the love of his life and the political leadership of his country, is one of the handiest metaphors for what has happened to the creative energies of mixed-race and black Jamaicans over the past six decades as their leaders and their fellow-citizens have, again and again, failed them at crucial moments of history.

Yet one cannot duck the reality that a good number of Hearne's Jamaican readers might well conclude that he fails them. It is all very well to suggest, fictively, that the barrier of race can be overcome by male bonding, whether out shooting birds in the mountains or surviving a hurricane. Others will say that we no longer live in a world in which it can be assumed that only men have agency. I don't think that Hearne's women are mere adjuncts to men: Sheila Brandt (Sheila Pearce as she was in *Stranger at the Gate*) is an independent-minded and physically tough lady; Eleanor Stacey is an energetic young woman who is trying to figure out where she stands in the world; Rachel Ascom is going to leave poverty behind, but somewhere along the line is going to develop the capacity to love; Bernice Heneky knows her own mind and is not going to be awed by mere religious verbiage; and Joan Culpepper may be in love with Stefan Mahler, but she's still going to sleep with Lester Pow because Stefan mistreated him. However, these women characters are, undoubtedly, limited by the world into which they are imagined, and it takes both some reading between the lines, and not assuming that what male characters have to say about these women is Hearne's view of them, to avoid the view that in his fiction women are invariably secondary to men. There is a character such as the bright young Barbadian biology student, Lois Gay in *Land of the Living*, who represents a future in which the West Indies will stand as equal with the West with regard to the ability of its people in the sciences. That she is a woman is an important point, for it means that Hearne recognised a central fact in the life of the Anglophone Caribbean: it was young black women, more than young black men, who took advantage of the postwar expansion in educational opportunities. It is these women who, in turn, will educate the first post-colonial generation. Hearne hints at this, but then lets it go.

His Cayuna as a post-World War II West Indian colony is a place of rapid economic development, a place where old, bad certainties are being undone. The new uncertainties, including the changing role of women, attract Hearne's attention, but all he can do is to hint at the future. I think he suspects that this future is going to involve far more radical change than has been seen so far, given what he evidently felt was being done to Cayuna's most creative and able people such as Rachel Ascom and Jojo Rygin, but there is also the anger that men like Marcus Heneky and Tiger Johnson express, a rejection of everything to do with Europe in the Caribbean, and this, I think, leads Hearne towards a more pessimistic view of the future and the valedictory tone of regret in his writing.

II

What we haven't noted up to now has been Hearne's mastery of style and manner. Consider the following passage from *The Autumn Equinox* that follows the consciousness of the elderly returnee to Cayuna, Nicholas Stacey:

> Nowadays I sleep lightly. Perhaps my body, apprehensive of the long sleep balefully hovering just beyond the horizon of my days, snatches me from oblivion to regard every passing wind, restive leaf, footfall, raised voice or amorous dog. The body never learns: it fights blindly, ludicrously, hideously to the last unconvinced rattle, trying to rally an army long since scattered, dead or surrendered, certain to the end that it can pull off some cunning ambush and surprise death as it waits in massed battalions along the road.
>
> I lie awake in this long night, listening to the light rain that has roused me as it advances fastidiously across the foothills and taps at the roof... my roof and Eleanor's. No, hers alone. As everything I have and do nowadays is for her alone. How ridiculous to try to live for another; and how impossible not to. The body again: with low, animal craft seizing this last chance for assertion, deceiving all the accumulations of experience; holding your intelligence to ransom with the thought of her alone in the world. As if we were not all solitaries. (p. 37)

We are drawn in and swayed by the beauty of the language, the elegance, the attitude classically Stoic enough to have appealed to Marcus Aurelius or Epictetus. This is so very clearly the mind of a man full of years and experience (someone like myself, who will never see his sixtieth birthday again). Hearne was thirty-three when the novel was published, evidence of his capacity to imagine characters beyond his experience. However, the declaration that it is impossible not to love, and the dedication of the novel to "Leeta", his wife Elizabeth, may have something to do with each other.

But it is also clear that, beyond experience and imagination, Hearne was a literary novelist who responded to the writing of others. It is easy to tell, for instance, when we read *The Autumn Equinox*, that Hearne had been reading the American Beat poets and novelists of the 1950s. That would certainly permit him to write a sentence of dialogue like "Our groove is really a grave", both gnomic and pompous, and so right for his character, Jim Diver, a young man who turns out to be out of his depth. Peter Conroy, the ganja-loving beatnik who, along with Diver, is printing a newspaper in support of Fidel Castro's guerrillas in the mountains of eastern Cuba, anticipates the hippies who would turn up on Jamaica's shores a decade later. We can also tell that Hearne had been reading Hemingway. The Latin American settings, and the formality of dialogue in parts of the novel, intended to convey the flavour of Spanish, echo the work of that writer. Hearne did not speak Spanish and gives that away by his weak grasp of Spanish onomastics.

III

None of the above explains why I, specifically, am writing this introduction. I had the good fortune to have had John Hearne as teacher, mentor, friend, and research informant at different points in my life. I am part of that first post-colonial generation, one foot in the past, the other landing in the future. Cayuna was a recognisable world because it was, to a degree, still the world I lived in in independent Jamaica at the end of the 1960s.

By the time I met Hearne and became his student, in 1976, Jamaica was moving away from that colonial model, and Hearne played a part in that. I was also trying to learn my way in a complicated, rapidly changing country and world. My friendship with Hearne meant that I had opportunities not often available to others. It landed me a job at the Gleaner Company, Jamaica's main newspaper publisher, and one of John Hearne's longest lasting employers, from which vantage point I had a fascinating view of a country in crisis at the end of the nineteen-seventies and the beginning of the nineteen-eighties. It was through Hearne, also, that I met the journalist John Maxwell, one of the most extraordinary figures in late twentieth century Jamaica, and another friend whom I cherished.

And John Hearne nearly got me killed. It was in early 1979. I was, briefly, unemployed, and at a loose end. Hearne had received a letter from a woman living on the western fringes of Kingston. It concerned the persecution of opposition supporters who lived in publicly-owned housing. At the time, Hearne was a newspaper columnist with *The Gleaner*, with a reputation for criticising the government, and so a natural recipient of such an appeal. He sent me, with the letter, to find out what was going on. No one at the sender's address or near it had heard of the woman or knew anything about her. They were very interested to hear that I'd received a letter from her, and wanted to see the letter, being pacified only by my assurance that I didn't have it on me. I found the whole affair puzzling. However, I did have a friend who lived near the area, so I went over to his apartment to see if he could shed some light on the matter. He could. He asked to see the letter, and when he read it he made remarks about various kinds of cloth in patwa that are as profane as anything in Jamaican speech. Then he compared the letter to "an atomic bomb" and said that if it had been found on me I would have been killed. Between the time the letter had been sent to Hearne and the time I visited the neighbourhood, there had been a forced transfer of population and where there had previously been opposition supporters, there were now government supporters. This had been managed without drawing the attention of the press (in other cases there had been considerable visibility). I then had to go back and explain this all to Hearne.

In all innocence, he had sent me to do his legwork on a possible story – and it remained only a *possible* story, for none of it ever got written until now – where the risk was truly greater than the reward. On the other hand, it was through Hearne that I had what may have been my greatest political impact on the world. I had read, in the *New Statesman*, of the arrest of the Kenyan writer Ngugi wa Thiong'o. I went to Hearne and asked if there was anything that could be done about it. At that point, in 1978, Hearne was alienated from the ruling People's National Party, though many of its leading members had been his friends for years. He did not hesitate, but phoned Dudley Thompson, then minister for national security, discussed the matter with him and asked for his good offices. (Thompson had been one of the lawyers who had defended Kenyan president Jomo Kenyatta when the British put him on trial for treason a quarter century earlier.) Thompson agreed. A few weeks later, Hearne called me into his office. He showed me a letter he had received from Thompson enclosing copies of letters he had received from Charles Njonjo, his Kenyan counterpart, and from Kenyatta himself, the latter in the man's own hand. Hearne was on the outs with the Jamaican government, but he was still influential enough to get Thompson to enquire about the condition of Ngugi, and receive assurances from Njonjo and Kenyatta that he was being well-treated.

Hearne's anger with that government, his alienation from a political party he had supported from the early 1950s onwards, had been triggered in 1977 by the report of a Commission of Inquiry into the so-called Orange Lane fires of May 1976, during which opposition supporters were forced back into burning buildings by pro-government gangsters and the fire brigade had been forcibly prevented from putting out the blaze at publicly-owned housing in downtown Kingston. Hearne's anger at his old friend, prime minister Michael Manley countenancing such barbarism led him to switch support to the opposition Jamaica Labour Party. Hearne felt that when he had joined the PNP it had been an organisation led by gentlemen. He hoped that the gentlemen would have migrated to the JLP. His hope was to be dashed.

His friend Morris Cargill – with whom he wrote the three thrillers about an imaginary Jamaican secret service in the late 1960s and early 1970s – left Jamaica and wrote a book called *Jamaica Farewell* (1978), in which he thoroughly washed his hands of the island and urged Jamaicans at home and abroad to do what they could to collapse Manley's government. Hearne felt that this was improper. Jamaica had not become a tyranny, and fleeing abroad and seeking to undermine the government from overseas was not acceptable. Cargill did return, and he resumed criticising the government in the pages of the *Daily* and *Sunday Gleaner*. As did Hearne. And the government changed, at the ballot box, at the end of October 1980, after one of the worst years in Jamaican history, with hundreds dead in armed clashes between political gangs.

I left Jamaica in 1982, and was only to see Hearne again twice. Once in New York, a few years later, when we talked about Hemingway – some newly-discovered stories of his had just been published – and happiness, and the best way to engage in writing. (Hearne believed in longhand on foolscap; I was enamoured of keyboarding into a computer for first, last, and middle drafts.) The final time I saw him was in Jamaica, in 1992, when I was a doctoral researcher, and it was Hearne's memories of political activism and activity in the 1950s, the very years when the Cayuna novels were being written, that I wanted to tap. By that time he was getting tired, though his memory was sharp and his judgment still clear.

Cayuna, the alternative Jamaica of Hearne's mind, unlike its creator, is one of those places that never dies. Like Austin Tappan Wright's Islandia, or Anthony Hope's Ruritania, it is a country of many dimensions. Its people are finding their own voices, and some of those voices are surprising ones. They are not all Othello, but their times are calling them.

F.S.J. Ledgister
Atlanta, Georgia
19 May 2017, 2019

Endnotes
1. These were published under the name of John Morris: *Fever Grass* (1969), *The Candywine Development* (1970) and *The Checkerboard Caper* (1975).
2. See the Perry Henzell 1972 film, *The Harder They Fall* and the 1980 novelisation by Michael Thelwell of the same name.
3. See "Wind in this Corner", "Reckonings" and "A Village Tragedy" in *John Hearne's Short Fiction* (UWI Press, 2016).

STRANGER AT THE GATE

1

During the night there was a sudden hard flurry of rain, twisting down from the mountains. It woke Brandt and he sat up among the warm sheets in the dark of his cedar and mahogany-smelling bedroom. For a while he listened to the frail, writhing columns of water rattle on the shingles and to the tinkling crescendos when the wind flung a burst against the windowpanes. Then he went back to sleep.

He was awake again before first light, and out of the bed almost before his eyes were open. The smooth teak of the floor was cool under his feet as he went out of his bedroom in his pyjamas to the big sideboard in the dining-room. In the dark he brushed his hand confidently along the surface until his fingers touched the glass-smooth side of the lignum vitae fruit bowl. He moved his hand and closed it on the fat, dimpled disc of a tangerine; then he went back in the dark, stripping the soft skin from the fruit and cramming the pegs into his mouth. The juice was thin, cool and sweetly astringent on his tongue.

In his bedroom again, he switched on the lamp beside the dressing-table. The soft pink light coming through the shade was reflected in the tall mirror and the heavy polished wood of the big bed and the chairs. It was an old, handsome room and the heads of the Brandt family had slept in it for two hundred years. He went into the bathroom which led off the bedroom and, in the dark, ran water over his hands and splashed his face. Before the mirror again, he pulled a comb through the thick coarse waves of his brown hair: from the plaited banana trash seat of the bedside chair he took a faded khaki shirt and a pair of dirty cord trousers: he stripped and put them on quickly and sat down on the chair, feeling on the floor beneath the seat for a pair of sandals. Then he went out of the room and through the big house where the echoes of his feet were muffled by the yard thick stone walls, across the back verandah and into the yard. A quivering, round-bodied bull terrier and four sleek mongrels pranced on stiff, eager legs across the yard to meet him. Grinning, they leapt as high as his waist and he cuffed them playfully.

Outside the house it was still and cool; the earth was damp and firm with the brief rain of the night. It was dark, but the purple sky had a white morning flush behind it and the stars were shrunken, pale flecks. There were piles of softly swollen cloud around the black tumbling mountains to the south. He walked across the big empty yard which smelt of chicken droppings, wet earth, charcoal and the scents of half a dozen kinds of fruit rotting on the ground. He went into the warmth and close, faintly ammoniac smell of the stable. There were casual, contented stampings as the beasts recognized him and he heard his big dun gelding, Caesar, snicker. He switched on the light above Caesar's box and took a head stall from a nail.

"Hello, boy; eating again? You're a greedy beggar, aren't you?"

He talked to the horse in the natural, matter-of-fact way of a man who shares his work with animals. The horse's big head butted him with insistent gentleness in the chest as he slipped on the stall.

"Come on, boy," Brandt said, "let's go and have a look at the dam before breakfast."

He led the beast into the yard and resting his hands on the broad back, heaved himself on to it, first balancing on his stomach across the glossy, wide-muscled spine, then swinging his legs astride.

A coolie man came to the door of the little hut beside the stables. He slouched down the steps rubbing his eyes with one hand and combing his straight, blue-black hair with the thin, exquisitely fashioned fingers of the other.

"Lawd King, Mass' Carl," he said, coming up to Brandt on the horse, "you up early, sah. What happen?"

"'Morning, Tom," Brandt said, "I'm going up the dam. You didn't hear the rain last night?"

"No, sah." Tom was stroking the shining great-muscled neck of the gelding with a sleepy, yet utterly abandoned tenderness.

"De beast dem did quarrel a little, though. I t'ink White Star have a bad dream."

"We had a shower," Carl Brandt told him, "and I want to see how the dam's holding it."

"You want me saddle up fe' you, sah?"

"Cho, no," Carl Brandt told him. "It's not worth it."

He took a crumpled red packet from his breast pocket and gave the man a cigarette and put one in his own mouth. Tom felt in his trousers pocket and brought out matches. Brandt leant down and took the light, then he rapped his sandalled heels against the taut sides of his horse and trotted out of the yard.

Going through the long grass of the steep south pasture it was still too dark to see anything clearly. There was mist and the scattered trees showed through, dark and indistinct, only when he was almost on them; the cattle lying with their legs tucked under were sudden looming blocks without a definite shape. But by the time he reached the gate, the white behind the blue in the sky was glowing with a pale lemon and the mist in the woods ahead was clearing, going away fast in thinned-out strips. Halfway up the bridle track, under the dripping trees, he could hear the sound of the swollen river coming through the leaves like a big wind. It grew louder and louder, then suddenly it was water; shallow fast water rushing over stones, with gurgling counterpoints as stray currents beat against the rocks. In a few minutes he was above the flat brown foam-spotted surface of the dam.

It wasn't much of a dam. He had built it six weeks before by stretching successive layers of lattice-worked bamboo and banana trash over wood: the first layers wide meshed, the meshes getting smaller till the last wall was of closely woven straw daubed with a thick coat of clay. From the dam a trench had been dug down through the wood to his fields below and to the east of his house. In these fields which he had terraced he was trying to grow rice. It was an experiment and the planning and execution of it had given him a great deal of pleasure. If it worked he meant to enlarge the dam and lead the irrigation down to the small settlers' fields in the valley. When he did this he would not ask any payment for his water or for the labour of his servants. It would become a part of the life around his property: like the casual fruit trees scattered in the pastures from which anyone could take when and how he wanted.

He slipped from Caesar's back, coming off the horse with no more conscious effort than he would have taken in rising from a chair. He scrambled down through the bushes to the diminished stream; a tall heavy figure, but moving lightly, with muscles conditioned by thirty years of habitual exercise, Caribbean sun and magnificent food. Standing in the mud of the bank he looked up at the walls of the dam and moved his broad hand over them in one or two places. Then he climbed up the bank to the path again, got on to his horse and rode back down the path.

2

The land was in full sunlight when he rode from the shade of trees. Below him, the grass still winked bright flashes of water but the mist had lifted with the sun. The great square house was white and delicate against the tawny green and all the trees had long shadows lying on the grass before them. The land sloped before him in big, tree-studded folds down to the coastal plain. There were humped, slatey white cattle, with long horns, grazing in this pasture; and before the house, in the north pasture beyond the great smooth lawn, a big herd of rich brown, plump cows, their hides shiny and wet looking, were being driven by two black men on mules. Over on his left, in the corner of a field that sloped out of sight down the side of the ridge, was a windmill for pumping water. The metal vanes had a dull glisten in the sun. Out on the coast were two powder-blue peaks and between them a wedge of grey flat sea. Then, on the side of the red dirt drive leading up to the front of his house, he saw a blue car, an old Vauxhall 14, parked under the grey, huge-spread ficus berry tree. Roy, he told himself. I wonder what he's doing here at this time? He jerked the reins of the head stall and tapped with his heels and the big gelding quickened into a soggily drumming canter across the wet ground.

In the yard he slid off and Caesar began to go to the stables before Tom had taken the reins to lead it. Brandt went across the yard and on to the back verandah near the kitchen: the hot, still air was heavy with the smell of coffee and baked flour. One of the maids, Elvira, met him at the door.

"Good mornin', Mass' Carl," she said. "Mister Roy came when you was out, sah. Him is waiting in the dining-room."

"'Morning, Elvira," he said. "Yes, I know. I saw his car from up the pasture. Tell Delia he'll want breakfast."

"Yes, sah."

"All right. You can bring breakfast in five minutes."

He went into the long, dark-panelled corridor which led through to the front of the house.

"Roy," he called.

"Hullo?" Roy McKenzie called from the dining-room.

"Come into the bedroom. I'm just going to shave. Have you eaten?"

"Not since last night."

"O.K. I've told Delia."

He went into his bedroom. The green jalousie shutters had been flung wide and the room was full of light. He stripped off his shirt and went into the bathroom.

He was lathering his face when Roy McKenzie came to the door.

"Hi, boy," Carl said.

"Hi. How's things?"

"Not bad. What are you doing here at this time of day?" He was drawing the razor round the hard, full curve of his jaw as he spoke and he didn't look round.

"I was over at Castleville. Came across last night and thought I'd look you up."

"Did you come for a case?"

He heard his friend's voice hesitate for a second, and then Roy said, "Yes."

"Good. I was coming up to town tomorrow, myself. How long are you staying?"

"I've got to go back to Queenshaven this morning."

"Pity. Be with you in a minute."

He heard Roy go into the bedroom and the creak as he settled into one of the big cane chairs.

He finished shaving and came out. His square, heavy-featured face was glowing with the cold hill water and the skin of his dark chest and shoulders was stretched tight, elastic and shining, across the great pads of pectoral and deltoid muscle. He grinned at Roy who smiled back at him.

"You make me feel old and decayed."

"This is nothing," Carl told him. "You should see me when I'm looking really beautiful."

He looked at Roy more closely. The thin face with its sharp, powerful bones, its too heavy jaw and curving, big nostrilled nose was tense and restive. Only the broad, fully cut lips were smiling: pulled back under the thick, close bristles of the black moustache. The widely spaced, small, quick eyes were remote from all the pleasantry.

It must be the case, Carl thought. Thank God I'm not a lawyer. Roy's small, compact figure was leaning back in the big white chair, but not really relaxed in it; he looked as if he were poised on the wood, ready to spring up.

"Come along," Carl said; he was at his bureau drawer, taking out a green cotton shirt, printed with yellow and crimson flowers. "Let's go and have breakfast and you can tell me the news."

In the big, high dining-room, where the long, deep-gleaming mahogany sideboard was bright with silver and crystal, Elvira had laid two places on large squares of coarse, starched white linen. Two centuries of polish had brought the table to a texture where the cloths looked as if they were floating on black water. There was grapefruit, cut and cored, with clear amber crystals of brown sugar soaking into the pale green flesh. While they were eating these, she brought in a heavy tray of eggs and ham on a thick, bone-white, blue-flowered dish, a big pot of coffee they could smell clear across the room, another jug of thick, faintly yellow milk, very thin, browned wafers of cassava gleaming wetly with patches of half-melted butter and marmalade in a chunky crystal dish. On the table before them, on a straw mat, was a long dish holding a cold, already cut joint of roast beef. There was the bowl of fruit, and a heavy, ugly, blue glass vase with yellow and scarlet poinsettias.

Carl cut into the soft warm yolk of an egg and watched Roy.

For twenty years, now, very little of importance had happened to either of them that the other had not shared in or known of; and he knew that sooner or later this morning he would hear what was worrying him.

"It's a pity you didn't come before I went out," he said. "I could have shown you the dam."

"What dam?" Roy looked up.

"You haven't been up for two months. I forgot. We've built a dam up in the valley. Where the stream broadens."

Happily, Carl began to tell him of the experiment.

"That's pretty good," Roy said when he had finished.

"But why did you start with a large mesh and make the next layers smaller and smaller?"

"That way you cut the force of the current gradually. You couldn't build it strong enough otherwise. It wouldn't last."

"It sounds pretty good," Roy said again. "Remember to show me sometime."

"We could go up after breakfast if you want to."

"I don't have the time; I'll have to be going pretty soon."

"O.K.," Carl said, "it'll keep. At least, I hope it'll keep. It stood up to the rain last night, but I don't know how it'll do when the seasonal rains start."

Roy said nothing. The stiff anxiousness had come back to his face. He was drinking his coffee too fast.

After a while Carl said: "I found something on Sunday that you might like to see. I was going to bring it up tomorrow."

"What is it?"

"One of the old maps. Seventeenth century. I was looking through the old packing cases in the storeroom and I found it in grandfather's papers."

He went out of the room and Roy could hear the pad of his sandals going up the corridor, and then returning.

"Here it is," Carl was taking a yellowing, folded oblong of thick linen out of a rusty leather container. "It's pretty good; must be one of the first maps the English made."

Spread out on the clear end of the big table, the map was about three feet by two. The colours were still very bright and it had been beautifully drawn; the mountains filled in as heavy, brown folds and the forests as a number of separate, bushy trees. The Caribbean was intensely blue and studded with precisely curling waves, In one corner the legend said, in fine Italianate script, "*Ye* Iland *of* Newe Cornwall (*formerlie ye Spanishe* Iland *of* Cayuna) *in ye* Caribbean Sea".

"This is very good," said Roy. He had come round and was leaning above it with his arms folded on the table.

"Not bad. There can't be many like this knocking about."

"It really is a beauty. It even has New Cornwall on it. You don't see many of those,"

Carl laughed. "Funny how that name never stuck. Grandfather once told me that they kept on calling Cayuna New Cornwall in official documents for nearly twenty years after they captured it."

"What are you going to do with it?" Roy asked. He had gone back to his seat. Slouched in his chair on the end of his spine, he slowly twirled the heavy, blue-patterned cup round and round in its saucer.

"Well, I'll get it photographed up in Queenshaven," Carl told him. "Then I think I'll send it over to Jamaica, to the University. It's the sort of thing they ought to have. That is if you don't want it."

"No," said Roy. "Thanks, though. The University ought to have it."

"I'll get you a copy of the photostat."

Carl went over to the sideboard. He opened one of the drawers and took out a new packet of cigarettes. He opened it and tapped the stiff, cellophane-covered container till the end of a cigarette jerked out. He took one and tossed the packet across the room to Roy. Roy absently and neatly caught it, one-handed, as it turned above his head.

"Let's go outside, Roy."

"O.K." Roy got to his feet, too quickly, too abruptly. "We can finish the cigarettes outside and then I've got to be going. I've a whole pile of work waiting for me in. Queenshaven."

"I've a lot to do today, too," Carl said.

3

Outside, it was already too hot to walk on the big lawn that sloped down to the stone fence: the stone fence separating the lawn which was for pleasure from the long grass of the north pasture which was the best pasture on the property for fattening.

They went along the red earth of the drive to the spreading, thin-branched Japanese sunflower. Underneath the tree there was a low wooden bench and around it were rocks filled in with crumbly black loam; the air around the tree smelt fresh and very clean because of the ferns planted in the loam. Above them the humming birds had begun their day-long business of sipping from the flowers; flinging themselves in unbelievable spurts from blossom to blossom or hovering in a blur of wings.

"Have you seen the paper today?" Roy asked him.

"No," said Carl. "It never gets here before eleven. Why?"

"You saw what's happened over in St. Pierre?"

"Hell, yes. I read it yesterday. I meant to ask you about that. How did it happen? I thought your friend Etienne was pretty well dug in. I never thought they'd stage a revolution against him."

"It wasn't a revolution," Roy said. "It was a war. St. Pierre was invaded and the whole business was paid for by the people who didn't like Etienne. The revolutionaries, as they call them, came across the border from New Aragon. They've been training and fitting up over there for months."

"I'm sorry, Roy. You thought a lot of Etienne, didn't you?" He paused. "What's going to happen now?"

"The war's over. They bombed the whole St. Pierre army to hell last night. Caught them on the road up to the passes. Eight fighter bombers. Napalm; heavy bombs; rockets. Then they came in with incendiaries and machine-guns."

"Jesus," Carl said.

"The invaders," Roy went on in a toneless, rapid voice, "the invaders came round by sea, their main army that is, and took Port-du-Roi after the town had been strafed."

"Jesus!" said Carl again. "Didn't Etienne's lot have anything to put up against the bombers?"

"Five Curtis fighters and an Anson trainer. Four of the

fighters deserted to the invaders yesterday; the other Curtis and the Anson were shot down over Port-du-Roi when they tried to break up the raid. Etienne's nephew was flying the Curtis."

Carl had leant back against the bench, one foot on the seat and his arm flung along the back. He looked at Roy; at the thin, heavy-jawed face which in the soft light under the tree was the colour of ivory, with the blue, sleek stubble showing on the cheeks, chin and around the mouth. If Roy didn't shave once in twenty-four hours he always looked rough and oddly dangerous.

"Don't take it so hard," Carl said softly. "What's happened to Etienne?"

Roy was feeling in the side pocket of his linen jacket for a cigarette. He brought out two and gave one to Carl. "It was bound to happen, of course. What St. Pierre was trying to do was scaring hell out of some of the big boys. They were afraid of it spreading. Not only to the independent islands, to the colonies too. They were bound to jump on it."

"I guess so," Carl said. Statements like this from Roy he took on trust.

"What happened to Etienne?" he asked again. "Is he all right?"

"He's O.K. for the moment."

"What's going to happen to him?"

"He's in hiding," Roy said. "They've indicted him for murder. As soon as du Croix set up a provisional government last night, he issued a warrant."

"God!" Carl said. "That's new, isn't it? I mean, they've always let the deposed President make his break, haven't they?"

Roy gave him a glance. "Etienne isn't just another president," he said. "He's a revolutionary and a communist, which is something different. The boys who have taken over don't intend him to make a come back. They've got a bitch of a case against him. I can show you the whole thing in today's paper if you want. I got a copy about four o'clock, just before I drove out here."

"Then you weren't at Castleville last night?"

"No," Roy said. "I'm sorry about lying; it was damn stupid. I came over to see you."

"To talk about Etienne?"

Roy got up from the bench. He was inhaling on the cigarette in a deep, greedy draw. His neat body in the crumpled leather and dust-stained linen suit was stiff with nervousness. He moved over to the rocks and ferns at the foot of the tree and broke the top from a long, thick frond which was moving in a lazy air current. Then he turned round and came over quickly and looked down at Carl.

"I need some help," he said.

Carl smiled up at him. "I've known that all morning. What do you want?"

"It's for Etienne."

"How much?"

"It's not money I want," Roy said. He stopped speaking, then went on: "Look, I told you Etienne's in hiding and du Croix's out to get him for murder."

"Yes."

"Well, they have a case, you know. If they get him, he'll swing."

Carl sat forward suddenly, putting both feet on the ground so that Roy had to fall back a step.

"You mean," Carl asked, "that Etienne really is a murderer? I thought you meant it was a frame-up."

"No, he's not a murderer," Roy said. "At least what he did wasn't murder. He had to kill a few people when the revolution succeeded ten years ago; and a few people have been killed since. And they're pinning it on Etienne. They've got most of his Cabinet already."

"What do you want me to do?" Carl asked.

"Etienne must leave St. Pierre sometime; they'll pick the place apart, stick by leaf, till they find him, They've broadcast a special message to neighbouring islands and to all Caribbean governments asking them to hold him for extradition if he tries to land."

"Can they do that?"

"For murder they can."

Carl leant his crossed arms on his knees and looked at the ground.

"What do you want me to do?" he asked again, in a flat, heavy voice.

"I want you to hide Etienne if he comes here," Roy said. He was looking straight into Carl's eyes.

"You mean *when* Etienne comes here."

Roy smiled. "Yes, when he comes here."

"No."

"You must. He's got to come here. And you're the only person who can help us. I'm not asking you to do it for the party; I'm asking you to do it for me."

Carl got to his feet, His heavy, blunt-featured face was slightly flushed.

"You're the goddam limit," he said. "I'm to hide out a man wanted for Christ knows how many murders. Just like that. If he was a straight political refugee, sure, you know I'd do it. Especially someone *you* wanted me to hide. But this is different. He's a murderer."

"The people he killed," said Roy, "had to be killed."

"I know, I know," Carl said. "We've had this before and I've told you I don't believe that's the way to do things. I know what sort of people ran St. Pierre before Etienne and his party took over, and I know some of the things Etienne was trying to do. It still doesn't make it all right for Etienne to commit murder. I'm not getting dragged into it."

The two men were facing now: the bull-heavy, gracefully moving bigger man, with the ash-blond, long, German hair on his thick forearms and the blunt, Negroid nose – and the smaller, ivory-pale, wing-nostrilled one who had drawn his lips flat against his teeth: Roy's mouth was a pale, inflexible scar, and to Carl watching it seemed to cut the thin, used face from ear to ear.

"Listen, Carl," Roy said. "Listen, please, because I really don't have much time. In St. Pierre, when du Croix ran things, fifteen thousand babies died in Port-du-Roi one year because they couldn't get anything to eat three days after they were born. That's how long their mother's milk usually lasted. The sugar companies declared dividends of 51 per cent that year. The same year, the unemployed had a protest march in Port-du-Roi and the police took the leaders and hung them up in the prison from big fish hooks. That was the year the two aluminium companies paid the government nine million dollars in royalties…"

"And when your friend Etienne took over," Carl said, "he still couldn't do without the killing. Not in the same way maybe: but he still got rid of anybody who criticized the way *he* ran things."

Roy McKenzie swung away from Carl, then with a savage abrupt twist he faced him again. He had raised his hands and they were clenched and when he turned back it looked as if he was going to hit the other man. But instead he put one hand in his pocket and used the other, slowly, while he talked.

"Yes," he said, and his voice was curiously urgent, with a note of dispassionate, serious interest. "Yes. A number of people were shot. I can't begin to explain all the reasons. Etienne was up against a wall. Du Croix was playing hell across the mountains, in New Oragon. And the sugar and bauxite people were giving them money. Things weren't pretty in St. Pierre for a while; but the revolution was just beginning to build a decent country for most of the people. It'll be hard for du Croix and the old gang to wipe out the memory now, and it'll be easier for the next revolution to start... Will you hide Etienne? It won't be for long. But if you don't, and they catch him here, they'll send him back."

Carl sat on the bench again. Now he too was looking straight into Roy's eyes. Roy stood still, with his hands deep in the pockets of his trousers, the small, neat back and shoulders a little bent, the long heavy lashes raised stiffly from the small, dark, too-bright eyes. He's tired, Carl thought; he's as tired as hell; he looks as if he were going to drop. But I can't help him with this. He shouldn't have asked me to do it. He smiled gently at Roy.

"Sit down," he said, "you make me nervous standing about like that."

Roy sat down. "Will you do it?"

"You know I can't," Carl told him.

"You're scared."

"That's not fair. You are trying to use me. You're using the fact that we've known each other a long time."

"If you're scared," Roy said without any passion, with leaden, unavoidable emphasis, "say so. Don't pretend about it. I know this could do you a lot of damage."

"Stop it, Roy. I'm not taking that even from you."

"If you're not scared then," Roy said, "it means you think Etienne and du Croix are the same kind of people."

"No, I don't," Carl said.

"Then help us."

"Why me?" Carl leant towards him and said the words in a soft shout.

"Because you have places here where we can hide him. Because I can trust you. Because all of us in the party will be watched as a matter of course until Etienne is captured. And because Carl Brandt is one of the wealthiest, most respectable planters in Cayuna and his uncle is the Commissioner of Police. Will you do it?"

"Roy, it isn't my business. I've never taken part in politics and that sort of thing. I leave that to people like you. I'm as sorry as hell Etienne has lost out in St. Pierre and I hate the idea of du Croix and his boys; but you just can't come along and ask me to put up a murderer, just because you say it's important."

"O.K." Roy got up from the bench. He rose with the uncertain, cautious movements of a very tired man. His face was without much expression and the eyes had suddenly taken on a flat, cloudy sheen. "O.K., boy. If you won't, you won't. You were right; I was trying to use you. Not for me, though, and not even for Etienne. But for what Etienne means. Etienne isn't important. It's only that what he knows and what he can do isn't easily replaced. But I can't stop to explain that now, and anyway you wouldn't understand."

He walked out of the shade of the tree. Carl watched him as he went briskly down the drive to his car.

"Roy," he shouted, and began to run after the small, compact, white-suited figure. Roy turned and looked at him, completely expressionless, as he came up.

"Yes?"

"What the hell are you doing?"

"Going, of course."

"Like that?"

"Where shall I call for you tomorrow?"

"Nowhere."

"Why? Are you busy all day?"

"Yes. But I don't want to see you anyway. Don't bother to call."

"Are you mad?"

Roy turned and went on walking to his car and Carl reached out a thick arm and closed his heavy, broad hand on the soiled linen of Roy's shoulder.

"For Christ's sake," Carl said, "don't be such a goddam fool."

"Let me go," Roy said. Carl could feel him stiff and trembling under his hand.

"You mean to say," Carl said, "that you're just walking out like this because I won't hide Etienne?"

"Yes."

"Walking out for good? You mean you and I are finished because of that?"

"Yes."

"Why?"

"I've told you."

"Why?"

"Because when you believe the things I believe and have to do the sort of work I do, you can only make so many concessions to your friends. Sometimes something happens and you can't be friends any more. That's all. Now let me go; I don't like this any more than you."

"Why hasn't it made any difference before?"

Roy smiled briefly.

"I tried to have it both ways, I guess. You; and the work I did. I suppose I always felt that if something like this ever did come up, I could count on you. I could count on *you*, I mean. I forgot your surroundings or rather I pretended they didn't matter; that you were different. It was damn stupid of me."

They had begun to walk to the car because the sun was too much for one tired man and another disturbed man to stand talking in. And because they had both known each other too long and too well to think that this could be talked over and shelved without action.

"You mean," Carl said, in a slightly bewildered voice, "that if I won't hide Etienne, you'll leave here thinking I'm like du Croix?"

"Yes."

"You must be crazy."

Roy's face was uninterested. They had reached the edge of the shadow flung by the big ficus berry tree. There was the sound of voices from the pasture beyond the wall, and a whip crack came to them, very loud and curling lazily in the hot, still air.

"You know I don't want anything like that."

"Sure." Roy opened the door of the blue Vauxhall. There was a pleasant smell of warm leather from inside the car.

Jesus Christ, Carl thought, he means it. He'll leave just like that.

There was a hollow in his stomach as he thought of Roy driving out of the gate, and as he thought of the years they had known together going with him.

"When do you want me to put him up?" he asked,

Roy's face suddenly bunched and stretched in a grin. It was a big, face-splitting smile that made him look about sixteen. He put his hands on Carl's shoulders.

"You big bastard," he said. "You big, stubborn, stupid bastard."

"You knew you had me," Carl said. "Did you really think I'd let you go out of here like that?"

"You had me worried. For a minute I thought you meant it."

"You're a —"

"I know. You're not, though; you make up for it."

"How did you know so quickly that Etienne was going to come here?" Carl asked him. He was looking away from Roy as he spoke: looking down across the great sloping lawn, across the gentle dip of the broad pasture, over the lip of the wide ridge on which the house, lawn and pasture stood and which, high up under the foot of the true mountains, was higher than all the other tree-thick, long-grassed ridges and hill slopes between the house and the sea. Over the sea, a hundred miles north of the sudden bright bar of light which was the blue and white of the shore, was St. Pierre, the independent republic where Etienne was hiding and from where he would come.

"We got the news about one o'clock this morning," Roy told him. "But I don't want to tell you how. Do you mind?"

"Of course not."

"It's only that it's safer for the man who brought it. It's not that I don't trust you."

"When's Etienne coming?"

"Tomorrow night."

"You must have been pretty sure of me, eh? You must have been dead sure your bloody Etienne would get bed and board."

"That's true," Roy said. "I knew you'd do it. I've been sure about you for twenty years."

"O.K.," Carl said. "He's coming tomorrow, then. Where's he going to land? How are you going to get him up here?"

"I can't tell you now. I have to do all that in town this morning. I can tell you tonight, though. Can you put your trip forward and come up to Queenshaven this evening?"

"Sure. I had to come up tomorrow anyway to see about the polo finals and get that map done. I'll come up this evening instead. It won't make any difference."

"That's fine, that's exactly how I'd want it. I'm glad you've business in town; that'll make it look natural."

"Come off it, Roy. Cayuna isn't a police state yet. Why the hell shouldn't I come up if I feel like it."

Roy laughed. It was a soft laugh, with nervous strain in it.

"I know," he said. "I'm being silly. It's just that your Uncle Hector's going to keep a bright eye on me and anybody who might hide Etienne if he comes here. They don't *know* he is coming, of course."

"You hope not."

"Brother, you can say that again."

"How do you aim to get Etienne out of here?"

Roy sat on the edge of the seat and slid over under the driving wheel, lifting his legs over the gear shift. He smiled at Carl.

"I'll tell you later," he said. "I'm not sure. It's one of the things I have to see about today. Where are you going to put him? What's the best place around here?"

"In the old woodcutter's place, I think. You remember the one where we had the landslide. We don't use it now, and there's the hut. Nobody goes there; it's too difficult."

"That sounds fine. I'd like to tell you how much it means, your doing this. How much it means to me, that is."

"Forget it," Carl told him. "I shouldn't have said no the first time."

"The damn thing about you," Roy said, smiling gently, "is that you really mean that. Anybody else, me included, would say it, but we wouldn't mean it. When will you be up?"

"About eight, I guess. I have to go over to Sheila this afternoon; when I'm finished here."

"Good. How's Sheila?"

"She's fine. She was asking after you the other day. She wanted to know when you were coming up again."

"She's a nice girl; I must come up when I'm not so damn busy. How are you making out with her?" He looked with frank curiosity at Carl. Carl shrugged briefly.

"Not any different," Carl said. "Everything's the same as it ever was. She thinks I play a hell of a game of polo and she asks me what to do whenever she's in trouble with the property. She's a sister to me, to coin a phrase."

"I don't get it," Roy said. "You're ten times the man that fool husband of hers is. I know she doesn't love him, and she more than likes you. What's wrong?"

Carl said nothing.

"Have you ever tried to make love to her?"

"Yes."

"What happened?"

"Nothing."

"She doesn't hold it against you?"

"Of course not."

"I didn't think so. She's a good girl. You keep trying. If you want to marry her afterwards, I'll handle the case for you as a wedding present."

"Thanks, you're a great little pal all right."

Roy grinned again. He looked much less tired than when he came, although he was further from his last sleep. His face, in spite of the heavy moustache and the quick knowledgeable eyes, had the virginal, intensely curious alertness that can be seen, sometimes, on the faces of thin, unafraid adolescents.

"Close the door," he said, and as Carl did so, "I'll see you about half-past eight. You better come to my place."

They waved briefly at each other and Roy took the car out from under the ficus tree and into the drive in a tight, fast, reversing circle. He went out of reverse and into second very quickly, and had impatiently changed into fourth before he was very far down the drive.

Carl watched the handsome solid old Vauxhall as it was taken down the winding drive in abrupt, skilful twists. Too fast, he told himself. One day he'll have to kill himself to avoid killing somebody else. He drives so damn well he'll be able to do that, but he goes too fast all the time.

From his driveway he could look down over the ridged, rolling land to where, at the top of the coast plain, stood the big house of Sheila Pearce. He could see the bright smear of the zinc roof showing through the coconut tree tops which at this distance looked like the tops of green umbrellas. For a minute he looked only at the house, then he looked back at Roy's car which was now out of the gate and going up the road. There was a lot of dust, thick then thinning out, behind the car.

I could tell you, he said silently to the car, why she won't have me. I could tell you, but you ought to find out for yourself when you can spare the time. His throat felt suddenly thick and sour as he turned and went to the wide, shallow steps of the verandah.

4

He went straight through the house to his office. This was at the back of the house, down the long, dark-panelled cool corridor, and built in the corner where the back and side verandah joined. Carl Brandt's great-grandfather had built it there. He had wanted a plain, private place where he could be away from his women and the guests that had always swarmed at Brandt's Pen; and he had wanted a place where he could smell the cooking and overhear the talk of those he employed or owned.

It was a square room, built of cedar planks which had been painted only on the outside, to match the rest of the house. There was a wide cedar desk, with a mahogany, cane-bottomed chair before it: the bottom of the chair was permanently sagged by the weight of four generations of big men. There were two other similar chairs in the room and a worn, treacherously holed coconut mat just inside the door. About fifty books on law, agriculture and surveying were on some rough shelves around the walls, or stood in dusty piles on the floor beneath the shelves. Most of the books were bound in limp, greying leather and the tooled gilt of their titles was fading; but some of them were modern and still had their dust covers. In one corner there was a big curve-topped tin chest giving off a strong smell of camphor and which was full of old papers. Near this was a pile of surveying instruments: a theodolite: a tape in a coarse-stitched, brass-centred leather drum, a big compass in a leather case, a plane table, a pole for marking levels, and a plumb line on a big tripod. On one of the chairs there was an Ivor-Johnson 12-bore, disassembled, in its case: any room which a Brandt man used a lot almost always acquired, as a more or less permanent part of the furnishings, a gun, or a saddle, or a piece of harness.

Carl went to his desk and sat down, picking up the top letter from the thin pile held down by the ugly, brass elephant paperweight which hadn't been polished for a hundred years. The letter was from a man in Venezuela who wanted to buy a bull and some cows which would improve his own herd and give him more weight in a tropical climate. This was the problem which people who raised cattle south of Cancer were always fighting: how to keep beef on the mixed Angus and shorthorn stock in a climate that never had any spring or autumn but only wet and dry and steady, lather-producing sun. Carl Brandt's herd with its infusion of Indian stock was one of those which had almost nearly solved the problem.

He answered the letter, writing it in careful, punctilious Spanish. When he had finished it he read it again. He spoke Spanish pretty well, but there was always something you found out later that should have been put a little differently.

Then he wrote to a firm in Barbados which made cattle cake out of sugar-cane trash. This was a different sort of letter because he knew the man who ran the firm. After this he answered the third letter in the pile, which was from a Canadian lawyer asking for an interview. The lawyer represented a company who wanted to buy five hundred acres of Carl Brandt's land because they thought there was bauxite under the grass. The lawyer suggested tentatively that there was a great deal of money in it for Carl Brandt. Carl said that he didn't think he wanted to sell just now, that the organization of his property at the moment wouldn't permit any other operations without inconvenience, He had written four such letters to the same company during the past two years.

Only once during the morning did he think any more about Etienne and of the place where he was going to hide him.

By eleven o'clock he had written five letters and made rough notes for the programme of the polo finals afternoon.

While he was sealing and addressing the fifth letter, Elvira came in with the morning's mail, the newspaper and a big pint glass of milky looking soursop drink with clear, sharp edges of ice chinking against the glass at the top. This was something that was done on all the mornings he worked in his office.

She put down the tray and left the room in a hurried, anxious scuttle, not lifting her eyes and looking around with oblique, hasty glances.

This, too, was part of a pattern. The Brandt men when the office was built had begun a war with all the women, wives, daughters, sisters and servants of Brandt's Pen. It was a formal, half-declared but constant action, with no compromise. The issue was whether the office should be cleaned and tidied to match the ordered, gleaming luxury of the rest of the house. It was a struggle turning on the relative strengths of both sides. Sometimes there would be too many women in the house and the place would be swept, polished, trimmed, full of flowers, almost uninhabitable as a place of work. This occurred, too, even when the sides were numerically a rough match, but when there was some fanatical, utterly devoted cleaner and tidier in the women's camp. Then the fortunes would turn, and a great warrior for the tidiers would die or leave to get married, and the Brandt men in occupation would reduce the office, in a frenzy of liberation and happiness, to the state it was in now and no woman in the house was supposed even to open the door except on certain strict conditions of a moment's service. At those times, the women of the house had a real fear and guilt about entering the office. This was how matters stood at present: but it was a very recent state. Just before Elvira, who was poor material as a shock trooper, there had been Louise, one of the fiercest, most tireless tidiers in Carl's memory. He had been hopelessly defeated in every major battle and every casual skirmish with her, and when she left to go up to Queenshaven to marry his uncle's chauffeur, Carl had taken two weeks to get used to the idea that the office was now his. He still, occasionally, had a bad moment when he thought that she might come back one day.

He picked up the letters from the tray and fanned them to see what he had got and put them on his desk. He took a cigarette from his shirt pocket, fumbling it loose without taking out the pack. He removed the little muslin cover with its edge of glass bead weights from the tumbler, and as he opened the paper he took a long drink from the cold, thick, sour-sweet drink.

It was all in the paper as Roy had told him. Front page, headlines and four half columns of news about the taking of Port-du-Roi and the short air fight and the murder charge against Etienne. Sipping his drink and smoking, he read it all. There was a large picture of Etienne on the front page, too: a good picture, carefully printed, showing the flat, broad, slightly tilt-eyed black face, the short, stubby nose, the close-cut, coarse hair and the neat, bristly moustache that grew down on either side of the thick sensitive mouth to the tufted beard that fringed the round jaw and chin. It was a newspaper photograph, so you couldn't tell much about the eyes. He didn't look his age, which was given as fifty.

He leant back in the chair and smoked, looking at the picture and thinking of Roy and himself and how it had been this morning. Outside, Mae, one of the maids, was feeding the fowls: he could hear the sweet thick voice calling, "Chi-chi-chi-chi-chi! Come fowl! Come fowl!" and he could picture the white drift of fine, grated coconut meat, arcing through the air as she threw it. Delia was telling Ralph, one of the yard boys, a long story of the hideous consequences which had overtaken a nephew of hers who had gone with women before he was married. Delia was very religious and she had lost a son when he was about Ralph's age and Ralph was sexually one of the most enviably endowed males on Brandt's Pen, so there was a maternal as well as evangelical warmth to Delia's voice. Tom was in the stables, because Carl heard him at the stable door, once, saying something in an exasperated, sarcastic tone to his little brother who helped with the horses. There were a lot of other noises, too, faint, busy, organized, from the pastures and drifting down on the mountain breeze from the pen. He did not listen to these. They were simply part of the day and he could have told as quickly if one of those sounds went wrong as he could if the oxygen in the room were suddenly to disappear.

It was really hot now, with the sun climbing to the top of a pale, hard sky. There was the midday feeling of stillness, the slowing down and rest. Carl Brandt went out of his study and into the wide drawing room with its bright mats and crisp, flowered slip covers and dark, cool-looking floor and the seven, wide open french windows looking out on to the broad verandah and big trees and the lawns. He went to a cabinet and took out a bottle of rum and called out for one of the maids to bring him some ice and water. When this came he mixed a drink and sat in a big, low-slung, wooden chair on the verandah, looking out over the lawn. He scarcely ever acknowledged it to himself, but he was often a very lonely man.

5

By twelve o'clock, in Queenshaven, the tar on the roads had ribbed tyre marks in it and the iron railings outside the Government buildings were too hot for a man to lean against. The fans were going in all the offices and the breeze coming down from the mountains was raising little flurries of dust at every corner. There was a lot of sweat and greasy shine on the faces you passed and shirts or dresses had big damp patches at the armpits and in the long hollows of the spine. The trees, even the big Royal palms outside Government buildings, looked limp and sluggish and the leaves were grey with dust. Everywhere there was a smell of gutters and if you tried to look up, even to roof level, your eyes watered with the white glare.

Roy McKenzie saw his last client for the morning at about ten to twelve. He had tried to persuade the man not to take his brother into court over the non-delivery of some bottles which he, the client, used in his preserves business. It had been obvious that the man's brother hadn't done what he should to deliver the bottles, but Roy had thought that if he could get both of them in the office he would be able to arrange something. The client had promised to think it over and had left looking disappointed. Roy knew that it would be a fight in the man between the passion for litigation and a fear of losing money. He didn't think that brotherly feeling would come into it much.

His office was high and square, with green-painted walls, a dark, highly-polished floor of thin boards and a tall, glass-fronted case of fat books. There were three plain, upright chairs and an old comfortable roll-top desk. A telephone stood on a little table beside his roundbacked swivel chair.

Roy swung his chair on its metal spine and put his feet on the corner of the desk. He stared through the window on to the harsh, blistering mirror of a zinc roof. Tilting back in the chair he closed his eyes. In the outer office he could hear his two clerks and the stenographers getting ready to go for lunch. The boy who was articled to him had already gone.

The door opened, and because the person hadn't knocked and because of the step, he knew it was Linda Hu-Sen, his secretary. She came across the room and leaned her arms on the front of the roll-top desk and looked at him. Still leaning back, Roy opened one eye and looked at her and said, "Hi!"

"Hi!" she said. "Tired?"

Roy nodded and heaved his feet off the desk and swung the chair round straight and looked at her.

She was a short, very dark, Chinese girl, with the elegant, delicate stockiness that only her race show. She was a very good secretary and knew almost as much law as Roy himself. She was excellent at handling women clients who were having trouble with their men and got hysterical or loudly sad in the office. Once Roy and she had been lovers. But that was over. They had quarrelled and made up, quarrelled again and made up again before they had accepted the fact that it was over. Then they had been embarrassed, and finally they had built that sort of friendship which is only possible to a man and woman who have been lovers and ceased to be lovers without too much bitterness.

"I saw Mason," she said now. "He saw the man we want. He's the carpenter on that French boat at Number Three. His name is Lauront and he'll meet you in the Spanish Jar in an hour."

"Good," said Roy. "Thanks, Lin; you and Mason did a good job."

"I wish it was over," she said. "I'm not made for this sort of stuff."

Roy smiled. "Me neither," he said. "It's like one of those things you read about but that never really happen."

"What'll happen if they find out?"

Roy shrugged. "Nothing much to us, personally," he said. "A short term, at most. They'll ban the party, though. They've been wanting to do that and it'll be the excuse they're looking for."

"Is it worth the risk?"

"Etienne says so, and the party in St. Pierre. They ought to know. I think so, myself."

"Me too; but I wish it was over."

Roy nodded. "We were lucky," he said. "Luck's really with us. Having that sailor to take the message and having Carl's place to hide him out till the ship passes next week. All luck. We could never have hidden him in town."

"How did Carl take it?" she asked.

"It was bad at first. But I expected that. It's all right now, though."

She sat down on the chair that was nearest the desk and pulled her dress up over her round knees and half way up the plump shapely thighs. She pulled the front of her lace fronted cotton blouse away from her chest with one finger and blew down between the flesh and the cloth.

"Carl's a nice, nice man," she said. "If he ever becomes politically conscious he'll be a knockout."

They smiled at each other. Then Roy looked serious and said: "Sometimes I wonder if it isn't a mistake for me to like him so much, Some day we might – we just might – find ourselves fighting on opposite sides."

They were silent for a moment; and then Linda said, "You'd better get some money. Just in case. Get it from your own account."

"Yes," he said.

"Fifty pounds enough?"

"That should be plenty."

"It's going to be all right, isn't it? You're not worrying about it and not saying?"

"No," he told her. "I was worried last night when it came all in a rush. It's all right now, though. We only have to go careful."

"You'll call off the demonstration?"

"The one for Sunday? Yes, that'll have to go. We couldn't risk one of us getting into trouble before Etienne gets away."

"How are you going to explain it?"

"I'll think of something," he said. "You think about it, too, while I'm out. I can't think about it now."

"I'll be glad when he's out of this," she said.

"So will he. So will I. Stop worrying, Lin."

She went back to her seat. Roy lit a cigarette and sprawled across his desk smoking, propping his head on a hand held open against his face, his elbow jammed against the raised ledge of the desk surface.

When he had finished his cigarette he got to his feet.

"I'd better go and see this sailor," he said. "How'll I know him?"

"Mason said he was short and fair. He'll be wearing a blue shirt and a black beret. There'll be a boy with him."

"Oh hell!" Roy said irritably. "The Spanish Jar'll be full of sailors this time of the day. What's the name of his ship?"

"The *Anjou*."

"O.K. If I don't spot him I'll ask one of the boys talking French."

"Yes, that's a good idea," she said. "Have you eaten?"

"I ate at Carl's this morning."

"You eat at the Jar. Get a couple of patties and some milk. You hear?"

"O.K. O.K. I'll get something."

"Eat before you drink, mind. Don't go drinking up a lot of rum on an empty stomach."

"Jesus!" Roy said. He was taking his coat from the hanger on the door hook. "I'm up to my ears in all sorts of illegal intrigue and all you can think about is whether I've eaten."

"You'd look nice," she said, "intriguing with an ulcer."

He made a rude gesture at her and left the office. He passed through the outer office and through the little swing gate in the waist-high railings, down the narrow stairs with their musty smell of law books coming from the outer offices and out into the harsh, overwhelming glare of the one o'clock sun.

He turned down the street outside his office and began to walk along the dirt-crusted, cracked pavement to the waterfront. There was a chemist's shop on the corner across from his office and he went in and bought a Benzedrine inhaler: the sort one uses for colds. After buying it, he stood at the door in the shade, sniffing at the white cylinder to clear the tiredness from his head and looking at the city. The dingy square-frame houses, with the plaster peeling from the walls and the green shutters caked with dust, looked frail in the white heat of the great sun. And the tin roofs gave everything a hurried, temporary appearance. He glanced at his watch and walked on down the street. At the end of the street he could see the harbour: the water by the shore near the wharves and the big warehouses was dull and heavy, but out in the stream it was suddenly a glittering, lively mirror with a blue glow beneath the brightness. There was a heat haze over the low, fuzzy, green strip of the Barricades which shut in the harbour.

This is a good place, he told himself walking along. And if I'm lucky I might live long enough to see a city here instead of this. That would be nice. A good city, white and green with plenty of trees and red roofs and coloured door-ways and walls. It would have to be something, though, to match this light. Something between Rio and Palermo.

He was past the offices now, and walking quickly because he had suddenly remembered that he wanted to eat before he talked to the sailor. He was in that part of the city between the uptown offices and the warehouses, shipping offices and bars of the waterfront. The air was loud with the sound of bicycle bells and motor horns because it was a narrow street, built for buggies, and never intended for this sort of traffic. As Roy looked around him, eyes squinting against the fierce beating glare, at the sun-polished skins and gracefully moving limbs, he felt very happy. It was a sudden happiness which came to him occasionally and gratuitously, like the momentary glow from the first drink. A mixture of intimacy, familiarity and love, it was something he had never felt in any of the other cities he had been happy in. Whenever it happened, it seemed to affirm that this was the place where he ought to be: the one place where he could, completely, share and suffer and grow with the people and things around him.

Stop that, he told himself as he turned off the street into a lane where the gutters left only a thin strip of dry tar on the crown of the road. You've had your ration for today. When he turned down the narrow street that led to the Spanish Jar, he was thinking of what he would do if his present plan failed: turning over and rejecting half a dozen schemes in turn. Each one as it was measured and thrown out, he was able to dismiss absolutely from his mind.

6

The Spanish Jar was a long, low-slung, narrow building on a corner about fifty yards from the water. It was a good bar and all sorts of men came to it, stevedores, clerks, sailors, even tourists if they were with someone who knew a good bar.

Roy McKenzie approached it, walking past the big, steel-shuttered, concrete front of the Mendoza Ltd. warehouse. There was a hot, sweet smell of rum, pimento and sugar coming from the open door of the warehouse that was almost like a solid body in the stuffy air. It didn't go too badly with the smell of the gutters and the salty pungence from the harbour. There isn't another smell like this anywhere, Roy thought. This is our own special brand. He grinned to himself. There were a lot of men squatting on the gritty sidewalk under the shade of the overhanging roof. Some of them were pretty ragged because they weren't working, but the others, those with overdeveloped, muscle-ridged forearms or big, full necks and shoulders, were the draymen and stevedores from the wharves. There was a flat dray, with iron-rimmed wheels and open sides and rope-work flooring, standing outside the doorway of the Mendoza's warehouse. It was dusted with flour from its last haul before lunch, and the huge, sulky looking mule in the shafts had white flour dust all over its haunches and tail. At the end of the street, by the breakwater, four crows with raw red necks and dull black feathers were ripping up a dead dog: you could imagine the hard, lifeless sinews tearing like calico as the yellow, powerful beaks tugged ecstatically at the flyblown meat. Roy pushed on the spring-hinged half doors of the Spanish Jar and went into the bar.

Inside it was all dark glimmering wood and a bright bank of glasses behind the long bar. There were four electric fans hanging from the ceiling and they made it cool and gentle after the fierce whiteness outside. There were four neatly-shirted brown men and a white man at one end of the bar and a group of white sailors in the middle of it. Two customs officers were at one of the tables with their big helmets on the table next to the glasses. They were drinking beer and Roy nodded to them and they waved at him. He went to the bar and smiled at the huge, shapeless, strong-faced Chinese woman who came up. Her bright cotton dress was dark with sweat under the arms and there were small drops caught in the scattered hairs on her top lip and under her chin.

"Hello, Mrs. Ching." Roy took her soft, powerful hand "How's things?"

"Mr. McKenzie, sir. We haven't seen you in a long time." She was smiling at him and held his hand.

"No," he said. "I haven't been down much since the wharf strike. I've been pretty busy."

She let go his hand. "You work too hard, Mr. McKenzie. Business good?"

"Pretty fair, Mrs. Ching. How's with you?"

"Can't complain. What would you like, sir?"

He ordered two meat patties and a half-pint of milk and bottle of beer. While she was getting the patties out of the tin box which had a plate of red coals in the slot beneath the safe, he went over to a table in the far corner.

In a few minutes one of the barmaids came over with the flaky, golden-crusted patties on a plate and a brown, damp bottle of beer, with the glass upended over the neck of the bottle.

"Miss' Ching send out for the milk, sah. It soon come."

"All right," Roy told her. "There's no hurry."

He broke the patties with the fork to let them cool, and looked around. He didn't think the sailor he wanted was in yet. When his milk came he drank it slowly and ate the patties which were rich and hot with red pepper. Then he poured half a glass of beer and lit a cigarette.

He had nearly finished it when Mason from the Customs, the man Linda had seen that morning, and two sailors came in. Mason was a tall, knob-headed man, the colour of Turkish tobacco, and he looked thin and lofty against the two sailors. Both the men with him were short and fair, and both were dressed in clean blue shirts and blue trousers. One of them, the elder, was bearing a faded black beret. The younger one, whose face had the slightly lumpy, unfinished look of adolescence, was carrying a white drill jacket slung over his arm. They were both wearing blue canvas *espadrilles*. Anywhere else in the city they would have looked exotic and alien; here on the waterfront they fitted.

They sat down at the table next to Roy. Mason lifted his hand in greeting, and Roy said, "Hello, Dick." Then Mason sat down. He and the sailors were speaking English, but the sailors were having difficulty with it, and Roy knew that Mason spoke no French.

It's a pity, he thought as he listened to the laboured conversation at the next table. Being on the waterfront the way he is, Mason should have French or Spanish. I wonder if he could learn one of them? I must suggest it to him next time I see him. It could be useful.

At the next table, the young sailor, evidently an enthusiast for six-day bicycle tours, was trying to explain them. Every so often the words would fail him and they would gesture at each other. They were both drinking beer, but the older man was drinking rum and ginger.

After a while Mason finished his beer and got up, putting on his big helmet. It looked like a whitewashed coal-scuttle stuck on the knob of a bedpost. He and Roy nodded to each other and smiled. Mason left, stopping at the bar to pay for the drinks. The talk from the other people in the room came in fragmented murmurs. Roy took out his Benzedrine inhaler and sniffed it. He felt that the grittiness had gone from underneath his eyelids. Outside, the drays had begun to roll again after lunch; they made a clattering thunder down the lane to the wharf.

"Will you and your comrade join me in a drink, sir?" he asked the older man. He spoke in French. It was a long time since he had used it. Not since he had gone to St. Pierre a year before. He was pleased with the sound of it, as he always was when he spoke it, and he was glad that he was speaking it well. You can break English, he thought, and mispronounce it, and still sound romantic, but bad French only sounds illiterate.

The older sailor looked pleased, too, and relieved.

"You speak French well, sir," he said.

Roy got up and sat down at their table. He signalled for one of the girls behind the bar.

"Thank you," he said. "I do not speak it much now. But I have lived in France."

"You have lived in France?" He's really pleased now, Roy thought. The waitress came up. She was scratching her head and rapping the big round tray gently against her thin leg.

"What will you have to drink?" Roy asked them.

"I will have rum with ginger," the older man said, "and will you order beer for my comrade." Roy ordered these and a rum and ginger for himself.

The boy smiled. "He will not allow me to drink rum during the day," he said. "Only at night, and then only a little. He says it is bad. But he drinks it."

"It is because I feel responsible," the older sailor said. "For young men, in this heat, rum can be bad. For me it is different. My stomach and I know each other." He had settled himself in the chair, sitting very straight, with the stubby hands clasped. There was an air of assurance about him.

"It is better to be careful," Roy told him. "Especially when the drink is not of your country."

"Exactly what I tell him," the older sailor said. "What your own country produces must find something in you to agree with, if you don't commit excess. But in a strange place, have care until you know your stomach. Like me." He slapped his flat, firm belly and laughed at the two of them. There was a mesh of fine, deep, weather wrinkles round the pale, clear blue eyes when he laughed. Quite suddenly and easily, he had relaxed. He was eager and compelling, looking at the two younger men with bright, interested eyes.

The waitress came back with a sweating brown bottle of beer and two glasses with the rum pale around chunks of ice. She put these on the table before them and put a small bottle of ginger-ale in the middle, opening it one-handed as she did so with the opener held in her right palm.

Roy poured a little of the ginger into his companion's glass and a little more into his own. The boy poured his beer but didn't tilt his glass enough, so there was a sudden froth that mounted to the brim before the glass was half full.

"I like this rum," the older sailor said. "It is not as good as the rum of Martinique or Barbados, but it is very good." He sipped his drink slowly and carefully.

"Good," Roy said. "The beer is not very good but I am glad you like the rum. Have you ever called here before?"

"No. The other islands, yes. But never Cayuna." He was looking about him as he spoke, the wrinkle-meshed eyes and the shapely head moving slowly in a calm, thorough exploration.

"It is very poor here, yes?" the boy, Andre, said. "I do not like seeing the things we see in these ports. In France we have many poor, but not like here."

"What do you expect to see?" the older man said roughly. "You are a comrade. They are the reasons for revolutions."

He turned to Roy, "What is your name, comrade?"

"McKenzie. Roy McKenzie."

"I am Paul. And he, I told you, is Andre."

They shook hands across the table.

The comrade who brought us here," Paul continued, "said that you had work for us to do. I did not understand very well. I know German and Spanish and a little Swedish, but no English."

"You have heard of what happened in St. Pierre?"

"Only from the ship's wireless."

Roy told him the details. Paul nodded when he was finished.

"It was to be expected. We called at Port-du-Roi two years ago. They had made a good start. It was a better place than here. What do you wish me to do?" He was holding his drink between his hands and the short, spare-fleshed body was still. The face was calm and watchful.

"Last night," Roy said, "the comrade you know from the

wharf, the man who brought you here, told us that your ship leaves here for Panama."

"Yes. We leave tonight."

"There is a Polish ship coming into the Canal in two days. Maybe a little before, but it will arrange to wait. Can you get a message to it for us?"

"Certainly. What is the name?"

"The *Kosciuzko*. They should have received word last night, or they'll receive it when they get to Panama, that Etienne will need help to get away. But they won't know when or where. It had to be arranged by the party here. And I could only do that this morning."

"I understand."

"The *Kosciuzko* is not calling at Cayuna, but it is passing north of here next week. Will you say to whoever is politically responsible on the ship that we will have Etienne twelve miles dead north of Colombus Head at twelve-thirty in the morning of whatever day they pass Cayuna. It will be easy to get the information on that point, but they must arrange it that we can take him out in the dark. Can you do it?"

"If the *Kosciuzko* is in the Canal I can do it. Are you sure that it has been arranged with them?"

"So we were told. The arrangements were not made by us but by comrades in other countries. Our work is only to hide Etienne and get him away."

"Is there no danger in this for you?"

"No," Roy told him. "The people here know me, and they know I would hide Etienne. But if we are careful they will never know that he has even been here. They will be watching for him, of course, but no more than anywhere else in the Caribbean. No, the danger is all for Etienne if he is caught."

"Your worst time, of course," Paul said, calmly, matter-of-factly, "is while he is here. You have a good place for him?"

"Yes."

"Good. I wish you luck. You and your party and Etienne." He finished his drink with the same slow consideration, put the glass on the table.

There was an explosion of laughter from the five clerks at the bar. One of them was not laughing but had the smug, delivered smile of a man who has just told an obscene joke. Paul gestured to them with a blunt thumb.

"That's good," he said. "That's one of the good things about your country."

"What?" Roy followed the direction of his finger.

"The four black men and the white one, all drinking together."

"It's one of the best things," Roy said. He smiled and jerked his head at the five men. "It must have been a good joke."

They had another round of drinks and drank them slowly. When they had finished Paul rose and held out his stubby, competent hand.

"Goodbye, comrade," he said. "Good luck once more."

"Thank you. Will you be coming here again?"

"Perhaps. It is possible."

"Then I will see you."

"Naturally."

He shook Andre's hand and the men walked across the floor, moving with an unmistakable, easy-balanced sailor's swing. The doors closed behind them and the last he saw of them was the black beret. He looked around the room. The people in the bar, except for the five clerks who were making a party of it, had all changed while he was talking to Paul and Andre.

He went over to the long bar and paid for the drinks, then he went out into the street. His watch said twenty-past two. It was hotter, now, than at one o'clock. Hot with the accumulated heat of several hours' refraction from zinc and whitewashed concrete; the wind from the blue hills north of the town had dropped. The harbour was like a basin full of flashing liquid metal and when he tried to look at the sun it seemed to swell slowly and fall on him. People in the street were shinier and more listless than before lunch, and he could smell the day's sweat from their clothes if he passed too near them on the sidewalk.

He went slowly uptown to Queen Street, the main street of the capital, and drew fifty pounds from his account with the Colonial Bank. He didn't think he would need the money, but he knew that in a thing like this not having money ready might spoil it all.

Halfway up Queen Street, near the sprawling, white Government buildings, he saw a tall paunchy man standing in the cool, shaded doorway of a store. The man was dressed in a crisp white shirt and a silk tie with the discreet colours of a good club on it. He was wearing a soft, smooth pair of grey gabardines and there was an expensive alligator-hide belt round the big stomach. The sign above the man's head, over the door lintel and under the bright awning, said *McKenzie's Furniture*. There were two windows on either side of the tall plump man, with good furniture smoothly gleaming behind the plate-glass. The man in the doorway was Roy's father.

Roy sucked his teeth in a slight twinge of annoyance. For a moment he thought of turning back before the other man saw him, and of going across to his office by a side road. Then he walked on. The tall plump man smiled as he came abreast of the doorway.

"Roy," he said. "What are you doing over in this side of town? Isn't it a scorcher, eh?"

"Hello, sir," Roy said. "Yes, it is. Had a good day?"

He looked with embarrassment into the plump folds of his father's face. Oh hell, he thought, I should have gone round the other way. He *would* be standing at the door just as I passed. I'll have to give him five minutes. Five minutes of nothing. It's always worse when we're alone.

Until he was twelve years old Roy had accepted the sleek, self-indulgent man who was his father in the way that any child does, as part of the unquestionable order of nature, They had never played or done anything together since Roy was five and his father used to drive him up to the Botanical Gardens on Sunday afternoons to hear the military band. They had treated each other kindly, and on Roy's part respectfully. But when Roy tried to think of him, the pictures that came most readily to his mind were of a soft, curve-stomached, remote body reading a newspaper in one corner of the big verandah, or a petulant voice complaining about money and food, or a bridge game with three other men who all looked very like him, talking of things which were boring and incomprehensible. There was also a picture of Christmas and birthday jollity and playfulness that began awkwardly, grew quickly to a point of carefully ignored strain which was near hysteria, and ended in mutual, bottomless relief.

At twelve, he had gone to Brandt's Pen for the first time and seen Arthur Brandt, Carl's father. To Roy, this man whose body had felt hard and huge and wonderful as the body of a great horse, who could shoot the stem of a mango at the top of a tree without touching the fruit, who seemed to cover about six feet with every loping stride, had been something new. An aura of tremendous and controlled physical force had come from him that made even the prospect of his company raise a thick excitement in the boy's stomach. Even his roaring bad temper when you rode a horse badly or carried a gun dangerously had not frightened. You understood them completely as things which must be learnt. And no one, certainly no boy, could come within sound of that deep, happy voice without wishing to share in whatever Arthur Brandt was doing. He had lived on a level of physical efficiency and sensation, with no problems except teaching his son to do certain things so well that he would be able to enjoy them. And when his son's friend came into his simple picture, he had taught him, too, with the same unthinking love and carefulness.

"You weren't home last night," Mr. McKenzie said, looking at Roy with timid, groping fondness.

"No, sir," Roy said. "I had to go over to the north coast on business. I left a note for mother."

"You couldn't have slept much," his father said. "You look tired."

"I stayed with Carl," Roy said. His face was getting stiff and twitchy from trying to smile naturally.

"How is Carl?" Mr. McKenzie's dull, incurious eyes had brightened. Roy's friendship with the old, socially distinguished Brandt family was one of the few things about his son that did not make him uneasy.

"Oh, he's well," Roy said. "Look, sir, I must go now. I only sneaked out to go to the bank. I've a lot of work waiting for me."

"Of course, of course, my boy. See you tonight at supper."

"Yes, sir," Roy said, turning away.

The elder McKenzie watched his son's brisk, compactly functional body go up the street in the bright sun. The old man's soft face was troubled. He looked like a large, broad-faced fish that has sensed a change in the climate of its tank.

7

This was Friday; and every Friday afternoon Carl took one of his ponies over to Sheila Pearce and coached her in polo. He didn't approve very much of women playing polo, and his father would have thought it ridiculous, but Sheila had begun to play two years ago, at the time Carl was falling in love with her. She had persuaded several of the other property wives and sisters for miles around to take it up and the idea was spreading. There was talk now of having a Ladies' Cup, and Carl Brandt as president of the All Island Polo Association was going to propose it at the next general meeting. He did not like to see women playing this game because it was a dangerous sport that to be done really well required certain physical qualities women did not have as completely as men; and the better you played it the greater became the possible risk. But he had given in. And to reduce the danger he had spent a great deal of time teaching the game as well as he knew.

It was a good afternoon, now; the freshness had come back into the day and there were some small, shining puffs of cloud. The hills looked cool, with vivid splashes of yellow and crimson among the green bush. Coming out of the foothills, the coast plain was suddenly packed, rich and bright, with bananas and coconuts, and he knew it was going to be a good year. When he drove across the bridge he could see the river, brown and silted, and running over big grey rocks like bathing elephants, and the trees bent above the river with the leaves glossy in the hard light.

He was driving the big black Humber he had imported from England the year before. Tom, the coolie man, was driving the jeep behind him. The jeep was towing a horse-box he had made himself that year: it was a good box, with spring blades and pneumatic tyres, and he was proud of how well he had made it. Jamshid, the oldest and cleverest of his ponies, was inside it.

For him, this time was the best and happiest of the week. These hours when Sheila relied on him and surrendered freely all her energy and judgement to his guidance. He knew it to be a substitute for the thing he wanted and could not achieve, and he was thankful and happy to have that much.

At the coast, it always seemed as if the huge, rushing tyres of the Humber had exploded a hidden mine of paint before his eyes. It was always and suddenly a bursting blue and white and green carved unforgettably, and always forgotten as it really was, against the aching purity of diamond hard, clear light. Out among the black sharp stumps of rock, the water had a deep, vivid glow, as if it would stain cloth. And all along the deep curving bite of the shore the coconut trees were close-packed, bent in stiff, tapering bows over the yellow-white sand and the lager beer froth of foam, with the glossy-feathered crowns touching and making a soft-lit, green layer between the white air and the blue, glassy water. The air coming into the car smelt clean with salt.

A mile up the coast road there was a little village; a few clapboard and zinc houses on either side of the road, a post office with green steel shutters, a Chinese grocery with a concrete piazza and a bar; it looked sleepy and relaxed and there were people sitting in the doorways or on the small, thin-railinged verandahs. Two men were stretched out the width of the piazza on their backs and asleep. Just beyond the village was the gateway of Tolliver, Sheila's house.

It was a sprawling, two storey building built fifty years before by the grandfather of the man Sheila had married. It was white and there was no particular handsomeness about the design, but it had been built solidly. It looked cool, pleasant and comfortable set among the closely-packed, regimented rows of coconut trees. The black roof of the soap factory showed among the trees about quarter of a mile from the house; and there was a heavy sweetish smell of copra in the air. Beside the house was a field of brown, stubbly, dry-looking grass, with the basketwork goals at either end.

He drew up at the low verandah, set about a foot above the ground, and blew his horn. Sheila came to the railing of the top verandah and waved and he waved back at her from the car. Tom was coming up the drive and turning off into the brown field, pulling up in the shade of a huge, rough-barked guango. Carl got out of his car; he was wearing jodhpurs and a closely-knit blue shirt which had been washed so often that it looked like a white shirt from which an ink-stain had been not quite removed.

"Get him out," he called to Tom. "Walk him around a bit. Don't saddle him yet, though. I'll be down soon."

"Right, sah," Tom yelled back.

He knew that Tom needed no instruction as to what to do; but neither of them would have liked to start the afternoon without these words from him and Tom's recognition.

He went across the driveway and into the house.

She was a tall girl, and standing on the stairs, as he came into the dim coolness of the hall, she looked even taller. She was dressed in jodhpurs and a shiny, fine-meshed shirt, and these made her slim, heavy-breasted figure seem thinner; and fuller in the places where she was round and full. Her big, strong-boned hands and long feet accentuated her tallness. And the slight sway at the waist with which she carried herself made him think now, as it always did, of the awkward, touching gracefulness of a two-week foal. As he came, quickly and smiling, up the stairs to her, he could see that her round soft cheeks and neat, tilted nose were pink with recent sun: there was the red of salt water sting around the rims of her deep, widely-spaced, greenish eyes; and the waving thick brown hair was drawn back smoothly from the high, mannish forehead and clubbed with a black velvet ribbon at the back of her long round neck. When he was close beside her on the stair and looking down, gratefully, at her upturned, smiling face, he could smell the clean, dry grass scent of her hair, and see that the sun and salt had faintly bleached it.

"Were you out in the *Nisba* today?"

"How did you know?" she asked. "Were you watching from the Pen?"

As they turned to go up the stairs, he told her.

She touched her hair with a brusque careless gesture.

"I'll wash it tonight," she said. "I was only out for an hour. Just to try the new carburettor. She goes beautifully now that it's in. Twelve knots without even trying. I went in for a swim when we were beyond the reef."

"You're still doing that, eh?"

"Carl. Don't get cross about it. It's wonderful out there. You can really feel the sea. You never get it like that near the shore."

He looked at her anxiously as they passed on to the top verandah. And yet he was glad to have, temporarily, something as deep as anxiety between them.

"Sheila," he said, "I keep warning you about that open sea bathing. It's dangerous. And no matter how clean the *Nisba* is, she's had enough fish blood spilling over the stern for some of the scent to stick. You never know what might be trailing you."

She laughed and flung herself into one of the big chairs which, painted green and white, were cut so that you half reclined in them. On the floor beside her chair was a pile of drawings on big stiff sheets: they were advertisements for soap, and he could see the notes she had written in the corner of the top sheet. A pair of horn-rimmed spectacles and a fountain pen rested on a file of papers which lay on the small table between her chair and his.

"It's not as bad as that," she said. "I swim close to the boat, and Jackson has better eyes alone than you with your big glasses."

"Sure, sure," he grunted. "And bigger teeth than a tiger shark."

"Anyway," she said. "You do it sometimes."

"I swim better than you."

"And I know more about the sea."

"Go ahead," he told her. "I'm only telling you what I think."

He was suddenly and momentarily angry with her, with the whole warm afternoon, with their tense, sparring relationship.

She was looking at the little watch on her flat strong wrist.

"You're over early today, aren't you?" she said. "I didn't expect you for about an hour."

"I'm going up town this evening," he told her. "I'll shower and change here."

"That's fine. Would you like to start now?"

"Whenever you like," he said. "Not too hot for you?"

"No; it's a nice afternoon." She was getting to her feet.

"I'm seeing some of the committee members tomorrow," he told her as they were going down the stairs. "I'm going to put in some spadework for the Ladies' Cup."

"Oh good, Carl. Do you think you can push them?" They were crossing the verandah to the drive.

"I think so. I'm president and half of them shoot at my place during the season. And after all, we play the north coast matches here at your place."

"Not my place: Lloyd's." She named her husband, smiling thinly.

"Lloyd's," he agreed, matching the way she had said it.

They were walking across the dry, hot smelling grass now, with the fine loose dust turning crisply beneath their boots. Under the guango tree Tom and Joshua, Sheila's stable boy, were saddling the ponies.

As they came into the shade of the trees, Carl turned to Sheila.

"Why aren't you riding Grey Gal?" he asked. "Why have you brought out Turco?"

"We always use Grey Gal," she told him. "She's a nice clever little thing, but Turco's faster."

He went up to Sheila's pony. It was a fine beast to look at, with plenty of chest, a short powerful neck and legs almost as good as those on Jamshid. Carl looked at Tom who was staring at Turco with a sour, disapproving concern. Tom shook his head faintly. Carl turned back to Sheila.

"I'd ride Grey Gal if I were you," he said. "Turco doesn't know enough for you to learn on. He's good for a game, but Grey Gal is the one to learn from."

"I'd really like to ride Turco," she said.

"I know," he told her. "Ride him all you want when you're exercising alone, but Grey Gal's the best for this."

"Can't I ride him?" she put her hand on the supple glossy neck.

"Joshua," Carl said, "take Turco back and saddle up Grey Gal. Hurry up, eh?"

He was only faintly irritated as he mounted Jamshid. In this game that he played as well as he did anything in his life, he was only concerned with learning to do it better. He knew he was right and that she was wrong; and that was all.

He put the pony in a long, easy canter that swung them, almost gliding, into the middle of the field. When he turned, it was by pressure so slight that the beast was loping round almost at the instant his thigh muscles began their contraction and his hard knee sent the message to the skin beneath it.

He listened to the intricate thudding on the dry ground; felt the easy, rocking dip and rise under him. Come on, boy, weave a bit. That's it. Near side. Off side. Now straight through, boy. That's it. Right away. Just gather and out. All right boy, easy now. Canter; walk up to them.

As he was walking the pony up to the tree, he suddenly thought of Roy and Etienne and his promise. The thought came without warning; it fell heavily into the warm-bodied, cool-headed confidence and sense of power that was the familiar condition of being on this three hundred yards of dusty grass. It spoilt it; spoilt it with a quick savage blow.

I won't think of it, he told himself riding under the tree and dismounting. It's done. I promised and it's done. I can think of it later.

Sheila was standing at the furthest edge of shade; away from Tom. She was looking sulky and trying not to. From round the back of the house, at the opposite side of the field, Joshua was riding a steel-grey, lean pony whose hooves, even at a walk, moved like the feet of a dancer. Carl went up to her.

"Here she is," he said. "We'll get started now."

"Yes," she said.

"What's the matter?"

"Nothing."

"Look," he said. "When I'm teaching this game, I only want to teach it. I'm sorry if I sounded short back there; but you've got to do as I say in this till you can play really well."

"I'm being silly," she said. "I'm sorry. I really am sorry, Carl."

"Forget it," he said. "It's good to learn on a pony like Grey Gal. Every good player has his own way of playing and when you're just learning it's a great advantage to have a horse as clever as that. It'll learn to know all the habits you're forming, almost as well as you. Better, perhaps, because you'll never know all of them. By next season you'll be glad to have a pony like Grey Gal. She'll know all your weak points. She'll know all your good ones, too."

She turned to him and put her big warm hand on the long

muscled ridges of his hairy forearm. He looked quickly down at her hand.

"You're a good teacher, Carl," she said.

They went over to where Tom and Joshua held the ponies.

8

They had been playing, with rests, for half an hour: practising some of the quickly taken, difficult shots which, with team work, always won a game, if you could do them one more time than your opponents. Practising these; and learning something more about the use of their ponies which was the thing, more than any other, you never fully learnt in this game; the one part of it where luck had no weight or importance, unless it was bad luck, and where understanding and habit and instinct were the only means by which you could ever know something about, or act with, the six hundred pounds of brave, trigger-nerved muscle beneath you.

He waited, feet hanging out of the stirrups, as Sheila came up the field dribbling the ball.

Not bad, he thought. Not good, now. She's jamming the bit against her mouth. Stop that, Sheila. No, not that way. Too hard. Too hard. She knows, she knows. You'll just hurt her pride.

When Sheila came up, he said, "You'll have to stop that wrenching on the bit. It's becoming a habit now that you can ride fairly well."

"Was I? Oh, dear. I was trying not to." She was a little breathless and her cheeks were brilliant with warm blood beneath her fine skin.

"It's one of the worst things you can do," he told her, "when it's not necessary. It's like not trusting a trained soldier to clean his rifle."

"I'll remember."

"One more", he told her, "and then we'll finish. Let's try that play where we're both riding up for the ball with me on your offside and you back hand up the field on your near-side. Remember what I told you about leaning your weight on me, so I don't ride you out of line with the stroke."

He swung his stick, and it was effortless and sure as a swordsman making a cut. The ball lifted fifty yards in a clean, true curve and dropped, spurting up dust, and rolled before coming to rest.

"Now," he said.

Galloping up the field, with her light seeming, soft, woman's weight pressing against him, shank, knee, thigh and side, he knew she wouldn't make it. They were going hard, and he was crowding her, but with discretion, remembering the difference in weights, but he knew she would fail this shot. And when she made the shot, and missed because her left elbow and knee were way out, forcing the stick and arm from the clean line of the stroke, she began to slip. He had begun to pull away as soon as she started her stroke; when he knew, without question, that she would never connect: and now she began the slide out of her saddle that would begin as one slow, jerking bounce and end in a fast helpless tumble.

He brought Jamshid in beside her again; doing the things that would change the beast's course, before his mind had properly registered that she was falling. He put his arm around her waist and pulled her clear, carrying her with him in full gallop. Then he stopped the pony and slipped off, still holding her.

She was breathless, and her face was glowing. He bent and kissed her on her open, fast-breathing mouth. And for a few seconds she was too out of breath and bewildered to do anything.

Then she twisted a little, not struggling but quite firmly twisting away, and said: "No, Carl, please."

He let her go. She began to walk over to Grey Gal who had come trotting up in a wide half circle across the field.. Carl took Jamshid's reins and followed her.

"I'm not sorry," he told her, catching up. "You looked damn wonderful."

"That's all right, Carl." She didn't look at him.

"I know you don't love me," he said, "but why don't you want me to kiss you?"

"Not out here," she said. "There's Josh and Tom, and they can see us from the house."

"I don't mean here only." His voice was flatly determined. "You know what I mean. You're not in love with Lloyd and we've known each other for two years. We do a lot of things together and you like me. Why do you always stop me trying to make love to you?"

"Please, Carl. It's just that if we did that sort of thing... well, we just wouldn't enjoy it, or like each other any more."

"That's not it, Sheila." His voice was hard, and a little vicious now. "Stop fooling around. You want a man as much as I want you. What's wrong with me? What are you afraid of?"

"Please, Carl."

You bastard, he told himself. You know why. You know how she looks when she comes up to my place and Roy's there. Or when I bring him down here. Or when I see him in town and tell her about him.

"Come on," he said gently. "We're both pretty hot and wet. Let's go and change and you can give me a drink."

They rode back to the tree. Tom took the froth-spattered pony, with the wet dark patches all over its sides and belly, and looked at Carl with troubled, compassionate eyes.

"O.K., Tom," Carl said, "you can go straight back now. I'll be back from town tomorrow night. Tell Delia to leave something cold for me as I'll be late."

"Him didn't look too happy on the right fore, Mass' Carl," said Tom, pointing to the deeply snorting Jamshid. "You didn't feel it, sah?"

"No," said Carl, "He felt all right to me. You sure?"

"Him didn't look too right, sah. Not right at all."

"Look at him when you get back. If you think you ought to, phone for Dr. Scott. He felt happy enough, though."

"Right, sah."

He joined Sheila and they walked across the field to the house. At his car, while she went on upstairs, he reached into the front seat and took out his old, officer's holdall. Then he went upstairs to the shower.

She was sitting on the verandah when he came out. Her dress was of green cotton, with a flared, pleated skirt; there were big gold flowers and crimson stems in the pattern of the skirt, and some of the flowers lay across her breast.

Her hair was still damp from the shower, and it was loose and cloudy at the front over her forehead, framing her face closely and curling on her neck. She was staring out over the tall, curved trunks and the gently stirring, thin-bladed leaves of the coconut trees. Her face was thoughtful, but not sad any more. There was rum, ice, glasses and a pitcher of water on the yucca table between the two cream and green chairs.

"That was quick," he told her. "I thought I'd be the first out. You look nice."

"Thank you. How's my sunburn?"

"It suits you. It doesn't spoil your skin like it does so many English girls."

"That's the Celt in me," she said. She was mixing two drinks as she spoke; dropping the chipped ice into the tall glasses and pouring the clear, amber rum over the ice. "Do you think I'll ever get a tan like you?" She looked at the glazed, deep-layered brown of his face.

He smiled. "Not unless you find a few black men among your ancestors. My tan had a good base to work on. Besides, you have to start getting this sort of tan as a child. It's hard to catch up on." He took his drink and poured a little water from the pitcher into it, and sipped at the cold, damp rim.

Sheila was looking at him curiously.

"You know", she said, "I've sometimes wanted to ask you something."

"What?"

"You are one of the few men of your sort, out here, who don't seem to mind being coloured. I mean, all the others I've met like you, the ones from the old families, they all want to pretend it doesn't exist. They don't deny it, but they'd rather go on as if it wasn't there. Why isn't it like that with you?"

"It used to be. I was just like that when I was young."

"But why not now? You even seem proud of it sometimes."

"That's Roy," he said. "At first he made me feel ashamed of not recognizing it. He made it seem contemptible. And then he made me feel it was rather a good thing, all this mix-up of races."

There was a pause; and then she said in a casual, painfully

distinct voice: "He means a lot to you, doesn't he? And you to him? It means more than just being old friends to both of you."

"It's more than that," he said slowly. He was close now to the thing that had given flavour to much of his life; and he had seldom talked with anyone about it.

"Yes", she said, "go on, Carl." She had leaned forward eagerly in her chair, with the drink tilted nearly to the edge of her glass.

"At first it was just being new boys at the same school," he told her. "You know what it's like at that age. Every day seems about a week, and at the end of the term you seem to have known a chap for years. Then he used to come to stay with me for holidays. I went to his place, too; but it wasn't much fun there. My old man and he got to like each other really well. When the old man died during the war, Roy took it nearly as bad as I did. He just sat there, looking at the cable lying on the table in the room we were sharing. Anyway, it wasn't only school. I think it was going away together after. We just got to know each other better and better, I guess; and by the time the war was over we'd shared so many things that it became like it is now. Even when we don't see each other for a while we always pick up where we left off."

Her face was alert, intent.

"After I came back from England," he went on, "I was afraid we might lose it. Roy stayed behind for three more years. He hardly ever wrote. He always seemed to be busy or going off somewhere. I used to get news from his mother. But when he came back it was just the same. Better, really. He was the same old Roy, but more so in a way. The night he landed I went over to Queenshaven to meet him, and we sat talking on his verandah till four o'clock in the morning."

"I'd like to have seen the two of you at school. What did he look like as a boy?"

"You won't believe it," he told her, grinning, "but he was fat. Small and fat."

"No," she said in a tenderly delighted voice.

"Yes, really. He looked like an egg on toothpicks. And he had a double chin. But he's always had those eyebrows, and they made him look interesting."

"I can't imagine Roy as a fat boy. Didn't the other boys tease him?"

"They started to, but they stopped it."

"Why?"

"He had a filthy temper when he was roused. And besides he was so interested in what other people were doing that they got to like him. He wasn't nosey. Just interested and pleased when they told him about themselves. He could make anybody feel important."

"He can look pretty fierce now, sometimes."

"That's how we first met," he told her. "Just after we got there, we both got caught up in a hell of a fight."

Her face was bright and utterly interested. He suddenly felt embarrassed and jealous and pleased, all at the same time.

"The second day we were there," he told her, "the third formers took us into their class to make us sing. They always did that to the new boys. My old man had told me about it. He seemed to think it was one of the things that made it a good school. None of us would have thought of refusing. It was just one of the things you had to do, and which you did to new boys when you became a third former."

"It sounds awful."

"It wasn't too bad, really. Just to show you your place. We all felt embarrassed, and one boy got excited and wet his pants. But so long as you tried to sing they let you go."

"And Roy was in this, too?"

"Yes. They took him first, because he was the fattest, and stood him on the master's desk; and then they crowded around saying, 'Sing, boy, sing'."

"What happened then?" She was smiling softly with open possessiveness.

"He wouldn't sing," he told her. "He just stood there looking frightened but grim. Then they began to twist his arms and one boy, a big chap, from the country like me, began to hit him on the head with the edge of a ruler."

"You mean to say they allowed things like that to go on?"

"Roy looked as if he was going to cry when they began hitting him with the ruler. But he still wouldn't sing. The rest of us new boys stood there looking at him; we thought he was brave as hell, but we felt that he was spoiling the tradition. We didn't exactly think he was wrong; but we felt he didn't fit in with what we'd been told about the school."

"I'm glad he didn't," she said indignantly. "It sounds awful to me."

"They must have hit Roy too hard, because all of a sudden he started to cry and then he kicked out and caught one of them flush in the mouth. Jesus, that was a kick. There was blood all over the place."

"What happened then?"

"Everybody was so astonished that they didn't know what to do for a second. No new boy had ever done anything like that before. And when I saw him start to cry, I knew I had to do something to help him. I knew he wasn't crying because he was scared; he was making a sort of angry noise. I was a pretty big chap for my age and I'd been fighting since I was three with the black boys on the property; so I flung myself on the smallest of the third formers and dragged him down. Then I gave him one in the eye."

Sheila gave a thrilled laugh. "Good!" she said. "I hope you hurt him properly. Go on."

"They beat us up, but not too badly. Bumped us and poured ink over our heads and emptied the pencil sharpener over us. But they couldn't think of anything to do. Short of killing us, they couldn't do anything that would match what Roy and I had done. It was too outrageous."

Sheila was looking like a small girl; excited and impressed.

"When they were putting us in the dirt box," he went on, "a queer thing happened. They were putting me in, and holding Roy ready to go in next. Roy had stopped crying but we were both feeling pretty serious and sad and... and abandoned. Suddenly we looked at each other and began to laugh. We laughed like hell. When they let me out I took up the blackboard pointer and flung it through the window and Roy and I laughed harder than ever. They let us go then because they began to get frightened in case we did some more damage. Maybe they thought they'd hurt us and we were getting hysterical. They allowed us to go without running the gauntlet and we went across to the toilet, laughing like two maniacs and blue with ink. We weren't hysterical though: Roy once told me, later on, that the reason we laughed was because we realized we'd won. They couldn't do anything to us as bad as we'd done to them."

"What a life," she said. "If I ever have a son, I won't send him to Cayuna College."

He smiled at her. "It wasn't too bad," he told her. "At least it didn't do us any permanent harm and we had a lot of fun there. Besides, they tell me it's better now; they go in for psychology."

"I should hope so."

She was smiling at him, and he was aware that they had been closer over the past hour than they had ever been: less cautious and defensive. He glanced at his watch and saw that it was half-past five and knew that he would have to leave.

"I'll have to be going now," he said, getting up and stretching. "I have to see Roy in Queenshaven at eight-thirty; and I want to call in at my uncle's before I go to his place."

"You're seeing Roy?" She wasn't looking straight at but past him.

"Yes. Just a little business matter."

The discomfort in his stomach which he had felt on the field had come back as he thought of Roy and Etienne. "Give him my regards." She spoke with elaborate indifference.

"I will."

Going down the stairs she said to him: "I'm sorry you have to go now. I wanted to have a talk about things."

"I'll be back tomorrow and I can see you Sunday. Is there anything wrong?"

"No more than usual." Her face held a thin smile. "It's just the same. I just wanted your advice on some of the things I had in mind."

"Sure." He turned to her in the half-light of the dim hallway. "You're doing a good job here, you know. I'm not saying that because of the way I feel about you. To come out from England without any training, and do what you've done to keep this place going, is a damn fine job."

"Thanks," she said. "But it's only limping along, and you know it. We spend too much money and we only keep going because this place is established."

"That's Lloyd," he said. "The fool. This was one of the best properties in the island when old Pearce died. And between Lloyd and his father they've brought it to nothing. He's damn lucky he had you to take over for him."

"Lloyd isn't too bad," she said in a tired, tolerant voice. "He's just lazy and a bit spoilt. He likes having a good time without working for it."

"A-a-h," Carl said angrily and went out to his car. He wrenched open the door and chucked his holdall from the front seat to the back. His sweaty polo clothes were lying there where he had put them after his shower. Sheila came up to him.

"You musn't be too hard on Lloyd," she said kindly. "I know you don't think much of him, but he's kind and rather nice in his way."

Carl got into the Humber and closed the door. He looked at her through the window.

"How many days has he spent at Tolliver this month?" he asked. "He's been to England on holiday five times since the war, and to Canada once. Do you think a man can run a place like this if he doesn't work. The company over at Long Harbour had nearly put him out of business before you took things in hand; and yet in old Pearce's day half the island used to wash with Tolliver's soap. If it wasn't for you, and me helping you, he'd have had to sell up by now. Fancy a man leaving his wife to run his land. It's not right."

She gave a small false laugh.

"You're sweet, Carl," she said. "That's really what's bothering you. You think women ought to stay in the house and cook and have babies. I like all this, you know. All that stuff upstairs, and seeing to the factory and going round the trees. I like it and the people I work with. I hope they like me."

"They respect you," he told her, "because you work hard and you're not afraid to learn. They probably like you, too. But don't try to pass it off just because you feel bad about being disloyal to your husband. Where is he now, by the way?"

"He went up the coast for the day."

"Business?"

"Yes," she said, not looking at him.

Carl started the engine and she stepped back from the window. He reversed and brought the car forward, pointing down the drive. Sheila came up to the window again and he took her hand. She let it lie in his, but she didn't look at him and he could see that she was still embarrassed.

"I'll see you Sunday," he told her.

She nodded quickly and drew back. He let the Humber into second and drove off.

Going through the gate, he wondered if Lloyd Pearce was ever unfaithful to Sheila with any of the hard-drinking, sleek, very rich women in that set of luxury class tourists and winter residents he frequented and who liked him for his fantastic good looks, his money and his amiable servility. He thought that Lloyd frequently was unfaithful, but only through snobbishness, the most casual, understandable lust and a need to convince himself that he, a highly coloured Cayuna boy, had really made the top. He was pretty sure that Lloyd loved and admired Sheila from a comfortable distance, and, in a way, this was the nicest thing one could say about Lloyd.

As the big humming car turned off the broad, banked tarmac of the coast road and began to climb the white, twisting road which led across the island, he was thinking again of Lloyd and Sheila; and of how two people so different could have found the one point in their lives where they thought they needed each other. He was thinking of the very young, shyly delighted girl Lloyd Pearce had brought back from England three years before; and of the woman who was being made, now, out of disappointment, work, and a hard, clear love for her new home. He was also thinking how strange it was that Lloyd Pearce, of all men, should be the one to bring into his life the only woman be had loved.

9

Late in the afternoon, the small wind from the sea that had blown through Queenshaven most of the day suddenly dropped. For a while it was clammy and the heat lay across the town like a leaden sheet. Then, a little later, the breeze from the hills began to trickle down; filtering quite faintly at first but getting stronger. By six o'clock it was pleasant to stand in the street; and down town it was quiet, with most of the people gone home, and no cars. The buildings were blank and flat with their steel shutters pulled down, and the offices were dark. They had lit the street lamps, but these did not show well against the golden-white haze over the harbour and the pale green sky above the town. There were a few, long stratocumulus clouds, blazing red underneath, but with the white glow from their tops showing against the green apple sky. For a little, just before the shadows in the doorways and the lanes began to go grey, there was a light yellow radiance that flooded the whole city. And after that, the blue began to grow thicker everywhere.

In his office, Roy was reading through the terms of a contested will. He sat hunched in his chair, curled like a question mark over the papers, with an easy light from the green-shaded lamp beating on his face. In the outer office everyone but Linda had gone home, and he could hear the sure fast chatter of her typewriter. Every so often he made a note on the glossy-papered, thick pad lying on the big leather-cornered blotter.

About five minutes later, Linda put her head round the door.

"Bob Daniel is here," she said. "I heard him bringing his cycle up the stairs."

"Good," he told her. "I'm about finished with this."

"What's it like?"

"It's a bitch. The way the old lady made this thing the only people who stand to collect are me and the defendant's counsel."

"As bad as that, eh?"

"Worse. She might as well have just left the lawyers their share and her relatives a little each, and saved everybody a lot of trouble."

In the outer office they heard the door open and the ticking sound of a freewheel bicycle being pushed. Linda looked over her shoulder.

"Hullo, Bob," she said. She turned to Roy and whispered: "For heaven's sake watch your language. You know how he hates it when you use those words."

Roy got up. "Hullo, Bob," he said. "How are you?" He moved from behind his desk to the middle of the room and shook hands. Then he drew up a chair beside the desk and went back to his own. Linda closed the door and came over and stood at the front of the desk, looking at the two men.

"I brought up my bicycle," Bob Daniel said, taking off his spectacles, polishing them slowly on a carefully folded, very clean cotton handkerchief. "It's not safe to leave it in the street at this time of night, even with a lock." He put his spectacles back.

"I know," Roy said. "They're going for the front tyres now, even if you chain it to the fence."

He looked at the man before him: at the neatly cut, close-curled, grizzling hair, the long, grave face, with the ancient, rolled gold spectacle rims very yellow against the black skin, at the dead straight, narrow lips, and finally at the long slim hands which might have been finely made from woven stands of thick, black telegraph wire. The hands still had patches of grease across the knuckles, from the day's work at the big garage where Daniel was a master mechanic.

Well, Roy," he said, "how did it go?"

"Not too bad. I've got Brandt's place for him to stay, and Mason put me on to the sailor this morning. He'll get the message to the *Kosciuzko*. I hope the Executive Committee will approve of the arrangements I've made."

"Of course, Roy. We gave you full authority last night. Where are you going to get him away from?"

"From Columbus Head."

"Columbus Head," Daniel said slowly. "I seem to have heard something about it. I can't remember what, though. Where is it?"

Roy turned the chair and got up and went to the framed, ordnance survey map of Cayuna which hung on the wall behind his desk. He put his finger on a point on the north coast. Bob followed him to the wall and stared at the spot with deliberate, slow carefulness.

"I don't know much about these things," he said, pointing to some marks in the sea area off the coastline, "but doesn't that mean shoal water? That was the thing I was trying to remember."

"Yes."

"That's dangerous, isn't it?" They went back to their chairs.

"Yes," Roy told him. "It's one of the riskiest bits of the coast. They've about three men up there who can get a fishing boat in or out at night. I think we should take him out to the ship from there for that reason. If anything happens they will probably watch places like that less closely and there's more chance of a getaway."

Daniel nodded gravely.

"I agree," he said. "I think you did right to decide on Columbus Head and the Committee are sure to say the same. You know anyone who can get him out of the Head?"

"A fisherman who has done it."

"A party member?"

"Yes. I don't think you know him; Jeffrey Summer."

"I've seen the name but I haven't met him."

"He's wonderful with a boat. Him and his three sons. There's one thing, though."

"What's that?"

"We'll have to transfer Etienne to a powered boat half a mile or so out."

"Why?"

"Two reasons. It's too far out for us to row him, especially in the sort of current you get off the Head. And we have to meet the *Kosciuzko* precisely at the right point at the right time. We must have a powered boat for that."

"Do you know how to get one?"

"I think so. There's a woman, a great friend of Brandt's, she has a boat and she's first rate at handling it. I think we might be able to use her."

"I don't like it." Daniel's long, serious face was disapproving, as if he was considering and rejecting a move in a chess game.

"We'd have to steal one, then," Roy told him, in the same way. "No one in the party owns anything more than a row boat."

"It's bringing another outsider into it," Daniel explained. "Could you trust her?"

"She'd do it, think, if Brandt asked her. And if she won't, she's the sort who would keep her mouth shut because of personal loyalty."

"You think this is the only way."

"No," Roy told him. "There are other ways. Steal a boat, as I told you; and we could probably think of something else. But we have to consider the possible risks; all the possible things that might happen between Etienne landing here and getting away again. In my opinion having two people like Carl Brandt and this woman, Mrs. Pearce, whom no one would suspect, will reduce the risks."

"Have you asked her yet?"

"No. I'll do it Sunday. That'll give us enough time, if she says no, to think of something else."

Daniel took off his spectacles, turning them slowly between his long fingers, and frowned. After a minute he turned to Linda.

"What do you think, Linda?" he asked her calmly. "You're on the Committee, too."

"I'm with Roy," she told him.

He nodded and sat in silence for another minute. Then he said: "I'm feeling like a pickney playing games. I've never done this sort of thing before. There are so many things we have to think of. I can't be sure if you're right, Roy. It sounds as if your plan's the best; but it's a dangerous best."

He said this in the steady, untroubled way he would have discussed a length of suiting.

"I know," Roy said. "If we had more time. If we had been given more time. The way it is now, this seems the only thing."

"You've done a good job. I think we had better get the opinion of the Committee, though. I'll do that tonight and tomorrow."

"How'll you do it?" Roy asked him. "See them separately and give them the facts?"

"Yes, that will be the best. I'll have the answer by tomorrow evening. I'm with you and Linda."

Roy nodded, got up and went to the window. Outside, it was dark, with sudden, sharply defined bright areas under the lamps. It was one of those deep, soft nights when the stars were huge and crowded. There were not many people in the street, but he could hear laughter and voices and glasses tinkling from the bar on the other side of the corner. A woman was quarrelling loudly in a yard behind the fence, but he couldn't hear what she was saying; some other people in the yard began to laugh, and the quarrelling woman became shrill and excited. It was cool.

"Now," he said, turning to Daniel. "What about the demonstration for Sunday?"

"It is being seen to. The group leaders have been told it's off as far as the party is concerned."

"It's the hell of a pity," Roy said. "It would have been a good rally and it would have made us a lot of useful friends in the Jungle. Do you think there'll be trouble?"

"Why? Because the party withdraws support at the last moment?"

"Yes."

"It will put us back a lot. We had done a lot getting this one organized. It's bound to put us back."

"I know." Roy was miserable, "But what else could we do? We couldn't have it without the leaders there and that's too much risk. If we got hauled in now, Etienne wouldn't stand a chance. How do you think the members will take it?"

"You mean the ones who don't know why we are calling it off? We'll lose a few and we'll know where we stand with the others. You know that, Roy."

"I'm sorry, Bob. It's just having to go and see Tiger Johnson tonight. It took us three years to get him to the point where he trusted us. If we lose him tonight because he thinks we're scared about Sunday, we'll never get him again. And all we can tell him is that it's off. We can't tell him why."

"We will have to go gently with him," Daniel said. "He's the boss in the Jungle, and we had just begun to make him useful to the people round him. We might even have to tell him why we're calling it off."

"That's impossible," Roy said flatly. "Even if he understood he wouldn't sympathize. He's only a gang boss. And we can't be sure enough of him. He's on too fine a balance for us to trust him that much."

"You are quite right." Bob Daniel had got to his feet. "I'll go home and eat now, and you can call for me in three-quarters of an hour."

"O.K. I'll call for you at about half-past seven, and we'll go and catch a tiger."

Daniel gave the polite, unpretending grimace which served him as a smile. He turned to the door and Linda followed to see him off. Roy heard their voices in the office and the ticking of the freewheel and the outer door closing. Linda came back.

"That's a man and a half," Roy told her, "but one day, just one day, I would like to see him smile."

"I know," she said. "He can make you feel pretty frivolous sometimes. What are you going to say to Tiger?" She was putting on a linen jacket and her handbag was on the chair beside her.

"That depends on how he takes it."

"Good luck," she said, taking up her handbag. "I'll see you tomorrow."

"Good night, Lin."

She went out of the room and he turned to the window again, leaning against the wall and resting his forehead on the edge where the wall ended. His mind felt empty and he had that easy, unshakeable sadness which comes with exhaustion. He was hardly seeing the street below. Linda passed under the lamp, walking towards the bus stop. She turned and waved in the hard yellow light. He lifted his hand back at her.

10

In the middle of Queenshaven, east of the main street, there was a low dusty hill. It was the Jungle. At one time it had been called Section Three; but during the last twenty years its present name had spread, so that only a few people now knew the official name, the one they had on the city maps.

It was densely populated. But none of the houses had been built by a firm or by the council. These shelters were made of old kerosene tins, motorcar chassis, old trucks without the engines, the bigger packing-cases, and rusty sheets of zinc leant together to form tents. It grew more crowded every year, and it was harder to find space on which to build. There wasn't any water except for two standpipes on the edge of the area, and the dust smelt sour and blew through the shacks. Forty thousand people lived in the Jungle, and five hundred of them had jobs to go out to in the morning.

At half-past seven, Roy and Bob Daniel walked up Junction Street, near the railway, and turned off at the end of the road into the Jungle. Roy had left his car outside Daniel's house, in a quiet lane near the main street.

Climbing in the dust of the Jungle it smelt bad, and the people they passed gave off the sweetish stink of bodies which don't get enough food, and which is like smelling, from a distance, the room where a man is ill with jaundice.

There were plenty of children playing and fighting in the dust: they showed up briefly in the light from the kerosene flares which burnt in some of the shelters; or they would as suddenly disappear into the black spaces between the shacks and lean-tos, like stones dropping into a dark pond.

There was a lot of noise; of people quarrelling and laughing; and once over on the left, they heard a man's ugly, exulting roar and, after a couple of seconds, a woman screamed. In some of the larger spaces there were fires, and smaller fires burnt before many of the shelters, with tins resting on stones above the flames. There was a lot of light, but fitful, and you passed from glare and heat to shadow unexpectedly. Most of the men sitting in front of the shacks, or drifting past in the dust, were ragged. And when the women passed before the fires you could see they had nothing on beneath their dresses. They were, mostly, wearing the sort of clothes you remember as grey.

Roy McKenzie was one of the few people in Cayuna, of his colour and class, who could have come here tonight, or any other night. Sometimes he and Bob Daniel were greeted from a fire as they climbed up through the closely packed shelters.

Near the top of the hill, the shacks began to thin out; then you could see the blurred dome of the hill and behind it a soft sky, with the stars so thick that it looked black and gold. Close under the crest of the hill, in a big space which felt underfoot as if it had been swept, was a large, solid shack. It had a door, and a small glass window, and the zinc sheets of the roof were well fixed on. This was Tiger Johnson's place. There was a big fire burning in the yard.

A small, tightly held brown man, in a good pair of blue jeans and a sweaty, flowered shirt, came out of the dark as they approached.

"What you want?" His voice was dry as two stones clicked together; and in the dancing light from the flames, Roy could see the flat, blank, unfriendly eyes. He carried a huge, nail-studded, coco-macca stick.

"Hullo, Trouble," Roy said. "We want to see Tiger."

"Oh, it's you. All right, wait here."

He went up to the door of the hut, seeming to bounce across the ground. He went inside without knocking and they could see his head against the window. After a while he put his head round the door and said, "All right. Him say come in."

They walked across the fine, sour dust of the yard and entered.

Inside, there was a table covered with a green-flowered shiny oilcloth. Four strong upright chairs were placed round the table, and an old-fashioned cane rocker stood in a corner. There was a big, glaring kerosene lamp in the middle of the table and its light flickered on walls which were covered with four different patterns of wallpaper. A blue and cream kitchen cupboard stood against one wall, with a lot of cheap tumblers on it and three pint enamel mugs. They could see the top half of a patchwork quilt on the bed in the other room.

Tiger Johnson sat at the head of the table: his dead, black eyes stared at them with the emotionless concentration of a wary carnivore. The eyes were reddened across the whites, and Roy could smell the faint, dead flowers' scent of ganja.

A slender, beautiful, half-coolie girl, in a clean, print dress, lounged against the doorway to the other room, with one perfect, thin foot resting on the knee of her straight leg: her face was half hidden in the long wild curls of her hair and all they could properly see was the steady, quick glitter of her eyes which followed every movement they made.

Tiger smiled as they came up to the table. When he smiled it went no further than the edges of his mouth. The inside of his thin, rubbery lips peeled back and showed so bright a red that you half expected to see fainter, red stains on the small, flawless teeth.

Roy looked at the man's wild, black head: the great bush of hair sweeping back from the high forehead, and the harsh lines and sharp planes of the small face in its frame of tufted wirey beard, looked as if it had been passionately cast from rough, black iron.

Jesus, he thought, they know something's wrong. They've sensed it before we've spoken. This is going to be hard climbing. I wish Bob would stop looking like a deacon in a whorehouse.

"Hullo, Tiger," he said. "We had to come and see you. O.K.?"

Tiger nodded and flicked his head swiftly at the chairs nearest him. Roy and Bob sat down. Tiger shifted his head imperceptibly again and looked at the girl. She seemed to flow away from the door jamb and Roy could not hear the pad of her bare feet on the floor behind him. She went to the cupboard and there was the sound of clinking glasses. Then with a quick gesture of fierce shyness she put a bottle of white rum and three glasses on the oilcloth before Tiger. She went back to her position in the doorway.

"You want water?" he asked them.

"Christ, yes," Roy told him. "That stuff burns me without it."

"No, thank you," Daniel said.

Tiger slid his eyes briefly to Trouble who was leaning rigidly and watchfully against the wall next to the door. He jerked away from the wall, went stiff-legged to the kitchen-dresser and took one of the pint mugs. Roy watched him dip it into the tin bucket beside the dresser and bring the dripping mug to the table. He still carried his big stick; it seemed to fit him like an extra long arm.

Tiger poured three half-glasses of the rum; it was the colour of clear water in which there is a faint trace of light oil. Roy filled his glass and sipped carefully, preparing his throat for the first burning choke. Bob and Tiger drank half their straight drinks with brief, expert swallows.

"You want a smoke?" Tiger asked them. His voice was sly, and he pulled his lips away from his teeth in a slow, red smile of impersonal malice.

Bob Daniel looked pointedly into his drink; his long face was severe and pained.

"You and your bloody ganja," Roy said. "Every time we come here you want us to try one, and every time we say no."

Tiger smiled again. He still seemed to be enjoying that solitary joke: some ferocious, gay music which he heard all alone.

"What do you want, Roy?" Tiger asked him.

Roy drank another careful sip, feeling the heat of it spread swiftly through his stomach and rising to his chest. What a boy, he thought. If I was to jump him with a knife, now, he would take it as natural as if I spoke.

"We have some bad news, Tiger," he said.

"Police?" Tiger's body was tautly balanced in his chair.

"In a way," Roy said. "We have to call off the rally for Sunday. We've got some news which means we can't do it."

"You don't want de march?"

"Not now. It would be a bad time for it. There might be trouble, bad trouble."

"Police?"

"Yes. There might be trouble with the police, and the party and the unemployed can't afford what might happen; not just at the moment."

"You don't have money?" Tiger's voice relaxed into bewilderment for a second.

"No, Tiger, not that sort of afford. It isn't a matter of cash..."

"Then how you mean you can't afford?"

"I mean that we have news that would make it dangerous and stupid to have the rally at the moment. We want to put it off for a little, until it's a better time."

I'm not doing so good, he thought. I'm bitching it up.

"What news you hear?" Tiger asked in a cold voice. "I don't hear any news. Trouble, you hear any news?"

"No, Tiger."

"What news you hear, Roy?"

"It's something to do with all of us, Tiger. It's something very important and it would be foolish if we were to give them what they want by having the rally."

He was sweating with the rum, and with the glaring heat from the lamp in this little, metal-roofed room. He knew that if he raised his hand with the glass, it would tremble. Behind him, in the doorway to the bedroom, he heard the girl draw a deep, steady breath.

"I don't hear no news, Roy. What news, Bob?"

Tiger was pressed, now, against the back of his chair in a tense crouch: his flat eyes glowed with a sombre, cold light, and they switched from Roy to Daniel repeatedly.

"Tiger," Bob said, "we've known you for three years, and you've known us. You know that we're the only party who have tried to do something for the people in the Jungle. Why don't you trust us in this? If we could have the rally we would. If we did, though, it might mean a bad thing for everybody."

"I trust you," Tiger Johnson said. "I trust you when I tell you say my boys would help you have de rally. What news you hear dat I don't hear?"

"Why did you offer to help us, Tiger?" Roy asked him suddenly. Get him answering, he thought. He's driven us all the way, so far. Get him answering. It might help.

"Because you say your party help de African man get something: just like de brown man or de white man."

"And do you think we mean it?"

"You say so. Mebbe you mean it."

His indifference, and the unrelaxing, savage gaze were a little terrifying. The girl brought him a cigarette rolled in brown paper and put it between his lips; she reached into the breast pocket of his gaily patterned shirt and brought out a box of matches and struck a light for him. Then she went back to her place in the doorway. Tiger never took his eyes from the two men before him.

"We mean it," Bob Daniel said. "We want something for all the men in this island; work and food and homes. We have shown you we mean it in the last three years."

"I got food and a house, and her," Tiger's eyes twitched towards the girl. "You get them for me?" He fixed his implacable stare on Roy and Bob Daniel again.

"No," Roy said. "You got them for yourself. How many men in the Jungle have them, though?"

"Dose? Out dere? Dey do what I tell dem. I tell my boys an' my boys tell dem."

"And you offered to help us," Roy said in a gentle, calm voice. "You knew what we hope to do and you offered to help us. You think we've changed?" The blood was singing in his ears and he could feel the sweat starting out under his armpits, running down his ribs.

"I tell you say, my boys will get de people out for de march and de rally. Ask fe' work. Dat's what you tell me an' dem. Why you change?"

"We have not changed, Tiger," Bob Daniel said in his slow, careful way. "We want the same things we always did. But now is a bad time; we could suffer plenty if we had it now. Another time it will be good. Hear me, no, man?"

"You frighten of de police?"

"Not frightened; we just want to be strong when we need strength."

"My boys won't let de police rough you up." There was an unsurprised contempt in Tiger's voice, more depressing than anger.

"Tiger, we don't mind the police. You know we've taken risks before," Roy told him. "But if we made a mistake now and held the rally it would put us back too much."

"What news you hear?"

"Why don't you trust us?" Roy said, ignoring the question. "We need your help and we have a chance of working together if you believe us."

"I don't need your help," Tiger said.

"Don't you want to help us find work for the people in the Jungle?"

"Sure. Black man in dis country have to take too much beating. I want de African man to get somet'ing."

"If you want that, then believe us now that we're not selling out. We only waiting for the best chance."

"Now is a good time."

"No it isn't. I'm telling you true, Tiger. We know it would be a bad time now."

"I don't need you, Roy. I don't need dat party of yours. I do fine before I know you."

He reached into the table drawer under the oilcloth and came out with a little canvas bag in his hand. The hard small fingers picked deftly at the knotted cord around the neck of the bag. Then with a quick jerk of his wrist he shot a heap of money on to the shiny cloth: there was a lot of silver and several small folded notes. Roy knew that there was no pride in all this: that he had done it as his namesake in a jungle would have roared.

We've lost him now, he thought. It took us three years to get him to the place where he felt we could help him. And we've lost it in a few minutes. We don't even interest him any longer.

"Here, Trouble," Tiger said. He chose a half-crown piece and flicked it off his thumb. Roy saw the dull glint twinkle in the air; then Trouble's hand closed surely on the gleam. Tiger had not looked away from them during this. He chose another coin and tossed it to the girl and Roy could hear the sudden rustle of her movement behind him and imagine the fumbled catch. Tiger poured himself three inches of the white rum; he did not offer to fill Bob Daniel's empty glass.

"Is de same t'ing," Tiger said, in a flat emotionless voice. "Is de same t'ing all de time: only African man is good fe' African man."

"Our party is for all men, Tiger," Bob Daniel said, speaking with deliberate, emphatic conviction. "This island is for all men and we want all men to share it."

"I don't know 'bout dat. Me only know 'bout de African man."

Roy got up, and looked at Bob. The other man nodded, the slightest movement of his chin, and got to his feet.

"You gawn?" Tiger asked them. His eyes were wide and baleful: they searched the two men with unworried, ferocious attention.

"Yes, Tiger," Roy said. "We have to go now. We'll come again, eh? We'll be able to explain about the rally then, perhaps. What you say?"

"Come if you want." The supple, glazed rubber of his lips pulled aside in that private spasm of unshared laughter. He drawled, with heatless, uncommitted malice: "You want a cigarette, Roy? Tek it wid you."

"Cho, no, Tiger. I couldn't smoke your cigarettes. They're too strong for me."

There was no ill humour in Tiger's face as his eyes followed them to the door, and no good humour either. He had dismissed them utterly.

They didn't speak until they were in Junction Street again. The breeze from the mountains felt good on his back after the yellow, glaring heat of Tiger's room.

"If we ever get into power," Bob Daniel said, and from his voice you could know that he had been turning this in his mind with unhurried calm, "if we ever get in, that Tiger Johnson will be a bad trouble for us. I don't think we really figured him out tonight."

"We need him, though," Roy said.

"We have to use him," Bob Daniel agreed. "But I think we ought to consider what he is, more carefully. We will make bad mistakes if we don't. Someday we're going to have to stop him."

"I know," Roy said. "But when that day comes, we'd better have a big tough boy to do it."

They crossed Queen's Street, deserted at this hour, with high lamps glimmering on the black tar. At Daniel's house Roy went in and got the wallet of money he had left there. He refused a cup of coffee, because it was late, and went out to his car.

"I'll see you tomorrow," he said to Daniel, and drove off. He turned the car out of the narrow, respectable lane where Daniel lived and drove up Queen Street, going to his home in the suburbs.

He was yawning: wide, stretching yawns that brought water to his sore eyes. He was sorry he had not taken the coffee.

As he was coming to the edge of the suburbs, he had a sudden, detailed vision of Tiger Johnson and his woman in bed. It was unexpected and involuntary and it went very quickly. But while it lasted it was formidable and disturbing.

11

Carl reached Queenshaven just after eight. He had driven over the high climbing, steeply descending trunk road which cut across the island, joining the two coasts by way of the damp forested mountains where the air always had a clean, bitter scent, and where, if you stopped the car, you could hear the solitaires in the valley calling their sad, liquid notes to one another.

In Saragossa, the old, faded Spanish capital, fifteen miles from Queenshaven, he had stopped to eat a large meal of fried rice and shrimps. This was in a little, shabby room behind a Chinese grocery, and the rich, tantalising smell of the food was mingled with the smells of raw saltfish and rice sacks and hard cheese. He always stopped here to eat when he came through after four in the afternoon: it was one of the regular, nourishing habits of which his life was made.

After eating, he came into town, driving fast on the flat, straight road between the big sugar estates.

His uncle's house was in the suburbs; on the plain, but close under the foothills. It was low, thick-walled and neat, like the other bungalows in this section, with white sides and heavy, red tiles. It had a good lawn and a wide verandah, and when he braked the big Humber by the steps he could smell the delicate, permeating sweetness of the night jasmine.

His uncle, Hector Slade, came to the head of the steps. He had been having dinner; Carl could see, in his hand, the white blur of his napkin. His uncle's big round head, and frail seeming, tall, stooped body looked incongruous in his stiff trim uniform.

"That you, Carl? I thought I recognized your engine."

"Yes, Hector. How are you?"

"Didn't expect you till tomorrow. Have you had dinner?" Carl was getting out of the car and locking the door. He said, over his shoulder, "Yes, I ate in Saragossa. Tell Hubert there's some oranges in the boot. I'll leave the keys in the door."

"I'll see you inside." His uncle went back into the house. Carl followed; passing through the cream tiled drawing-room, with its bright rugs and sleek, modernistic furniture and many books, into the dining-room. Hector Slade and his wife Kathleen and his daughter Janice were having dinner. They sat at one end of the long, gleaming cloth of their table, like people grouped protectively on the edge of a snow-bound, empty plain.

"Carl," said Kathleen Slade, "we didn't expect you until tomorrow. What a nice surprise."

She held out her slender, dry-fleshed hands eagerly, and he went to her quickly and bent to kiss her gaunt, eccentrically handsome face, hugging her fondly and feeling the quick, nervous strength of her hands on his shoulders.

"I finished early," he said, as he straightened and ran his hand softly on the shining, smooth hair, which was still black and youthful, but caught in a heavy bun. "I thought I'd come over tonight instead."

"I'm so glad."

She smiled up at him with an abrupt, fluttering tenderness that had nothing to do with timidity, but was, you felt, the result of some darting, too eager effort to meet life, and which was matched by those big, shy eyes which dominated the off-centre planes and proportions of her face and looked at the world with a gently puzzled, inept eagerness and trust.

He smiled at her, holding her hand for a moment. As long as he lived he could never forget or repay this woman who had been, in her own gentle, completely faithful, slightly askew fashion, mother and aunt to him since he was nine, and with no call to have been these except for an accident of marriage and the summons of her warm, clumsy heart.

"I'm so glad," she said again. "We haven't seen you for ages."

"I brought you some oranges," Carl told her, "and those double hibiscus cuttings you asked me for."

"Thank you, dear, it was sweet of you to remember."

He turned to the sallow, fading blonde who was his cousin Janice. She raised the cheek of her slightly sullen, defeated-looking face for him to kiss.

"Hi, Jan," he said.

He sat in the chair beside her and looked at his uncle.

"Good to see you," his uncle said. "How're things at the Pen?"

"Not bad. It should be a good year. I got a nice order from Venezuela yesterday."

"Good. What is it?"

As he always did, Carl felt happy in the comfortable warmth of his uncle's precise, intelligent interest. With Hector Slade, you felt your responses heighten at the sound of his sharp, high voice, picking answers out of you like a hen's beak snapping corn from the ground.

"They want a bull," Carl told him, "and six heifers. The new stock."

"Can you spare it?"

"Oh, yes, I can spare it all right."

"They'll ask for more. You're the only man in the West Indies who has the sort of stock they need."

"Go on," Carl said. "There's plenty of good stuff all over the place now."

"Not like yours, man."

The maid came into the room from the back verandah which led to the kitchen. She was carrying a tray with a plate and cutlery and a little leather case of keys.

"Good evening, Mass' Carl," she said. "How you is, sah? Hubert say, please here is de car keys."

"Good evening, Gwen," he said. "I'm fine. No, don't lay for me. I've eaten already."

He took the car keys from the tray and put them in his pocket.

"Carl," Kathleen Slade's voice rose on a happy, possessive wail. "You must eat something."

"I couldn't, Aunt Kay. Didn't Hector tell you? I ate at Dora Ching's in Sargossa."

For a minute she nagged lovingly; he would have been disturbed had she not.

"I'll have some dessert," he said, "when you're having yours."

"Good," she smiled, satisfied. "It's pineapple ice-cream."

He grinned faintly at Hector, whose small stone-grey eyes behind the thick spectacles twinkled in mock sympathy.

"I can't stay long," Carl said. "I promised I'd see Roy tonight."

"How is Roy?" asked Hector; looking at him, then, you did not notice the large, globular, scholar's head, and the thin scalp and fine hair which gave it an appearance of fragility. You only saw the shrewd, smooth pebbles of his eyes, the rigid, decisive nose and the small, firm mouth under the neat, grey moustache. The meagre neck did not look scrawny, but was suddenly pliant and ready to thrust, like a snake's neck. And you were aware that the thin, round-shouldered body, under the starched khaki uniform, was lean as vulcanised flex is lean, for efficiency and control.

"He's fine," Carl said carefully. "He came over to see me this morning. He was up at Castleville for a case."

"One of his poor people's cases I suppose," Janice said in the faintly bitter, petulant voice she had begun to use during the last three years. "I saw him the other day, downtown, with the roughest looking black man you could imagine. You should have seen them, talking like old friends."

"Maybe they were old friends," Carl said.

"I wouldn't be surprised," Janice said. "I'm only sorry for his poor mother; they say he brings all sorts of people into her drawing-room. Can you imagine it. If I were her, I'd have given him his marching orders long ago."

"Now, dear, she couldn't do that," Kathleen Slade said worriedly, catching at some fresh puzzle. "But, Carl, don't you think he could find some other place to meet his friends? Some of them are very common, and it couldn't be pleasant for poor Mrs. McKenzie."

"They don't steal her silver, do they?"

"No, dear, no. Nothing like that. But, after all it isn't comfortable to have them there."

"I'll tell him," Carl said.

"Will you, dear? If *you* put it to him I'm sure he wouldn't mind."

"All right, Aunt Kay, I'll mention it to him."

"Cho," Janice said. "He's a rough. He was all right when he went away; but he came back a real rough."

"What do you think of this business in St. Pierre?" Hector asked him.

"It sounds dreadful," Kathleen said. "And that Etienne; I don't know why those places always seem to have men like that."

"I don't know much about it, Hector," Carl said. "I read about it this morning in the *Gazette*. It seems pretty bad."

"It had to come, man."

"I hope they catch Etienne," said Janice with tired anticipation.

"I hope they do," Hector said. "Save me the trouble if he comes here."

"Hector," his wife said. "You don't mean to say he's coming here?"

"No, Kay. They'll find him before he can leave St. Pierre. I was only saying that if he did try to land here we'd have to send him back." His eyes were gentle with understanding as he looked at her, and the deep grooves of his face pleasant with fondness when he smiled.

"You'd have to send him back, eh, Hector?" Carl asked. "I thought he could claim political asylum. They all do it, don't they?"

"He's a gangster. Saw the charges this morning. They flew them down with the request for extradition. Damned gangster and nothing else, whatever Roy and his friends would like us to believe."

"That's what your precious Mr. Roy will be like," Janice said, "if he doesn't watch out."

"Janice," said her mother, "you mustn't say such things. You've known Roy for years and he's Carl's best friend. Just because he calls himself a communist it doesn't mean he would be a murderer."

Gwen brought in four goblet-shaped blue dishes, with smoking, pale yellow mounds of ice cream above the glass.

"I must eat and run," Carl said, looking at his watch.

"What time will you be back, dear?" Kathleen Slade asked him.

"I don't know," he said. "About eleven, I guess, but we might go on somewhere."

"You'll be in for dinner tomorrow, won't you?"

"Of course," he said. "And we'll have breakfast together in the morning."

"Have lunch with me tomorrow?" Hector asked him.

"Sure. I'll be seeing about the polo in the morning, and we should be finished by twelve. I'll wait for you there."

"I'll be at the club about one."

He finished his ice-cream and smoked a cigarette and had coffee with them. Then he went out to the car.

Hector came down the steps with him.

"Got some good news for you, man." The high, snapping voice was affectionate and proud.

'What sort of good news?"

"They're going to make you a Justice of the Peace?"

"Me?"

"Don't say anything yet, of course, Unofficial. But it's quite definite. Good work."

"But how can I be a J.P., Hector? I don't know a damn thing about law."

"Nonsense. You can learn enough for that. Nothing to it. They were just waiting till you were old enough."

"I hope they know what they're doing."

"Of course. Recommended you myself, man. Unofficially, that is. I'm not supposed to have anything to do with it."

"Thanks, Hector."

"Nonsense. Nonsense. You're the best man for the job up there now."

"Thanks again."

"That Roy is causing me a lot of trouble," Hector said. The brusque voice was reflective and tinged with exasperated concern. "Can't understand what's come over the boy. Didn't like to say it before Kay, but he's getting into hot water."

"What do you mean?" Carl asked him. He was slowly turning the key in the handle of the car.

"He's organizing some damned march on Sunday. Lots of hooligans from the jungle. The worst elements in Queenhaven. He's going to march them up through the suburbs and have a rally at Cotton Tree Corner. Calls it the march of the unemployed."

"I didn't know that," Carl said. His legs felt watery with relief and he put one foot on the running board and leaned his weight on the handle.

"Tell him to be careful. Between friends, you know. Tell him that if anything happens I'll have to arrest him. I'd hate to do it to a boy of good family like that, but I'll have to."

"I'll tell him," Carl said. "Cheerio, Hector. I'll see you at breakfast." He got into the car, "Oh, by the way, I almost forgot." He fumbled in the locker of the dashboard and took out the map in its leather case. He passed it through the window to his uncle.

"You'll want to look at this," he said. "It's one of the old New Cornwall maps."

"Where did you get it?"

Carl told him.

"I'll have a good look at it," he said delightedly. "This is a find. What are you going to do with it?"

"Send it to the University. I'm having a few photostat copies made, though. I'll give you one."

Hector was turning the case over between his hands.

"I suppose we must do that," he said. "It's too good for us to keep now we have a university. Pity, eh? Good night, Carl."

He went up the steps quickly with that spring-kneed, mountain climber's stride which was so much younger than his sixty years.

Reversing the big Humber up the drive, Carl felt light and empty in his stomach. As he straightened in the road, he gave a soft laugh of eased tension.

12

The McKenzie's house had verandahs that bordered the front and half of one side; and Roy's bedroom was at the end of the half-length, opening on to it by opaque, double doors.

When Carl drew up at the steps he could see the light in Roy's room and he was glad that neither Mr. nor Mrs. McKenzie were on the verandah. He never knew what to say to Mr. McKenzie and he liked Roy's mother, but he did not want to see either of them just then.

He went along the verandah to the light. The doors were open and he could see Roy sitting at his desk, and part of the low shelves which were placed against three walls and filled with books.

Roy looked up over his shoulder as he came in from the dark.

"Hello, boy," he said.

"Hello. Am I late?"

"A bit, but I haven't been in long."

"I'd have got here before, but you know what it's like when you haven't seen them for a couple of months."

He straddled a chair by the heavy, executive-style desk, leaning his arms over the back. The desk was covered, but for the big square of blotter, with letters, files, magazines, an ugly glass ashtray filled with stubs and old ash, and the leather-framed photograph of a dark girl in a Royal Air Force uniform.

There were several good reproductions on the walls, mounted on big sheets of white cartridge paper; most of them were modern, but there was a large one of Rembrandt's "Butcher's Shop" above the head of the bed.

"You look beat up," Carl told him.

"I can believe it. I couldn't look as beat up as I feel, though. You want a drink?"

"Good idea. I better come and say hullo to your old lady."

"It's all right. She and the old man have gone out."

Roy got up from the shabby old cane chair he had used for working in ever since Carl could remember. At first it had stood before a small kitchen-table, then, since his sixteenth birthday, before the desk which had been his father's gift.

Roy went out to the drawing-room, and Carl heard him opening the liquor cabinet. Then he heard him in the back of the house, but faintly, getting ice from the refrigerator. He came back carrying a bowl of ice, and holding a bottle of clear, pale amber rum in his other hand.

He poured two drinks and put ice into them and ran water into the glasses at the washbasin in the corner. He gave one glass to Carl and sat again in his chair before the desk. It was a basketwork cane chair and it fitted him like a suit of clothes.

Carl looked at him as they drank the first sip. Roy's pale face was dead, bluish-white with tiredness, the small quick eyes were cloudy and there were sore red smears across the whites. His springy black hair was wild, and Carl knew that he had been rubbing his hand nervously through it from time to time, as he always did when he was tired.

And suddenly, seeing Roy slumped and small in the protective, work-hollowed cave of his chair, and with the first, easy warmth of the drinking spreading through his body, Carl knew that he could have done nothing else than agree to help him. That he had made a commitment, irrevocably, a long time ago.

Some of this knowledge was the drink, and some of it was this silent, relaxed, utterly confident moment which was one of the things he and Roy had enjoyed most in their friendship.

It was these, and it was the product of the other things that had happened to them and which they had done together over the years.

"Do you ever hear from her parents now?" he asked Roy, pointing to the photograph of the girl with the little finger of the hand which held his glass.

"I get a card every Christmas," Roy told him.

"Have you ever written them?"

"When Linda heard about her, she made me send them a letter and a little parcel. That was the first time. I didn't know what to say after all that time, but she nagged me till I did it."

"Were they pleased?"

"I got a nice letter back. They really sounded bucked. I was glad Lin had made me do it, then. But we only exchange cards at Christmas now."

"It was a damn shame," Carl said. "She was a nice girl. You'd have married her, eh?"

"Jesus, yes."

"You ever miss her? Miss her like I miss the old man, I mean?"

"I used to, but I stopped it. It's no use missing the dead."

"It was a damn shame," Carl said again.

"It's funny how it works, eh? If Shirley hadn't broken her leg and had to sit with it up on the back seat then Dorothy wouldn't have gone in Nolan's car and it would have been all right. Maybe Nolan would have got away with it, even. You remember they found him with his arms around her."

"Nolan was a good boy."

They finished their drinks in silence, Then Carl got up and mixed two more, putting in the water at the tap as Roy had done. He came back and sat on the edge of the desk and handed Roy his drink. He lit two cigarettes and gave Roy one, and looked steadily at the sleepy-lidded man below him in the lopsided, comfortable chair.

"Well," he said, "what about this business?"

"It's tomorrow night," Roy told him, "about half-past twelve."

"Yes."

"We're going to pick him up halfway along the Barricades, on the open-sea side."

"But Roy, why are you taking such a chance? It's so close to town, and there's cars coming and going from the airport out there."

"It's Etienne's idea; not mine. He knows what he's doing, though. First of all there's the dunes and the bush which hide us from the road. Second, nobody ever lands a boat there because of the surf. Third, it's six miles long and except for the lighthouse and the airport facing into the harbour there isn't a hut the whole length of it until you get to Old Port."

"That's true; but suppose you're followed. They might, you know, just as routine."

"Can't we use your car? They'll think we're going for a midnight bathe. We can go a few places before we go for him. Everybody in Queenshaven knows that we go around together when you're in town; and you're Hector Slade's nephew."

"Yes, you can use my car; but what if there are a few more midnight bathers out there? It's a popular place for that, you know."

"We're picking him up at that bend where the current is bad. We'll have to park the car near one of the bathing spots and walk to where we're meeting him."

"How is he coming?"

"Schooner from St. Pierre. They'll bring him ashore in the schooner's dinghy."

"They'll have a job in that current, won't they?"

"Yes, but they must know how to handle it or they wouldn't have picked that spot."

"It sounds all right."

"I hope it is." Roy was rubbing his hand through his hair, pressing down flat and hard, moving the hand slowly and jerkily. "I didn't make the arrangements. I only have to meet him and hide him."

"And get him away."

"That too."

"How are you going to do that?"

"I'll tell you tomorrow; when I'm sure of it. O.K.?" He looked steadily at Carl.

"Sure. I don't want to know too much."

"You'll have to know most of it. You're our key man."

"I feel it. You are a hell of a man to know, aren't you? How did I get mixed up with you?"

"Because you're a good lad."

"You better make the most of it. The next time you ask me to do something like this, I'll have to arrest you. They're going to make me a J.P."

Roy whistled, and sat up straighter. "That puts you on a spot if anything happens."

"We'll be all right."

Roy had slouched back against his chair. He was staring past Carl at the wall above his desk. There was a Medici print there: Corot; Avignon; the olive fields and grey stones and the bridge broken across the big green river which separates the old town and the new. Except that there was no bewilderment in them, Roy's eyes had the same bright, quick sheen of pain and sadness that Carl had seen in his aunt's eyes earlier on this evening. He looked at Carl again, turning his head slowly.

"I'm sorry," he said. "This isn't a nice trick to play on you. It's important though. It's important to everybody. You know what I mean?"

"It's important to you," Carl said, smiling at him gently.

He got up from the edge of the desk and went to the open door and looked out on to the blurred fuzz of the garden and the glittering, golden fret of the black soft night.

"I'm glad there isn't a moon," he said, not turning round. "It'll make it safer. You remember how we used to like a good moon that showed up the target?"

"Yes," said Roy. "I remember. The same thing isn't always good at different times, I guess."

"What do you mean by that?"

"Nothing," Roy gave the quick grin that stripped his face of its years. He got up and stretched in a shivering, tired way. "I was trying to be philosophical and I couldn't add two two's now, I'm so tired."

"O.K., boy. I'll leave you to it. When do I see you tomorrow?"

"After dinner all right? If anything happens, like Etienne getting picked up, I'll get in touch with you."

"That's fine for me. I have to have dinner at Aunt Kay's anyway. I promised."

"Give my love to Hector," Roy said, sitting on his bed and beginning to take off his shoes.

"I will. He gave me a message for you, too."

"What?"

Roy was still and rigid on the bed, holding one shoe stiffly in his hand.

"It's this march of yours for Sunday. You didn't tell me about that. He says for you to be careful or he'll have to arrest you. He sounded worried. I think he likes you. He always did, you know? He was always telling me that I ought to study like you."

"The march is off," Roy said. He was busy at the laces of the other shoe, his fingers fumbling a little. "It was too dangerous with this other business. I like Hector, too. It's only that we want different things from life. Tell him that I've finished with that book about the slave trade. He'll know the one: they told me at the institute he was asking for it the day after I took it out. If he sends round to the office he can get it, that'll save time." He was taking off his jacket and shirt as he spoke. He stood in his vest and Carl could see the first signs of the round shoulders that would pull the neat, well-trained boy out of straightness.

"Right," he said. "See you tomorrow. Sweet dreams."

"Brother," Roy said, stepping out of his trousers, "I won't even know it when I lie down."

13

It was early yet; and as he drove out of the quiet, tree-bordered avenue on which Roy lived, Carl decided he did not want to go back to his uncle's house. He turned the sleek black car down the long road which led to town. About a mile further on, he came to a knot of bright, overhead street lamps and a cluster of Chinese groceries, cafés and gas stations, with one or two houses. There was the shuttered bulk of a post office next to one of the service stations. People were still about, talking on the piazzas of the shops or waiting at the bus stops. In the gloom of the big post office verandah as he drove past, he could see the sprawled, wrapped forms of the country people who had come down for the Saturday markets, and beside each body, the bulky, rounded shape of a fruit basket.

Just past the post office, he turned the Humber into a tarmaced yard with trees in it. Coloured lanterns hung among the leaves and there were cars parked. He parked his own car near the gate and went across the yard to the lattice-work entrance of the nightclub. Above the entrance there was a softly glowing neon sign which said, The Pickapeppa.

"Mister Brandt, sir." The white-jacketed doorman was very

pleased. "How nice to see you. We haven't seen you for a long time."

"Hullo, Charles," Carl said. "How are you?"

"Well, thank you, Mr. Brandt. Are you in town for long, sir?"

"Going back tomorrow, Charles. Anyone in I know?"

"Mrs. Gordon, sir. She came in about half an hour ago."

"Good. Mr. Gordon, too?"

"Oh, *no,* sir."

You son of a bitch, Carl thought, looking at the smooth, pleasant face and the cynical eyes.

He went inside.

It was a good club. There was a big dance floor, faintly lit, and with a band in red, satin shirts and tight, black trousers. The tables were out in the open under small coconut trees, but there was a long, thatched roof gallery with more tables along the high, pink plastered wall. The bar was round and had a thick, mirrored column in the centre of the circle, with bottles all round it reflected in the mirrors. The lighting was discreet and clever; it could make any woman look her best, and it had the soft glow which persuaded people to feel a little sad if they were alone and so to drink more.

There were six couples dancing and some of the tables had people, but not many. The bar had five people sitting round it: two men in good gaberdines and flowered shirts which hung out of their trousers like smocks; a lonely-looking, English army officer; and Joan Gordon, sitting next to a squat, expensively dressed brown man.

The barman was pleased to see him, too; Carl ordered a rum and water and asked him to have one as well. The man mixed one drink and put the money for his in a little box under the bar. He lit Carl's cigarette with practised swiftness.

Carl looked toward Joan and waved slightly, as if to indicate that she didn't have to take it up if she were busy.

She left her companion and came round to his stool. She was staggering a little and he could smell the whisky on her breath when she came close.

"Carl, darling," she said, putting her face near to his. "Where have you been?" She sat down clumsily on the stool beside him, rumpling the skirt of her elegant, heavy-silk print. Her rich brown hair was escaping in floating wisps from what had been a good coiffure, and there was a faint sprinkle of sweat on her forehead and upper lip. Her face – it was still beautiful – looked as if something had clawed gently but persistently at the flesh around the mouth.

"How are you, Joan?" Carl said. He put his broad hand lightly on her fine one, which lay along the bar. She was wearing very thick, bright bracelets and her arm looked too thin against them.

"Buy me a drink, Carl," she said, "and we can have a nice talk."

"Scotch and soda," he told the barman. "What about him?" he asked her, pointing to the squat, big-bellied man she had left. "Wouldn't he like to join us?"

"Hi, Froggy." She half-turned and spoke with her head dangling back, speaking with her face almost upside down. "The gentleman is asking you to have a drink." Her neck in that position looked broken.

The man slid in a fast quiver from his stool. He walked eagerly over to them. He was smiling and holding out his hand before he was halfway to their stools.

"Froggy," she said, "this is Mr. Brandt. Carl, this is Froggy." She turned to her drink.

Carl looked at Froggy's buttonhole. He didn't want to meet the man's eyes. Froggy moved his hands in a wide meaningless gesture, and Carl caught a green dull, glow from the square emerald on the wedding finger of his left hand.

"I am Eustace Wright," he said. "I am honoured to make your acquaintance, Mr. Brandt. Honoured."

It was sad and irritating to watch the uncertain, twitching smile on his big face; the dull, uneasily searching eyes.

"How do you do, Mr. Wright," Carl said. "What will you have?"

"Whatever you are having, Mr. Brandt."

"You mean", Joan said, "that you're going to drink from his glass. Have a heart, Froggy; Carl can afford two drinks."

Looking at Eustace Wright's face and hearing the laugh flounder from his throat, Carl was sorry that he had allowed himself to smile.

"Another rum and water, please," he said to the barman.

"My card, Mr. Brandt," Eustace Wright said.

"Eh? I beg your pardon?"

"My card."

Carl looked at Eustace Wright's hand and saw that it was holding a small, white oblong. There was a wallet in the other hand, of limp, dull, expensive leather.

It was a nice card, with gilt around the edges. It read: *Eustace C. Wright,* and underneath, in handsome, thick print, Representative, Pan American Assurance Ltd.

"Thank you," Carl said. He put the card in his pocket and picked up his drink. There didn't seem to be anything else to say.

"Carl," Joan said, "how long are you up for?"

"Just tonight and tomorrow. I came about the polo finals."

"When are they coming off?"

"Next month, at the Barracks. We should have a couple of good matches. The army have a red hot team this year."

"I'll come to see you," she said. She turned to Wright. "You must come too, Froggy. You ought to see Carl playing polo. He looks like God."

"Joan," Carl said, "if Mr. Wright will excuse you, may I have a dance?"

"Certainly, certainly, Mr. Brandt." Eustace Wright gave his permission with a hurried, unctuous benevolence. Joan was already walking towards the dance floor.

As soon as he held her he knew that she was just too drunk to dance properly.

"Ease up on your friend," he told her. She was sagging against him, and they were not quite catching the sharp, lively rhythm in their changes.

"What have I done now?" Her thick, smooth eyebrows were raised and the delicate, brown velvet of her forehead as wrinkled in pretended astonishment.

"You don't have to go out with him, you know. So if you do, ease up. You're spoiling my drink."

"Oh, Carl, I'm sorry. I'll be nice when I get back. Men don't like it, do they, when women go on like that to other men?"

"No."

"Even if the other men are like Froggy?"

"No. It looks ugly and it makes me feel uncomfortable. And stop calling him Froggy."

"You're sweet," she said, and leaning against him, so that he had to hold her very tight, she kissed him on the mouth. He could taste the whisky on her tongue.

"Don't do that," he said. "You know how people talk."

"Are you afraid of Ian?" she asked him; referring to her husband.

"It's not that, Joan; but it's damn silly to have all sorts of gossip when there's no reason for it."

"I forgot," she said viciously and bitterly. "I'm sorry; I forgot it was all over. You remember when we used to leave here and go out to the Barricades? You didn't mind gossip then, did you? Everybody knew your car, but you didn't think of that then, did you?"

"Will you stop this, Joan. I didn't break it off, you did."

"You mean that time; with that Canadian?"

"Oh, hell, Joan, what's the matter? Can't you just forget what's over and done with, and let's have a dance and a drink."

"It's because I'm drunk, isn't it? If I wasn't drunk, would you take me out to the Barricades now? Like you used to?"

"Please, Joan. Stop it. What's wrong tonight?"

"You're a bloody fool," she said. "You're such a bloody, goddam, stupid fool of a man. Am I looking older nowadays?"

"You look wonderful."

"Your eyes go all shifty when you tell lies," she told him, "and your mouth goes all funny." She gave a small laugh that made him feel as if someone had drawn a knife across a window pane.

He was glad when the drums rolled for the end of the set. When they reached the bar again she drained her whisky in a quick swallow.

"I'm going ashore for a little," she said, taking her bag from the bar. "Come and hold my hand, Carl."

"They threw me out of there the last time I came to the Pickapeppa," he told her. "I can't get in there any more."

He and Wright watched her going across to the little door of the toilets. Once or twice, her ankles twisted a little under her and the high spike of her gold sandals skidded on the floor.

"Mrs. Gordon is a fine lady, Mr. Branch," Eustace Wright said.

Carl made a small, discouraging noise in his throat.

"A very fine lady," Eustace Wright continued. "Her husband is a fine gentleman. We are business associates."

"Oh, yes."

"It is one of the advantages of insurance. You meet such interesting people."

"I'm sure you must."

"I had the pleasure of driving past Brandt's Pen last week, Mr. Brandt. You have a beautiful place."

"Thank you."

"It is a pleasure to see a property kept like that. I am often up that way."

"You must travel a good deal in your business."

"Oh, yes, Mr. Brandt. All over the island. Our company has some of the best life and company policies in the Caribbean."

"That's pretty good," Carl Brandt said.

He felt Joan Gordon's cool hand on his wrist, and then she slid past him, pressing closely, to her stool; when she sat down the skirt of her dress wrinkled unattractively. She sat with one foot on the floor, and the other swinging free. Her sandal hung from the toe of her free foot.

"So there you are," she said. "I've been looking for you all over. Did Froggy try to sell you some insurance?"

"No, we were just talking."

"You're lucky. I remembered that he tries to sell everybody insurance, so I hurried back."

"I thought you couldn't find me," Carl said.

Hell, he thought, why doesn't he just slap her and leave? I don't know what he's getting from her, but it isn't worth it. I wonder where he picked her up tonight? She must have been loading her tanks since afternoon.

"Would you care to dance?" Wright asked her. He had got from his stool and was standing before her half-bowed, in an attitude of uncomfortable, studied formality.

"Not now, Froggy," she said. "Let's have another drink first."

Carl stayed until he had finished the drink Wright bought for him.

"Good night," he said to Joan. "I've a lot to do tomorrow. I only came in for a drink."

"You're off, then?" Her voice was unsurprised and resigned.

"I have to. I promised Aunt Kay I'd come in early and talk to her."

"Good night, Mr. Brandt," Eustace Wright had taken his hand and was shaking it vigorously. "It has been most interesting to meet you. When you're next in town perhaps we can have lunch."

"Froggy," Joan Gordon said in a tired voice, "he already has all the insurance he needs. The Brandts have always insured with Lloyd's."

"Yes, perhaps we can do that," Carl said to him. "I'll drop you a line."

He left them quickly. At the entrance to the bar, he went into the toilet.

When he came out, he turned for a moment and looked toward the bar. Neither Wright nor Joan saw him.

She held a cigarette and she was trying to stab the tip into the plump hand Froggy kept moving about on the black, glass surface of the bar. Her face had the remote absorption of a person scratching an itch. And even at that distance, Carl's eyes caught sudden flashes from the great emerald Wright was wearing, and the foolish embarrassed smile clamped across his broad, soft face.

14

Saturdays in Queenshaven, during a hot spell, it was always as if the sweat and sun and dust of the week had coagulated and formed a layer, sealing off any freshness from outside.

This was in the morning. At twelve o'clock it felt different. Then, everybody was coming out of the offices, and the young men were joining in groups and filling cars. You could hear them talking about the afternoon and the cricket or tennis they were going to play, about the fish they were going to catch, about the birds they were going to shoot, and about the clubs they were going to drink at. The girls coming out of the offices were talking less loudly but you knew they were thinking of the men they were going to watch playing cricket, of the men from whom they were going to get offerings of birds or fishes, of the men who would come for them at the end of the afternoon's drinking to take them bathing, of the dresses they would be wearing when the men called for them to go to parties, that night, in houses where there was plenty of bougainvillia and night jasmine and tiles rubbed smooth as glass with a stiff, abrasive coconut husk end, and where the chairs stood in the shadows under lignum vitae and poinsettia and angel bells.

The rules committee for the Cayuna Polo Association sat until half-past twelve.

As Carl had expected, there was opposition about the Ladies' Cup. It took a long time to wear it down to the point where they agreed to consider putting it to the vote of all members. If it had not been for the support of Colonel Long, the officer commanding the English regiment at Barracks, he would not have got it that far.

The colonel's pleasant voice, as mellow and inhuman as a musical instrument had gone on, bearing down on the opposing members of the Committee with a precisely calculated, cunningly staged confusion of reminiscence, reasonableness and thirty years of habit of authority. At the end he leaned back and the hard, weathered face had creased like the upper of an old shoe as he smiled at Carl. The pale eyes had glinted wetly with conspiratorial, secret amusement.

After the meeting, which had been held at the Cayuna Club, Carl went over to him.

"Thanks," he told him. "You carried the day. They'd never have seen it our way if it hadn't been for you."

"It's the colonies," the colonel said. His musical, resonant voice was bright with amusement. "It's only in the colonies you get people like our committee. I like it. They're like the men I used to hear in my father's library."

"You'll be popular with the women after this, anyway," Carl said. "I'll spread it discreetly that you're the hero."

"Thank you, Carl, thank you. You need a boost when you're my age."

Again the bumpy, long nose lifted above the broad, expressionless mouth, and the thin, tough skin creased with amusement.

Carl went out to the high, wide verandah. He sat in one of the chairs which stood along the dull, gleaming tile. From here he could look out across the cropped green lawn, where the water sprinklers were spinning a slow, rainbowed mist in the sun. There was a double line of Royal palms along the grey drive and a thick aurelia hedge around the fence. There were many trees and tight-packed, bright cannas in circular beds. Five miles away was the long, broken spine of the mountains; they were softly blue up among the clouds and fuzzy green in the hard light of the foothills.

Except for the clouds around the peaks the sky was clear and hard as a glazed plate. He thought of how the sea near Tolliver would look today, and then he began to think of Sheila Pearce. A man he knew came to the doorway and said, "Hullo, Carl," but didn't stay. A few minutes after he saw his uncle's black Chrysler turn into the drive.

He watched Hector park the car under the tall, black-mango tree and then walk with that stooping, springy lope across the lawn. He was in a bush jacket, and as he came up to the verandah steps he was unbuckling the Sam Browne belt and wrapping it round the whistle-topped stick he carried.

"Well, man," he said, sitting beside Carl, "how did it go?"

"All right: Colonel Long backed me up and we're going to have a general vote on it. Would you like a beer?"

"Thank you. Wonderful day. Just the day for the hills."

"It's a nice day," Carl said. "Shall we eat out here?"

"Good idea. I'm hungry. Let's have the black crab."

Carl signalled the white-jacketed club servant who was standing in the open double doorway of the lounge. He ordered, and the man went away. A couple of minutes later a boy came out and put a light table before them, with the tablecloth folded stiffly around the cutlery. He laid the table, and they waited until the man came with their food and the drinks on a big, round, silver tray.

There was black crab baked in the shell and seasoned with sweet and red peppers, avocado salad, boiled brown rice, and tall, frosted glasses of pale Danish beer.

It was a good lunch. Hector was pleased with it; and with the map he had studied the night before. While they were eating, his rapid, incisive voice talked about it and the old history of the island.

"... what we have to remember," he said as they were eating smooth, yellow, Bombay mango, "is that in these islands we have no long, careful growth of one culture to make us timid. We have almost no nostalgia. Our principal import has been history... What are you smiling at?"

"You," Carl told him fondly. "You sound like Roy. But I don't understand what you mean by importing history."

"It's simple, man. Every West Indian has had to learn to live with a dozen different pasts. We've attracted everybody and we've had to live on top of each other. We can't afford to resent it when new people come, and we've learnt to absorb them and use them. It takes any willing man only three years to become as West Indian as if his family had been here as long as yours."

The man who had served them came from the lounge carrying cups and coffee on the tray. The silver pot and milk jug were stamped with the club crest. Carl watched the deft brown hands pouring the milk and coffee in two mingling jets. He went away, leaving a red earthenware bowl of brown sugar between them on the table.

"All the same," Carl said, watching Hector's alert, flung-back face, the yellow teeth clamped on the short stem of the old black pipe he always smoked, the hard, compelling light in the grey eyes behind thick lenses, "all the same, you still wouldn't like it if Janice wanted to marry a black man. You would raise hell." He had become interested, as he generally did when Hector talked, even though Hector talked of things he hardly ever thought about.

"No, man. You're wrong. I wouldn't be pleased and I'd try to break it up. But I couldn't raise hell with conviction. I'd have a slightly uneasy conscience about feeling like that. And if she did, it wouldn't take long for me to feel that any children were part of the Slades too."

"A brown man would be all right, though?" Carl said, teasing him. He knew that his uncle liked to be gently teased, and he suddenly realized that he liked it because he was shy. And because it struck him so suddenly he also realized that he must have known this for a long time. "A brown man like me would be all right, eh?"

"Yes, man. That would be all right. Like you; even much darker."

They grinned at each other, and Carl felt happy in the warm, lubricating air, the smell of warm, sprinkled grass under the sun, and in this whole familiar pattern of verandahs, bright flowers, airy, dark-polished rooms and intimate relationship.

"By the way," Hector said, "I see that Roy and his friends are calling off the march for tomorrow. I hoped he would."

Roy took Linda Hu-Sen for lunch at about half-past one. He had not meant to leave his office until Bob Daniel came: but when Linda began to nag him with serene implacable righteousness he had known that he might as well give in and take her.

They shut the office and went down the stairs. They walked over past Queen Street into a long street of shops with Chinese lettering on the signs. Linda's brother had a restaurant here, above a wholesale business. They went up the stairs and sat at a corner table next to some yellow silk curtains painted with green dragons. Linda ordered the meal for them, speaking in fluent Cantonese.

While they were eating, she said: "You're feeling it, aren't you? You're worrying about it?"

"Yes," Roy said. "The nearer it gets the more nervous I feel. Every time I see a policeman I wonder if they're moving in on us."

She selected a fat, rich cube of pork from the little dish between them and put it on his plate with her chopsticks. It was one of the customs of Chinese eating which had shocked him at first.

"I dreamt about Dorothy last night," he told her.

"Oh!" She looked at him with understanding. "Why? You haven't done that for a long time."

"Carl and I were talking about her before I went to bed. I was dead beat, and I suppose she slipped over the threshold."

"What did you dream?"

"It was an odd dream. She and Etienne were on a beach and

I was on a sailing ship in a sort of lagoon near the beach. The ship was racing up and down the lagoon and there was a storm because the waves were high and breaking over the bows, and the deck was slanting. Finally the boom knocked me overboard. I wasn't frightened though; I just swam through the waves at a hell of a speed. There was a shark coming after me, but I didn't mind that either. I could see Dorothy's face, and Etienne's, quite clearly, on the beach. They looked as if they were very good friends, and I knew that I was going to be with them in a minute."

"I wonder what that means," she said. "I never told you, but when we first met you used to dream about her a lot."

"No, Lin."

"You did. You know you did. You used to cry in your sleep sometimes and call her name. I ought to remember, because I used to lie there feeling cold with jealousy."

"Jealous? Why?"

"Because I couldn't do anything about her; I couldn't touch her; and because I had to pity you now that she was dead and you couldn't have her, except when you dreamed about her. Sometimes I hated her and then I'd feel ashamed of myself."

"Well, it's over now." Roy said. "I'm sorry I mentioned it. It isn't healthy to keep going back to something you have left behind; something you can't get back."

"It's never over like that, Roy. Don't you know that? It's the serious thing about love, it keeps going on and going on, no matter what happens."

"Yes, maybe. But you shouldn't brood about it or think about it too much."

He watched her face trying to find in its calm, compassionate interest some hint of what she had tried to tell him. For a moment in her eyes, and in the slight movement of her lips, he saw what might have been an appeal, or a message begun and ended, quickly. As if the sender had realized that the one who would hear it would not understand the language.

Roy finished the beer in his glass; he could feel, distinctly, the glare from the zinc and tar beyond the window gently striking one side of his face, and on the other cheek he could feel the faint, cool stir from the big fan whirring above their heads.

"Come on," he said. "We ought to be getting back; Bob will be there soon."

They walked back to the office through the quiet, untroubled, Saturday streets. The bars were full of people who did not have to hurry over their drinks. You could tell that from the voices and by the unhasty clinking of the glasses.

In the office they waited for Bob Daniel: Linda reading, with her feet on a chair, and Roy working on one of the cases he would have on Monday.

At three o'clock he came. They heard the ticking of his bicycle in the outer office, and then the long, deliberate strides coming to the door.

When he came in, and they both looked at him, they could see the exhaustion on his face. There was grey, dried scum at the corners of his straight lips and his skin had the dull, metallic sheen of bloodlessness. His khaki jacket was crumpled, with huge sweat stains under the armpits, and the blue shirt was limp and sodden. Even the neat, hard knot of his tie was damp.

He sat in the chair beside Roy's desk; the same chair he had sat in the day before. From the way he sat, shuffling heavily into the seat, they could measure his tiredness. He looked like the exhausted elderly man he was; and the stout, thick-soled black boots, with their turned-up toes, and the bicycle clips which folded the trousers tightly around his thin ankles, made him look oddly pathetic and respectable.

"Well, massa," he said to Roy, "the committee says you're to do as you think best."

He had taken off the old-fashioned, rolled-gold spectacles, and he was slowly kneading the damp hollows under his eyes and massaging the shut lids. When he opened his eyes, they looked naked and tender without their lenses.

"How did it go?" Roy asked him. He was referring to the meetings the party had held that morning in the Jungle and the slums.

"We did our best. It was hard going, Roy."

"Was there any trouble?"

"No. Thank God. There was a lot of anger, but there was no trouble."

"Tiger's boys all right? Were they around?"

"I recognized some of them, but they didn't do much except talk to people here and there. They didn't trouble us at all."

"I should have been down there too," Roy said.

"No, Roy. There was no need. You have your work here and you wouldn't have made any difference. What you have to do is still ahead. You'll need to be fresh for that."

"You boys had a rough job."

"Dick Mason was good."

"Not shy any more?"

"He doesn't show it as much as he used to."

Roy looked at the weary, grizzled face held still in the bright, soft afternoon light of the room. He could see quite clearly, behind his friend's brief, factual words, the heat; the confusion of poverty tangled in the narrow, stinking lanes; the drifting, unfocused crowds of furious or puzzled faces. And he could see the slyly smiling, cynical faces of those who were disillusioned beyond any possible surprise. The sad, almost useless ones in whom bitterness had become a dull, chronic habit, without the stimulus.

Linda came over and rested her hand on Bob Daniel's shoulder.

"We'll get back what we've lost," she told him. "Maybe not right away, but we'll get it back. You mustn't feel like that, Bob. You've done as much as you could, and that's what matters."

"Mix us a drink, Lin," Roy said. "See if there's any ice left in the cooler outside."

She went out, and came back with three glasses from the cupboard where the typists kept their water tumblers. There was a pitcher of water in her other hand.

"There wasn't any ice," she said, "but the water's still quite cold."

She took a bottle of rum from behind a copy of Blackstone in the bookcase. She mixed three drinks.

"Go on," Roy told Daniel. "Drink that. I know it isn't up to your speed, but it'll do you good."

They drank. Daniel seemed stiff and preoccupied still. His face was hard and grave.

"Can you come over to the Jungle now?" he asked suddenly.
"Yes. What's up?"
"Bring the car; you can stay with it in Junction Street. Campbell's woman is going to have a baby very soon and I told her we would take her to the hospital this afternoon."

"Sure. Poor Campbell; no job for three months, and now a baby. He must be feeling bad about it, eh? How did he do this morning? He's a good man."

"He wasn't there. He has left her, Roy."

"Campbell?" Roy was incredulous.

"Why not?" The anguish and humiliation in Bob Daniel's eyes were not easy to meet. "A lot of men leave their women just before the time."

"I know, I know. But Campbell. I thought we'd taught him more than that. Do you have any idea where he is?"

"How could he?" Linda answered in a cold, weary voice. 'When the men leave they always vanish completely. How near is she to her time, Bob?"

"I don't know," he told her. "Quite near I expect. She told me it was any minute now."

"We better go now," she said. "She might need help."

They finished their drinks, and then they went out to Roy's car in the parking yard beside the office. They left Daniel's bicycle in the building and locked the door behind them. Driving across the quiet town towards Junction Street, Roy thought that this was one factor in the lives of the poor of Cayuna that he would never learn to accept and relate. It was bound up, in his mind, with the women he saw sitting on the kerb outside the Government buildings, under the palms, and who tried to sell their babies to any white lady who looked kind enough or new enough to the island: the babies wrapped and cocooned in layer after layer of bright, cheap-looking wool got from God alone knew where, and with their faces inside the petals of the unsuitable over-hot woollen caps looking sad and resigned, as if they had already learnt all about life they would ever need to know.

He thought about Campbell, the ex-sugar worker, ex-garden boy, ex-postman, ex-wharf labourer, who had been a good worker for the party, and who was now an ex-husband (he thought of him as that although he knew that Campbell and his woman had never been formally married) and who with this sudden, frightened denial of all the people who had needed him and trusted him was now an ex-everything.

At Junction. Street he parked near Campbell's shack which was across the road in the blowing, hot dust of the Jungle. There was an acrid, bitter tang of coal in the air, coming from the railway on his right. Bob Daniel and Linda went across the road in the hard light, and he watched them disappear among the shacks. He lit a cigarette and waited. Five little boys, in trousers as holed as fishing nets, seemed to grow from the ground like plants and surround the old Vauxhall, touching the hot, glistening metal with their fingers and picking the dirt out of the tyre-ribs. Two men sat on the bankside across the road and watched stolidly.

After a while he saw Linda and Bob coming through the rusty zinc and frayed boards of the shacks. They were walking on either side of a very slim woman whose distended belly, under the faded cotton dress, looked as if it had been stuck on grotesquely, as an afterthought. She was balancing a red brick on her head to keep herself straight: one of the red bricks that were made in the penitentiary over in Saragossa. The three of them were walking slowly, and the woman's bare feet seemed to pick doubtfully at the ground before she would trust her weight to them. He got out of the car and opened the back door. As they came up to him he could hear Campbell's woman groaning: full, unconstrained moans coming from deep in her chest. She was tall, with very long, slender legs and arms, a lean, very short body, and a thin face. Her nose was too large for the fine face bones and delicate, pointed chin.

"Easy now," Linda was saying. "Walk easy now. It's not far. You can soon rest. The pains have started," she said to Roy.

Her eyes had a remote, angry pride as she took the brick from the woman's head and helped her into the car and got in beside her. Roy behind the wheel again and Bob Daniel sat with him in the front seat.

All the way over to the Coronation Hospital, Linda talked softly and confidentially to Campbell's woman. The groaning was less frequent now; but every few minutes a heavy, sharp gust of breath was flung from her: it sounded like a war cry, or the response in a cathedral. Once, at a stop sign, Roy stole a glance over his shoulder at them. The woman's face was drawn and fixed with solitary concentration. It was a frightened face; but it was a strange, knowing terror, as if she were sharing in some tremendous, inexorable ceremony from which she had no desire to escape and for which her whole life had been selected. Her thin, long legs were spread wide, the feet pushed against the back of the front seat on the floor; her hands were open and expectant in her lap under the swollen belly, and she was leaning against Linda's shoulder. They looked like two trees interlocked above a pool.

At the hospital Roy went up the steep, wooden staircase ahead of them. On the long, narrow verandah, beside one of the sharp-scented wards, was the doctor's office. Roy went to the open door of the office and looked in at the olive-skinned, blue-eyed Sikh who was working at the desk. His name was Katha and he was a good doctor.

"Hi, Robbie," Roy said. "I've got two new customers."

The tall, stout, sleepy-eyed man came to the door. He walked with the ponderous yet delicate stateliness of an elephant.

"Thank you;" he said. "That's just what we need. They've been coming since morning; one after another. You didn't bring her bed by any chance, did you?"

His eyes widened, and then were hooded by the sleepy lids, as he swept one rapid glance over the body of the woman who had reached the top of the steps. He nodded and looked pleased. The woman was panting, and when she groaned there was a long, uncoiling shudder in it. There was thick sweat on her face and she was squeezing Linda's hand very tightly and resting full against her.

A nurse came out of the wide-open double doors to the ward and walked up to them. She and Linda and Campbell's woman went away slowly and through the doorway. There were two babies yelling in one of the other wards along the verandah.

"Another mango season baby," Doctor Katha said. "It'll come out looking fine. Any father?"

"No," Roy said.

Doctor Katha shrugged and his lips flattened as the corners of his mouth were pulled down in a grimace.

"She'll do it all right," he said. "She should have a fine baby. They always do after mango season. Did you pick her up on her way here?"

Roy told him about Campbell.

"She'll want a girl," Doctor Katha said. "When they have a girl they know they've got someone they'll have always. Girls are faithful. The boys slope off when they can take care of themselves."

He left them and went through the wide doors into the ward. Roy and Bob Daniel waited for Linda; they leaned against the wooden railings of the verandah outside the office and smoked without talking.

Another baby, in a ward downstairs, and then what might have been a dozen (or any number) more, began to yell in confident, demanding voices. A minute later a woman's bawling scream burst between the two men with the sudden, shocking fury of a hand-grenade. It came from somewhere in the back of the hospital and it seemed to rip apart the rhythmic, understandable confusion with which the babies' howling had surrounded them. It was repeated with a savage, coughing grunt at the end of it. To Roy it sounded as if it were coming from her throat on a thick, choking fountain of blood. He and Bob Daniel looked at each other with frightened blank faces, and when the scream came again they could not meet each other's eyes. Not many of the babies were yelling now, and from the ward beside them, in the silence between the screams from the woman, they heard another woman say something incomprehensible and give a low, private laugh. Roy could feel his heart beating so hard that it seemed to jump against his ribs. He lit another cigarette from the stub of the one he had smoked. He didn't want it, but there didn't seem to be anything else to do with his hands.

When Linda came out they went ahead of her down the stairs and waited by the car.

"Well," she told them, smiling, "her pains are coming nicely. She should have it in a few hours. There's a girl she knows in the bed next to her who has just had a beautiful little boy. You should see him, he's just perfect. I promised I'd take them back a few things; you know, grape juice and things like that."

Roy and Linda went across the street from the hospital and into the big Chinese grocery on the corner. Under her direction, he bought grape juice and condensed milk and some talcum powder. Then they went down the street and bought two boxes of face powder, two lipsticks and two pads of rouge in the chemist's shop. On the way back, they stopped at the Syrian store, which was open, and Linda chose two pink satin nightdresses with blue lace at the breast, and some white cotton babies' clothes. He had both his arms full on the way back to the hospital.

He went up the stairs with her and she took the parcels from him outside the office. The woman who had been screaming was silent now, and he went back to the car.

When Linda came back he drove out of the hospital yard and turned the car downtown, towards his office.

Halfway there, he said to Bob Daniel: "How about a beer?"

Bob nodded, and Roy stopped the car outside a grocery which had a bar. They went in and sat down at one of the cool, enamel-topped, white tables. When the beer came, he drank his very quickly. He had reached that stage of thirst so that when he drank the liquid seemed to sink into his gullet, like water thrown on flat, cracked earth. He ordered another beer for himself.

Bob said: "That Campbell!"

"It shook me," Roy said. "I'd never have believed it of him. You remember, Bob, he was one of the first to join us. When it really took something to join us. I'd have sworn we'd taught him better than that."

"Discipline," Bob Daniel said. "Until we have discipline, Roy, we can do nothing. Most of us do not know what it means, and the rest who have any idea of the word forget it when they please. Look at us now. Everybody is against us, from the governor down to most of the workers. We get smaller every year and every day we find it more difficult to tell people what we believe. Until we learn discipline that is what is going to happen."

Linda gave a raw chuckle. She looked at the two of them and Roy could see a sparkle of malice in the depths of her eyes.

"You should tell that to her," she said. "She could teach us about discipline. She knows all about it. She won't pull out from the Coronation Hospital one night and leave her baby behind. She'll feed it some way until it's a big strong boy like his daddy; and she'll probably adopt one or two more and look after them as well. You better go back, Bob, and tell her all about discipline. Tell her, and all the poor women in Cayuna who bring up three or four kids that don't belong to them."

Roy and Bob Daniel said nothing.

They drove back to the office and Bob collected his bicycle. Downstairs, in the street, they separated.

"I'll see you Monday," Roy told Bob. "Unless anything goes wrong. I better not see you before then. I'll spend tomorrow at Carl's place; I expect Slade will have put a watch on your house. Just as routine."

"Good luck," Bob said and Roy was surprised at the sudden tight grip of his hand.

15

Carl was sitting on the lawn, in a light, cream-painted wicker chair, watching his aunt. She was putting in the double hibiscus cutting he had brought her the day before.

"I don't know how you do it," he told her. "Every time I come up this place looks better. You make me feel ashamed of the garden at the Pen."

He got up and shifted the hose which had been set to sprinkle a bed of Provence roses. He moved it to a bed of gerberas, cotching a stone under the nozzle so that the jet tilted, rising then falling like rain on the earth of the bed.

"I have some lovely hibiscus now," Kathleen Slade said. "There are those yellow ones I got at Christmas and Hector's friend in Jamaica, you know, Major Murphy, sent me a beauty. In the morning it's cream and by midday it has turned to a sort of pink."

"You can't beat hibiscus," he said.

She got up from where she knelt. She came over and sat beside him in the other chair.

It was almost cool now; all the heat there had been was fallen to a gentle pleasant warmth. There were four small clouds very high up and shining pink against a very pale, whitish blue sky. The garden was bright with that clear, softly golden light of late afternoon which, in Cayuna, always seemed more luminous than midday.

As she sat down she passed her hand lightly and quickly over his which lay along the arm of the chair. She was wearing the light silk, black and white dress he had always liked. It had a pattern of black palm leaves against the white. When she passed him he could smell the *cous-cous* which was practically all the scent she ever used.

"Would you like a drink?" she asked.

"Yes," he said. "That's a good idea. Hubert!" He lifted his voice in a powerful shout. "Sorry," he went on, smiling slightly at her. "I forgot I was in town. That's a country habit, shouting when you want something."

Kathleen Slade shot a quick, sidelong, happy glance at him.

Hubert, the garden boy, came round the corner of the house and Carl sent him for the drinks.

When the drinks came, on a satinwood tray rested on a small drawing-room table, she mixed two glasses of rum and ginger: a large one for him and a very small one for herself.

"Oh, I forgot," she said, "you like it with water, don't you?"

"This is fine," he told her.

They drank in silence for a little. Carl lit a cigarette and watched through casually lowered lids Kathleen Slade's constant, tender and happy examination of his face. She never looked directly at him for long; her gaze would slide to the ground and then back to him swiftly.

"It was sweet of you to spend the afternoon here," she said. "Wouldn't you have preferred to go to the club with Janice?"

"Nonsense," he told her with mock severity. "I like spending afternoons with you. Anyhow, I didn't feel like tennis today; if I'd gone to the club I'd have just sat and had a drink; and the company's much better here."

"You ought to go out more," she said, looking out across the lawn, into the red-flashed hedge of Barbados pride.

"What do you mean, Aunt Kay? I go out a lot. We have a social round over on the coast, you know?"

"I know, darling; but I worry about you sometimes."

"Worry about me? Why?"

"I know it seems silly, but you're getting so set, Carl. You have your work at the Pen, and your polo, and your friends, but you don't seem to want anything else."

"But, Aunt Kay, what else is there to want? That seems a lot for one man to have."

He was amused and warm and happy with her, all at the same time. And flattered, in what he felt, obscurely, to be a pure, good fashion, by her concern and the love that was prompting this concern.

"You ought to be thinking of getting married," she said with a nervous yet resolute determination.

"I knew it," Carl told her, laughing. "I knew that was what you were driving at." He closed his broad hand over her thin, dry one. "You mustn't worry about that," he said. "There's plenty of time to think of getting married. I'll just wait until she comes along and then you can have a lot of fun getting a wedding ready and telling her all about the Pen."

For a moment he wondered whether he should tell his aunt about Sheila Pearce; then he decided that this was not the time.

"You know what the black people say," he went on. "'Man never ugly, man never old'."

"No, Carl," she said, and from the gently implacable lilt in her voice he could tell that she knew she had him against the wall. "You mustn't laugh it off. You're not getting younger, you know, and you are the last of the Brandts. I shan't be happy until I hold your child in my arms."

"What about Janice?" he asked; and immediately he told himself that it had been a cruel, unnecessary thing to say. He could feel a tingling, tight heat of blood swelling under the skin of his face.

"Janice, too," she said quietly. "But it's different for a girl. *You* can get married and you ought to. You shouldn't try to avoid your responsibility."

"But I'm not in love with anyone," he said, in a fast, clumsy stammer.

"Because you don't want to be," she told him. "Men always get lazy and set in their ways when they reach your age without marrying. They get too comfortable."

"You really want to see me married off, eh?" he said for the sake of something to say,

"More than anything. I don't like to see the flame flicker down so low in one family; like it has with Hector's family. I'm almost resigned to that now, that Janice won't marry; but it would break my heart if it happened with you, Carl."

Because he knew what was behind her words, Carl put his arm around her. He looked into the gentle eyes which were dark, shining smears, now, in the thickening shadows of the garden.

"Don't worry," he said. "I promise I'll give you a chance to hold a little Brandt. It takes time, though; you can't rush these things."

She touched his cheek. "I know you will," she said. "But do be careful, Carl. Every time you go out on that polo field I don't really expect to see you again. I wish you didn't play it."

"It's not as bad as that," he said softly. "Think of all the fat business men who play it for years without a scratch."

"Yes," she said, "and think about that nice boy from England, Captain Digby, who had his neck broken and his head kicked in last year. Hector told me they wouldn't let his wife see him afterwards."

"That was just luck, Aunt Kay. Honestly. It's a very long chance of that ever happening twice on the same field. And you know how carefully I play."

She got up and he rose as well. "I know you don't take foolish chances," she said, "but please be careful."

"I will," he said. Then suddenly he wanted to tell her about Roy and the woman he had lost. He didn't know why, but he felt it would give Roy a protection he badly needed.

"You ought to get on to Roy," he said, keeping his voice light. "I'm not the only one. Maybe some day we can court two sisters and have a double wedding."

"I often think about him, too," she said. "At one time I almost used to think of the two of you as brothers. But he has got so strange and hard since he came back from England, and then this dreadful thing he has taken up with. I wonder if he would ever be able to love a woman properly."

"I think so," Carl said. They were standing by the chairs, and he could just see her face in the dusk. "He was going to get married once, just after the war. I never told you; but he was in love all right. She was killed in an accident. The most stupid damn thing you ever saw; she was driving from one house to another, about a mile."

"No." He could hear the shock and the pity in Kathleen Slade's voice. Even a thing like this, he knew, told casually, she could see clearly and feel almost personally. So long as she had the least connection with those people involved she had an instant, biting knowledge of the implications of any tragedy.

"Don't ever tell him I told you," he said. "He's put it behind him. At least he says he has, and with Roy if he acts a thing long enough he can make it real."

"Of course I won't tell him, Carl. Poor boy. If you really love someone, especially when you're very young, it must be hard to replace them when they die like that. I think it must leave a sort of need unfulfilled, no matter who you find afterwards."

"I think you're right," he told her, taking her arm to walk across the lawn. "Let's go and hear the six o'clock news."

"I don't bother with the afternoon news," she said. "It's always the same thing as the morning. If there is anything new, Hector tells me about it at dinner. He should be in soon. Did you two enjoy your lunch?"

"Yes," he told her, "we had a good lunch. He talked a lot."

"What about?" They were going up the steps past the night jasmine.

"Oh, you know Hector. It needs him to tell it, but it was interesting."

"I always said," she told him, as they went into the drawing room, "that Hector should never have gone into the police. He should have been a professor... What was Roy's girl like, Carl? The one he lost?"

16

He left his uncle's house at nine o'clock. Until then, after dinner, he had stayed with the two of them in the cool, flower-scented shadows of the verandah.

Hector and Kathleen had sat side by side on the stripe-awninged swing, occasionally touching hands and locking their fingers.

As they always did when they sat like this, they had told each other the old tales which had passed down in the Brandt and Slade families. All three thought they knew every legend or anecdote passed on by six generations of maiden aunts, mothers and nurses; but somehow, no matter how often they reminded each other of them, another tale would come up which was new to everybody but the one who had suddenly dredged it from some buried layer of awareness.

At nine, Carl had gone down the steps to his car, carrying the old officer's holdall which had been to nearly all the places he had, and which had no travel-stickers, only stains and marks.

Now, he was sitting with Roy in the bar at the Pickapeppa where he had come alone the night before.

It was Saturday night and the table space was pretty full. Most of the people at the bar were the men who had come without women, like Roy and himself. It was a good night; there was a thick studding of huge, close stars, and the first silver of the new moon hung above the high pink wall. If you closed one eye and squinted with the other it looked like a nice bit of lighting the management had stuck on the wall itself.

Roy and he were drinking the pale, powerful Mount Ida rum, which Bob Daniel considered all right as a pleasant refreshment, but hardly the thing a man would bother to drink if he were really drinking.

"Maybe we ought to act a little drunk," Carl said to Roy in a low voice, "just in case they're feeling suspicious."

"No," Roy said, and his voice would not have carried a foot past Carl's head. "We don't have to do that. Just act natural; like we always do when we come here together."

"O.K.," Carl told him. "I was only joking. Try and relax, boy; ride it out easy until you have to do something."

He looked at Roy with a fondness in which there was a little slightly smug malice. He knew that for this sort of thing he began with better equipment. That there was an area of massive, calm efficiency inside him which had nothing to do with how he was feeling, or what he was thinking, but had become a matter of practised habit. He knew also that Roy would never have the muscular and nervous control he had learnt so thoroughly.

"I saw Joan last night," he told Roy. He did not mention the man she had been with.

"How was she?"

"She's beginning to go. She wasn't too sober. I felt sorry for her. She was carrying on a bit."

"Cho!" Roy said, in a cold, impatient voice. "I can't bother with people who go around making you feel sorry for them. People like Joan who start off with so much, shouldn't allow themselves to get like that."

"I don't think she could be too happy with Ian. He isn't much, you know: he's harmless but, God, he's dull."

"Maybe," Roy said. "But all the same it's bloody silly to let yourself go to rubbish, like Joan. It's a sin. It's the worst sort of sin. She didn't have to marry him, and she doesn't have to stay with him. Even if she does, she could work it off like Sheila. That's what people like that need: something to work at."

"I agree with you there," Carl said. "I wasn't trying to excuse her. I was just explaining why she was like that."

"We waste too much time understanding and explaining people like her. There's not enough time to spare."

Carl did not want to go on with this. He swung round on the stool, his glass in his hand, and watched the people at the tables outside and on the floor. The music from the band sounded nice in here: not too obtrusive and yet close enough for them to catch the tangy beat of the calypso it was playing.

Suddenly Roy laughed. He had come out on the crest of one of those unpredictable, gay moods where he would joke about everything, or sometimes go out to the edges of a light craziness.

"I'm going over to beg old man Dunfield to let me dance with his daughter; I haven't had a dance in three months. You come too and ask Mrs. Dunfield to dance; it'll make her feel good."

He was already going towards the tables outside, walking with a loose easy swing: Carl grinned at his bobbing back and followed.

Dancing with Mrs. Dunfield was not nearly as bad as he had expected. She was stout, too tall, too tightly corseted, but her feet retained a precise, neatly moving memory of her girlhood. It was like dancing with two people at once: the effortless, responsive one she was below the waist, and the heavy-breathing, banally talking one whose great curve of bosom pushed him too far away.

And he could watch Roy moving about the floor with Evelyn Dunfield. Among the dancers who filled the floor, Roy had a fluid, natural vividness, like a bird among a flight of shuttlecocks.

When they had danced, Roy and he sat at the Dunfields' table and had one drink. Roy told two funny stories about Carl and himself and everybody began to laugh, as much at the stories as because Roy was grinning with pleasure at his own jokes. Then he told them a clever obscene anecdote and for a moment Carl thought it wouldn't come off as Mrs. Dunfield and her daughter looked at the old man with anxious attention. When he began to laugh, they did too, with a relieved, bursting suddenness. Carl and Roy left them then: old Mr. Dunfield was dabbing his eyes with a linen handkerchief, shaking the stiffly ironed folds so that it spread out as big as the sheet for a child's cot.

When they got back to the bar Roy said: "We'll have one more drink, eh, and then we'd better be going."

"Right," Carl said.

"What's the time?" Roy asked him.

There was no clock in the bar.

"Quarter to eleven," Carl said. "I told you it was no use buying one of those thirty-shilling watches."

"Plenty time. I wonder why they never have clocks in night clubs. At least I can never find them."

"What would you want a clock for? If people saw how late it was they might feel they ought to go home."

Roy rubbed his hand in a familiar, slowly grinding motion across his hair.

"You want to go now?" Carl said.

"One more," Roy said, "and then we'll go. We've got to be there at half-twelve."

"That's all right," Carl said. "It's only half an hour at the most to get out there."

"Oh, hell," Roy said, "here comes Morty."

Carl turned his head, looking over his shoulder, and watched the small man coming through the dim, bluish light towards them.

It was Mortimer Barrow, an old school friend, a man they both liked. He came across the smooth blocks of the floor with a dapper, precise twinkle of his small feet which showed the sort of athlete he had been. His square body was well padded with hard, plump flesh, and when he came up beside them they could smell the strong, piney shaving lotion he always used on the round firm jowls of his sleek face. The eyes were small and green and danced quickly in very clear whites, and the coarse straight hair was slicked down flat on the round skull and cut very short at the sides. Nobody in Cayuna could ever get his trousers as sharply creased as Morty Barrow, and not even the Chinese laundries ever washed and starched a shirt as white as the old woman who had been one of the Barrows' maids for thirty years.

"Carl," he said, in a loud, quick voice as blandly cheerful as the flourish of a trumpet, "Roy, you old commie. How's things?"

"Morty, you old scoundrel, what are you doing here?" said Carl, "You look as if somebody has just left you the Bank of England."

"Hi, Morty," Roy said.

Mortimer Barrow pulled a stool round from the bar and set it between them. He sat on the edge of it, in that nervous, light way which made him look as if he were ready and balanced for instant departure. He never rested in any other way, but it never made you restless, you accepted it as you accepted a child's momentary, friendly stillness and attention. Carl handed him a glass with rum and ice in it.

"Water or ginger, Morty?"

"Water. Well, what are you two up to?"

"Just drinking, Morty," Carl said. "How's things?"

"Oh, not too bad. I've been looking for you, by the way. I heard you were in town and your aunt told me I'd probably find you here."

"What's up?" Carl asked.

"I need your help in a little business I'm trying to swing."

"What sort of business?" Carl asked him cautiously. He watched Morty with narrowed eyes. Whatever it was that Morty wanted him to do, he knew that there would be money in it for Morty. He didn't mind that. It was one of the things you understood about Morty. It was part of him that he had made money since he was nineteen, in the same cheerful, brilliantly competent way he played football or tennis or any game he chose to take up.

"You know the beach at Tolliver?" Morty asked him.

"Yes. What about it?"

"Well, there's a man who wants to buy it and the land behind it, up to the road. He wants to build a hotel there. Not one of the dollar-a-day shacks for the two week tourists. A posh affair. Cottages and a fishing club and that sort of thing."

"Sheila didn't tell me," Carl said.

"I bet she didn't. Goddam it, do you know I've been over there three times in the past month, and still the woman won't sell?"

"But, Marty," Carl told him, "some of her best trees are in that strip along Tolliver beach, and anyway it's Lloyd's place, not hers; why don't you try him?"

"Oh, God, Lloyd! She just looks at him with those damn schoolmarm eyes of hers and says in that silky voice, 'No, Lloyd, I don't think we ought to consider selling any part of Tolliver'; and he stands there and looks like he's nine years old."

Carl and Roy gave a simultaneous burst of delighted laughter at Morty's imitation of Sheila.

"You can laugh," he said with comic, artificial bitterness. "I tell you, Lloyd's dropping down to sell. You know how much my man is willing to pay?"

"No," Roy said. "I can't guess. How much?"

"Five hundred a yard frontage. That's bigger than in the Miami land boom."

"Then where do I come in to all this?" Carl asked.

"You speak to her. Everybody knows that the sun rises and sets by you, as far as she's concerned. If you say it's all right, she'd sell. There'd be a commission in it for you, of course."

"But Morty, I told you, the beach has the best trees on Tolliver.

She gets better than five hundred pounds of copra in the thousand out of the nuts there."

"Lord, Lord, Lord," Morty Barrow said, his eyes rolled to the ceiling. "You bloody country boys. Can't you understand, man, that she would have to grow coconuts for about a million years to get the lump sum she'll get from this. Roy, you're a business man, make this damn farmer see reason, can't you?"

"You heard the man, Carl," Roy said. He nodded his head slowly. "You never believe me when I tell you," he went on, "but you're just an ignorant farmer. Tell Sheila she's holding up the tourist trade."

"Cho!" Morty said, without resentment. "I should have known better than to ask you, you bloody red. What do you say, Carl? Will you ask her for me?"

"I'll tell her that you asked me," Carl said, getting off his stool and looking at his watch. "I'll see what she says."

"Thanks, man, thanks. I'll come over to see you some time next week about it. You two going already? I haven't stood you a round yet."

"We want to go out for a while, Morty," Carl told him. "We'll probably come back later."

"Well, thanks again, eh. You're a good boy." He gave them the energetic cheerful salutation that he would have given them even if Carl had not agreed to help him. He dug Roy in the ribs and said, "Up the revolution", and laughed his loud, ringing, trumpet laugh.

They went out of the club, walking quickly, and got into Carl's car. Roy had left the too familiar Vauxhall at his home where Carl had called for him two hours ago.

"That damn Morty," Roy said, "he held us up like anything. What time is it?"

"It's all right," Carl said. "It's only half-eleven. We'll make it easy."

They drove out of the club gates, swinging left into the long, overhead lit street which led three miles into town. Down there they would turn east on to the long, curving road, which ran along the harbour's edge for five miles before it reached the place where the sandy, thick-bushed strip of the Barricades joined to the mainland. It was late at night, and a weekend; the roads would be nearly empty: Carl knew they would reach their place on the Barricades a long time before half-past twelve.

17

About a mile beyond the airport, on the harbour side, there was a long stretch of mangroves, their multiple spider-leg roots thrust into flat water which smelt bitter and salty. It was one of the smells Carl remembered most vividly from his childhood.

Half sunk in the black flat water, caught in the roots like some tattered fly in a web, was the wreck of an old dredger that had been carried ashore and broken one night in a hurricane. Just beyond this point there was a bend in the road; and here the Barricades were at their widest. Thick scrubby bush grew in the sand, coming right down to the roadside. And it was here that Carl parked the Humber; driving off the road for a little, the big car lurching through the loose sand, with the hard bushes swishing and scratching along the metal. He drove until they were out of sight of the road; then he stopped, switching off the lights.

"Roll up your window," he told Roy. "I don't want any prowler making off with my bag."

"What's the time?" Roy said.

Carl looked at the green glow of his watch dial.

"Not quite twelve," he said.

They got from the car and Carl locked it. They went through the bush, walking heavily in the loose sand, the dry *macca* crunching beneath their shoes. They could hear the slow crashing mutter of the surf. It grew louder as they climbed to the crest of the dune.

On the other side of the dune the beach had a steep slope. There were rounded, close-packed stones at first, then loose sand, then firm, wet sand. The sea was faintly luminous and they could see the white of the surf like a line of thin gauzy cloud. It was dark and the breeze was warm and out to sea there was that faint luminous paleness gradually getting darker and becoming black. The stars were so huge and near that you were surprised they cast no light.

They sat in the still warm, loose sand, beyond the line where the surf-wetted, firm sand began.

"How are you going to do it?" he asked Roy. "Are you going to flash a light or something."

"No," Roy told him. "He'll just come ashore in the schooner's dinghy and walk up the beach till he meets us."

"That was taking a chance, wasn't it? Suppose there had been somebody else here: real bathers out for a midnight swim?"

He sensed rather than saw Roy shrug beside him.

"He arranged it," Roy said. "We only got the message. Anyway, this is less risk than flashing lights about the place. This is a good spot too; there's a hell of a current here."

"Oh, yes," Carl said, "I remember. Do you think he thought of that when he chose this spot to land?"

"I suppose so," Roy said. "Either he or somebody else who knows Cayuna."

They waited for quarter of an hour. Then for another half an hour. Once Carl asked, "Is it O.K. if we smoke?" and Roy said, "Yes, there's no reason why we shouldn't," and they lit from Roy's lighter which was made out of an old cartridge case and which had a grill shield against wind. They didn't talk at all, and once, about two miles out, they saw the red glimmer from the port light of a ship going east. Three planes came in behind them and landed at the airport, roaring low over the harbour. Carl tried to tell them from their engines, as he had once been able to identify nearly fifty types of aircraft by their engine sound alone. But he couldn't do that now. It was nine years since he had been even inside an aircraft and they had changed too much. He tried to recall the mnemonic, which he had once used to ensure that his cockpit drill was correct, but he could hardly do that now.

"There he is," Roy said suddenly and got to his feet. Carl looked hard, down to the water, and saw a darker, solid blur of shadow among the shapeless shadow above the luminous, faintly white line of the foam. He got to his feet too and watched the shadow coming across the beach in a line to the left and away from where they had been sitting. Looking straight behind it, at the sea, he could just distinguish a vaguely shaped blur bobbing on the unseen ground-swell. The shadow on their left had stopped. It was hard to see it now that it was not moving.

"Over here," Roy said in French, and the shadow was easier to make out as it came towards them. Roy went forward to meet it. His outline became indistinct as he walked away from Carl, and the shadow coming nearer was growing more definite.

Carl watched Roy and the man he knew to be Etienne meet on the beach. He saw their figures merge and realized that they were embracing, French fashion. They were coming towards him. The dim, thick figure that was Etienne was carrying a squat, shapeless bundle under the left arm.

"Carl," Roy said, "this is Henri Etienne. Henri, this is Carl Brandt: you will be staying with him."

He still spoke French and Carl could follow it, but not easily. It was a long time since he had used any French, and he seldom read it now.

Henri Etienne came closer. It was too dark to do more than make out the shape of his face. He felt for and grasped Carl's hand. His grip was not the heavy, solid closing of a strong hand, but firm and decided with nervous energy.

"I am happy to meet you, comrade," he spoke in English. "Thank you." His voice was steady and pleasant, rather deep, and Carl could sense the years of practised modulation in oratory.

"Carl isn't one of us," Roy said in French. "He is my friend. He had the most suitable place."

"Thank you again, Mr. Brandt," Henri Etienne said to him and, turning to Roy, "Speak English, Roy. If anything goes wrong it would be safer if I am practised in speaking and thinking English."

"You're right," Roy answered. "Let's go, eh? The sooner you're at Carl's place, the better."

The three of them turned and climbed up through the powdery, dry sand, going toward the fuzzy outline of scrub against the sky.

Carl led the way. Roy and Etienne walked a few steps behind him, Etienne still carried his bundle. He was wearing a dark suit. Nobody said anything more.

At the car, again, Carl unlocked the front door, reaching inside, over the back of the front seat, and twisting the handle to open the back door locks.

"Etienne better ride in the back," he said to Roy, and to Etienne, "I would sit back if I were you: the seat is pretty deep and at night you won't even be seen."

Etienne got in very quickly, flinging his bundle in ahead of him. Even in the dark of this bushy place it had a dull, black gleam. Carl realized it must be wrapped in oilcloth.

He and Roy got into the front seat. He getting in first and sliding under the wheel, Roy following.

He backed the car out slowly, swinging the rear round to the left when he felt the hard scrunch of the tyres on the fine, stony sand at the side of the tarred road. He shifted the gear into second and pulled away, driving over to the left of the road. When the green dial on the dashboard showed sixty he took his hand off the knob of the gear lever.

They passed the lit-up airport. Flashing past, they saw an aircraft, red and green wingtip lights glowing, about to lurch round on the runway for the hurtling rush of a take-off.

Then they were past the airport and the flat black sheen of the big harbour was on their left and, across the harbour, a few lights on the waterfront, with long, broken reflections in the water. Etienne leaned forward slightly.

"Excuse me, Mr. Brandt," he said in a calm, pleasant voice, "may I ask you something?"

"Yes," Carl replied. He did not turn his head, but leaned a little further back, his eyes watchful on the headlamp lit stretch of road before the car.

"What is your place like?"

"It's out in the country," Carl told him. "It's quite big; on the side of a hill. You won't be in the house, of course. We'll put you in an old hut back of the property; in the bush."

"That sounds excellent," Etienne said. "What I meant, though, was how many people do you have in your house?"

"Just me," Carl said, "and the servants. There's a lot of outside people, workers on the property, but they never go to the hut now. I'm afraid it won't be very comfortable. It's just a shelter and it hasn't been used for two years."

"That does not matter. How are you going to feed me?"

"I'll take stuff up to you late at night," Carl told him.

"Your own food?"

"Yes. It's all right."

"Please don't do that," Etienne said. "It isn't safe. The other people in your house are bound to notice if another person is eating your food. Women always notice a thing like that."

"Oh, hell," Roy said, "I never thought of that. I should have bought some stuff today."

"He's right, Roy," Carl told him, "and the bloody shops are closed now, of course. What shall we do? I can't buy food down in the village for the same reason: they'd think it damn queer."

Roy was thinking hard and angrily. It's these little things in this sort of thing, he told himself. It's the little things that screw it up. I should have thought of that.

"I'm sorry," he said, turning round in the seat and speaking to Etienne. "I made a bad mistake there."

"I know," Carl said, "we'll buy a load of frankfurters at Uncle's Parlour. It's open late on Saturday because of the soldiers coming out of the dance over at the Blue Bucket. I'll make out I'm buying for a beach party. I'll get some beer and chocolate too."

He heard Etienne give a low, pleased chuckle in the back.

"Good," the man said. "It's not absolutely safe, but I think it is the best. I am glad I don't have to go hungry. I have blankets and clothes with me, by the way." In the dark they could hear the slight smack of his hand on the oilskin covered bundle.

Carl turned the car at the road where the Barricades joined the mainland.

"Your place?" he asked Roy.

"Yes," Roy said. "Like I told you tonight when you called. I'll pick up my car there and follow you over to the Pen." He turned to Etienne again. "I often spend a Sunday with Carl," he said. "We usually have a night out and go over on Sunday morning early, like this, and sleep late and ride and talk all Sunday. He has a nice place there."

"How long have you known each other?" Etienne's voice was pleased and relaxed and warmly interested.

"Lord," Roy said, and Carl, his eyes fixed closely on the road, as they went past the dark gardens and houses, noticed how his voice had lost its thin, edgy tautness and had taken its tenor from Etienne's. "Carl and I have known each other for about twenty years, eh, Carl? We were at school and in the war and everything together. We've just stuck with one another."

"I like to hear that," Etienne said. "You are both very fortunate."

You bastard, Carl thought, you come here with a price on your head, you land as cool as a cucumber and set off in the back of *my* car as if you'd hired it, and then tell us you're glad we're friends.

He turned the car up the long road which led past the Pickapeppa Club and which would bring them, finally, to the avenue where Roy lived. He looked at his watch; it was nearly half past one.

"We'll have to drive like hell," he said to Roy. "We won't be at the Pen till nearly four, and he must be settled in long before daylight, so that we can get back to the house."

"I know." Roy's voice was tense and anxious again. "It's a good thing we know that damn road so well. Drive like a bitch, eh? Don't worry about me. I'll keep up. You think we can do it?"

"Yes," Carl told him. His mind had considered, calmly and efficiently, all the physical factors involved. The time they had left before daylight. The miles they had to do. The times they had taken to drive those miles before. The distance from the house to the old woodcutter's shelter. He had considered all these things, and he knew that they could just do it.

He stopped at the crossroads where the big post office was; pulling up beyond the cluster of overhead light. He got out quickly.

"I'll get the grub," he said shortly, and walked across the road to the little, vine-hung, tree-shaded ice-cream parlour on the other side. From up the road he could hear faint, thin sounds of music coming from the Blue Bucket, the big, rowdy club where the English soldiers went to dance on Saturday nights with the professional or amateur prostitutes of Queenshaven.

He bought three dozen frankfurters and rolls, and eight bottles of beer, eighty cigarettes and two big slabs of milk chocolate. He wanted to buy more chocolate but he didn't think it would look right. He chatted casually with the man who owned the parlour, a squat, black man with very short arms. He was glad that people like himself sometimes came here late at nights to buy hamburgers or hot dogs for impromptu picnics on the beach. The man put the food and cigarettes in two large brown paper bags, and the perspiring, cold bottles in another. Carl scooped them in his long arms. He could feel the bottles, which had already wet the paper, pleasantly cool against his chest, the cold striking through his shirt. He went back to the car and Roy took the bags, passing them to Etienne in the back. Nobody going by on the sidewalk could have seen Etienne in the back of the deep, black car.

Carl drove very fast to Roy's house.

He swung the Humber into the drive and parked halfway up it. He and Roy got out and went up the drive, up the steps, and along the verandah to Roy's room. When they went in they left the door open.

Inside the room, Roy turned on the light. There was a small, green, canvas and leather bag, already packed, on the chair by the bed, but he and Roy drifted idly about the room for ten minutes: he sitting on the edge of the bed, Roy moving and straightening the papers on his desk, opening the wardrobe door and feeling in the pocket of a suit, closing the door, washing his face at the basin. This was in case anyone was watching the house from the shadows of the bank across the road. They didn't think there would be, but they had decided earlier that this was what they would do.

Carl lit a cigarette while Roy was brushing his hair.

"Your people know you're coming over with me?" he asked. He said this for something to say. He already knew that Roy had told them.

"Oh, yes," Roy said quickly and jerkily. "I told mother before she went out tonight. She was sorry she missed you both nights."

"Yes", said Carl, "you mentioned it earlier on. Let's go, eh?"

He went out and Roy followed, flicking the switch by the door. Carl walked along the verandah, past the big, red clay pots of ferns: he could hear the glassy bang of the door as Roy drew it shut. He went to his car and got in and turned the key. From the yard round the corner of the house he could hear Roy's Vauxhall start up, and as he reversed down the drive he saw the two, blinding white spots of the Vauxhall's headlamps glaring through his windscreen, and coming closer. The two floods of hard light, from his car and Roy's, made the thick hedges on either side of the drive look naked and colourless.

When they reached the road that turned north, going towards Saragossa and leading out into the country, he was already going at seventy miles an hour.

He didn't have to look back to see if Roy kept up.

18

The wide flat road was empty because it was a weekend and all the slow-moving ox or mule drays which, on other mornings, might have been on it (coming out of little side turnings, lurching unpredictably and inexorably across the main road, stolidly undisturbed beasts tugging in their own time, unencouraged by the hunched up drivers, the dim lanterns hung on the back of the drays more an added uncertainty than a help) had long since been driven home.

Roy kept the red glow of the Humber's rear light at a steady distance: never allowing it to draw too far ahead, nor to get too close. They had often driven across to Brandt's Pen like this, at two o'clock, or later, on a Sunday morning, but hardly ever so fast.

They were in Saragossa; the town still, badly lit and shuttered. They had slowed down. He could see the red light turning the corner by the rococo cathedral. They were nearly out of the town, now, going past the high, floodlit walls of the big penitentiary. They were out on the open road, the cane fields dark and bristly, like huge hairbrushes, on either side. The road flat and white looking. It was the last stretch of flat. Soon they would begin the long, twisting climb over the centre of the island, over Mount Angeleno, forty-five miles to Brandt's Pen. Roy was glad there had been no rain: that the tar was dry. He hoped that there had been no rain on the northern slopes. It could be a deadly, testing drive if the road was wet, and sometimes the steep, loosely packed hillside bordering the road cut away with rain and blocked the way with earth and rock and trees.

He was passing a white, stone-built house. It was built of heavy, irregular stones joined by thick seals of mortar. He couldn't see this, but he knew the place well. Headlights shone briefly on trees and then on the house, built high up off the road on a bluff of rock, and on the trailing rice-and-peas vine which covered the house in front. Just ahead the real steepness began, where you changed down, and then changed down again as your car made the steadily twisting, straining climb to the crest of Mount Angeleno.

He changed down to second and the engine began the deep, groaning hum it would hold until the top of the hill. It was a good car and he had looked after it well. The bankside was very steep, now, and thick with trees and bush; down below, on his right, where the wide plain bit into the mountain range, he could see a solitary light burning in an isolated house. I wonder what it is? he asked himself. Somebody being born? Somebody dying? Maybe just a man who can't sleep and is reading out the night.

Ahead of him, Carl's car had begun to draw away. He did not try to catch him up. He knew that, on this part of the hill, the Humber would leave the Vauxhall. Going down on the other side, he would close the gap again. The red gleam ahead suddenly vanished round a bend.

He was at the top of Mount Angeleno now: he could see the road surface falling away before him in the white light. Far down the hill he saw the lights of the Humber glare for a moment against the bank. He began to drive very fast.

They reached Brandt's Pen at about quarter to four, after some of the most reckless driving Roy had ever done. He always drove a little too fast, especially in the country, late at night, but when the big Humber ahead of him slowed up about three miles from the Pen, so that they could arrive together, he realized that Carl was a better driver. That, even allowing for the superior car, Carl had more endurance, faster reflexes, surer judgement of distances than he. Going up the steep, stony drive to the great house he knew that so far in his driving he had enjoyed a lot more luck than he deserved.

They parked the cars under the lignum vitae tree which grew in front of the house, a little to one side of the verandah. The big house was dark and shuttered, and Roy was glad there wasn't a moon. It was late enough so that the unattached young men on the property had come in from the villages and were now a long way down in the first, heavy sleep of sexual satisfaction. And it was too early for anyone to be getting up. Four o'clock in the morning was probably the stillest, loneliest time of the day anywhere, and in the country, with the next day being Sunday, they were pretty sure to have the next hour to themselves. The dogs had barked when they first drove up; but as Carl got out they began to whine delightedly and scuffle around, nosing at the legs of the men.

Carl was fumbling with the lock on the boot of the Humber; Roy could just make him out, and the gleam of metal as the boot lid swung open. He heard Carl say to Etienne, who was still inside the car, "Put 'em in there," and saw him pass a crumpled shapeless blur through the window. He realized this must be a gunny sack that Carl had taken from his car, and when he heard a chinking of bottles, he knew that it was the food Etienne must be wrapping up.

The big door of the Humber swung open and he saw the blurred darkness Etienne made against the dark of the morning. He saw Carl take one of the big parcels.

"Come on," Carl said, and swung away across the drive in front of the house, with Etienne close behind him. Roy followed, almost walking on Etienne's heels. He knew how Carl could walk when he wanted. When Carl was really stretching his long, constantly practised stride he, Roy, had to trot occasionally to keep up. He didn't want to fall too far behind in this sort of darkness.

Carl led them across the front of the house, across the garden beside the house, and out into the long, wet grass of the pasture. He was leading them away from the house and the low line of the servants' quarters behind it.

Out in the pasture he turned right and they began to climb with the coarse calf- and knee-high grass swishing damply against their trousers and with sudden squelchings as they stepped on the pats of cow dung.

It was still; a dark, breathing quietness. Ahead of them were the black, blunt edges of the mountains against the sky. The stars were paling. Roy could smell the freshness of the dew and the green, crushed grass smell and the faintly bitter, very clean scent that you always had at Brandt's Pen when the breeze was blowing down from the mountains.

He knew that they were near the fence of the top pasture now. He had learnt this place too well and too hungrily, as a child, to forget that. He even knew, sensing it, that if he were to walk fifty yards to his right he would come to the old ebony tree that he and Carl, watching from the back verandah, had seen split and tormented into flame by a bolt of lightning. That was the year of the big storm, when a piece of the rocks on Tolliver beach had washed away and uncovered a cave full of rat-bat droppings and Huntley Pearce, Lloyd's father, had made a nice little packet selling the stuff to every planter within thirty miles.

There was something like a great stone wedge driven down his gullet into his lungs, and he was trying to breathe round that. His throat felt cold and dry, as if he had sucked peppermint and drunk water afterwards. He could hear the harsh, gulping sob of Etienne's breath, the grunting stumble as he tripped occasionally; ahead of them both, he could hear the clean, deep snort of Carl's breathing and the regular, thudding swish of his well-lifted feet.

Walking behind them, he would have liked to run forward and touch Carl. He wanted to chuckle as he felt the racing, tight-stomached tension of the past two days, and of the drive, run off him like sweat. He would have chuckled, but he didn't have the breath, and when he tried it came out as a painful, chest-burning wheeze.

He touched Etienne's arm and took the oilskin bundle.

The old shelter was up the mountainside and off the path, about a quarter of a mile from the dam.

Carl led them up the narrow, loose-pebbled, rain-rutted track at a fierce walk, almost loping. They passed the dam where the held water was only a broad, faint sheen in the darkness and went on up the path with the trees all around them. On a bend in the path, the stream crossed the road; and here Carl took a flat bicycle lamp from his pocket and with his big fingers folded across the glass shone a light on the flat, wet stepping stones set in the shallow, rushing water.

Roy could hardly hear the fast gurgle of the water, now, for the blood which hammered in his ears. His feet, crossing the stones, were uncertain, and Etienne slipped and put one foot in up to his ankle.

"Down here," Carl said, and turned off the path, pushing his way between the bushes which grew at the lip of the little valley bordering the path.

They went down the old trail where the bush, at stomach, waist and face, had grown up since it was no longer used, but where there was enough clear ground left to move. Roy's knees felt weak and uncontrollable as they plunged down the valley side. It was very dark, and he had run upon Etienne before he realized that Carl had stopped.

Carl shone the light and they saw the sheer cut, and the path fallen away, and the steeply slanted drop. It was all loose, crumbly shale and soil and at the bottom, on the valley floor, was the little shelter with old earth piled over one half of it.

Up to two years ago they had cut timber in this section of the valley and rough dressed it in the hut, because this was an easy place to make a trail up to the path. Since the landslide they cut wood further down, below the dam, and had left this place alone for the raw wound in the earth to heal. It was a clear sixty feet from where they were standing to the half-buried shelter on the valley floor.

"Right," Carl said, "let's go down. Roy, you wait here." He turned to Etienne. "I'll go first," he said. "Walk sideways, dig the edges of your shoes in and get plenty of give at the knees."

Etienne nodded and took his bundle from Roy. Both of them were trying to breathe again. No matter how hard they tried they couldn't seem to get more than a shallow, burning cold trickle of air into their lungs.

"Tomorrow," Etienne gasped. "See me tomorrow... better... night... late."

Roy nodded, and sat in the damp leaf mould of the little trail.

Carl stepped carefully over the cutaway edge of the path, facing sideways to the line they would take as they went down. When Henri Etienne's hand touched his shoulder, he said, "All right?"

and felt the hand tighten and the slight tremor of the man's instinctive nod. He began the descent, digging his feet into the crumbling surface, putting them one after another, leaning sideways against the slope, bending his right knee fully, the left leg stiffening to keep him pushed back against the slide. Etienne was following him precisely, and the bundles they were both carrying helped their balance.

About fifteen feet above the shelter the slant became sheer, and they did this in a furious, falling over scuttle, their legs scissoring hard to keep pace with the bodies which were being pulled away from the earth they had tried to hug. As they reached the bottom Carl put up his hand, and a second later he felt the smack of it against the rough, tarred board of the shelter and the shock being taken up by the muscles of his arm and Etienne piling heavily against him.

He took the bicycle lamp from his pocket again and moved along the wall to the sagging door of the little hut. He pushed it open and shone the light on the damp, packed earth of the floor, and the rough table which they had not bothered to dismantle. Etienne followed him inside.

"Well, this is it," Carl said quickly. "It's a bit damp but you can't be seen from the path. I'll leave you the light." For the first time that night he saw Etienne's face, briefly, in the light of the lamp. It looked strange, and then he saw that the beard and moustache had been shaved.

"Thank you, Mr. Brandt," Etienne told him. "I have my own light in my pack." He was still having a hard job of it to catch his breath.

"Right," Carl said, putting down the gunny sack of food. "You don't have to worry about water, by the way. There's a twenty-gallon drum outside this corner. It's full of rain water and I think it's pretty safe to drink. No mosquitoes this far up. I think that's all, eh? Anything else you want to know?"

"No," Etienne said. "I think I know everything I need to know."

"Good," Carl said. "I'll see you."

"Good night, Mr. Brandt, and thank you again for all this."

"That's all right," Carl told him. "You don't have to thank me. Roy arranged it all."

He went out of the hut and gathered himself for the first rushing hand-over-hand scramble up the wall of the slide. He made it. Then with lunging, steady heaves he worked himself up to the lip of the slope where Roy was waiting. He was breathing heavily now, but he liked the feel of the power in his legs as he took the slope of the landslide.

They set off again without a word. It was still dark but they knew it was the pre-dawn blackness. When they reached the path and looked out across to the black, forested peaks in the distance, at the head of the valley, they could see a blue brightness in the sky around the mountains.

Carl looked at his watch.

"We'll do it before five," he said in a panting voice. "We'll have to run."

They trotted most of the way back to the pasture. When they reached there they stopped and wiped their shoes clean with bunches of wet grass. It was darker here than where they had looked towards the peaks which were high enough to get the first glow from the east.

They went back to the house in the same wide, skirting movement they had used coming up. They both got their bags from the cars, and Carl opened the small passage door. They went inside and into Carl's room. Carl turned on the light and looked at Roy.

"Well," he said, "I told you we'd do it."

Roy smiled at him from the foot of the bed where he was sitting, his small weekend case in his hands. His linen suit was crumpled and there was a green bush stain across the front of it. His face was pale and sweating, but it looked happy and relaxed. He needed a shave.

"I'll see you tomorrow," he said, getting up.

"What time?"

"About ten."

"Good. I don't think there are any sheets on your bed; you want some?"

"God, no," Roy said, going to the door. "I don't even need the bed, really."

"What now?" Carl asked as Roy was opening the door. "How are you – *we* going to get him out of here?"

"I'll tell you at breakfast," Roy said. "It's a long story. I'll need you for that, too, if you'll do it."

"Sure, boy," Carl said. "I'm in it now."

Roy went down the passage to the room which he always slept in whenever he came to Brandt's Pen. It was a smaller room than Carl's and it had the same fragrance of old, very fine wood, and of linen which had been packed in *cous-cous* for hundreds of years; the mattress was flat and firm and resting to the body as only a good coir-filled mattress could be.

He took off his suit and put it in the bag so that the maid wouldn't see it in the morning. He put on his pyjamas and lay down, wrapping himself in the soft, warm lightness of the eiderdown. His legs felt heavy, and when he stretched them he could feel the big muscles of the thigh stiffen and the calf muscles twitch and hurt.

He tried to imagine Etienne up on the mountain, in the little, battered shelter, spreading out his oilskin and his blankets, but it only heightened this luxuriously tired, heavy-resting sensation.

For a moment he tried to think of how he could best ask Carl to get Sheila Pearce to help them with her boat: but he was asleep before he had even got a proper image of Sheila's face in his mind.

19

When he woke he felt as if he had slept round a whole day; and he got up quickly and went to the jalousies and opened them. When he saw the sun and how it stood above the big peaks to the east and how the shadows lay in the garden, he knew that it wasn't late. He felt good, and there was a faint stiffness in his legs that was, somehow, clean and comfortable. His mind was very clear. It had been one of those short sleeps where the brain seems to sink to the bottom of a black, warm well and to rise slowly again, absolutely restored. He didn't often sleep like that.

He leaned on the broad, white-painted sill and looked across the heavy-awninged verandah with its line of chairs in linen slip covers and its elegant ironwork pillars into the bright garden.

There was the smell of Brandt's Pen in the still, warm air. It was a smell you really got on Sunday and it was made up of warm grass, dung, flowers, the stale odour of sheep from up the fold, the cheap jasmine scent and powder the servant girls used, flowers again, warm red earth, the heavy, sweetish smell of cattle dip, and then half a hundred other scents, each of which he knew, all eddying briefly and lingering among the baked, grassy, food, hide and flowers smell of the Pen. Whenever, in other places, he had thought of this one, it was always with the memory in his nostrils of these odours and the clean, comforting smell of warm earth; and the whispered hint of blood somewhere in the blue-gold, green and silver brightness of the air.

He could hear Carl talking to Tom somewhere round the corner, on the back verandah, and then their voices lifted on two shouts of laughter.

"Carl," he called, "what's the time?"

"Half-past nine, just gone. We'll have breakfast on the front verandah. Nearly ready?"

"Five minutes."

"O.K. I'll tell Delia."

Roy showered in the small bathroom down the passage; the water was cold from the tank on the roof. He went back to his room with the towel round his waist. He dressed and went out to the front verandah; to the wide corner where there were ferns in tall, red, clay pots and orchids hanging from the ceiling in small, slatted boxes filled with black earth.

Carl was sitting at the small breakfast table which had been spread with stiff, glistening linen and laid with the heavily elegant cutlery. There was a silver bowl of roses in the middle of the table.

"Hi, lad," Carl said. "Sleep well?"

"Never better."

Carl looked at the small, neat figure before him. There was a blue, stiff bristle along the jaw and over the lips. Roy was wearing blue jeans and the old bush jacket that he had been issued a long time ago in the East: it was faded and there was a big, fine darn along the left breast, but it was starched so that the cloth showed occasional gleams, and where the wings and flashes and medal ribbons had once been sewn it had something of the old colour left.

"How is it your jacket has lasted so long?" Carl asked. "I gave mine to Tom two years ago and the last time I saw it, Tom's little brother was wearing it like an overcoat."

"I don't wear mine much," Roy said. "Only when I come up here."

Delia, the cook, came through the drawing-room carrying the large silver tray, and the white, blue-patterned service on the tray, with a smell of coffee coming out before her. She was a big, solid woman, and her hair under the cap was the real, iron grey and forced flat against her head with many hairpins. The broad, seamed face, which had never seemed to grow any older since Roy had first known her, was smiling.

"Mass' Roy," she said, in her heavy, singing, authoritative voice, "how you do, sah? What a long time you no come an' look fe' me."

"Hullo, Delia," Roy said. "How you do?" His face looked bright and happy.

"I well, sah. But you mustn't stay so long nex' time. Old woman like me you have fe' see plenty time, else dem dead between visit."

She put the tray on a low, wide, oval table beside theirs and brought two big glasses of pineapple juice over to them. She looked at Roy, smiling broadly with possessive fondness. Looking at her healthy, powerful face, you realized that it was lined and scored only as the bark of a tree gets toughened.

"Cho!" Roy said. "You'll put me and Mister Carl out in the sun yet. You wait."

"He was drunk last night, Delia," Carl said, joking her. "You should have seen him. I could scarcely get him here."

"Lawd, Mass' Carl," she said. "How you stay bad so, eh, sah? You know Mass' Roy can't drink like you an' you Daddy. Why you lead him into bad ways, eh, Mass' Carl? Time an' time I tell you say, 'Mass' Carl, don't make Mass' Roy tek up him waters too much.' You feel all right, Mass Roy?"

"I feel fine, Delia," Roy said smiling. "Mister Carl is a wicked man. I only had three drinks last night."

Carl was laughing and drinking his pineapple juice. He never knew how much Delia believed the tales of sin and wantonness he told her about Roy and himself, but he knew she enjoyed being shocked by them and getting the chance to offer a little good advice.

"You can leave the breakfast," he told her. "We'll help ourselves when we want."

"Yes, sah. Eat good, eh, Mass' Roy. How long you stay dis time?"

"Just today, Delia," he said. "I have plenty work in Queenshaven to get back to."

"Cho!" she said. "Dat place not good fe' stay too long. You mus' come an' stay longer, Mass' Roy. Like old time. You need feedin' up."

They watched her long, beautiful back and broad buttocks and straight, slender, black legs as she went through the door. From behind, with her hair under the cap, she looked like a powerfully built thirty, but she had been nearly that when Carl was born.

"Do you know," Carl said, "that you are the only one of my guests for whom Delia will carry a tray? She wouldn't bring anybody else a glass of water. I've heard her call one of the maids in from the yard to fetch somebody a towel when she was standing right next to the bathroom."

"She's a one all right," Roy said. "I don't think she really regards any man as a man, though, unless he owns a property like you, or at least works on one."

"She thinks you're great stuff," Carl said. "She probably just feels sorry that you missed your vocation. And talking of her and men: did you know that Hector's yard boy, Hubert, is her son?"

"No! Delia! But isn't she the second pillar from the left in the Methodist Church here?"

"Yes. I didn't know myself until a few months ago when Hector told me. Tom's father was responsible."

"I'd never have thought it," Roy said. "Hubert doesn't look the least bit coolie. I guess you need plenty to swamp the sort of stock Delia has."

He went over to the oval side-table and brought back a steaming, salty smelling dish of fish and ackee. He put this down and went back for two plates and the salver of sliced bread. Carl was pouring coffee into the big cups.

And this, Roy told himself, as he chewed the first forkful of salty, shredded fish and smooth, yellow gobbets of ackee, and this is the thing that could really corrupt me. Not the wealth of it, he thought, feeling the solidity of old polished wood beneath his feet, looking at the spacious bright interior (where the flowers seemed to have stood, fresh and beautiful, for as long as the old, winking silver) regarding the strong, nourished, confident face of his friend opposite. No, the wealth and luxury I can handle, he said to himself, rubbing the unbelievably sensuous smoothness of the old linen between his fingertips. But it's the closeness of it that could change me. This incestuous, happy, kindly closeness where every personal contact is never let go, and where everyone fits into his place like a cork into a bottle.

"Any coffee left?" he asked, and as Carl was filling the cup, "What did you think of Etienne?"

"He was all right," Carl said. His face was set and uncommunicative.

"No, really, Carl. What did you think of him? You know what I mean. What did you two talk about driving over last night?"

"Not a goddam thing. I was going too fast to worry about chatting, and it's hard to talk to someone in the back seat when you're driving. Besides I didn't want to. He's a man, right enough, but as far as I'm concerned it can stop right there."

"It's a pity: he's an interesting chap. He's had a hell of a life and can talk about it well."

"Maybe. He talks good English."

"He taught himself when he was sixteen. He once told me that he used to know all the major Shakespeare tragedies by heart."

He studied Carl's face and knew that nothing he could say would break down that stubborn, unhappy sullenness.

"How are you going to get him away from here?" Carl asked then, "Have you fixed that up yet?"

Roy took out his cigarettes and gave Carl one and took one himself and lit them both. Then he told Carl, briefly and economically, about the *Kosciuzko* and Jeffrey Summer, the fisherman. And, at the end he asked him about getting Sheila Pearce to help them. He watched the serious interest with which Carl had listened to the first part of the plan change to sullenness once more: but this time it looked dangerous and he could see the hard flecks at the back of the other man's grey eyes.

"You must be crazy," Carl said, in a cold disgusted voice.

"Sheila's not coming into this, you understand. I'm not going to go pimping for you and Etienne; and if you try to get her into it I'll tell Hector."

"You wouldn't do that, Carl."

"No," more slowly now, feeling a little ashamed of the jealousy which had been half responsible for his words. "No, I'm sorry I said that. But it still stands as I said: Sheila is not to get mixed up in this."

"Why?"

"Oh, for God's sake, Roy, this is too nasty, and she's a woman. It's dangerous too: Columbus Head offshore's some of the worst water on the coast."

"She could do it. You've told me how she can handle that boat of hers."

"If it's a power boat you want I'll hire one. I'll tell them we want to go fishing."

"How would we explain Etienne to the owner? His picture was in the papers yesterday, remember, and everyone knows that the police want him if he lands."

"We'll handle the boat ourselves."

"We couldn't. You know that. It's not just running an engine. This is going to take skill."

"We'll think of something," Carl said. He won't get away with this one, he told himself.

"What can you think of, Carl?" said Roy urgently. "If you can really think of something, tell me. I don't want Sheila in this. I only want you and me and the few party members who have to know. I don't even know if Sheila would do it. She doesn't approve of Etienne any more than you do, I guess. But if you asked her and told her to keep it secret, she would. She's that sort."

"Yes," Carl said bitterly. "She is. You seem to be depending a lot on that sort, don't you? What you call the bourgeoisie. You seem to find them valuable when the pinch comes."

"I'm depending on men, Carl."

They sat and smoked in silence while Elvira cleared the breakfast dishes. They waited until they could no longer hear her footfalls from the drawing-room.

"Well," Roy said, "can *you* think of something else?"

"Not yet," Carl said. "When does this bloody ship pass?"

"Tuesday or Wednesday. Late at night. It all depends when it clears Panama."

"How do you know it will stop?"

"If it's possible it will. If we are there, it will pick Etienne up."

"Sheila mustn't get mixed up in this," Carl said.

"Why, Carl? She's not an idiot or a child. You've got to ask her."

"I can't. If anything happened to her it would be my fault. *I* can help *you* and that's all right. But I'm not going to drag somebody else into it. No, Roy, we'll have to think of something else."

Think now, Roy told himself. Think hard. If this fails then the whole thing fails. He's not angry any more, but he could get angry any minute. I've got to touch him now; like I touched him Friday morning.

"You're leaving me halfway," he said to Carl. He looked down and took another cigarette from the red packet. He put it in his mouth but he did not light it.

"I'm with you," Carl said. "Anything I can do I'll do for you. Not murder or stealing or anything like that, but help you any other way."

"Not with Sheila though?"

"Sheila is out."

"It means that the whole thing has failed, you know. There isn't any other way we can get him out. You might as well go in and phone Castleville for the police now. He'd be more comfortable in a dry cell; until they send him back to be hung."

"He's hung a few, himself."

"Sure. But didn't particularly like it and it probably saved more lives than you could imagine."

"O.K.," Carl said. "Don't let's go into that. It doesn't really matter. He's on my land and I promised to help him. But she didn't. Why her?"

"I couldn't think of anyone else. Not with the same tie-up; and not anyone I could trust because of you. Can you?"

"No," Carl told him. He spoke very slowly and his face was stiff and expressionless. "I guess you have me, eh, Roy? If I don't do this I'll be really letting you down, eh? You have me coming and going."

"It's not like that," Roy said. His eyes were bright and steady. "What we're doing, what has happened, is not as simple as the two of us. We're in a situation and we're acting with it. Once you make the first action the rest follows."

"Did you know about Sheila when you came on Friday?" Carl asked. "Did you decide not to tell me in case I refused?"

If he lies about it, Carl thought, I'll hit him. Then I'll put him and Etienne in his car and tell them to find their own way out. If he lies about it we're finished.

"I knew about it," Roy said simply. "I got the idea coming across Friday morning. Up till then I didn't know how we would get him out. Then I thought about Sheila and you; and about her boat. I didn't mention it to you on Friday because I didn't want to scare you off."

"You're a lucky little bastard, aren't you?" Carl said, smiling gently at him. "You get into trouble and you have me, and God knows who else, sitting in your lap begging to run errands."

He saw Roy give a spasmodic heave of relief and delight.

"What would you have done if I hadn't told you the truth?" Roy asked him. He asked the question in the steady dispassionate voice he would have used in an academic discussion. "Would you have killed me or what?"

"I wouldn't have meant to but I might have by accident."

"When are you going to ask Sheila for me? It will have to be today."

"I'm not going to ask her," Carl said. "You'd better ask her."

"But why, Carl? It would come much better from you."

"You bloody fool," Carl said, "she's in love with you. She'd blow up the Houses of Parliament if she thought it would make you look at her."

"What?"

"You think I'd make a joke about it?"

"Jesus, Jesus, Jesus," Roy said. "I never bargained for this. How do you know? I mean, I know she liked me and we've always got on fine when we meet; but *this*. Jesus, Carl. How did you find out? Did she tell you?"

"Don't be a goddam fool. Of course she didn't tell me; but I know it when I see it. I'm not blind."

"Lord," Roy said. "What am I going to do?"

"You aren't any way in love with her yourself, are you?"

"She's a woman," Roy said, "and she's a very nice person, but until now I've never thought of her any way but as your girl. That's the truth."

"It's your problem now," Carl said, and got up. "I've finished with it. Friday, I kissed her and it was like kissing a child who doesn't want you to. It was as bad as that."

He was standing by the low, broad parapet of the verandah, looking out across the hillside down to the plain where Tolliver was. It isn't too bad, he thought. It's like getting a dildo thorn out of your foot. You can feel the flesh hugging it close and you want to leave it there. But if you make one swift tug it comes out all right; and the last part is much easier than the first.

"I'm sorry, boy," Roy said from the table behind him.

"You've got nothing to be sorry about."

Carl turned round from the parapet and faced him. Standing there, with the sun behind him, he looked huge and indomitable: it was hard to imagine that anyone so physically impressive could ever be hurt.

"What now?" Carl said. "It's quarter to eleven. I told Sheila I'd see her today sometime."

"Let's go down to see Jeffrey Summer first," Roy said. "He has a small beach past Tolliver. We can bathe there and talk to him. Then we can see Sheila."

"All right," Carl agreed. "I know Summer, by the way. He's an old friend. I didn't know you'd roped him in. You're lucky to have him: he's a marvel with a boat."

They went through the house to their rooms and got their trunks and towels. Then Carl went to tell Delia that they would be a little late for lunch. While he was doing this, Roy shaved quickly. He drew the razor across the hard stubble and nicked his chin and had to put a patch of toilet paper on to stop the blood.

They went out to the garage, where Tom had put the cars early that morning while they were asleep, and got into the Humber.

There were small clouds, high up and wispy, and it looked like a nice day to go to the sea.

20

About two miles west of Tolliver, where the main road swung in a little, was the beach where Jeffrey Summer lived. It was a rocky part of the coast and two coconut-tree-grown, jagged headlands enclosed the narrow strip of hot stony sand. The water was shallow and very rough, except for one deep channel, rough also, up which Summer brought the boats. There were many stubby, brown, coconut trees with dark, flecked leaves growing in the warm loose sand behind the white strip next to the sea. Underneath the trees were a few tables, made by nailing packing-case lids across barrel tops, and some benches round the tables. It was not the sort of beach where many people came: you had to drive down to it over a narrow dirt road and there was better sand and water in a lot of bays near by. Having it as a bathing place was only the casual part of Summer's business: the regular, serious work of his life was contained in the two long, black boats, with full bows, high thwarts and narrow sterns, which were drawn far up the beach.

Carl drew up in the gravelly, coarse grass at the edge of the trees. They could see a little, neat house with a tiny verandah set among the trees about a hundred yards from the coconut frond changing huts. It was very hot and bright, but under the trees the sunlight was faintly green, diffused and pleasant and the wind moved the long, hard leaves with a continuous, soft scraping.

A little boy was coming to them among the ringed, curving boles of the trees. He was wearing only a ragged pair of damp khaki shorts. When he came up to the window, they could see the rich, shiny, dark beauty of his face; the up-tilted, round nose, the big, wide mouth with its curled-back lips, the soft, glossy black hair and the huge black eyes and thick lashes which seemed to glitter almost on to his cheekbones.

"Good mornin', Mr. McKenzie," he said. "Good mornin', Mr. Brandt, sah."

"Hullo, Lionel," they both said, and Roy continued after a moment, "Is your Daddy at home, Lionel?"

"Yes, sah. Him up de house."

"Tell him we're here. We're going to have a bathe and he can see us on the beach. How is your mother?"

"She well, sah."

"You still skipping school, Lionel?" Carl asked him as they got out of the car.

"Sometimes I go, sah. But I prefer go out in de boat wid Pappa."

"He gets a beating about once a month," Carl told Roy, "for trying to sneak into the boats at night. If he goes out with them he's only fit for sleeping the next day."

The little boy giggled and lowered his lashes and drew a sweep in the loose sandy gravel with his toe. When Carl ruffled his hair brusquely, he twisted against the big hand like a cat.

They watched the tautly sprung, shining small body trot lightly to the house among the hard slender trunks of the trees.

Then they changed in the hot, thick air of one of the huts and ran across the sand, lifting their feet quickly and putting them down lightly, going quickly because of the heat in the fine sand.

The water was pale blue and it felt smooth and clinging, like warm milk. But when they swam out and dived to the white seabed, it was cool and there was a dim, glassy, blue light around them, and coming to the surface again they could feel the salt stinging their eyerims, as they blinked the water from them.

They swam up and down for a quarter of an hour; they were far out, beyond the edge of the shallow shelf near the beach. It was rough, tumbling water and Roy, who had a great fear of sharks, would never swim there alone; but with Carl he always felt safe. It was irrational, he knew, but he never felt afraid of things in the open sea when Carl was with him. They both swam with the confident easiness of men who could hardly remember learning to swim. Carl with a great thrashing trudgeon that seemed to fight and master the waves, and Roy with a silkier, neater, very fast movement, slipping through the water and using it.

When they came out they could see Jeffrey Summer and one of his sons, the eldest one they both knew as George, sitting on the fallen fronds under a tree at the edge of the coconut grove.

Carl and Roy walked across the beach to the two men. Their feet were cool and wet now and they did not mind the burn from the sand. They could feel the water drying on their bodies in the full sun, and the salt tightening the skin pleasantly. They were both breathing hard from the swim and they sat in the shadow with Jeffrey and George Summer before they spoke.

"Hullo Jeffrey," said Roy, stretching out to take the flattened, wiry, dark brown hand Summer had offered him. When they squeezed on the grip he could feel the long thin scars of line cuts which had healed quickly because of the salt. "George," he said, taking the bigger, darker hand of the son. It was the same sort of hand: flattened and very hard with rowing, but the scars were less noticeable.

"Hullo, Summer. How are you, George?" Carl said. He shook hands also.

"Good day, Mr. Brandt, Mr. McKenzie. I is glad to see you, Mr. Brandt; it's a long time since you come here, sir. How you getting on?"

"Good day, Mr. Brandt, Mr. McKenzie," George said.

"I'm pretty well, Summer," Carl replied. "How are things with you? Had a good season?"

"Not bad, sir. Kingfish run bad so far dis year. Snapper is good, though."

Roy squinted against the hard glare beating up from the sea and looked at Summer. He had often studied the older man's face with fascinated thoroughness; and yet there always seemed to be something new to be discovered in the long thin head with its sleek, salt-faded black hair, the small brown eyes set in wrinkles that meshed around the sockets, the long scimitar curve of the nose and the two very deep grooves that ran down from the nose on either side of the wide, big-lipped mouth. The edges of his lips had curling, carved edges like the little boy's and like George's. The chin was small, pointed and had the deep cleft that Roy had seen in the chins of most stubborn, brave men. He was wearing a brightly clean, soft, blue shirt and blue canvas trousers. He had no shoes and his bare, broad feet were tucked under him as he sat in a thin, loose-muscled huddle. George, who was much bigger and very much darker, rested on one elbow. He was mending a large piece of net, his powerful, quickly moving fingers plaiting and knotting deftly and surely. He was so handsome that you knew he had once been beautiful and angelic like his brother, Lionel. Lying there, in his gaily patterned shirt, he had the utterly relaxed arrogance of a glossy, flower-decked panther; but it was all physical; when he smiled his face had the sweetness that they had seen in the face of the little boy.

"I came over to see you, Jeffrey," Roy said. "I have a job for you, if you can do it."

"Surely, Mr. McKenzie, I should like to help you, sir. What is it?"

He's being polite, Roy said to himself. It's because of Carl. He knows it would embarrass Carl if he were to call me Roy; like he does when we're alone. George too. A Queenshaven man would have "Roy-ed" me twenty times by now.

"You've heard about Etienne?" he asked Jeffrey Summer. "And the invasion over in St. Pierre?"

"Yes, sir, It was sad news. I pray for Etienne's safety. Do you think he will escape, Mr. McKenzie, and go back one day?"

"He has," Roy said flatly. "He's here. That's why I've come to you: we need your help in getting him away."

Jeffrey Summer stiffened and his suddenly hard eyes flickered from Roy to Carl and back to Roy again. He looked puzzled and suspicious and, without looking at George, Roy knew that he had stopped working on the net.

"It's all right," Roy told them, "Carl is in it, too. He is helping me; that's why I brought him."

Jeffrey Summer slowly went loose again. He still seemed a little puzzled, but the hard suspicion had gone from his face "Leave it a minute," he said, "de bwoy coming."

Roy turned his head and saw Lionel walking to them among the trees. He was carrying a dish in one hand and bottle in the other. He walked delicately, looking at the dish with intense careful concentration, and you knew that he felt the world turned on this errand being well done There was a machete held under his arm.

He came up and smiling shyly put a dish of cold, escovitched fish between them on the fronds. There were strip of pickled onion and red pepper on the brown fish, and five thick slices of bread. He gave the bottle to his father, and George took the machete from under his arm..

"Good bwoy," Jeffrey Summer said. "You gwine climb de tree for us?"

"Yes, Pappa," he said happily.

He went to one of the stunted, curving trees near by and clasped the rough, ringed bark and curled his feet on each side of the trunk. He squatted on his heels, holding on, and began to hitch himself up. He didn't seem to find it any harder than walking across the ground.

"Lionel!" George called, and winked at Roy.

The child stopped and looked down over his shoulder.

"Lionel," George said, "suppose rat hold you, eh? Suppose rat jump out 'pon you like last time?"

He was grinning to himself. Lionel had stopped halfway up the stem. His face was thoughtful.

"George, you is wicked, you know," Jeffrey Summer said. "Go on, son, you brudder fool you, ah. No rat up dere... Him did climb a tree wid a rat nest in it on Wednesday," he explained to Roy and Carl. "When dem feel him climbing dem did get frighten an' jump out of de leaves, past his head. Dem frighten him bad."

"Ai-ee, Lionel!" George called, laughing lazily. "Suppose rat jump on you like last time, eh? Suppose dem hold on to you nose. Dem might bite you, eh?"

Lionel had stopped again. You could see him thinking hard. He looked very doubtful. Carl got up and went to the foot of the tree. His head came just under halfway up it.

"Go on, Lionel," he said, smiling up at the boy. "Don't make your brother *ginal* you. If you see any rats, jump down; I'll catch you."

The child flashed him a brief white smile of gratitude and went up and into the leaves. He vanished into the stiff, feathery crown like a mongoose going into high grass. Then they could hear him twisting the stem of one of the green nuts and a second later it came down and hit with a thump beside Carl.

"Hoy!" he shouted. "Wait! Let me get out of the way." He jumped back and came over and sat with the laughing men.

When there were six nuts on the ground George rose and taking the machete flicked the hard green fibre from the tops of four of them. Holding the heavy nuts in the palm of his left hand and cutting them casually with the big machete, as Roy would have sharpened a pencil with his penknife.

Each one he cut he passed to one of them, and gave the last to

Lionel as he came down from the tree. Then he cut the fifth for himself. He came over and dug a hole in the white fresh cut of the tops, the clear juice spurting around the file-scratched blade. They tilted a little of the juice out and Jeffrey Summer poured rum from the bottle into each of the men's coconuts and they swirled the juice inside the nuts to mix the rum with it.

Summer took a piece of the bread and put fish and pepper and onions on it and gave to Lionel.

"Thank you, bwoy," he said. "Go and see if you mamma want anyt'ing else."

"He's growing nicely," Carl told him. "He's really a fine boy." He watched the man's tight, pleased smile.

"Him is bad, though," Jeffrey Summer said proudly. "Him is bad, you see. Him is worse dan George was; an' him was *bad*. And now what you want me do, eh?"

"We hope to get Etienne away on a ship; we want you to take him out part of the way."

"Yes, sir. When?"

"Late at night. Fishing time. It should be early next week; this week, rather; today's Sunday."

"I can do it. Me an' de boys can do it easy. Where you want it, sir?"

"It will mean going into Columbus Head and taking him out from there."

"Lawd King!" George said in a slow, thoughtful voice. Jeffrey Summer's face became very serious, as he nodded his long, thin head gently.

"Columbus Head!" he repeated. "Mr. McKenzie, sir, do you know what it like dere?"

"Not as well as you," Roy told him. "Is it impossible?"

"No, sir; but it is bad water."

"Can you do it?"

"Twice I do it. Once when I was younger dan George, an' one time four years ago. You remember, George? Bot' time I have fe' do it, because of storm."

His voice was clear and steady and Roy knew that the old man was not afraid for himself but was simply and calmly stating the conditions under which the job would have to be done.

"If I remember?" George said rhetorically. He held out his flat, wide, calloused hand at a slant. "Look, Roy. Dat current off de Head stay so. It tilt like a bankside and it faster dan waterfall. Going in, it all right. It hard, but me and Pappa an' me brudders do it. Coming out it hit you broad on. Like so," he smacked his clenched right fist into the palm of his hand "an' beyon' dat de water dance up an' down on de rocks. Why you pick Columbus Head, Roy?"

He asked this with interest and without any resentment or petulance.

"Because if they suspect Etienne has come here, or that we're trying to get him away, they'll get us for sure. They can't watch the whole coast, but we couldn't know where they would set a patrol. The good bays and clear water are too risky."

Summer nodded and looked at his son.

"Columbus Head is de best, den," George said.

"Yes. You think you can do it?" Roy asked him. He bit into a piece of the bread and fish. The dried bird pepper was very hot.

"Me an' Pappa? An' me brudders? Cho, yes. If Pappa steer, we can do it."

"What do you say, Jeffrey?" Roy asked the old man.

"George say it," he said in a tranquil, utterly decided voice. "We can do it. It not easy, but it can be done. How far out you want us to go?"

"How far in could a launch come; a cruising craft? How big, Carl?"

"Thirty feet I think. I don't know how much she draws."

"Good sailor on her?" asked Jeffrey Summer.

"Yes, very good."

"A mile and a half, mebbe. Mebbe mile an' quarter. It could come in nearer, but it would be fool to do it at night; even wid a good sailor."

"O.K.," Roy said, "that's how far your bit is. The launch will take over from there."

"Who you have for de launch, sir?"

"You know Mrs. Pearce?"

"Miss' Pearce of Tolliver? De lady who have de *Nisba*?"

"Yes."

Summer drew a low, astonished whistle through his yellowing teeth. George opened his eyes widely for a second.

"De *Nisba* is a good boat," he said, "an' Miss' Pearce can manage her good." He looked at Roy questioningly.

"I don't know that we have her yet," Roy said. "But I think we might. If we don't, then we'll have to think of something else."

All right, sir," Summer spoke again. "When you want us?"

"Either Tuesday or Wednesday. Between nine and half-past on the beach. How long will it take you to row out to the *Nisba*?"

"T'ree-quarter hour in dat water."

"How long for a boat like the *Nisba* to go another twelve miles?"

"Cho, an hour an' a half easy."

"That's fine. Make it between half-past nine and ten on the beach. We'll come to you there. Either Carl or I will tell you the day by tomorrow. Probably Carl as we don't want people to see me too much around your place. How does it sound to you?"

"Plenty people in it, but you can't help dat. It sound all right. Which of de boat dem you t'ink we should use, George?"

"*Rose* ride better, Pappa, but *Selina* answer better. Which you t'ink?"

"Which of dem you want, George?"

"Lawd, Pappa. I like go in *Rose* because she ride light. *Selina* heavy, but she always do what you want. It hard to say."

"Which of dem you t'ink, George?"

"You have fe' steer, Pappa, an' you know de boat how dem stay. You know what dem can do. What you say?"

"Which of dem you t'ink, George?"

The old man's eyes were hard and bright as a bird's eyes and his voice was thin, inflexible and patient.

You better tell him something, George, Roy thought. He'll keep you here till seven o'clock tonight if you don't say what you think. Go on, George, say something. Any damn thing. I don't want to be here all day.

"Which of dem you want, George?" Jeffrey Summer asked. And this time, hearing him, you knew that he was not going to ask again.

"Tek *Selina*, Pappa. In dat water it better to have a boat dat answer all de time. What you t'ink?"

"I t'ink *Selina*, too," Jeffrey Summer said, and smiled his tight, face-wrinkling smile and clapped his son on the knee.

They finished the coconut and water rum, drinking between mouthfuls of the bread and fish and shrivelled, burning pickles and talking. When Roy was sure they understood, fully, everything, and remembered it, he and Carl went to change. Jeffrey Summer and George were standing by the car when they came out.

"You've got it all, then?" Roy asked Summer. "Carl will get in touch with you when we know which night for sure. Be careful, eh? Don't say anything to Mrs. Summer even."

Lionel ran from the house as they drove into the little road. He followed, trotting beside the car, for a few yards. Roy signalled to him and Carl slowed the engine until they were not going faster than a walk: Lionel jumped on to the high, black sweep of the front mudguard and clutched the window-ledge and Roy held him by his bony, smooth-skinned shoulder. When he had got his ride Carl stopped and the child hopped into the dust. He stood there, waving after the car until it went round a bend in the road.

21

When they went inside the house at Tolliver they saw Lloyd, Sheila Pearce's husband, sitting beside the telephone table at the foot of the stairs, in the cool, dim hallway. He was listening in on the telephone and he waved at them and pointed up the stairs. They waved back without speaking. As they went up they heard him say, "Yes, that would be splendid, I'd be delighted," and then he gave a polite laugh.

They went out on to the verandah and sat down. Neither of them said anything to each other. Now that they were here they both felt a little stiff embarrassment, and Carl was wondering if they could get rid of Lloyd for a while, until they had talked to Sheila.

Lloyd came through the door; he made a slim, gay figure in his bright shirt and creamy flannels: his very dark, heavy features were handsome in a way that reminded Roy of some old Mediterranean bronzes, with everything a little too full, indulged and soft.

"Well, boys," Lloyd said. "Long time no see. How are you, Carl? Roy?" He shook hands. "Sheila is just coming," he continued. "She was out in the kitchen. Are you staying for lunch?"

"We can't, Lloyd," Carl told him. "Roy's only over for the day, and Delia would be mortally offended if he didn't eat up at the Pen. She always has something special when he comes up."

They all sat down. Carl was glad that he heard Sheila's long, quick footfall coming from the passage.

She came to the doorway. She was wearing white shorts and a green linen halter which went very well with her tan. Her gaze slid from Carl's face, even as she was smiling at him, and went to Roy and stayed there. When she shook Carl's hand she kept looking from him to Roy, and Carl knew that she had got to the stage, seeing Roy again after two months, where she didn't mind being careless about it before her husband. One of the maids came out with four brown bottles of beer, rum, glasses and two big bottles of ginger ale, all on a tray.

"What will you have?" Lloyd asked them.

"Beer, thanks," Carl said. "I'm thirsty."

"Rum for me, please," Roy said.

"Evadne," Sheila Pearce said to the maid, "bring some water: I think Mr. McKenzie prefers water with his rum. Isn't that right?" she asked Roy.

"That's right," he told her. "I am not fussy about it, but you don't lose the taste when you have it with water."

Lloyd was opening one of the beer bottles.

"Darling," he said to his wife, "guess who just rang up?"

"I can't guess," she said. "Who was it?"

"Lady Hampton. She called up from Resurrection Heights. They want us to come over after lunch and take them up to Assembly Bay for the afternoon."

"I don't think I want to go," Sheila said in a pleasant, profoundly disinterested voice. "I asked Carl to go over some work with me today. You can make excuses for me, can't you."

"Why don't you come?" he asked her. He said it as if he were repeating a lesson. "They're such charming people. Have you met them?" he said to Carl.

"Yes," Carl said. "They were over last month to look at my ponies. He wanted to buy one."

"I didn't know Lord Hampton played polo," Lloyd said. He sounded a little worried.

"Yes," Carl told him. "He tried out a couple at the Pen. He's not bad at all. Getting a bit heavy but he knows what to do on a horse; he must have had a good teacher."

"He was in the Blues," Lloyd said with the air of a man producing the trump card in a friendly game of whist.

"Oh, yes!" Carl said. Lord Hampton had told him this when they had come up to Brandt's Pen, but he didn't want to spoil Lloyd's winning hand. He had a feeling that this sort of thing was about all Lloyd ever won in life.

"Yes," Lloyd said, pleased now. "They're really charming people. Have you met them, Roy?"

"No," Roy said in a solemn regretful voice.

"Why don't you all come out this afternoon?" Lloyd asked them. It was like watching a small, beautiful, much spoilt child offering sweets to the company in a sudden access of self-conscious generosity. "Why don't you all do that, eh? They would like to see you again, Carl, and Roy would be able to meet them."

"That would be nice, Lloyd," Carl said, "but we have to get back to the Pen. Roy brought up some work from town and I have a few things I want to go over with him."

"You go alone," Sheila told Lloyd gently. "I'll come next time. But I really want to see Carl this afternoon, and we did arrange it. Ask them for dinner one night next week, and then we can have Carl down. Maybe Roy would come across too?"

She looked at him, and Carl saw the slow surge of colour start under her thick, smooth, sun-darkened skin. After a second, Roy looked away over the verandah railings.

"You're staying for lunch, aren't you?" Sheila said, turning her eyes briefly to Carl.

He explained to her about Delia.

"I tell you what," Roy said and Carl wondered if the voice sounded as sudden and harsh to the others as it did to him. "If Lloyd has to go out, and Sheila wants to see Carl, why doesn't she come up to the Pen for lunch?"

"That's a good idea," Carl said. "Why don't you do that, Sheila?" He felt that he was now responsible to both of them; that

167

he had given up his claim and adopted theirs. There was a queer, numb excitement inside him, as if he were watching an accident about to happen but which he was powerless to stop.

Sheila turned to her husband.

"How about it?" she asked in a polite, remote voice. "Do you mind having lunch by yourself? It would be nice to go up to the Pen, and Carl and I could talk in the car going up."

"I think that sounds fine," Lloyd said. His big beautiful eyes blinked at them and they could sense the relief in his voice now that he knew he would have the Hamptons all to himself. "What time will you be back?"

"We'll bring her back after dinner," Carl told him. "I guess you'll want to dine with the Hamptons?"

"Well, yes; they probably will ask me," Lloyd said happily.

They had another round of drinks and Lloyd talked. He never made the sort of conversation that needed much attention. You could listen to it with half a mind, and sometimes he could be quite funny about the people he met.

Carl listened to him and watched Sheila trying not to look at Roy for too long, and Roy trying to sit comfortably under her eyes. Neither of them was succeeding very well, and he was glad that Lloyd was such a fool.

When Sheila left them to put on a skirt, and to get the things she wanted him to advise her on, he and Roy went down to the car.

Turning the car in the drive, with Sheila's warm, fresh-smelling body between him and Roy in the front seat, he suddenly thought that Lloyd's bright, immaculate figure, lounging against one of the verandah posts and waving at them, looked lonely and abandoned. He didn't think Lloyd felt like that at all; but against the bulk of Tolliver's great house, he looked little and inefficient and in need of protection.

22

They were going up past the yellowish brown river, with the grey rocks shining in the sun. The green tops of the trees were bright, and ahead of them the mountains were a pale blue-grey behind a heat haze.

Carl was driving very fast. When the big car dipped smoothly round a bend on Roy's side, he could feel the warm pressure of Sheila's body move against him. He was gripping the back rest with his outstretched hand and whenever a twist in the road made to pull him on to her he would stiffen his arm and press against the door.

If I leant my head back, she thought, my neck would touch his forearm. He has very thick hair on his arm.

"Isn't it a lovely day?" she said to him. It was the first time anyone had spoken since they had driven out of Tolliver.

"It *is* nice," he said, looking at her glowing pink face, with its faint dust of tan, and into the greenish eyes in the very clear, ice-blue whites.

"I like it when you can feel the heat coming up off the road," she said. "Don't you?"

"I know what you mean," Roy told her. "You can feel it even with the windows open and going very fast."

"Why are you stopping?" Sheila asked Carl. He had pulled the car over the side of the road and was slowing it. They stopped in the shade of a huge, grey, cotton tree. It was very still and the heat was sending up hard bright little waves from the fields. They could hear a goat from somewhere up the hillside; and at this distance the river sounded like a gentle breeze stirring among thick leaves.

"Roy and I want to ask you something," Carl said.

"Do you have to stop for it?" she began to say with light, happy carelessness; and then she saw how his face looked and she became serious too.

"Carl and me are in a bit of trouble," Roy said quickly. "We thought, I thought really, that you could maybe help us. You don't have to. But if you can't, don't say anything about what we asked. O.K.?"

"Of course," she said. "I'd do anything to help you two. But what is it, Roy? You're not in real trouble, are you? Please tell me."

Her voice was anxious and alarmed and Roy, whose living depended partly on his ability to sense undertones and reservation in the voice of a witness, could hear the sudden, pleased intimacy in it. Carl's right, he told himself. Well, he registered with another part of his brain, that will make it easier.

"Shall I tell it?" he asked Carl.

"Who else?" Carl said, looking out through the windshield, his big hands curled and flattened on the rim of the driving wheel.

Roy told her about Etienne, and about Carl and himself, and of what they hoped she could do to help. He told it well, as if he were giving the synopsis of a very short story. He had told it all in about four minutes.

At the end, she said: "Yes. I'd like to help you very much. If there is anything else I can do, tell me now."

Roy saw Carl turn to her as he said in an uneasy voice, "Sheila, don't do it unless you're sure you know..." and Roy said, "You mean, you'll do it? Just like that?"

"Yes," she said. She was looking straight at him, as she had never turned her eyes away all the time he had been telling her. Her eyes were very bright.

"Well, I'll be damned," Roy said and laughed a soft, astounded laugh.

"Why?" she said. "What's the matter? Did I say something wrong?"

"No," he told her, grinning with the sudden relief. "No, you didn't say a damn thing that was wrong. It's only that you're the first person I've got into this that has said 'yes' straight out like that, with no hesitation."

"Did you think I'd say no?" she asked him. Her lips lifted in a slight smile.

"I didn't know how you would take it," he said. "After all, you don't like our brand of politics."

"I don't like some of what I've heard," she told him. "But that has nothing to do with this. If you and Carl are in it, then I want to help, that's all."

"God, Sheila," Roy said, "I don't know how to begin to thank you."

"Cho," she told him, and he reflected that she was one of the few English out here who had learnt the proper cadence of that word, "You don't have to thank me, Roy. Think how I would feel if Carl and you asked me for help and I didn't help you."

He realized how much he had been depending on her answer. She had been the one uncertain factor in the plan he had made.

And now that factor was fitting with the rest. Now he wouldn't have to worry about the plan any more. He had only to make it work. He slid his hand from the back rest and pressed her bare shoulder. "You're wonderful," he started to say; and then he felt her give a startled, shivering jump as his hand touched her. He put his hand back quickly to where it had been. He could see the colour in her face, and he suddenly felt excited and uneasy.

23

There was too much glare for it to be comfortable on the front verandah; so they had lunch in the clear, soft light of the dining-room.

It was a fine lunch. They had a chicken roasted and stuffed with breadcrumbs, rice cooked with chopped sweet pepper, strips of golden, fried plantain and a huge salad which Della had tossed the way Carl had taught her to do when he came back from abroad. There was sweet-potato baked in a crust of brown sugar, baked green bananas split open with white butter melting on the grey meat, slippery calaloo, a large dish of boiled corn, a big cold ham, huge, purple garden eggs stuffed with cold minced meat and pepper, a covered dish of brown oatmeal cakes, new peas, roasted coco the colour of pearl, and shrimps in a silver chafing dish. Twelve people could not have finished the food that had been provided for three. And that was the way it had been done at Brandt's Pen for two hundred years.

Roy knew that if he was to lunch here tomorrow he would see nothing left over from today's meal. Except, perhaps, the ham.

It must have a strange effect on a man, he thought, (half-way through the meal, when they were not talking), to have always known this much food on his own table. And most of it his own food, too; lifted or killed outside his own window. I've had a comfortable, secure sort of life, but this one thing I don't know. This is not just money. Food is different. Always being able to command so much of it, to take this amount for granted every time you sit down to eat, it must give a man a basic assurance that very few people can have. This is the world on your plate, all right.

Dessert was simple: long pink slices of paw-paw, dusted with sugar and sprinkled with lime juice; and after this they went into the bright drawing-room where the patterns on the slip-covers made a big gay pattern with flowers in the vases. Elvira brought coffee, and while they were drinking this Carl mixed a pale golden rum punch.

Outside, it was very clear, white dazzle, and when they tried to see into the depths of the sky their eyes ached with the hard, intense blue. All sounds seemed to drift and twist in lazy spirals across the air and their voices sounded hushed to their own ears. They could feel time going by in a warm, undulating, endless crawl. The furniture was cool and dark and gleaming in the gay, silvered softness of the room's light.

"Tell me," Roy said to Carl as they tasted the first cold, sour-sweet, gently tingling smoothness of the drink, "is this just you, or do all you planters inherit a formula? If I lived a thousand years I could never make a punch like this?"

"This *is* a wonderful punch, Carl," Sheila said. "I think it must be inherited: Lloyd mixes one just like this."

She was on the deep, highbacked couch and Roy, sitting on the low chair opposite, was watching the long, powerful curve of her legs and the smooth brown knee under her flowered skirt.

"It isn't me," Carl said, "it's being in the country. The limes have just been picked, I used spring water, and I keep my sugar in a keg not in a brown paper bag."

"Haven't you ever wanted to be a country man too?" Sheila asked Roy, and he noticed that she broke the word, "country-man", quite naturally into two words, as they did in Cayuna. Her eyes were bold and steady and very bright; and suddenly she blushed and tugged the skirt lower over her crossed knees.

"Not me," he told her. "I like cities. Any city. I enjoy being in the country, but after a couple of months I always get bored."

"I don't know how you can like living in Queenshaven all the time," she said. "I used to be a great one for cities myself – when I lived in London. But not since I've had Tolliver."

"You ought to see him when he gets back to a city after he's been buried in the country for a while," Carl said to her. "He's like a dog sniffing at a butcher's shop. Or like an Italian we once met."

"What Italian?" she asked, smiling because the two of them sharing a suddenly remembered, private joke made a pleasant sight.

"Oh, he was a little P.O.W. we met in Eritrea," Carl said. "He was very anxious to let us know how much he loved England and the English and English culture generally. He kept telling us how superior England was to everywhere else and how much he had loved it when he lived there. How beautiful it was and all that. Finally we asked him where he had lived in England, and he spread his fingers and said, 'Manchester, *bella* Manchester'."

They all laughed at that and Sheila asked: "Is that how you feel about cities, Roy? Even Manchester?" She laughed again, remembering the Italian.

"Well, not quite *bella,*" he said smiling at her. "But I admit that after three months in the country I get a bit hungry for two miles of paved streets and people living in each other's pockets."

"But why?" She was serious now.

"Habit, I guess. It's a matter of the air I grew up breathing. And all the new things happen in cities nowadays. You can feel history moving and changing when you're in the city."

"And what would you do without us in the country? What would you do without us to feed you and grow the clothes you wear?"

"We'd be stuck," he agreed. "I was only telling you what *I* preferred."

"You come and work with us in the country for a while," she told him. "Not just as a tourist. You'd change your mind then."

"Maybe," he said. The bold, scarcely concealed challenge in her eyes had suddenly made him uncomfortable and a little frightened.

They became silent. The warm, fresh air combed gently through the quiet house, and the blue and white-gold of the day outside was like a faint, beautiful stain in the room.

"How about some music?" Carl said. He did not wait for them to answer, but went over to the huge rosewood pick-up and switched it on. He took some records from the deep slot in the machine and put one of them on the turntable. It was a record he and Roy liked very much: a hard, knowing, sad yet triumphant woman's voice singing *Oh, Careless Love.*

You old bastard, Roy thought, looking at Carl's casually expressionless face, you chose that on purpose.

When the record was finished Carl put a few more on the spindle. He sat down beside the pick-up and they listened to a sharp, involved, searching trumpet from the old New Orleans period. Carl went out of the room, before it was finished, in the manner of a man going to the lavatory.

Roy and Sheila waited, listening to the music and not talking. He refilled her glass and his own, and lit a cigarette. After another ten minutes he went into the long passage.

The house felt empty as he went through to the back. It was silent there too. Elvira was seated on a box by the kitchen door; she was bent over the Sunday paper, her lips moving silently as she read. All round, there was the drowsily dragging feel of Sunday mid-afternoon: hot and sleepy and fitfully broken by lazy, contented murmurs. The smell of fallen, half-rotted fruit was very strong from the yard.

"Have you seen Mister Carl?" he asked Elvira.

"Yes, sah," she said, looking up from the paper. She sounded faintly surprised. "Him go out on de big horse. Him mus' be go to de peak."

She gestured, with a wave of her hand, out to the pasture and to where the track led from the fence, up past the dam, up past Etienne's hut, up beside the valley, getting steeper and narrower until it gave out among the tangled, cloud-wet forest of the peaks. It was a ride that Carl and Roy had often taken, and he knew that was where Carl had gone.

"Yes," he said. "I remember now; he said something about it at lunch."

He went to the lavatory, and then back to the drawing-room. The pick-up was playing a cool, sardonic clarinet solo.

"Carl has gone out for a ride," he told Sheila. "He's gone up to the peaks."

"Oh!" she said.

"Would you like to go out for one?" he asked her. "I could get Tom or Aubrey to saddle up for us."

"No," she replied. "I don't think so. I only have a skirt, and it's too much trouble riding in that. I do it sometimes, but not for pleasure."

Now he could see that her face had paled, even beneath the tan; and her eyes were not bold any more, but shy and darkened behind the short, thick lashes. When she looked at him her eyes made a shifting flicker, and she would not look straight at him for long.

"Well," he said, "let's have another, eh?"

"Yes," she said, "I'd like one more."

He poured the drinks and sat down opposite to her. She was looking at him in swift, brief glances and then staring at her sandals which made her strongly-arched, too big, English feet look neat and smaller. There was a tight, excited knot in his stomach. He knew that he wanted her and he didn't know whether he ought to.

"Was it you, really, who thought of asking me to help with the *Nisba*?" she asked him.

"Yes," he said. "Carl nearly killed me this morning when I told him."

"I'm glad," she said. "I mean I'm glad you thought of asking me. Did you really think I'd refuse?"

"Yes," he told her. "At least I couldn't be sure. Because of the political part of it."

"This is different," she told him. "I want to help because you – because Carl and you asked me to. Politics don't come into it."

"I'm glad," he said. "And thanks again."

"Would you like another drink?" he asked her. He got up and went to where the tall, nearly empty pitcher stood on the table.

"No, thanks," she said. "I've had enough. I like how I feel after three of these. If I have any more it would spoil it."

"How do you feel after three?" he said.

"Oh, just nice. Relaxed." She smiled up at him. Her lips looked dry and swollen. "I feel talkative and clever."

"Baudelaire said that a man should be always drunk on something or the other. Anything at all, so long as he went through life drunk."

God, he thought. Listen to me. What are you playing at? You sound great. You know you want to go to bed with her. But you

175

don't want any emotional mix-up. I want her, though. She looks wonderful sitting there.

He came over, with the glass in his hand, and sat on the arm of the sofa beside her. She was not looking at him and he could hear her breathing in long shallow sighs. The palms of his hands felt empty and tingling and there was a thick stiffness in his throat and he could feel the pumping of his heart. The whole day seemed to have gone absolutely still, except in the place where they were. He took the hand which lay in her lap. It was warm and the palm was moist; he felt her tremble violently, once, and there was a little beating pulse somewhere in the hand he held. He put down his glass on the round table behind the sofa and with the tips of his fingers turned her chin so that she had to look at him. Her lips were twitching and she was very pale and scared-looking. Her face was tragic, masklike, and yet triumphant, and it reminded him of the voice on the record. There was a swollen pricking behind his eyes.

"I want to kiss you," he said.

"Yes," she told him.

When he moved his hand from behind her back she gave a long, heaving squirm against him and he could feel her heavy taut breasts flatten, even through the thick, starched shirt he was wearing.

"No," she said; her lips were brushing jerkily against his ear. "No. Please, Roy. No. Please. Roy. Roy." Her hands were gripping his shoulders and then her long arm went behind his neck; it was heavy and warm and firm. He moved his lips across the fresh-smelling cheek and kissed her again. He was being driven by a most terrible urgency and his moving hand seemed unable to be filled. And suddenly she was consenting and softly bent against him.

He lifted her to her feet, one arm around her waist. Her eyes had a shining blind look as he took her to his bedroom.

He was very glad that, following the custom in the country, the jalousies were shut against the heat, and that the room was dark, and that they could go straight to the bed, and that he didn't have to let her go in order to close the shutters.

24

Carl had not meant to leave the house when he left them in the drawing-room. But when he was coming back along the passage and heard the music, he understood fully, for the first time since he had told Roy about Sheila, that they did not need him with them.

Going out to the stables there was a confused pain inside him that was half hate and half weary sadness. It was an odd feeling to be able to hate the fact of Roy and Sheila, the two people he really needed in this world.

He saddled and bridled Caesar himself and rode out of the yard and across the south pasture, glad that he had a lonely, sure to be deserted place to which he could ride.

When he was going past the dam he saw that the rain of two nights before had weakened the bank of the channel they had begun to dig down to the fields. He noticed this by the fresh colour at the edge of the trench and he knew that if it wasn't strengthened it would break the first time they ran water through it. He thought that he would tell Haig, his overseer, about this in the morning. He could judge, almost to the hundredweight, how many stones they would need to fortify the trench.

Up on the peak he could look out across another, broader valley at the high mountains to the south. At this distance the sea was grey and the plain hazy, with bright patches glinting through the haze. It was very cool and thin grey cloud was blowing across the summit and hanging in patches above the forest in the valley. There were a lot of cedars on the peak opposite, and cinchonas on this one, which was known as Brandt's Peak.

He thought about Roy and Sheila. And then he didn't think about them. He thought about Etienne; and that was better. Thinking about Etienne he could think of the specific things that would have to be done to get him away.

Caesar was grazing on the coarse, sweet grass and Carl scrambled up to the knob of the peak where there were no trees but a bed of wild strawberries. He picked and ate some, and came down again with a handful for Caesar. The loose, powerful lips slobbered them up from his hand and the big head butted him in the chest as it always did when Caesar wanted to be affectionate.

He stayed up there for an hour. Then he mounted and rode down the path.

About half a mile from the old track which led down to the hut he turned Caesar off the path and into the bush. The big gelding, sure as a mule and much less temperamental, chose a way down on to the valley floor with precise, certain steps. Carl bent low against the taut neck, to avoid being switched by the branches. At the bottom he rode towards the hut; Caesar's hooves made rustling thuds in the heavy mould. When they were a hundred yards from the hut he dismounted and flung the reins over the lowest branch of a sapodilla tree and knotted them. He went the rest of the way on foot.

He could walk very silently when he wanted to and when he appeared in the doorway of the hut, Etienne jumped to his feet. Carl could see the alarm in his face.

"I'm sorry," Carl said. "I just wanted to see if you were all right. Did I startle you?"

"You frightened me, Mr. Brandt," Etienne said simply as he climbed back on to the table where he had been sitting.

Carl came in. He saw Etienne's pack on the table beside him, neatly roped up in its oilskin. Except for a grey blanket, which he must have had round his shoulders before he jumped from the table, there was nothing to show that Etienne had spent the night there. His cigarette stubs and burnt matches were in the top of a plastic soap dish. The gunny sack with the food was on the table too; and a thick book lay on the blanket.

"I'm sorry," Carl said again. "I've been up the top, by the peak, and coming down I thought I'd look in. You needn't worry about anybody seeing me. How did you know it was me, by the way? You haven't seen me in daylight."

The flat, broad black face before him bunched into polished knobs as Etienne smiled, and the slanting eyes became narrow like a cat's. When he smiled the wide nostrils showed very clearly, and Carl saw that he had big, yellow teeth. There was a puckered, sunken scar low down on his left cheek, spoiling the jelly smoothness of his skin.

"I do not think there could be many men of your size in Cayuna, Mr. Brandt," Etienne said in his clearly, too clearly, articulated English. "And the shape of your head is characteristic. It is very marked. I recognized your voice, too, of course."

"Are you all right?" Carl asked him. "You weren't cold last night, or anything."

"I was most comfortable, thank you. And I do thank you, Mr. Brandt, I did not have a chance to say it properly last night."

He looked so incongruously relaxed and ordinary, sitting there in his very dark, tropical tweeds, that Carl nearly smiled. The only signs of his circumstances were the dried mud on his shoes and the filthy unbuttoned collar and the tie with its knot slipped down from his throat. Also, the carefully rounded nails of his small, frail looking hands were blackened, and there was an untidy, sparse stubble on his chin. He sat on the rough table, small feet dangling, his hands folded over the edge and the plump, broad face, its plumpness made smooth by firm muscle under the skin, was turned to Carl with tranquilly attentive pleasure. With his head tilted like that Carl could not see much of the scarred cheek.

Carl looked around the hut. "Where did you put the food?" he asked.

"In here," Etienne tapped the bundle on the table. "I buried the empty bottles in the loose earth outside."

"I'm glad you weren't too uncomfortable," Carl said. "This couldn't be very nice for you. I think you'll soon be out of it, though. Roy and I arranged for you to get to the ship. We've found someone who'll take you out."

He came over and stood by the table. He took out his cigarettes and offered Etienne one and took one for himself.

"I am glad to hear that," Etienne said. He smoked in rapid short puffs. "I should like this to be over so that no one will get into trouble because of me. Who is going to take me out?"

"A friend of ours," Carl said. "She has a very good boat and she's a fine sailor. She'll pick you up from a fisherman who is going to get you beyond the shoal water."

"A woman, eh?" Etienne shook his head, and smiled briefly at Carl. "You see, Mr. Brandt, how one's early prejudices linger. I should not be surprised to hear that there is a woman in this. Not in these days, and after the things I have seen and heard; but I am. Well, that is one more reason for hoping that this business is over soon. How is Roy? Is he coming to see me tonight? I have things to tell him."

"Yes, he'll be up," Carl said. "He's down at the house now."

"Yes, that is best," Etienne nodded. "You can move about your own property, Mr. Brandt. But I am glad Roy did not try to see me this afternoon. In these affairs we should not take any but the necessary chances. I am glad you came to see me, though. It gave me an opportunity to thank you properly, and I was feeling in need of someone to talk to."

He was looking at Carl with friendly calm interest. The confidence and self-possession of his face was quite different from the way he smoked, and from the way he had shaken hands the night before.

You little brute, Carl thought. You're the coolest one I've ever met. Sitting there as if you were in the lobby of an hotel. You're efficient, though; I've got to give you that. You could move out of here in a second without any bother. I wonder if you killed those people as calm and friendly as you're talking to me now? Probably. You probably did it in the same way that you planned to have a bundle ready for when you had to move on. You even put a book in it. Just something to pass the time.

"What's your book?" he asked Etienne.

Etienne picked it up. It was a thick, closely printed volume, with a stiff green cover. It looked as if it had been read a lot. Carl saw, by the typeset, that it was poetry.

"An English book, Mr. Brandt," Etienne said. "One of the English poets. William Blake. A tremendous man. I find something new and rewarding in it every time I read him. Even in those poems I know by heart."

Carl remembered what Roy had told him about Etienne teaching himself English so that he could read Shakespeare. He had not read any Shakespeare himself since he was at school, although he had seen some of the plays acted. All he knew of Blake was the hymn they sometimes sang in church. The one about arrows of desire and the spear of burning gold. Or was it a bow? The words gave you a nice feeling when you heard everybody singing them, and the organ taking the words up to the roof.

He tried to find some connection between what he knew Etienne to be and the poetry of William Blake.

"May I ask you something, Mr. Brandt?" Etienne said. The flat, smooth face was intent and serious.

"Yes, certainly."

"Why are you doing this? Why are you putting yourself into this position for me? Roy said you were not a member of our party."

"It's like Roy told you," Carl said. "I've known him a long time and he was pretty desperate for help. There wasn't anything else I could do."

"You would not have done it if Roy were not your friend?"

The voice was emphatic and deeply interested; and the widely-set, slanting eyes were gentle and reassuring and brilliantly watchful.

"No," Carl told him. "If it wasn't for Roy, I wouldn't have helped you."

"I understand," Etienne said gently. "Please do not think I am being rude, Mr. Brandt. But I like you. I like you and I am interested in you because of what you are doing. Knowing people such as you, and liking them, is a luxury I have had to forgo during the past fifteen years." He smiled up at the big man lounging against the rough table beside him. "This is a sort of holiday for me, you understand. A personal holiday. This is the first time I have had to sit still and wait, for a long time. I feel... how do you say it in English? Uprooted? No. Cut-off. Ah, yes; cut-off. Irresponsible."

My God, Carl thought, you're a peach all right. You've lost your country. You've left your friends to be hung or shot. You are sleeping out on a mountainside in a crummy hut. And yet you talk about holidays. Where do they dig boys like you up?

"Yes," Etienne continued. His voice was musical, practised and quite empty of the self-absorption of the obsessed chatterer. "I am glad to have had the opportunity to meet a man to whom friendship means more than political allegiance. Who will do something for his friend when he probably hates the thing his friend believes in."

"You're lucky then," Carl said dully. "The other person who is going to help you is in the same position as me. She is doing it for ... for friendship, too."

Etienne gave him a hard, searching glance.

"You mean the woman with the boat?"

"Yes."

"She is not a party member?"

"Of course not."

"And she is doing this because of friendship for both of you?"

"Yes."

"What is she like?"

"She runs a property down on the coast. She's an English-woman who married the man who owns the place. He's a Cayunan, but she really manages things down there."

"I understand. Is she young?"

"Yes. Younger than me or Roy; about twenty-five."

"She sounds a fine woman."

Carl said nothing.

"Is she beautiful?" Etienne asked him.

In the moment before he answered, Carl could hear a woodpecker, among the trees outside, tapping loudly in a startling, concentrated flurry. He had never asked himself whether Sheila was beautiful. He had not expected the conversation to take this turn and he wondered why he did not resent it.

"No," he said, "I don't suppose she's beautiful. She is handsome, really. If you passed her in the street you'd want to look back at her."

"Which of you is she in love with?" Etienne asked him.

"How did you know that?" Carl said thickly.

"So I guessed right," Etienne was smiling. "Which of you is it?"

"She's in love with Roy," Carl told him.

How the hell has this happened? he thought.

"And you are in love with her yourself?"

They were close, now, in the heavy, damp, earth-smelling air of the hut, and it was all dreamlike and incomprehensible to Carl. His answers to Etienne were involuntary and natural.

"Yes," he told Etienne, "I'm in love with her. But she doesn't want me; she wants Roy."

Etienne nodded briefly and heaved himself off the table and went to the door and looked out on the raw, crumbling slope, with its fringe of bush, and down through the gloomy, shadowed green of the tree-choked valley. When he came back to the table and leaned against it Carl could see that his face was serious and hard.

"Is Roy in love with her?" Etienne asked.

"No. He likes her. She is the sort of person he would like."

"I hope he does not fall in love with her," Etienne said in a voice that sounded a little sad.

"Why?"

He was taking part in this, now, without being able to control his share of it. He knew that he would remember every word.

Etienne shrugged.

"It is hard to explain," he said. "Roy would understand, but I find it difficult to explain to you. For him to fall in love with a woman who does not share his belief might mean danger one day. Not only for him, but for the work he does."

"Why the hell should it?" Carl asked. There was a sour satisfaction now that he could feel angry. That this last remark had broken the trust of a few seconds before, and that he could dislike Etienne again. "What do you think she is? Some sort of disease that's going to kill him? Don't forget that if it wasn't for her you'd probably be caught here."

"No," Etienne said. "I see you do not understand. It is simple, though. If you love someone, that means an extra weight to carry. If you are both going in the same direction, at the same pace, then the two weights together become lighter than one alone. If you only have the love, however, then one day you will have to make a decision between it and your work. And for someone like Roy, that moment when he stops to decide could be fatal."

"Does Roy think like that?"

"Yes. I'm sure he does. Very often we have to forget our love for the one man or woman whom we need for ourselves."

"Is that why you left your friends in St. Pierre?" Carl asked him harshly.

He saw Etienne jerk as if someone had slapped him, and then, almost as quickly, he relaxed. The slanted eyes were shadowed, however, when he looked at Carl. And the flat, broad face was thoughtful and remote and sad.

"Yes," he said slowly. "That is why I had to leave them. Would you believe me if I told you that I did not leave but was told to go, by them? That it was not my choice but an order?"

"Yes," Carl told him. "I believe you. I'm sorry."

Etienne waved his hand briefly.

"It is a good thing you asked," he said. "It is an illustration of what I meant. You see, for us, there was no conflict in making the decision. Pain and grief, yes. And some of us were afraid. Me for one. But we knew what had to be done and we had practised it together. In a way it was easy."

"I'm sorry," Carl said again. "I shouldn't have said that."

He looked at the bent, thinking figure, leaning, with folded arms, against the table; and he quite suddenly wanted Etienne to escape. He had not really wanted it before, but now he did.

"Look," he said gently, "I've just thought. If anything happens, and you have to leave this place, I'd better show you where you ought to go."

Etienne looked up and Carl saw that the sadness had gone from his face. The eyes were alert and friendly and calm once more. Whatever he had been thinking he had put aside, as he would have taken off his shirt.

"Yes," he said. "I should like to know that."

"Come on outside, then," Carl told him. "It's quite safe; we can't be seen from the path."

They went outside, into the gentle, golden brightness and the deep, soft blue of late afternoon.

"If anything happens," Carl said to the trim, dark-suited man whose head was nearly a foot below his, "go straight up this valley here. It comes to a saddle; and on the other side there is another valley. Go down into that. Get well hidden; and wait. I'll find you. The house is south from here in case you have to come to me on your own. You'll see it; or if it's night, you'll see the lights. My room is in the front, on the right."

"I understand," Etienne said. "I feel very safe in your hands."

They went inside the hut.

"I should have got you some rum last night," Carl said, "but I forgot. Beer is a cold drink up here. I'll send you a bottle tonight by Roy. I can't take from my house, I'll have to buy it outside."

"Yes," Etienne said. He sounded pleased. "I would like that, thank you. I cannot burn a light here at night and I do not sleep very well. I should like a drink to keep me company."

Carl had the sudden conviction that this was the only part of himself that Etienne had permitted to remain – the only selfish part. This appreciation of good food and drink. All the rest he had abandoned somewhere along the road he had chosen to follow. Even the interest he showed for everything around him was a little inhuman, though it wasn't unpleasant.

No, Carl thought. I don't understand you, Etienne. I don't understand you and I don't want to. I hope you get away, but I hope you never come back to where I am.

"I'll be going now," he said to Etienne, and he was surprised to see that the man looked sorry when he said it.

"Goodbye for now, Mr. Brandt," Etienne said. They walked to the sagging, rusty-hinged doorway, "If you have the opportunity, I should like to see you again. I have enjoyed your visit."

Riding down the path to the house he began to ask himself how long it would be before Roy became like Etienne. When that happened he knew that they would no longer be friends. He did not think there was anything either of them could do about it.

He reached the house when it was getting grey in the yard. There were lights in the kitchen and on the back verandah. Tom was in the stable having an involved, if one-sided, dispute with the stallion, White Star. They were cooking over the open coal stoves before the servant's quarters and he could hear some children laughing. Aubrey, Tom's little brother, and Sammy, who was his chief cow-man's son, rolled from round the corner of Tom's hut, writhing in a desperate, hard-grunting embrace of rage. They were always fighting: about food, about who should ride in front with the truck when it went down to Castleville, about which of them was the strongest, about anything. He went over and separated them and cuffed their heads. Then he followed Caesar into the stable. He was suddenly very happy.

25

The room was full of shadow when Roy awoke, and looking at the jalousie slits he could see a shining, purplish-grey light and he knew it was late. Sheila was awake, her head turned to him; he saw the glitter as her gaze moved over his face.

"God," he said, "it must be late! What's the time?"

"Not too late," she whispered. "Going on for six. You've only slept about an hour."

"Did you sleep?"

"A little. I've been watching you."

He sat up. They were on top of the eiderdown, she lying on her side as she watched him. He pushed her shoulder gently and turned her on her back and bent down and kissed the hollow where her throat joined her chest. Then he kissed her lightly on the mouth and on her eyes.

"Hullo," he said, and: "Has Carl come in yet?"

"I haven't heard him," she said. "He may have, when we were both asleep."

He was softly, almost unbelievingly, stroking her body. Where sweat had dried on it, he could feel a faint roughness on the very smooth, thick skin. She was smiling; a slight smile that lifted the corners of her mouth and did not show her teeth. Sometimes she put her hand on the back of his, or squeezed his wrist with her fingers.

"Are you cold?" he asked her.

"No," she said, "I'm fine."

"You're not sorry?"

"No. I love you."

His hand stopped moving. He wondered what he should say.

"It's all right," she said. "You don't have to say anything. You don't have to say you love me, too."

He felt awkward and embarrassed as he searched his mind for something to say. He could not think of anything.

"Don't leave me, though," she continued. "Try and see me sometimes. Will you?"

"Of course," he said gladly. "I wouldn't have started this without meaning to make something of it. You're too nice for that."

She reached up her long, powerful arms and pulled him down to her.

"I'm glad," she said: she was whispering this. "I'm so glad you said that: you don't have to say anything more. Roy, I love you so."

"Just like that?" He lifted his head from the pillow to look at her; they both smiled as they remembered when and why he had last used those words to her.

"Just like that," she said. "From the second time I met you. Do you remember the second time you saw me?"

"Yes," he said, trying to remember. "It was two years ago, up here. One Sunday like this."

"No," she said, laughing throatily. "It was in Castleville; at the Yacht Club. You and Carl were in the bar; you were both drinking that Dutch beer and you told me it tasted like nuts."

"God, yes," he said, "I remember now. I wasn't too sober. I wasn't drunk, but I'd been trying to keep up with Carl."

"That's right. You looked sweet. I suddenly wondered what it would be like if I were driving you home afterwards, and how you would look when you flopped on the bed and went to sleep. And of how I would take off your shoes so you wouldn't dirty the coverlet. I knew I was in love with you then."

"You're sweet," he said, hugging her. He kissed her mouth.

And then they were together again. Without warning, with an explosive rushing that began as a tremor and suddenly became the familiar, enclosing, light-centred darkness, shutting out everything but the faces of each other. Rising. Rising. Rising to the last unbearable, uncontainable shudder of pressing, holding and wanting. And then the slow, cooling release; the clamour of nerves and muscle dying to easy, half-sad, half-grateful murmurs, and once more the face beside you, seen against the background of the whole room.

Her fingers combed through his hair.

"You're the only man I've had except Lloyd."

"Why did you marry him?"

"I don't know. I was in love with him I suppose. I was, really. After I met him, and we'd been going out for a little, whenever he touched me my knees felt watery. He is very attractive to women. It's only that he's so... so limited; and he seems to get more so every year."

"He doesn't," Roy said. "It's you who are growing every year. How do you think he'll take this?"

"I don't know. Does he have to find out?"

"He probably will, sooner or later. Every servant in this house knows by now that we've spent the afternoon in here. Every other servant in the parish will know by tomorrow."

"I don't know," she said again. She sounded utterly tranquil. "I'll think about it when the time comes."

"If you have to leave him, though," Roy insisted, "how will you take losing Tolliver?"

He felt her stiffen in the bed beside him. When she spoke again she was keeping her voice flat and unemotional.

"I won't like that," she said. "But I suppose it had to come eventually. I was just pretending that we could go on the way things were. I don't want to lose Tolliver, though."

He was very sorry, now that it was too late, to have brought this out. It was something that could have kept. If it had kept even for one more hour it would have saved this moment from being spoilt. He would have liked this afternoon to end as it had begun. No, not as it had begun. As she had made it.

He turned to her and squeezed her tightly in his arms. So tightly that she gasped as she kissed him.

"Sheila," he said.

They heard Carl's long, solid footfall go past the door.

Roy got up and went to the wall switch. When the light came on, he saw her lying on the bed as he had left her. It was the first time he had seen her naked in a full light: her body looked long and big-boned, and much fuller than he had imagined it. Her face was very calm and it had a glowing lightness he had not seen before. She sat up in the bed, with her legs tucked under her like a figure of the Buddha, and watched him as he picked his clothes off the floor from beside the little heap of her things.

"Is that your Air Force shirt?" she asked.

"Yes."

"I can see where the wings were. Is that patch below it where you put the medals?"

"Yes."

"Did you have a lot?"

"Hell, no," he said. "Only the usual ones. Carl's the boy for the medals. He got the D.S.O. He should have got the Cross. I don't think he was afraid very often. That's very unusual, you know, to be really brave like that. They're a special breed."

She got out of the bed with a swift graceful flash of her long legs, and the tall, slightly stooped body swayed lithely across the floor to him. Even without her shoes she was a little taller than he. Her naked body felt strangely exciting and new against his clothed one.

"Kiss me," she said and, as he did so, her arms went round him in a hard, joyous hug.

"I'll be out in a minute," she said, watching him as he combed his hair at the mirror. "You have nice hair."

He went from the room and into the passage. He thought that he would find Carl on the verandah. It had got quite dark outside now and he could see a segment of star-filled sky against the open doorway at the end of the passage.

26

When he went on to the verandah he could see Carl in one of the deep, cushion-seated wooden chairs at the far end, under the orchids. The drawing-room was lit, but the light from it only stained the darkness of the verandah with a faint glow. Carl was smoking, and Roy knew from the size of the tip that it was one of the strong, heavy-flavoured "big copper" cigars they both liked to have in the evenings sometimes.

As he came across the verandah to Carl he saw the red cigar tip lift and grow bright as the man drew on the smoke. For the second that it flared Roy could see his friend's features very clearly: the broad, blunt, straight nose, the delicate curve of the mouth which had always been more the shape of a girl's mouth than a man's, the flat hollow of the cheek and the deep eye-socket. But the glare made the skin seem bloodless and polished: it was like watching some important transfiguration where all the inessentials of the face were stripped away and only the significant, immortal core remained to startle and disturb him. For a quick, painful moment which seemed to be cut out of the day, and suspended for all eternity independent of him, he knew the sad, precise and illimitable quality of Carl's humanity. It was nothing he could have foreseen, or arrived at by scientific analysis; he knew it as he experienced the slight, cool night wind on this cheek. Looking at Carl then, he forgot Sheila, forgot Etienne, forgot everything in the tremendous, nourishing assault of love and confidence that was not really for Carl but for the fact of being alive in a world where two separate fleshly envelopes of appetite, strangers within their enclosing skulls, could still find this strength in each other.

He came up and sat beside Carl in another of the verandah chairs and put his sandalled feet on the knee-high parapet.

"Hi, boy," Carl said, "You want a cigar?"

"Thanks," Roy said, and took the one Carl was offering him. He bit the end and spat the bitten-off piece over the parapet, felt in his breast pocket for a nail file with which to pierce the tobacco, and lit it with his own lighter.

"This lot isn't too bad," Carl said. "You remember the last batch we got wasn't so good?"

"They were green," Roy told him.

"Green as bloody grass. They didn't wait to cure them properly."

"Well," Roy said, "you know how it is with the cheap cigars. They have to make a big turnover or they don't show a profit."

"Yes, I suppose so. They must have got caught, last time, with not enough cured tobacco in hand... you hungry?"

"What, after that lunch? Not yet. Let's have a drink first."

Carl went into the drawing-room and called for one of the maids. One of them, not Elvira, but the one called Isobel, came through and Carl told her to bring glasses and water and a bottle of ginger ale. He came back with a bottle of Mount Ida in his hand and sat beside Roy again, putting the rum on the broad sill of the parapet.

When the glasses and water and ice came, he mixed two drinks and poured rum into a third glass.

"Shall we wait for Sheila?" he asked.

Neither of them felt any embarrassment. Roy hadn't been sure if there would be any. He hadn't thought there would be; but he hadn't been dead sure that there wouldn't. Now there was none and he felt glad.

"God, no," he said. "She'll probably be all night in there, fixing up. You know women."

They were drinking their second drink when Sheila came out. She came out walking very quietly, because of her sandals, and it wasn't until her body blotted out the light behind her that they realized she was there.

Roy drew a chair for her from against the wall and put it beside his own. Carl was fixing a drink. As soon as she sat down she took his right hand, so that he had to transfer his cigar to his left. He liked the honesty of her action, but he felt it was a little tactless.

Then he squeezed her hand in a sudden rush of happiness and gratitude; and he felt an animal, restive energy tingle under his skin. He got up and stretched abruptly and sprang to the sill of the parapet; he was hugely, widely alive and merry, and he began to do a grotesque, hopping dance on the sill, waving his glowing cigar butt and singing at the top of his hard, resonant voice. The song was one he had heard and didn't remember, but he liked the opening which went:

In the cool, cool, cool of the evening
Tell her I'll be there.

"Roy," Sheila said. "What's the matter? What are you doing?" She was laughing.

"He's crazy," Carl told her. "If you fall off there and break your goddam neck," he said to Roy, "I'll let you lie until the ants carry you away."

"Tell her I'll be there," Roy sang.

He jumped off the sill and sat on it, grinning at them both. His face was pale and excited in the soft, diffused light. It glowed like marble in a dim room and they could see the stiff feathers of his hair against the luminous sky.

"Do you know," he said to Sheila, "that you're a rich woman? At least, potentially rich. At least, Lloyd is, potentially."

"How?" she asked him.

He told her about the proposition their friend, Morty Barrow, had made to Carl the night before, on her behalf.

"Oh, *that*," she said.

"Talking of Tolliver," Carl said to her, "do you want to go over your business with us after dinner? You know: the advertisements and the plans for the new factory?"

"Yes, let's do it then," she said. Her throat was thick with happiness; the men could hear it dripping from her voice, like honey from a tree in a dark wood.

They sat in silence while they finished their drinks. There were hardly any noises except the sound of the mountain breeze through the leaves, like the rustle of many petticoats heard from a distant room. When bulky shadows blotted against the dark luminous sky before them, they knew that was cattle moving in the pasture. A dog was howling in the village and the sound came to them, lonely yet domestic, laid hard across the soft night. Once or twice they heard the clink of cutlery inside, and a throaty laugh. After a while Isobel came out to announce supper, and they went in for the light, colourful, cold meal which was what people like them generally ate at this time on a Sunday in Cayuna.

After supper they laid the stiff artist's copies of the advertisements out on the big dining-table and discussed them. Roy sat in the highbacked ugly, massive chair at one end of the table, studying them with the fierce, solitary concentration he could put on like a hat, and Sheila leant against the chair with one long, heavy arm across his rounded shoulders.

"This is the one," he said, finally, tapping hard and quickly on the sheet. "I'd play this one all you ran. What do you think of it, Carl?"

"I liked that one, too," Carl said.

"That's it," Roy told them. "That's it."

"Perhaps," Sheila said. "I'm not sure, though. Let's leave it for now."

Then they began to look at the estimates and the plan for the new factory that Sheila was hoping she could build.

While they were talking, Haig, Carl's overseer, came in for a drink. He often did on a Sunday, walking or riding up from his little house down in the fields half a mile away.

He was a tall, very thin half-Syrian. His knobbed, lean flesh looked so hard that it almost hurt to think of touching it; and he had the bluest black hair any of them were ever likely to see. His head and face were as slim and savage as the head of a hatchet.

"Hullo, Tony," Roy said as Haig came in.

"Hullo, Roy: they told me you were over." They shook hands.

"Good evening, Mrs. Pearce. How are you?" Haig turned to Sheila.

"Good evening, Mr. Haig. Very well, thanks. And you?" Sheila answered.

"Tony," Cad said, "we'll have to shore up the trench at the dam. It's weakening. You better get the men on it tomorrow, first thing."

"I'll do that," Haig said. "We'll need boards for it, I guess. Why don't we use the timber from the old shelter? We might as well use it up."

"I wouldn't bother," Carl said casually. "It's too much trouble getting it out now. Use the stuff we have stored. You know, the ironwood."

"All right," Haig said. "We'll use that. The stuff from the shelter is tarred, though; and it's just the right size, for part of the job anyway. What do you think?"

"No, Tony," Carl said. "Don't bother with the shelter. We'll probably need it later; when we start cutting there again. Take the ironwood planks."

Roy realized that he had stopped breathing, and he could feel Sheila's arm tense as a post across his back. Carl was mixing a rum and ginger for Tony Haig.

Haig stayed for two drinks, and left.

When they couldn't hear him going across the yard outside, Roy said, "What would you have done if he'd really wanted to use the timber from the shelter?"

"Nothing," Carl said. "I'd have gone up with them. They wouldn't have found anything. Etienne is all ready to move out of there at a moment's notice. He wouldn't have left any more trace than a lizard."

"How do you know that?" They were both speaking very softly.

"I saw him this afternoon."

"Oh! Do you think that was wise?"

"It's all right," Carl told him. "It's my place, and I am always up there anyway. Besides, I wanted to tell him where to go if anything *did* happen."

"Yes," Roy said. "Perhaps it was good to see him. Jesus, when this is over I'm going to get so drunk. I don't like this business. How was he?"

"Cool as ice. I promised him some rum. You can take it up when you go."

"Yes," Roy said. "I'll do that. We'll have to buy it near Tolliver, though. Don't send him anything from here."

From the way he was relaxing he knew how frightened he had been by Haig's remark. He looked back at Sheila and smiled; her arm tightened across his shoulders and he could feel her fingers press into his shirt.

"O.K.," he said. "Let's get on with your business."

They stayed at the Pen until nearly eleven, finishing Sheila's plans and discussing, briefly and thoroughly, what to do about Etienne. Then they went out and got into Carl's Humber for the drive back to Tolliver. They sat as they had done coming up; but now Sheila had Roy's hand in hers and was looking at his face in the green glow from the dash-board light.

Halfway to the coast road, she said: "I don't want to go back tonight. Can I come up to town with you?"

Roy's hand, over hers, stiffened.

"I don't think that would be a good idea," he said. "If it was any other time I'd say yes, but not now. Not until this is over."

"You're right," she said. "I wasn't thinking. I'm sorry."

He squeezed her hand. He would have liked to say that it was a nice thought on her part, but he didn't want to say it with Carl next to them in the car.

"Be careful," he told her, "when you're off Columbus Head. Do be careful; we don't want anything to happen to you."

"I'll be careful," she said. "I am pretty good with the *Nisba* now, you know. And she handles marvellously. I'll go out tomorrow afternoon, just like I do all the time, and I'll take her up to where I'll have to meet Summer. That will make sure I do it all right when the times comes. Can you come out with me, Carl? We'll do some fishing to make it look good."

"Yes," Carl said. "I'll come down after lunch."

At Tolliver they didn't go in because Roy had to get back to Etienne. Lloyd had not come in yet.

Roy got from the car to let her out, and she kissed Carl lightly on the cheek before she stepped on to the drive. The house was dark, except for the landing light. They saw it yellow inside, but it cast almost nothing on to the verandah. Roy and she walked across the dark verandah to the shadows of the doorway leading into the hall. There she turned and faced him very quickly and her arms went round him before he could take her in his. Her cheek was warm and firm and closely nuzzled against his.

"Good night," she said. "Thank you. Whatever you do about us, thank you for this afternoon. I love you, Roy. I love you."

He could not think of anything to say, and he kissed her. It was not passionate or hungry, as it had been this afternoon. But it was not bored either, as it could be, so often, after you had got what you desired from a woman. It was sweet and comforting, and by the pliant, calm eagerness with which he fitted against her he knew that his body was quite prepared to love this woman, and that he already needed her.

27

On Monday morning in Queenshaven, about eight o'clock (around the time when Hector Slade, say, was having his breakfast and Carl had been up and busy for two hours, and Roy was still heavily asleep), a man called Scissors Clark came to see Tiger Johnson over in the Jungle. They called him Scissors because although he was no good with a razor, a knife, a big stick, a brick, or even a machete, he was astonishing and deadly with the pair of cheap, chromium plated household scissors he always carried in the back pocket of his trousers. One or two men, starting almost contemptuously to match him in single fight (they with a stick or a big switchknife, he with his scissors), had found themselves, five minutes or less later, jabbed to ribbons, almost senseless and shrinking with cold terror, wildly hoping that some of the men nearby would pull him off before he did anything worse. He was not afraid of the police, or of any man except Tiger. He feared the three women that all his world in Queenshaven feared, but Johnson was the only man who could make him feel afraid.

Besides all this, he was the most expert stealer from parked cars in Queenshaven.

Now he went across the fine, sour, hard-swept dust of the yard to Tiger Johnson's front door. He knocked and waited. A chair scraped inside and then Trouble's round, tight-skinned head looked out from the six-inch gap of the opened door.

"What you want?" Trouble asked, and his little, steady eyes travelled briefly and comprehensively over Scissors with impersonal hostility.

Scissors smiled embarrassedly and opened the breast of his shirt and pointed inside it. The shirt front was bumpy and edged with the concealed objects he was showing Trouble.

"I want to see if Tiger buy something," he said. He grinned ingratiatingly.

"Oh, dat," Trouble said. "Wait."

The door was shut loudly and abruptly. Scissors Clark leaned his short, broad back against the warm wood and waited. It was a good morning. The sky was clear and milky, the sun fierce and steady, and the air still had some of the fresh coolness from the night. There was no breeze yet and you could hardly smell the jungle below: only a trace of that smell came up to here at this hour, as an expensive woman leaves a memory of her scent after passing through a room. When Trouble jerked the door open again, Scissors almost fell in backwards.

"All right," Trouble said. "Him say come in."

Inside, there were three places set on the oilcloth. Coffee in big, pint-sized enamel mugs, bread and butter on cheap, rose-patterned china, a plate of red, pickled herrings between the three places. Tiger's woman sat at one place, looking smug and sleepy, with her thick, brown-tinted, black hair half-hiding her face and hanging cloudily to her waist.

"Hi, Tiger," Scissors said. "How you do?" He smiled uneasily as Tiger Johnson's remote, slitted, red-veined eyes fixed on him.

"What you bring?" Tiger asked. He had not combed his hair or beard yet and they stood out like knotted, carelessly piled wire bush all around the small beautiful skull. The harsh, gaunt, hawk sweep of his face showed no interest as Scissors neatly, almost apologetically, began to heap his loot at the clear end of the table.

There was a gold embroidered lady's handbag, small and heavy and stiff with the gold thread worked on black velvet; a nice, man's watch; a pair of silver lamé sandals; a silk stole which rippled liquidly on to the oilcloth; a prayer book with ivory covers and fine gilt along the leaf edges; a stamped, morocco leather spectacle case which Scissors opened to show the spectacles; a pair of 12-denier nylon stockings; a green, waxed, cardboard box of 12-bore shells, and a fine, silver cigarette lighter.

"Dat all?" Tiger asked. He had looked swiftly at each piece as Scissors put them on the table and now he was staring with unblinking closeness into the other man's eyes.

"Cho, yes," Scissors said. A stiff-muscled, uncertain smile quivered faintly on his lips. "Luck was bad dis weekend, you see, Tiger. Only a few car come out dere, and dem have a patrol, now, of de panhead cops. You have fe' careful, you see."

"Let me see de bag."

Trouble, who had sat down again and continued his breakfast without seeming to glance at what Scissors had brought, reached and took the bag and put it into Tiger's small, rigid hand. Tiger Johnson opened the catch and poked his finger against the velvet and rubbed at the gold thread.

"De book." Trouble passed the prayer book to him also.

He looked at it and riffled the pages delicately then put it down with gentle care beside him.

"Man," he said to Scissors Clark, "what you steal a bible for?"

"It feel good when I pick it up, Tiger. Me didn't know say it was a bible."

"Man, you don't 'fraid a bad luck hold you, no?"

"Cho, Tiger. How me fe' know. De man and de woman come out Sunday morning early. It still dark, though. Dem go into de bush where de soft sand is and me find de bible and dis in de car." He lifted the heavy, shot silk stole. "How me know say dem is gwine to church after."

"Dat's your business," Tiger grunted. "I don't pay you fe' de book, though. T'irty shilling." He gestured to the objects Scissors had stolen, with a crisp, dark flicker of his small hand.

"Lawd, Tiger, man," Scissors said in a complaining, mechanical voice. "You is doing me wrong, though. T'irty shilling for all dis?"

He was not hoping that he could raise Tiger's price. That is, he was not really hoping very much for this. He knew that Tiger's rates were flexible and eccentric, varying from much higher than a thing was worth to perhaps a tenth of its value; and he also knew that once a price had been offered by the iron-faced, disinterested man opposite him, it was never changed. He, Scissors, came always to Tiger, as did many successful thieves in Queenshaven, because the chances were that you might at any time get a month's high living for something almost worthless. Equally, you might get a few drinks and a meal for something quite valuable. You might even, as now, get what was roughly the fair price for stolen goods. You never knew exactly, but it was always worth the gamble.

"Dat's all right," Tiger said in a voice so low and casual that it was almost inaudible. "Tek it and gawn, den. I don't need your trash."

The woman looked sidelong at Scissors with her utterly contemptuous, coldly glittering eyes, and he knew that Trouble had stopped eating and was looking at him also. Tiger chose a chunk of bread from his plate and forked some herring on to it, holding the bread under the edge of the dish and spreading the fish on to it. After a few seconds the woman and Trouble looked away too. Scissors could feel their complete dismissal in the air as he could have smelt something bad. He shifted on his feet and sweat ran cool down his ribs from his armpits.

"Cho, Tiger," he said in a hesitant, soothing way. "Don't go on so. Give me de t'irty bob, den. I know you always treat me good."

Tiger put the bread and herring down and took his little money-bag from the drawer in the table before him. He took a pound note and two five shilling, Bank of Cayuna notes from it and tossed them across the table to Scissors.

"Here," Tiger said, and smiled the red, swelling-lipped grin which only pulled at his mouth and left the rest of his face still and carved. "Dis is extra." He flicked a two shilling piece in a twinkling parabola over the table and Scissors slapped it down against the oilcloth to stop it rolling. "Dat's not for de book, mind," Tiger continued, touching the graven, ivory cover of the prayer book. "I not buying de book. I don't want none of your bad luck. You can give me de book if you want. If you don't want, den tek it."

"Keep it, Tiger, keep it." Scissors' smile was loose and relieved and he was glad that he could leave this room as soon as he wanted, now that he had his money. "Cho, what I could do wid it anyway,"

The woman got swiftly to her feet and took the prayer book and carried it into the bedroom behind her. She came out and sat down again.

"You don't get much," Tiger said to Scissors. "What happen?"

"Like I tell you, Tiger. Not many car and dem have a patrol 'pon de Barricades now. 'Specially at weekend."

"You want go up de August Hill road," Tiger told him. "Dat's where de white man an' de brown man dem, tek de woman at night now. Plenty car up dere."

"You t'ink so, eh?"

Tiger's head moved a half-inch in confirmation.

"All right, I go dere dis week." Scissors was feeling chatty, now, with the money in his pocket, and the thought of the two pounds he had taken from the handbag before he brought it to Tiger, and with the knowledge that he could leave this room as soon as he wanted. "I see a friend of yours 'pon de Barricades Saturday night," he said as he made to move to the door.

"A friend of mine?"

"Yes. De little white man. You know, him little, but him hard. De one dat always mek de speech. Lawyer McKenzie. Him come out in one lovely car, you see; him an' anoder fair man, a big man. Dem park near de place where I always hide de stuff so if police pick me up I don't have nuttin' on me. Lawd, it was a nice car, though. I was going tek from it, but when I hear him speak I know him was your friend. It was too dark fe' see good, but when I hear him speak I leave it alone."

Tiger shrugged.

"Him is no friend of mine," he told Scissors. "Nex' time tek what you want."

"All right," Scissors said casually, half-regretfully. "I wish I did know dat den. It was a big lovely car; mebbe I would have got a big haul from it. An' de free of dem didn't come back from de beach for a long time,"

He went to the door and began to open it.

"Scissors," Tiger said.

"Yes, Tiger?" Scissors turned, his hand on the knob.

"How t'ree of dem come back? I t'ink you say dat McKenzie come out wid one oder man."

Tiger Johnson's hard, sharply-curved face looked as if it had been edged and faceted suddenly with a razor. Only someone who knew him really well could have told that this suspicion was as natural to him as breathing; that he allowed no odd, unfitting particular to pass without question; and that he was simply asking now as a matter of habitually cautious routine.

"No, Tiger," Scissors explained patiently. "Two of dem come out, but de t'ree of dem come back to de car from de beach."

"Who de oder one was?"

"Me no know," Scissors said without any interest. "Friend of theirs, mebbe. It too dark fe' see good. I t'ink him a black man, though; or brown like Trouble. I don't pay dem much mind. Lawd, it was a nice car. I wish I did know dat Lawyer McKenzie was no friend of yours."

"Dis oder man, him have him own car?"

"No," Scissors said. He was sorry now that he had mentioned this. He was anxious to get out of the room, and out of the Jungle; to go down town to the little room where his woman was waiting for him with a breakfast bought out of the two pounds he had taken from the bag. "No, Tiger, him go in de car wid de two of dem. A little man, like Lawyer McKenzie."

"All right," Tiger told him. "I see you."

"I see you, Tiger."

The door closed behind Scissors Clark.

Tiger Johnson sat finishing his coffee, his eyes narrow with thought.

"What I don't see," he said three minutes later, in the voice of a man who has been considering something which might be important but hardly urgent, "is what a man like dat do on de Barricades dat time of night widout a car."

Neither Trouble nor the girl said anything to this. Trouble, because he knew that if there was anything to be done about it, Tiger would tell him what to do. The woman, because she had not listened to the last talk between Tiger and Scissors. She had been thinking of how she was going to get the stole from Tiger before he sold it. She was thinking of that now.

28

Roy McKenzie drove into town at about ten o'clock on Monday morning. He was doing forty miles an hour in an area where he should have been doing thirty and he was feeling very good. Since Friday night he had slept better and deeper every night than he could remember for several months, and this was having its effect on him now.

When he got out of the car in the parking yard and the first heat of morning hit him, he felt even better. There was a positive, gentle pleasure in the sensation of his crisply starched, soft-clinging linen suit and the ground felt warm and springy under his white kid shoes. Walking across to the office, his muscles moved with an oiled, elastic briskness which had once been habitual but which had become unfamiliar in the last two years. As he always did when he felt like this, he promised himself that he would, seriously, take up some sport again: boxing, maybe, or riding; perhaps both.

He went up the narrow, musty leather-smelling stairs, taking them two at a time, and into his outer office. The three stenographers were busy, and the boy who was articled to him was looking busy. Linda was typing at her desk, which stood by the wall next to his door and which was separated from the rest of the office by a cage of thin, waist-high wooden railing. There was an inch-thick pile of the morning's letters that she had opened, beside her typewriter, and several other letters unopened in their envelopes. Five clients were already waiting to see him, sitting against the wall in straight, cane-bottomed chairs.

It looked like Monday morning and he had worked hard to get it looking like this. As he smiled his reassuring, professional smile at his clients, he realized that he would soon need a partner; that he had made more work than one man could handle.

Linda followed him into his office. She shut the door, and the frosted-glass half of it, which had his name in black letters across the white, opaque surface, made a faint, glassy crash. She stood, with the letters in her hand, watching him as he sat down at his desk and snapped open his brief case and began to take out his papers.

"How did it go?" she asked him, and he could hear how deliberately casual she was making her voice. This was a rule he insisted on: that during the hours when they were dealing with other people's business, and taking good money for it, they kept their party and political interests on a background level; only allowing them to intrude when there was no help for it.

"It was fine," he told her happily. "Everything went like a play. If we don't get him away now it isn't our fault. I've a lot to tell you; too much to tell you now, but everything's fine."

"I thought so," she said as she came over and put the letters on the big square of green blotter before him. "I worried all Saturday night, but by yesterday morning I knew it was all right. Good work." She ran her small, soft fingers across his closely brushed, freshly oiled hair.

"It was Carl, really," he said. "He was magnificent. I wish I could tell you all about it now."

"You look fine," she said and bent down and kissed him lightly on the cheek. "I like to see you when you look like that: it's like how you were when you first came back from England."

"Anything important in these," he asked her, patting the pile of letters.

"Yes," she said. "Mendoza is willing to settle out of court. You were right there; I thought we were going to have trouble with him. How did you know he would climb down?"

"I know Mendoza," he said absently.

He had searched for and found the letter they were talking about. "I remember him from school. He was a greedy, impatient little bastard even then. I guessed he'd jump at the chance of cash, without the fuss and trouble of a court case. O.K., Lin, send Bristow the good news that Mendoza will settle out of court. Anything else?"

"No," she said, then with tender mockery, "Is that why you're such a good solicitor? Because you knew half your clients at school?"

"Damn right," he told her. "Most men forget what their friends were like as children. I remember; and if I can't remember, I go back over every incident in which those men figured until I do. After he's twelve, a man only changes on the outside."

"What about women?" Her broad, darkly vivid face was attractive with fond mockery.

"I don't know a goddam thing about women," he said grinning at her. "Go on, Lin, tell the first one to come in. We've wasted enough time this morning."

At half-past eleven he was listening to the curious, involved, outrageously sad story of a man who wanted to divorce his wife.

He waited for a little after the man had left and then he pressed the buzzer for Linda to send in the next client. He was looking at the relevant papers (a straightforward entail; easy enough to break it) when Linda herself came in.

"Dick Mason's outside," she told him. "I think he must have some news about the *Kosciuzko*. Do you want to see him now?"

"Better let him wait," he said. "It looks bad when someone jumps the queue. If it's really urgent, he'll let you know." He dealt with the man who had the entail case. He did it thoroughly and well, not even thinking, except once, about Dick Mason outside. When the man left, he pressed the buzzer again and waited.

Dick Mason came in, bending his small, tight-curled head to pass under the door, carrying the ridiculous, huge, pipe-clayed helmet in his large, sharply knuckled hand. When he sat down in the chair beside the desk, after shaking hands, he seemed to fold in numerous, narrow angles, like a surveyor's ruler.

"Well, Roy," he asked, "how did it go?" His very young, attractively grotesque face was taut-skinned with excitement and his almond shaped, dark eyes were bright with nervousness.

"Damn good," Roy told him. "It couldn't have gone better, Dick. I think we'll get him away. I'm sorry I had to keep you waiting, but it wouldn't look right for you to come in before other people."

"That's your story," Dick Mason said, smiling his long-toothed smile, his heavy lips stretching flatly across the narrow face. "You just wanted to show me what a big shot you really are."

Roy smiled at him in turn. It pleased him to hear Mason making jokes.

"What about your side of things?" he asked. "Do you have some news for us?"

"Yes. I'd have come before, but I had to wait until I was off duty and I didn't think it was wise to phone. The *Kosciuzko's* loading at Kingston this afternoon and tonight. We got the Custom's signal two hours ago. She clears Kingston some time early tomorrow morning."

"Good. How long will it take for her to come across from Jamaica?"

"Under twenty-four hours."

"That's just right then. What did you and that sailor, Paul, arrange in case he couldn't get in contact with the *Kosciuzko*, or if they couldn't do it?"

"He was to send a cable to the wharf about a parcel of laundry he had forgotten at the Seaman's Hostel. He had left it there, by the way. If it's all right he'll send the cable from Antofogasta."

"It sounds all right to me then. Is there anything else I have to know?"

"No," Dick Mason told him. "Is it all fixed up about getting him out to the ship?"

"Yes," Roy said, and told him very briefly the bare details of what he had arranged with Jeffrey Summer and Sheila Pearce.

"Well," Dick Mason said when Roy had finished. "That's that, then."

He looked slightly disappointed and Roy knew that the boy was feeling the letdown which had been bound to come after three days of worry and responsibility, now that his part of the work was over: a part of the work which had been brief and remote, without any of the concrete satisfactions which he, Roy, had been able to enjoy in meeting Etienne and seeing him safely hid, and which he would be able to feel when he saw the conclusion of the work as Etienne climbed the side of the ship.

"Yes," he said gently, "You've done what you can do, Dick. And you've done it damn well. That's not just me, either; Etienne thinks so too. You'd better go now, though. There's no reason why you shouldn't come to see me, but we might as well be really careful until it's over."

Dick Mason left then. Roy took him to the door and when he opened it to let his friend out, the typists were putting the black, shiny covers over their typewriters and the articled clerk was straightening his tie at the mirror and looking smugly at his reflection. Roy realized it was lunch time. Linda looked up from the pencil-marked page of Theobald on Wills from which she was making notes. Roy and Dick Mason both smiled at her, and she nodded back almost imperceptibly, as if she had looked up and jerked her head as it bent again over the book.

Roy went back into his office. He had the used and completed feeling which always came to him after a good morning's work, and which was different in quality from the exhaustion at the end of the afternoon when the physical and emotional payment he had to make was heavier than this extension of himself he could savour, and take pride in, so acutely and truly now.

He went over to the window and looked on to the blistered, dingy walls of the buildings below; screwing his eyes against the splintered silver glisten of the zinc roofs and the whitish glare which beat up from the hot tar: the people in the streets moved with the languid, conserving slowness which they always adopted at this time of day. When he saw Hector Slade's black Chrysler turn out of the corner by the bar he knew, before it began to slow, that it was going to stop outside this building. He walked to and sat down at his desk; he waited until Linda opened the door and Hector Slade's thin, stoop-shouldered figure loped springily past her and into the room. Roy got up and took the hand which Hector had offered before he was halfway to the desk.

"How are you, Roy?" Hector said. His fine-skinned hand felt cool and knottily hard.

"Pretty good, Hector," Roy said. "Sit down, please. How's yourself?"

"Getting old, man," Hector Slade told him as his lean, crisply-uniformed body bent like a weathered cane into the chair beside the desk. The long legs crossed with smooth abruptness, effortlessly. He leaned from the waist and put his whistle-topped swagger stick and the black, silver-badged cap on the floor beside the chair. "Haven't seen you in ages," he went on, straightening. "You couldn't have been that busy: I feel hurt."

He smiled at Roy, the grey quick eyes twinkling with friendliness, and felt in the big side-pocket of his closely fitting khaki tunic. He brought out the short-stemmed, dented black pipe and very old, almost mildewed leather pouch, with a worn, flaking regimental crest stamped in gilt on the flap.

"This is a nice surprise," Roy said, "I keep meaning to come and see you one evening but something else always seems to turn up and prevent me."

He was, he suddenly realized, not breathing very easily as Hector Slade's round heavy head turned with slow thoroughness and the little, polished eyes examined the room.

Be careful, he told himself. Be very careful. Don't try to be clever and don't try to look for anything behind what he says. If he knows anything you can't do much about it now. And if he doesn't, then answering straight is the safest thing to do.

"I feel rather guilty myself," Hector told him. "I've really come for that book you told Carl you had for me. I was passing and thought I'd pick it up."

"Oh, yes," Roy said. "Lavant's *Slave Trade*. Yes. I have it here."

He got up and went to the bookcase and opened it and took a thick, red-covered volume from the lower shelf; and came back to the desk. He handed it to Hector Slade.

"What was it like?" Hector Slade asked him. "Any good?" He was flicking the pages with practised, competent fingers and he turned to the back of the book, where the bibliography was, and ran his glance expertly down the list of references which were printed in italics.

"Not bad," Roy said. "Not a great deal of new stuff, but it's very comprehensive and thorough. He hasn't missed much. I'd hoped he would have a fresh idea on where our Madagascars really came from, though; but he doesn't. He just gives a summary of the existing theories and an evaluation of each. I think you'll find it useful. There are some very good letters I hadn't seen before."

"Good, man, Thank you. Pity he hasn't found anything conclusive on the Madagascars. They're the only tribe I can't account for. I've sometimes thought that I've tracked them down, but there's always something missing."

Hector Slade was filling his pipe as he spoke, thrusting the big, scarred bowl into the pouch and fingering the flaky shreds of cheap, peasant's tobacco into it. Now he stopped filling the pipe and looked at Roy questioningly, with his long, blue-veined hands curved about the battered bowl.

"Yes," Roy said. "I'd like to find something definite on them, myself. I wonder sometimes if they weren't a group who were meant for the South African Dutch and pirated by one of our ships and brought across. It would have been worth going the extra two thousand miles for West Indian prices."

"Hadn't thought of that." Hector Slade sat up straight in the straight chair and his narrow face became brighter and sharper with interest. "That's an idea. Are you going to follow it up?"

"When I get the time," Roy told him. "But you have it if you want. I won't get around to it for months. If you find anything, tell me, though."

"Yes, certainly. We might find something really interesting. You sure you don't want it. It's your idea, really."

"No," Roy said. "You follow it up. I wouldn't be able to touch it for a long time."

"Thanks, man."

Hector Slade took the dented, white-scratched mouthpiece of the pipe from between his yellow teeth.

"By the way," he added, and looked at Roy with an odd, appealing pleasure and shyness. "They've asked me to give the Mandeville lectures in Jamaica at the University next term. Would you like to share them with me? I'm covering a lot of ground, and you know far more about the post-emancipation stuff than I do. If we did them together we could really give them something worthwhile. What do you say?"

Roy got up, then, from his desk. He wanted some relief from the tight caution in which he had held himself, waiting and expectant, for all the time that had passed since Hector Slade first came into the room. He went to the door and opened it. Linda was sitting tilted back in her swivel chair, swung round from the desk; when he smiled at her, her answering glance was anxiously inquisitive.

"You better go out for lunch now, Lin," he said and nodded slightly, pulling a small grimace, to show her that everything was all right.

"Yes, Mr. McKenzie," she said in the clear, neutral tone she always used before people who were strangers.

He came back into the room, closing the door behind him, and Hector Slade looked at him enquiringly, waiting for an answer to his last question.

"Yes," Roy told him, "I'd like to do those lectures with you, Hector. What's the theme, though. Might be something I couldn't handle."

"It's family patterns from slavery to the beginning of industry," Hector Slade said. "Up to about 1910, say. I thought of calling them *Work and Family in Cuyuna*. What do you think?"

"It sounds excellent," Roy answered. He was seated, leaned against rather, the edge of the desk, his hands in his pockets. "We could get some good stuff together for that, Hector. I'm glad you asked me."

Hector Slade made a brief, dismissing gesture with his hand and the lined, weather-cured skin glowed with delight as his tight, pleasant smile stretched his mouth briefly.

"Good, man," he said. "That's splendid. I'll tell them over at the University that I've asked you. We could plan it in four periods, eh? A Spanish period; after the English conquest up to about 1750; 1750 to the Napoleonic wars; we'll need a whole lecture on the period between 1800 and the emancipation; and then two for after emancipation. How does that sound?"

"Fine," Roy said. "You take care of the Spanish stuff and the early English, and I'll do the late nineteenth century. Perhaps we'll have to do some closer collaboration on the middle ground, though. How are you on that side? I'm rusty."

"Me, too. I'm depending on you for the donkey work there."

He put the pipe in the heavy, square, glass ashtray beside Roy, and leaned sideways to pick up his cap and stick, and the book which he had put beside them. He rose and straightened the creases in his tunic with two or three deft tugs and pats. He knocked the ash and dottle from his pipe and put it in his pocket. Standing there, with the cap set squarely yet at a confident jaunty tilt on his head, his lean, used body held easily and with light, supple poise in the close-cut khaki uniform, he looked pliantly fashioned, like an old sword blade which has been filed and polished and edged time and time again for a great number of years.

Roy heaved himself from the edge of the desk, and felt in the pocket of his jacket for a cigarette.

"Well," he said to Hector Slade, "this has been nice. We must see each other more often. Are you off now?"

"I have to go and get some lunch. Can I drop you anywhere? Or perhaps you could lunch with me? We could talk properly." He glanced encouragingly at the younger man.

"No," Roy said regretfully. "I'd like to, but I'm too busy. I'm just going to get a sandwich at the corner and come back here. But I'll see you soon, eh? We'll have to go over the plan for the lectures."

"Of course. You get in touch with me. Don't make it too long."

Hector Slade's bony hand rested for a moment on Roy's shoulder as they went to the door.

"No," Roy said. "I'll arrange something soon."

At the door, Hector looked closely at him for an instant: his narrow, edged face was wooden, but the lively eyes were questioning and sharp.

"I see Etienne's got away," he said casually. "Got a signal from Port-du-Roi this morning."

"Good," Roy said. "I'm glad to hear that. Thanks for telling me."

His skin was suddenly too tight, cool and prickly. So that's it, he thought. He knows, and he's about to let me have it. Then, looking at Hector Slade's face, he felt the heave of nauseating panic subside. No, he told himself, he isn't like that. If he knew, he would have declared his hand and done something. But he's no sadist; he wouldn't have played the old cat and mouse with me just for the fun it would give him.

"Didn't you know?" Hector Slade asked him,

"No," Roy replied. "How could I know?"

"Just wondered. Where do you think he'll head for?"

"Somewhere safe," Roy said smiling easily. "Maybe Mexico. He'll get asylum there, won't he?"

"I hope it's Mexico," Hector Slade said. "If he tries it here, I'll send him back. Don't try to hide him, eh, if he comes here?"

"You know I'll try, Hector," Roy said, still smiling. "If I get half a chance I'll try."

"I know, man. And I'll smell it out. Pity, really. Met Etienne once and quite liked him. I like him better than the rubbish who've taken over in St. Pierre now. Still, what to do, eh? He's a dangerous fellow. You can't imagine the trouble having him so close has been to me. Ring me soon, eh?"

Roy stayed on the landing until Hector Slade's tall, frail-seeming, body, bent, wide shoulders and big, thrust forward head disappeared around a bend in the stairs.

29

Carl Brandt went down to Tolliver in the early part of the afternoon. When he left the Pen he had done nearly all the things he had meant to finish that day. There were a few left, which would be done under Tony Haig's supervision, but not so many, nor of sufficient importance, to make him feel uncomfortable in his mind.

The hardest part of the morning had been just before lunch; when they were servicing the gigantic, evil-tempered, Mysore bull. His name was Rajah and he was the twelfth bull in his line to be called that at Brandt's Pen. He was the chief sire of the great, unbelievably strong steers Carl sold to the sugar estates for hauling the high, piled carts of cane from the fields to the factories during the cutting season.

It had started well enough, with the faintly trembling, apprehensive cow in the little stall which would hold her steady while they brought Rajah up behind her. Then, without warning, the enormous, slatey white bull had gone suddenly from its habitual brooding sullenness into an explosion of fury which pulled him free from the men on the ropes. Stanley, the head cowman, was close in front on his mule. It twisted away in a fast, intricate stammer of hooves and the first, blurred reach of the horns had raked the air where the mule and man had been a split second before. And almost with this, while Stanley, as tightly fixed in his saddle as a bat in a girl's hair, had been bringing his mule round, the whips in the hands of the two cowmen, (gripped as far along the handles as a fencer would hold his rapier), had snapped before

Rajah's face with that bursting ripe, fruitily evil, cracking curl which, the bull knew, could have lifted his eyes out of their sockets.

It had stood, except for two incredibly swift, quickly halted rushes, raging, coldly planning with hate, while the men had backed the mules through the gate. Then it had given a grunting, harsh yet sonorous bellow that was almost a scream and come charging across the packed, dung-splashed earth of the pen and hit the half-ton, five-barred mahoe gate a crack that could be heard all over the property. It had not stopped there. While the men, and Carl who had now joined them, sat on their mounts outside the gate, Rajah charged the gate again and again, till the humans, to whom this conduct was not unfamiliar, began to fear that he would drop dead of intense, mounting rage.

Then Rajah had charged for the last time and the great, sword sweep of thick horns had hooked firmly under the gate and the huge head lifted with the gate on it, taken off the bolt and hole hinges on which it swung. The head had tossed and the gate went through the air and fell ten feet away; and the glaring, anger-swollen creature had charged for the nearest man with the unstoppable, hurtling power of a boulder going down a hill.

It had taken them ten minutes of swift, carefully dodging manoeuvre to get him back into the pen; the full, savage explosions of the whips sounding all the time. So that when he was finally backed up, sullen, twitching and confused, in the pen, while twelve men were hoisting the gate back on to the hinges and lashing it to the fence with rope, Carl could feel the sweat thick under his shirt and his arm trembling from the long, heavy shuddering of the whip cracks. He had been riding Caesar, and the deep-drawn swelling breaths of the horse were pushing against his knees.

By this time, too, Rajah had been so used up and bewildered that he was no good for service that day.

Carl had gone back to the house and showered and changed. Then he had eaten his lunch quickly and got into his car for the drive down to Tolliver.

When he reached Tolliver they told him that Sheila was down at the factory and that Lloyd was not in. Carl told them not to disturb Sheila and went up the stairs and sat on the verandah to wait for her. He smoked a cigarette and sat wondering what it would be like when he saw her again, today.

After a while he saw her coming through the trees from the distant, black-roofed factory. She was dressed in a plain, full skirt which she had put on over her bathing costume, because he could see the neat, severe line of the top piece and her smoothly tanned, bare shoulders and chest. When she came near the house, and saw his car, she looked up to the verandah and waved. He came to the rail and smiled down at her. Even from here he could see how happy she was; and seeing her he knew that it would be all right, that he had, without realizing it, already accepted the situation which he had helped to make possible. He had hoped this was how he would feel; but he had not been sure until he looked down and saw her face.

She went out of sight under the verandah and Carl turned and leant against the railing so that he would see her as she came through the doorway from the landing.

Then she appeared in the doorway and came quickly to meet him, tall, shiny brown, her full skirt whipping back with the long, angular, graceful strides, the big sandalled feet planting decisively on the boards, and her high, neat head dipping to the bend of the slight, leant from the waist sway which was the thing that gave her an arresting, feminine delicacy of movement and which was like the women on the old fashion plates he had once discovered in a forgotten chest at the Pen.

"Hullo," she said. "Have you been waiting long?"

Her eyes had a deep, very bright gaiety as she put her heavy-boned, lightly holding hands on his shoulders and kissed him on the cheek. There was a raw, greasily acid smell from the vats of half-processed soap caught in her thick hair and he could smell the pungent, pleasantly sour odour under her arms from where she had sweated in the heat of the factory.

"No," he said, answering her question. "As long as this." He raised his hand to show her the cigarette stub in his fingers.

"Good," she said. "We can leave right away if you want."

She turned from him with an abrupt swing which swirled her skirt and which had no nervousness or tension in it, but was vivid and spontaneously full, like the sudden movement of a young girl.

"Yes," he said. "Let's go. What sort of a day is it for going out?"

"Not bad," she told him. Her voice had a gay fullness that he had never heard in it before. "It's a bit too bright for good surface fishing; but if you troll well down you should get something."

"What about the other business?"

"Oh, that." She smiled at him. "That's all right, too. There is a bit of wind, but not enough to make it really rough. It should be all steady going. Come along and choose the rod you want."

She turned and went into the house and he followed her down the stairs and into the wide, cream and gold day-room where she kept her fishing rods. There was a fine, stuffed blue marlin on one wall, and a huge, narrow, wicked barracuda on the wall facing it.

She went over to where the five rods stood in the rack.

"You better take this one," she told him as she lifted a tapering, seven foot, tip-quivering rod from the slots. "It's the best for deep trolling. Have you ever had it before?" She was not looking at him as she spoke, but selecting her own rod from the four left in the rack, her face intent and seriously happy.

"I can't remember," he told her. He lifted the rod, holding it near the shining reel drum and enjoying the astonishing, sensuous spring of its balance. "I think so; it feels familiar. I'm not sure, though."

He had not done much fishing before Sheila began to take him out in the *Nisba;* but he was beginning to enjoy it now, and he had decided that if he enjoyed it any more he would take it up seriously and perhaps buy his own boat.

"Oh, you philistine," she said. She turned to him and laughed with that welling happiness she did not seem able to keep from her voice today. "I ought to give you a string and a bent pin. Not knowing if you ever used a rod like that before. Come along. We'll walk to the jetty." They were walking across the room as she talked.

She turned her face up to him, and as she saw for the first time what showed in his eyes, though not in his carefully controlled face, she became serious with understanding.

"Carl," she said. She had stopped so that he had to stop now and face her too.

"Yes?" he said.

"I'm sorry that it had to happen like that yesterday, between Roy and me. I didn't mean to let it happen then, but I couldn't stop it once it had started. I wasn't sorry about it afterwards, only about you. But I didn't want to spoil it, so I didn't pretend. Is it all right now?"

She looked straight at him while she said this: her eyes never flickered from his face once and her voice was steady. Now, when she finished, she stood still, looking at him.

"It's all right, Sheila," he said slowly. "It really is all right. If it was going to happen, that was the place for it. You know what I mean?"

She nodded, very slowly. Her face had a look of tenderness, and something, also, that was almost surprise.

"Carl," she said, and put her long, smooth arm round his waist and hugged him with a powerful squeeze. He grinned embarrassedly.

"Come on," he said. "We'll never get where we're going if we don't hurry."

They went out of the house into the steady, metallically still pressure of the early afternoon glare. There was a little path in the grass, leading across the property, through the hard, sabre-curved trees and under the harshly rustling leaves, to the fence by the road. Across the road were the beachlands and more trees. Down by the beach was a little point; and in the lee of this point was the jetty and boat-house where Sheila kept the *Nisba*. That was where they were going.

They crossed the road about quarter of a mile above Tolliver village, going through the little gate in the wire fence. Beyond the shade of the trees it was very hot and the glare was thick and whitely opaque, beating up from the road in a hard dazzle. She walked before, with the heavy, springily nodding rod held on her shoulder. The trees over on the beachland had a soft, green glow. The tar of the road was warm and soft beneath his feet; it felt faintly and pleasantly exciting, as if the road led a long way through this hot, murmuring stillness to some place that it would be very good to know. Sheila, as she walked ahead of him, her skirt floating wide in the wind of her long, quick strides, the tapered rod dipping in the air above her sloping, sleekly powerful shoulders and firm flat brown back, looked like a warrior from some vanished tribe of fighting women, carrying her spear. The short tail of her hair switched from side to side on her long neck.

When they came to the point, they saw that Jackson, the boatman, had already got the *Nisba* out of the boathouse. It was moored at the end of the jetty: a solid, deceptively squat little craft, painted white except for the glassed-in wheelhouse forward of the cockpit. This was of dark, varnished mahogany and broadly edged with a pale, young leaf green. Jackson was sitting on top of the wheelhouse and when he saw them he got up and came along the boat to the jetty. He was a huge man, big enough so that even Carl always felt little beside him, and he moved with the shambling, fluid sureness of a great ape. His size, too, was all bone; the flesh was so thin over the roughly cut, gigantic frame that it was stretched like the skin of a drum; and even the muscles which bunched if he so much as lifted his hand were lean and flexible like hose-pipe.

"Hullo, Jackson," Carl said as they came up. "How are you?"

"Well, Mass' Carl." The lean, massive face smiled up at him from where the man stood in the cockpit. Jackson was one of the real black people; and there was a rich brown tint beneath his skin that somehow confirmed the blackness, making it stronger. "I glad you come out wid us today, sah. You don't come for a long time."

He took the rods from them in his wide, startlingly huge hands and they stepped down into the boat.

"All ready, Jackson?" Sheila asked him. She was lifting her long legs out of the skirt as she spoke, and now she folded it neatly and threw it on to one of the bunks below in the little cabin which lay beyond the small, latched open door.

"She all ready, missis. You wan' fe' cast off?"

"Cast off, Jackson," she said and went to the wheel.

The port engine fired and caught and then the starboard engine. She ran them in with a quick, steadily mounting pulse of power, and as Jackson cast off she took the boat out and up the narrow, darker water of the deep channel which lay between the shallows off the point.

Carl stood in the opposite corner of the wheelhouse and watched her large, beautiful, sunburnt hands on the wheel and her joyfully absorbed face squinting against the molten silver, flashing dazzle from the sea, and at her widely planted taut legs. It was very hot in the low, glass-set wheelhouse and after a few minutes he went and sat on the stern and took off his shirt and sandals.

When they were beyond the reefs she turned the boat west and called Jackson from forward.

"Keep her on two-eighty-five for a while," she said. They were going west along the coast and heading out to open sea. She came across the cockpit and sat beside him on the stern. There was a basket of small fish in one corner, and she began to bait Carl's line from this.

"What will we get today?" he asked her as he watched the powerful fingers drive a hook expertly and easily into the mouth of a little salt water mullet and work the point out behind the gills.

"Anything," she said, glancing sideways at him and smiling. "We might get something really exciting like a blue marlin or a swordfish or a ray. On the other hand we might only get a few miserable little tuna or at best a few good king. It's not really a good day because the wind is too small and because of the moon phase, but you never know with fish. You remember Mr. Savage and his wife, Jackson?" she added raising her voice.

Jackson glanced back.

"Yes, missis," he said. "Poor Missa Savage. Bad luck follow him, eh?"

He began to laugh silently. When he laughed like that, and his shoulders and back shook, he looked quite remarkable, a little awe-inspiring. Standing still, he seemed to take up most of the little wheelhouse. Laughing, you wondered if he might not shake it to bits.

"Who was he?" Carl asked, grinning at Jackson's amusement. "I don't know that story."

"A Canadian," she told him. "He came down here and fished from Castleville every day for a month and didn't get a thing. He knew how to fish, too. I'm telling you, Carl, he didn't even see anything. Then the last day of his holidays, Mrs. Savage who had spent all her time over at Resurrection Heights lying on the beach, and who didn't know a snapper from a shark, went out with him just for the ride. She trolled for five minutes and the third biggest blue marlin ever caught off Castleville struck her line. Goodness knows how she landed him, but she did. And do you know, she was so sweet; when they got in she told Mr. Savage he could have himself photographed with it and take it back home as his. She couldn't understand why he got into a temper and stalked off and got drunk at the bar in the Yacht Club."

When their lines were out and they were seated in the steel-framed, canvas chairs facing over the stern, he asked her in a low casual voice: "What about this other business? You know, smelling out the water up by the head?"

"We'll go up there shortly," she said. She was watching the place in the water where her line went into the little waves. "We'll go out to sea for a while, a bit beyond Castleville, and then turn in to the head. I don't think Jackson's going to like it."

"That makes two of us," Carl told her.

"It's quite safe," she said, without any boasting, but quietly and with complete assurance. "I'll be at the wheel. But if I'm going to do it at night I'd like to feel it out when I can see."

It was one of the best days Carl could remember since he had taken to coming out with Sheila. Beyond the broken water near the coast, outside the reef, they could feel the long, easy ocean swell. There wasn't much wind and the waves were small and bright, with little, flicking, white tops. You could see the warm, creamy yellow beach on the receding coast and the curled, shining line of surf and the cool green of the packed trees against the sky. When cars drove along the coast road you could see the hard flash of wind-shields in the sun. The mountains inland were damp-looking; a cool, dull blue, with a long broken belt of cloud wound about the peaks.

It wasn't a good day for fishing, though. Long after they had passed the glistening zinc roofs of Castleville and the white yachts in the basin, they still hadn't caught anything.

About three miles west of Castleville, and a good way out to sea, Sheila left her rod and went forward to the wheel.

"All right, Jackson," Carl heard her say, "I'll take over now. You go back to Mister Brandt, and keep an eye on my line."

Carl could feel the *Nisba* coming round off her course and he knew that Sheila was taking them into the water off Columbus Head. Jackson came up and sat on the stern near him and watched the lines with the same sort of expression Carl had seen on Sheila's face.

"Pass my shirt for me, Jackson," Carl asked him. The man picked it up from the deck and Carl took the cigarettes out of the pocket and gave one to Jackson and took one himself. Jackson lit for them both; the little match flame burning between his enormous cupped hands like a small camp fire at the back of a deep cave.

After a while Jackson, who had been watching the trolling lines, looked suddenly over the side and then swung round in a huge, flowing movement to stare out over the bows. An incredulous expression came to his great, long face.

"Missis," he said, "where you goin', eh? You know where we is now?"

Sheila looked back from the wheel,.

"It's all right," she said. "I'm going in off the head. We've never tried it there. Don't worry, I'm not going to take her in too near."

The disbelieving stare was now frozen on to Jackson's face.

"But, missis," he asked again, still not convinced that she was doing this, "what you goin' in dere for, eh? You know how dat water stay. Suppose de current tek you and sweep you 'pon de rock."

"Cho," she said, "the *Nisba* will do it easy, Jackson. A boat should be able to go anywhere she can draw water. And you never know, we might need to use Columbus Head channel one day."

"My King!" Jackson said in a glum disgusted voice, referring not to royalty but to Jesus Christ. He got up swiftly from his seat on the stern and went forward with that fluidly shambling pad. For a couple of minutes Carl listened as he and Sheila argued the point with the hot, bitter intimacy possible only between two people who have worked together for a long time at something they both like and who trust each other's skill and knowledge. It was very interesting, but he realized that it sometimes got a little too technical for him to appreciate fully.

Finally Jackson came out looking gloomy and resigned. He swung himself on to the roof of the wheelhouse so quickly and easily that Carl did not quite believe it when he saw him going forward to the bows, but was half persuaded that he must have missed some part of the movement. It was then that he felt what Jackson had sensed five minutes earlier: the fast terrifying solidity of the current pressing against the boat, and twisting in his chair to look over the starboard bow he could see the sheer, jutting bluff of Columbus Head covered with wild, knotted bush, and the stumpy jagged rocks shining blackly and then vanishing in the quickly chopping, tumbled, three-mile stretch of milky green, offshore water, and the sudden, blossoming, thick white and glinting silver explosions of spray when the seas crashed against a submerged bar of rock. There was more water like that on the port side, too, between them and the shore.

Then the stern began to skid, exactly as a car might do on a wet road, and he could feel the engines shudder, and sense the fight they were making to keep the bows straight on into the stream. He remembered what George Summer had said about the tilt of the current and he figured that this must be it.

"Reel in," Sheila called back to him. "If we leave them out the lines might foul."

Her voice sounded tight and she had hardly turned her head to speak and when he glanced at her he saw the stiff heave of her body and her arms move as she turned hard on the wheel.

While he was doing this, the stern slipped some more and from the sound he knew that Sheila had given more to the engines. He glanced back over his shoulder and saw the boat going down the current with a sideway tack on it almost like some horses he had ridden which always tried to move with a thrust on one side. This was all new to him and he wasn't sure that he liked it, but after he had brought in the lines he went up to her and watched how Sheila used the wheel. Her body was tautly hunched and the knuckles showed white under stretched skin.

The rocks were around them, it seemed to him, very suddenly. One moment the *Nisba* was straining with a heavy, beating shudder but going steadily enough along the wide road of the current, and then the boat made a big leap so that he saw the deck lift and heard the hull slap down with a hard splash. He saw the bow slew round very quickly but he couldn't decide how much of this was Sheila's steering and how much the surging backwash of the current from against the concealed rock bar. They were head on to the land, now, and round the head, so that he could see the small white beach set between two bushy, steep bluffs. The boat was going in, making fast, short, smooth rushes or pitching savagely on the jabbing crests of the waves. Once or twice they seemed to hang powerless for a second before being slung towards the rocks and Sheila would twist on the wheel and open wide on the throttle and the *Nisba* would crawl shuddering to an area where it could make one of its smooth rushes downcurrent. Jackson was stretched out in the bows looking ahead into the water, and once he yelled back: "Lay her off one point on de starboard."

The water looked hard, like green bottle glass; and the froth of air bubbles beneath the surface made it pale and bright. When the rocks showed out of the water it was as if they had come up from the depths with a clearing rush to leap at the sky.

He could see the land getting nearer now and they were in a big patch of almost smooth water, with the rocks through which they had come, behind them, and bad water ahead and around them.

Sheila cut down the engines till they were ticking over and kept the boat almost stationary, broadside on to the land, by racing the power against the drift of the sea. Her fingers looked pale and stiff and there were runnels of sweat down her face and side.

She kept the boat like this for two minutes, then she nodded to Carl and opened up the engines again and brought the *Nisba* round in a tight circle and headed out to sea. They crossed the current edge in a wild plunge that lifted the propeller out of the water to send a thudding, violent jar through the boat. When they were well on to the easy heave of the open sea, Jackson came back to the wheel house.

"You satisfy now, Missis?" he asked grimly as he took the wheel.

"Go on," she told him. "One day you'll be thankful if we ever have to run for it and need shelter in a hurry."

"So you say," he replied, refusing to be drawn into good humour.

"All right," she said, "sulk if you want to." She turned and began to walk to the stern. She stopped and looked back at the man whose great hands almost hid the wheel.

"How did she handle?" she asked him. "Did it feel good?"

He looked back at her, aloof with disapproval.

"She don't handle bad," he started to say coldly, and then his face slowly cracked in a wide smile. "Lawd King, she handle sweet, you see, missis. What a boat dis is. An' you handle her nice, you see. You handle her good, fe' true." He was grinning now and he gave the bulkhead a slap which seemed to shake the boat almost as much as the propeller had done when it raced clear of the water.

Carl went back to the stern and sat, enjoying the fresh afternoon afternoon breeze that had started quickly, as it did whenever it was very hot on the land. The waves were faster, now, and higher than when they had set out, and the *Nisba* lifted to them, as they went fast along her sides, with a long gliding swoop. She was a fine boat, all right.

They had turned north-east to go back to Tolliver in a wide circle, and now as he watched Sheila coming towards him he had to screw his eyes against the sun and her half naked body seemed bright, almost luminous, with the strong light behind it.

She sat in the chair opposite him and took the band from her hair and fluffed it out and then began to plait it into two braids. He realized that she was doing this for the same reason that he and Jackson were smoking, as a relief from the tension.

"Nice work," he said softly.

"Thank you," she said. Her voice was a little flat and limp. "You couldn't have enjoyed it, though. I mean, you didn't know what the boat could do, or how good I was. Jackson was different. He was nervous because he wasn't steering. But I'd have been the same way if he'd been steering, although we are both just about the same now. No, that isn't true; he's much better than I am, still. He's taught me nearly everything I know about this."

"He's taught you well, then," Carl told her.

30

They got back to Tolliver about six o'clock, coming up the channel on a broad bright golden spread of light.

Coming back they had trolled again and had better luck. Carl had taken four good kingfish and she had taken two and a big bonita. It wasn't anything of a day as far as fishing went but it finished the afternoon nicely.

They went back to the house the way they had come. There had been three little boys from the property down by the jetty when they moored, and they were on ahead carrying the fish.

"How about Jackson?" Carl asked her as they were crossing the road to the gate in the fence. "Do you think he really swallowed that tale about exploring the water in case you ever needed to know it?"

"I'm not sure," Sheila said. "Perhaps not. I think he feels that I wanted to see how good I was. He probably thinks I'm crazy but he'll forgive that."

"Yes," he told her, opening the gate for her and smiling. "There's that. It's a good thing you're English and what would be crazy for a Cayunan is quite normal for you. You look cute with your hair like that." He reached up and tugged gently at one of the stout, short, thick braids. She gave a pleasant smile and hurried past him.

When they reached the house they saw Lloyd's green convertible parked in the driveway behind the Humber and they could see him in one of the chairs on the top verandah. He came to the rail and looked over. It was getting dusk and they couldn't distinguish his features very clearly.

"Hi!" he called out. "Had a good day?" He sounded affable and faintly excited.

"Hullo, Lloyd," Carl called back, looking up. "Yes, thanks. We had a nice day. You should have come with us."

"Can you come over to dinner on Thursday?" Lloyd asked him. "The Hamptons are coming. I saw them today."

He said "the Hamptons" with the carefully casual, uncertain air of a man at a party doing a magic trick he hasn't practised. His voice was sleek with satisfaction.

"Fine," Carl said. "Thanks. You dressing for it?"

"I think so," Lloyd said. "I think we'd better, don't you?"

"Perhaps," Carl told him. "Yes, perhaps it would be best."

"Ask Roy for me, will you?"

"Yes. I'll phone him tonight and tell him."

"Good. Aren't you coming up for a drink?"

"No, thanks," Carl said. "I have to hurry up and get back. I'm going out tonight."

"See you," Lloyd told him.

Sheila came down the drive with him to the glossy, huge car. He gave her his rod and got in.

"When will we know about it?" she asked him in a low voice.

"That's up to Roy," he said. "He said he'd phone through to me. I'll tell you and Summer as soon as he does."

"Good," she said tranquilly. "I hope it's soon. I'd like to see it over."

"I wish you'd never had to get into it."

"Don't be silly," she said. "I couldn't do anything else. Now could I?"

"No," he said. "I suppose not. You can't let a chap down when he's really stuck for help. Cheerio. See you soon."

"Good night. Thanks for a nice day."

He started the engine and locked hard on the wheel to turn the big Humber on the broad drive. As he drove out of the gate he could see mist on the mountains behind his home.

31

That evening, about six o'clock, Tiger Johnson went up the steps and through the front doors of Police Headquarters in Queenshaven. It was the first time in his life he had ever gone there of his own accord.

There were three constables in the main office when he entered. They were sitting at broad, table-like desks. A thickset, dark brown officer was writing at a square executive's desk at the end of the room, under the stationary electric fan.

Johnson walked past the three constables without looking at them, ignoring it when one of them half rose and said, "Hey!" He went straight up the room to where the squat, heavy-necked, thick-armed sergeant-major was writing. Standing up, you could see how small a man Tiger Johnson really was: small, made with almost doll-like neatness, and tightly packed so that what he had inside him seemed to make the hard smooth skin uncomfortable.

"I want fe' see de chief," he said flatly to the sergeant-major, and stood before the desk with that unbearable, overpowering arrogance which had begun, forty years ago, as a gesture of defence (because of his size), and had grown now to a degree, not of pride, but of complete, final contempt for the whole human race.

The sergeant-major looked up slowly from the form on which he was writing and stared with angry, thoughtful eyes at the sharply-cut, metallic face which was not so much cruel as negatively unmarked by any memory or hope of kindness and trust.

"Chief?" the sergeant-major said. "Chief? I don't know any chief live here."

His name was Flower. He had joined the force fifteen years before and had performed his work with an impartial, unimaginative ruthlessness and energy which had brought him to his present position and done much to increase the criminal population of the island.

"Chief?" he said again, with cold dislike thick in his voice. "What *chief* you t'ink stay here?"

Tiger Johnson breathed a heavy, deliberate sniff to show his boredom with this sarcasm. The three constables were not pretending to work now; their eyes were fixed watchfully on the two men. One of them reached behind him, without getting up or taking his eyes off Johnson and Flower, and took a baton in a leather case from a peg on the wall.

"I want see de chief upstairs," Tiger Johnson said with unmoved, infallible contempt.

The heavy-jowled face below him tightened, and the short neck seemed to grow shorter. Flower's eyes became little and hot.

"If you mean Commissioner Slade," he said carefully, "what mek you t'ink he would want to see a dirty little dry-foot crook like you?"

Tiger Johnson's slow smile had the near beauty of anything

pure and unadulterated, even if it was, as it was in this case, a pure snarl of contempt and unadulterated savagery. He rested one hand casually on Flower's desk and lounged against the front of it.

"I got business wid him," he said.

Flower looked pensively at the small, hard hand on his desk top. He reached out and picked up a heavy, cylindrical, ebony ruler from the inkstand. He held it with a rigid, eager tightness and tapped the end against his open palm with unconcealed anticipation.

"Tek your goddam hand off a my desk," he said. His voice was raw and ugly. "Tek it off before I bruk your fingers."

Tiger Johnson removed his hand and stared at Sergeant-major Flower, his eyes glittering with amusement.

"How 'bout my business, eh, sah?" he asked genially. "I can see de chief?"

Sergeant-major Flower drew a very long, deep breath which sounded painfully in the still room.

"You mad?" he asked softly.

"Who? Me?" Tiger Johnson said. "No. I not mad."

"Den if you not mad how you t'ink a brute like you can come in here an' ask fe' see Commissioner Slade like you was Governor of de island?"

"Is business me want see him 'bout," Tiger explained patiently. He was enjoying this and he hoped that Flower would get angrier.

"What business?" Flower asked him, bringing the words out carefully and slowly. "If you have business tell me an' I will tell Commissioner."

"Dis is for de chief," Tiger Johnson said and smiled again, a slow, carefully executed sneer. "Dis is not for you."

He had no intention of telling Flower what he had come here to say: that he suspected Roy McKenzie of sheltering a wanted alien.

All morning, after Scissors Clark had left him, he had thought at intervals about Roy McKenzie and the third, unaccounted for person whom Roy had met at the Barricades.

It had not worried him much, because he almost never worried about anything; but it had made him cautious and wary. During the afternoon he had heard, like most people in Queenshaven, that Henri Etienne was in hiding or in suspected flight to any one of half a dozen places in the Caribbean.

How he had connected Roy with this, Tiger Johnson could not have told anyone clearly. It was not, with him, a conscious process, but rather an habitual suspicion and system of relating events that had ensured his survival long after he should have been in prison, considering the things he did and encouraged.

It would have ended there, as far as Tiger Johnson was concerned, if it had not been for the march that Roy had abandoned. To Tiger the march itself had meant nothing, or very little. As a gesture, though, and a threat against the class and colour he hated, and as a display of his own strength it had meant a great deal. When Roy and Bob Daniel had come to him and called it off, they had only confirmed his instinctive, customary belief in himself and the unrelaxed mistrust of others which were the things he moved by and used to protect his integrity. The sense of betrayal had come later, today, when that savagely wary intuition related what he had heard and seen into the correct pattern.

So that now he stood here, in the last place in Queenshaven that anyone would have expected to see him stand freely, waiting to commit his share of that ageless, universal treason to which every man contributes at least once in his lifetime, quite aware of the importance his news would have but unwilling to tell it to any but the highest of his enemies; knowing that if he kept it he could barter a reward before talking, but that if he so much as half-hinted to Flower what he suspected and knew, any chance of a cash return on his secret would be gone and that they would almost certainly hold him on suspicion until he told the rest. And even had there been no chance of money in it for him, he still would not have told it to Flower. Nor to any other policeman; but only to Hector Slade, and to his face; for the subtle and delicious satisfaction of standing in Slade's office as a requested visitor, the sole possessor of whatever crumbs of information he might, contemptuously, choose to offer and without whom, in this thing, they were powerless.

"No," he said, now, staring at Flower and feeling laughter crawl sweetly inside him. "I can't tell you. Me want see de chief."

"Listen," Flower said heavily. His face was grey beneath the rich, dark brown skin and the muscles of his jaw were like stones packed tightly in a bag. "Listen good to me, Johnson. If you come here fe' play games, me can play too. You hear? If you have somet'ing to say, mek your statement to me an' I will tek it to de proper aut'ority. What is it you want say?"

"Nuttin'," Tiger Johnson said. "Nuttin'. Is private business me have wid de chief... Conference," he added as if explaining something patiently to a very stupid child, showing his beautiful, red-shadowed teeth in a grin of relish.

"You want to walk out of here?" Flower asked him. The voice was grotesquely calm issuing from his stiffly moved lips.

"Hi, yes, sah," Tiger Johnson said. "Of course me want walk out of here an' go back to me yard."

"Den you better go now," Sergeant-major Flower told him seriously. "Go on, Johnson. You better get out now."

Tiger Johnson looked at him, calculating if he should chance another twist of provocation. He decided not. He made this decision uninfluenced by any fear, but simply as something that it would be foolish and profitless to risk.

Wordlessly he turned and went back past the cold-eyed police constables, walking briskly in that studied, bright arrogance without which he would have felt, and looked, nakedly incompetent and vulnerable.

When he was halfway to the door, his fantastic, matted bush of hair glinting under the harsh, yellow electric light, Flower called out softly: "Johnson!"

Tiger Johnson turned and saw Flower's face, rigid and shiny and sick-looking.

"Yes, sah," he said.

"You goin' to mek a mistake one day, Johnson," Flower told him with a brooding, morosely happy conviction.

"Yes, sah?"

"We goin' to hold you dat day, eh, Johnson? Dem is goin' to have you down at Lord Street Jail."

"Yes, sah?"

"I am goin' to be dere, too, Johnson. If I have to walk a hundred mile on macca thorn, I am goin' to be dere dat day. You know what I mean?"

"Yes, boss," Johnson said cheerfully. "I will look out fe' you."

He went on out, walking steadily, and disappeared through the door. They watched him go.

"Dat is a bad man," one of the constables, the one who had reached for his baton, said. "Dat is a bad, proud man."

"Cho," Flower said. He was feeling better now that Johnson was no longer in the room. "Proud. What is proud? Goat is proud. Cat is proud. Every dawg have pride. Proud don't mean a damn t'ing. De day we hold him down at Lord Street Jail, you come down, too. You will see how much proud is worth dat day."

He tapped the cylindrical, ebony ruler lightly, slowly and meticulously against the edge of his desk; then he carefully wiped his damp face and bent over the form he had been filling when Tiger Johnson came in.

Tiger Johnson went back to his house in the Jungle. He was neither surprised nor disappointed not to have seen Commissioner Hector Slade. He had hardly expected he would, the first time. He would go back tomorrow, and if necessary, the day after. If he went two or three times he knew Hector Slade would want to see him.

Sergeant-major Flower went off duty at seven o'clock. He got on his bicycle and rode hard and quickly to the neat little house out on Harbour Road where his wife was having one of her bad spells of rheumatic fever. When he got in he sponged her down with bay rum and remade her bed and tried to make her easy. Then he ate his supper.

After supper he switched on the green-shaded lamp beside the bed and read to her. She was a devout Catholic (although he was not) and when she was like this she took great comfort from the lives of the gentler, more comprehensible saints. He had a good voice and read aloud very well. Listening to him, and with the faint, regular crash of the little harbour waves sounding across the road and into the room, she very soon fell asleep.

32

It was quite dark when Carl got back to the Pen from Tolliver. As the car hummed deeply up the driveway, the headlights moving whitely on the hedges and the trees, he could smell the mist coming down from the mountain and he knew that by midnight it would be as far down as this, drifting round the house and lying in heavy patches on the bottom pastures. It often happened like that when the day had been very hot and clear and the wind blew in from off the sea and cooled quickly against the high mountain wall.

He went in and bathed in the cold tank water and put on flannels and a blazer because the night was going to be cool. While he was waiting for his dinner, he mixed and drank two glasses of rum and water.

When he was eating his fruit, at the end of dinner, he heard the telephone ring in the drawing-room; it was no surprise when Elvira came back from answering it and said, "Mass' Roy want fe' speak to you, sah. Him is calling trunk from Queenshaven."

He went into the drawing-room and picked up the telephone.

"Hullo, Roy," he said.

"Hullo." Roy's voice was imperfect and muffled across the sixty miles of wire, but distinct enough and very cheerful. "How are things?"

"Fine. Went out fishing today. Did you get back all right?"

"Sure. I made good time. Doing anything tomorrow afternoon?"

"No. Why?"

"I thought I'd take the afternoon off and see you and Sheila."

"Splendid. What time will you be over?"

"Oh, afternoon sometime. Look for me when you see me."

"Right. I'll be here."

He said goodbye and put the telephone back on the rest.

Well, he thought as he went back to the dining-room, here it is, then. It's tomorrow. Thank Christ. I wish it was tonight. It can't be over soon enough to suit me.

He finished his dinner and took his coffee into the drawing room. He sat by the telephone again and took it off the rest.

"Castleville two-six please," he said to the operator; then, "Hullo, Tolliver? Oh, hullo, Lloyd. Yes, Carl. Ask Sheila to come to the phone a minute, will you? ... Hullo, Sheila? How are you? Good. Look, can you and Lloyd come up for tennis tomorrow? Roy's coming over for the afternoon and I thought you'd like to come up."

"Yes, that would be nice," she said evenly. He was listening hard for how she would sound. "Tomorrow afternoon?"

"Yes," he said. "That's right. Tomorrow. O.K.? Fine. See you then."

So that's how it's done, he thought. Two telephone calls and a little careful arranging beforehand.

He got to Summer's place just before the men went out for the night's fishing. They were down at the beach, Mrs. Summer said, and he walked there in the dark, first over the crackling sun-dried coconut fronds, and then through the fine, yielding sand to where the men were preparing the beached boats by the light of two yellow kerosene flares.

Besides Jeffrey Summer and George, he could see the other three grown-up sons: the squat, long-armed, stupid one called Edward, the nineteen-year old Reuben, and the slim, quick-moving one, Aaron, who liked to catch sharks and who had already in his twenty-three years killed nearly forty. There was also the man that Summer hired to help with the second boat.

Carl greeted them as he came into the light and they could recognize him. He leaned against the gunwale of one of the boats and talked casually as they finished stowing the gear.

His presence needed no explaining to the man Summer employed. This sort of visit was a thing he often did with his friends up and down the coast and inland. And when his friends were of Summer's class and occupation, he could do it without any sense of patronising or embarrassment on either side. He had been doing it for a long time: from those days, in fact, when as a child he had spent nearly as many nights, and eaten nearly as many meals, in a score of widely scattered homes all over the parish, as he had done at his father's house. So that sometimes for two or three days he wouldn't sleep in his own bed, and would show up one evening as casually as he had left the Pen, and his father would say, unworriedly, "Hi! Where have you been?" knowing that it would have been impossible in the parish of All Souls, Cayuna, for a Brandt child to suffer a moment's danger without the news spreading faster than the telegraph or a hundred people hurrying to save him.

He helped them push the boats down the damp smooth beach, stopping short of the water each time because of his shoes. When the two boats were launched, Summer came back across the beach to him.

"You have some news fe' me, Mr. Brandt?" he asked quietly.

"It's tomorrow night. Mr. McKenzie phoned me about an hour ago."

"Good, sir. We'll be dere half-past nine to ten. What about de oder t'ing? Missis Pearce gwine fe' help us?"

"Yes. She'll meet you about a mile and a quarter out as we arranged. You know, where it's calmer."

"Yes, I know. It's good we have her."

"We were there today," Carl told him. "We went out fishing and she took the *Nisba* in to see what it was like."

"Dat was good. You catch any fish, sir?"

"A few king and a bonita."

"Nice, sir. What you t'ink of de water off a de head?"

"It looks bad. For Christ's sake, be careful, Summer."

"Cho! You don't worry, Mr. Brandt. It will be all right, you hear? I glad you is in dis. It will go good."

He put out his flat, very hard hand and Carl took it; he could just make out, in the faintly phosphorescent glow, the man's narrow, big-lipped face and the thin, blade-like curve of the nose.

"See you tomorrow," he said. "Good luck tonight."

"T'ank you, Mr. Brandt. I see you tomorrow, sir."

Carl watched him go down to the boats and stayed while they pulled steadily out to sea. When he could no longer see the white flash of oar froth on the shadowed water under the starlit sky he went back to his car.

He drove further east for about two miles, to a crossroads where the road from a valley came down to the coast: there was a Chinese shop there, and he bought five tins of sardines, a pound of Dutch cheese, two long loaves, some chocolate and a bottle of Mount Ida. He didn't want to buy any nearer to Tolliver or his own place than this, but he had reckoned that Etienne must be nearing the end of the food they had bought on Saturday.

Then he turned and drove back into the hills and spent the evening five miles from the Pen, drinking with one of his neighbours, Captain Stacey, who had caught polio late in life and still managed his property better from a wheelchair than most men could on their two feet.

33

It was midnight when he put the Humber into the garage. The mist had come down from the peaks. It was grey and damp, thinly veiling the house and luminously opaque on the fields in the darkness. It had a vaguely exciting smell, which stirred him with the same obscure restlessness as the smell of the hot, tar road.

He went into the house, carrying the supplies he had bought. In his room, he took off his good clothes and put on the ones he had worn that day, taking them from the tall laundry hamper. He put the food and rum into his old web sidepack and went quietly out of the house.

Out in the long grass it was wet with the mist: before he had gone very far his trousers were clinging to his legs from knee to ankle, and he could hear his feet squelch in their sandals as he went fast to the fence at the top of the pasture.

Up on the path the mist was really thick, and went past him lazily, going down to increase what was already on the fields. It was condensing on the trees and dripping steadily from the leaf tips on to the mould. The insect sounds from the forest came to him muffled and remote and there was a bitter smoky scent, clean and cold in his nostrils. When he passed from the noise of the stream it was like crossing a barrier to some lost, sleeping world. And by the time he reached the slide it was hard to remember, in this grey, clinging silence, what it was like outside. He could imagine time lying still here, or dripping slowly like the water from the leaves. He couldn't see the trees but could sense them, solid, close packed, growing and decaying and always growing in this silent, drifting water from the old sea. Life, here, belonged to the trees; and he was a small moving part of their life, walking among what he would one day nourish.

Below the slide lip, on the floor of the valley, the mist was dense and still, and he could see nothing of the shelter. He went down the slope slowly and carefully and when his legs began to move in the helplessly bounding, fast rush near the bottom, he put his hand up, palm and forearm rigidly straight and held a little before him. He hoped he had calculated right and that he wouldn't finish up in the pile of fallen earth or strike the corner of the hut. Then he saw the wall close before him, suddenly appearing, and his hand hit the wet boards soggily and his body hurled against the stiff spring he had made of his muscles.

Going along the wall to the door, he could feel the ground damp and greasy with surface moisture beneath his wet sandals.

It was dark inside the hut and he stood in the doorway trying to hear if Etienne was there. He couldn't hear anything.

"It's all right," he said. "It's me. Brandt."

A dim, livid red glow lit the hut and he saw Etienne on the table, sitting up in his blankets and holding a big torch which had red tissue paper covering the glass.

"Good evening, Mr. Brandt," Etienne said. "I thought it was you but I wished to be sure. I have been hoping you would come up tonight. I did not count on it, but I hoped you would."

His voice sounded husky, and by the torchlight Carl could see the shelter was full of thin fog. The little room was very cold and smelt dankly of wet, mouldering wood.

"How are you?" Carl said. He walked over to the bed and shook hands because he knew Etienne was French and would feel uncomfortable if the formality was neglected.

"Well." Etienne smiled up at him and passed his fingers through the little curls of his coarse hair, the way a usually kempt man who is particular about his appearance tries to keep neat in rough circumstances. "I am very well, Mr. Brandt. But cold. I have been hibernating since afternoon."

"Lord, yes," Carl said, looking at the fingers of mist drifting past the torch. "This is bad. It's no place to lie low with only cold food. It won't be for much longer, though. You're leaving tomorrow. Roy telephoned tonight"

Etienne sat up quite straight at this.

"Good," he said. "I am glad to hear that. In these things every hour spent like this accumulates danger in arithmetical progression. It does not take long for the one person who should not to suspect something."

"I think it's gone well up to now," Carl told him. "I think we're going to get away with it. Look, I've brought you some fresh food and another bottle of rum."

He put the web pack beside Etienne. He could see the oilskin bundle and the gunny sack on the far side of the broad table, the bundle not tied but flapped open neatly so that to fold over the flaps and knot the rope would have been the work of a second.

"Thank you." Etienne said. "I still have some food and a little rum left. What did you bring?"

"Some sardines and cheese and some pickled onions. Fresh bread, too, and a little butter. O.K.?"

"O.K.? It sounds like a feast for kings. Sausages are very good but I am relieved to know that the good earth produces something else."

He grinned widely at Carl, the skin around his eyes crinkling to make slits of the eyes themselves, the flesh on the broad cheeks swelling into big, gleaming knobs.

"Have something now," Carl urged him. "The sardines will be good for you. They'll get some oil between you and this bloody cold."

When he smiles like that, he thought then, as he looked at Etienne's delighted face, and his skin stretches tight, that scar on his face looks just like the top of a half-open rose bud. It must have been a hell of a wound. Bullet probably. Only a heavy bullet could leave a mark like that. Or the sharp end of a pick axe.

"Will you join me, Mr. Brandt?" Etienne asked. He had tucked his legs under him at his end of the table and put a blanket round his shoulders. Now he was taking a stubby, dull, army knife and fork set from his bundle.

"No, thanks," Carl told him. "I'm really not hungry. You go ahead and eat. Don't talk. We can talk afterwards. Just eat up."

He got on to the table, sitting near the edge so that the foot of his long left leg was on the floor and the other foot swung free. The air in the shelter was very chill, striking through his wet sandals and trousers.

"Here, Mr. Brandt. Please take this," Etienne said, leaning forward and giving a folded blanket to Carl. "Please put that around your shoulders or you will be getting sick. After that walk you have just taken it is not good to sit uncovered in this damp."

"Thanks," Carl said. He swung the blanket cape fashion over his shoulders and dragged it shut in front of him. It felt coarse and bristly like all the service blankets he had known, but it was warm enough.

"Go on," he told Etienne. "Eat something."

"I am. I am," Etienne said. "Or rather, I will." He was looking inside Carl's web pack with a pleased, hungry expression. "Will you mix us two drinks, please?" he asked. "The rum is on the floor beside you, by the table leg. And there is some water in a beer bottle."

He stopped taking the food out to hand Carl a small enamel mug and the flat, leather-covered, chromium top from a hip flask, both of which he picked up from the shadow of the bundle.

Carl bent down and felt for the bottles. There was about a third of the rum left. He mixed a strong one in the mug for Etienne and gave it to him. Then he mixed one for himself in the flask top.

"*A votre santé,*" Etienne said raising the mug. It was the first French Carl had heard him use since Saturday night on the beach.

"*A la vôtre,*" he replied, and smiled.

He watched, without speaking, as Etienne ate eagerly and intently, forking the sardines from the tin and the onions from the bottle, and taking large, appreciative bites from a thickly buttered chunk of bread. When he had finished the sardines, Etienne broke off another, smaller piece of the long white Chinese bread, and cut it down the middle and spread butter on it. He unwrapped the cheese and sliced a long, heavy wedge from it and put this between the bread. Then he put the bread and cheese down carefully beside him, wiped the knife and fork on a dirty handkerchief, wrapped the cheese and the butter in their papers, screwed the lid of the pickle jar tight, and stowed these, along with the food in Carl's pack, neatly and expertly into his own bundle. He finished his drink in one swallow, picked up the bread and cheese, and handed the mug briskly to Carl as he bit into the big sandwich. Carl took the mug. His own drink was nearly finished and he drained the flask top as Etienne had drained the mug, feeling the warm sharp bite of the liquid catch pleasantly in his throat. He mixed another drink for Etienne, and putting down the flask top he went outside to the water butt to fill the beer bottle. The water was numbingly cold on his hand he dipped in the bottle.

Etienne had nearly finished eating when he got back inside; and while he poured himself another drink, Carl watched him chew steadily and appreciatively on the last of the sandwich.

"Ah," Etienne said as he swallowed his last mouthful, "that was good. I'll remember that. These are the sort of meals a man remembers better than any other sort."

"I know what you mean," said Carl, who could recall many such meals."

He gave Etienne a cigarette and put one in his own mouth. Etienne leaned forward to take the light then settled back, drawing the blanket tighter about him with his free hand. Partially hidden in the folds the hand looked small and paw-like.

With a head like that, Carl said to himself, he ought to have a heavier body. You don't notice it until he is sitting all crouched and tucked in like he is now in that bloody blanket.

"Now," Etienne said. "What about tomorrow? What do I have to know and what do I have to do?"

"You don't have to do anything," Carl said to him. "You just sit here and Roy or I will come down for you about eight o'clock. We'll take you down to the house and from there down to the coast. From the coast you'll go out to the ship."

"I understand," Etienne said. "Yes. That sounds very good. I think we should succeed."

His face had become calm and bland again. He looked at Carl obliquely from under his lowered brows, then he looked into the mug in his hand.

"Have you read the papers today, Mr. Brandt?" he asked. "Or listened to the radio?"

"Sure," Carl told him. "I read the *Gazette* this morning. I should have thought to bring it up for you. I listened to the news tonight, too. Sorry about the papers."

"That is all right. I only wanted to know if there was any fresh news from my country?" His voice was dry and had the toneless calm of carefully held anxiety.

"No," Carl said gently. "There was nothing that you don't know already. There was hardly anything about it in fact. Just a few lines to say that order had been restored and that things would soon be back to normal."

"Thank you. I had not expected anything else."

"I'm sorry," Carl said. "And I'm sorry for what I said yesterday about you and your friends in St. Pierre."

Etienne gave him a sharp, questioning glance from the narrow, slanted eyes. Then he shivered and swung his legs over the edge of the table, still clutching the blanket round him. He heaved himself off the table and stamped on the damp, firm earth of the floor. Two little plumes of moisture fluttered from his nostrils when he breathed into the mist-filled air of the hut. He walked up and down slowly for a minute and came back to stand before Carl.

"If any of my friends manage to come here," he asked quietly, "would you help them as you've helped me?"

"I suppose so," Carl said. "If I've helped you I'd have to help them if I could. Are they likely to come here? I thought you were the only one who could manage it?"

"I don't know, Mr. Brandt. Some of them might be fortunate and escape. But it will be difficult now. I wanted to ask you, though."

"Don't worry about them," Carl told him still speaking in the gentle, reassuring tone he had learnt to use speaking to troubled nervous beasts.

Etienne gave him a long, probing stare which made him uncomfortable. He was glad when the man scrambled up on the table again and sat as he had before, legs folded, in the tent of his blanket. He watched as Etienne took the fresh bottle of Mount Ida from the bundle, broke the sealed screw cap, and poured two long shots into the flask top and into the mug.

"Tell me, Mr. Brandt," he asked suddenly, "have you ever a your life refused to help anybody who needed your help?"

"Jesus!" Carl said, "I suppose so. Nobody helps everyone he should. Not every time, I mean. Why?"

"I think you have refused help to others less than most. Less, perhaps, than almost any man I have met. You have a quality most of us learn slowly, Mr. Brandt. No, not a quality. A knowledge. You were either born with it or learnt it early. It is very unusual and I envy you for having it."

What the hell is he getting at now? Carl asked himself.

"There's nothing special about me," he said uncomfortably. He only spoke because it was easier than leaving Etienne's last statement to hang between them. "I don't have anything special."

"No," Etienne said smiling almost imperceptibly. "I did not say you had anything special. All men could have what you possess, but not many realize it."

"If you say so," Carl said shortly. "I haven't thought about it."

Etienne laughed softly. He raised his head and looked shrewdly and confidently at the younger man.

"Do not be offended," he said evenly. "And please do not be embarrassed. I am old enough to have earned a right to say this. I only learnt very painfully what you know. That is why I am interested."

Looking at him curiously, Carl had a sharp, undeniable awareness, deeper than anything he could have thought, that whatever conclusion this man had come to in life, whatever conduct of life he, Carl, could never approve or accept or condone, it had been come by passionately and bravely. It was something about him that Carl could understand.

"And how did you learn this... whatever it is?"

Etienne smiled very faintly. He touched the puckered bud of the scar on his cheek with tender, almost hesitating fingers.

"This helped," he said. "You were in the war, were you not?"

"Yes," Carl told him. "Roy and me went in together."

'Were you wounded?"

"Yes."

"Was Roy?" "No. He got through all right."

'Were you hit badly?" Etienne asked. "Where were you hit?"

"Arm and shoulder," Carl said, "and across the top of the chest here. It was a burst and I caught the fringe of it."

"How did you feel?" The face opposite Carl was gravely intent; and the eyes had a curious, steady flicker.

"Hell!" Carl told him. "It's difficult to say. I can't remember much about it, except that it seemed more violent than I had imagined it would be. You know: it felt tremendously heavy."

"Yes, I know. But did you lose consciousness immediately?"

"No."

"Then how did you feel? In yourself. Along with the physical shock of it?"

"It was so sudden," Carl told him. He was trying to recall what it had been like that morning: the appalling sudden violence on his body, like blows from a huge hammer: the crowded panel growing dim and unreal; the sheer disbelief in his mind as he fell against Matthews. "I suppose I couldn't believe it had happened. In a way I felt that I ought to be able to stop it."

"That is it," Etienne said. "You are quite right. That is what I mean. When I got this," he touched the scar on his cheek, "I felt like that. I wanted to protest against an outrage."

"How did you get it?" Carl asked, touching his own cheek on the place where Etienne was scarred. And you can have it, he thought. I wouldn't have that one for anything.

"It was a revolution," Etienne said. He shrugged wryly. "My first revolution. We were changing presidents. There was not much to choose between them, but one was a little better for our country than the other. I was fighting for the who was not so good. In the last engagement I was hit face by a ·38. It went in here, almost cut my tongue in two, and lodged in the jawbone.

"We were fighting outside the town in a field; and I lay trying to become unconscious. But I could not. I tried very hard, but I kept quite awake, feeling what I was feeling and listening to what was left of the battle. After a little, along with the pain and belonging to it, if you understand me, I felt as if the whole world, not only the man who had fired the shot, but the whole world, all of life, men, beasts, the grass I was clutching, even my mother, had joined in hideous, evil unanimity to throw a pan of boiling water in my face. I was not very clear in my head at that point, you understand. But I was clear about this: that there had been a rejection of one man, me, by others; a rejection for which I could find no excuse or explanation; a rejection that was totally meaningless and totally wrong. It was then that I suddenly knew all men are, from the first to the last, indissolubly one. I knew that just as I did finally lose consciousness. And I knew it when I woke. And I have known it since. It is a belief I could not have laid aside afterwards even had I wanted to."

He sipped his drink and looked steadily Carl, his flat, smooth face composed yet intent. Showing above the against the grey air of the hut, his face in the lurid glow from the torch had a hard yet spectral brightness, as if it had been expertly stained in a faint wash of blood.

He's like a black Mongolian, Carl thought, studying the face before him. Put a fur cap on him, and he would be after one of those Tartars Roy and I saw that time in Peking after the war. Except that he's a real black. If he has any white in him, it must be pretty far back.

Then Carl suddenly spoke. "It seems very sad," he said, "that a man who believes as you do, who feels that way about people, should have done the things you have done."

"What things, Mr. Brandt?"

"You know," Carl said calmly and definitely. "The things that happened in St. Pierre when you took over. The things you forced people to do, the people you had removed, the lies you put out for people to swallow."

"What about the other things, Mr. Brandt? The work we did. Solid practical work such as you could appreciate. The faith we gave to nearly a million people. Any words I have could never tell you what it is like."

"Maybe," Carl said. "But you chose the wrong way to do it. The other things, the force and the lies and the killing, that is going to spoil it. They're going to make it worse than what you replaced. You take them into whatever you do and they make it bad. You ought to have chosen a slower way. It would have been more difficult but it would have lasted longer."

"And yet you have used force, Mr. Brandt. You have killed. You have even used lies. Have you not?"

"Yes. That was in a war. We had to."

"How did you feel about it, then?"

"I didn't like it. But you have to do it if you want to win."

"We want to win a war, too, Mr. Brandt. When we do the things you say we have done, we don't like them; but we do them of necessity. It is part of a battle in which we are not even volunteers but conscripts."

"What battle is that?" Carl asked with an irony he did not trouble to hide, "Your class war? You think that is a way to get what you want for people?"

"No, Mr. Brandt," Etienne was speaking with serene, utter confidence. "Not the class war. That is only one part of it. I am speaking of the real battle the human race has been fighting since it began."

"And you'll never win it your way," Carl said. "If you keep on trying to do it your way, the whole world will go rotten with all the hatred and fear you breed. If people are to become what you hope – and I'm not sure they ever can – then you'll have to find another way."

He looked at his watch, got from the table, stamped his wet sandals on the earth and stretched. When he reached his arms above his head, the hands nearly touched the roof. He gave a half malicious smile at Etienne.

"It's a good thing for you, isn't it," he said, "that I don't see things the way you do? If I did, I'd have turned you in on Saturday night."

Etienne laughed. When he threw back his head and the wide face tilted its flat planes he looked more like a Tartar than ever.

"You are quite right, Mr. Brandt. I am very lucky. I must have led a good life to deserve such luck."

"I'm off now," Carl said, smiling and putting out his hand.

"You've got a clear picture of what we're doing about tomorrow? There is nothing else you want to know?"

"No. I will wait and hope."

"That's right," Carl smiled again. "It's going to be O.K."

They both went from the hut and stood side by side for a moment. Then Carl climbed the slide and loped down the path swiftly, keeping well into the bank because of the fog.

34

A few minutes after twelve on Tuesday afternoon, when the clerk and the typists had gone or were about to go for lunch, Linda Hu-Sen came into Roy McKenzie's office. He had a file of papers in his hands and he was standing by the desk, with the brief case opened on it before him. Now, as she came in, he looked at the top paper of the file and put it into the briefcase.

"Hullo," he said. "I'll be leaving in a minute. I won't be back this afternoon. I'll go straight over as soon as I've had lunch."

"So early? I thought you hadn't planned to leave till later?"

She looked at him with faint surprise.

"Yes, I know," he said. "But I thought just a while ago that it might be safer to go over and do something in Castleville. Business, I mean. I thought I'd see Harry Broome and then go up to Carl."

"Broome? You don't have to see him for another fortnight. I made your appointment with him for then."

"It won't do any harm to see him now," he told her. "And I really ought to have some good reason for being over there. Just in case. Don't you think so?"

She nodded so that the square-cut sleek, frame of her hair held a moving sheen of blue-black tints.

"Yes. You're right," she said. "Do you have everything you want for Broome?"

"Sure." He smiled fondly at her as he turned the papers in the file and took out a document of typewritten pages clipped together. "You had it all here. Get me Halsbury from the bookcase, though – you know the right volume; and I'd better have Anson. I may want to quote a few cases."

"Do you think he'll win?"

"He's got a good chance. I'm not sure yet. If he's telling me the truth, he should. Thanks."

He took the books from her and placed them flat in the front compartment of the briefcase, then he brought the flap over and clicked the solid springlock shut. He took off his linen jacket and his tie, hung them over the chair, and went to the back of his office. There was a little room, hardly bigger than a cupboard, let off here, containing a lavatory and wash basin. Linda followed and leaned against the jamb of the open door, watching him as he washed his face and hands.

"Where are you having lunch?" she asked.

"Up at the club," he said, his voice muffled behind the towel. He finished drying his face and looked at himself in the little mirror above the basin and passed his hand over his long, heavy jaw.

"Do I need a shave, you think?"

"Yes," she said. "If you're going to see Broome, you'd better shave."

He took the brush and safety razor he always kept here from the little white-painted medicine cabinet.

"I thought it would look more innocuous," he explained as he turned the tap and ran water over the brush, "if I lunched up at the club, had a couple of drinks afterwards and then went over to the coast. Probably not necessary; but I want everything to look just like any other day."

Linda looked closely at him as he began to draw the razor over his lathered chin.

"How are you feeling?" she asked casually. She did not realize it, but she had leaned forward a little and tensed as she said this.

He did not answer at once as he carefully drew the razor up his throat, then he said, "I feel all right."

It was a truthful but not an exact answer. What he was really feeling would have been harder to tell her.

Since this morning, when he had woken early, there had been a tight sensitivity on his skin and in his stomach. It was not uncomfortable or even unpleasant, but it was quite definite; as if his muscles and nerves had swollen imperceptibly during the night and stretched their coverings slightly. It made him feel oddly, lightly restless. Sitting down, he had wanted to shift his position often; and it had been difficult to find the normal slope and shape of his letters when he wrote. His brain was clear and very active, but he had found it hard to concentrate on his work. Like a flywheel he had thought at one moment during the morning, like a flywheel going round under full power but in free gear, with nothing to bite on.

"Yes," he said turning to her as he wiped the scraped lather from his cheeks and chin. "I feel O.K."

She smiled at him. She knew exactly what state he was in; she had learnt to recognize it very early in those days when they had been lovers and had always disliked it for the debt she knew it would claim from his body later on. But now she was happy to hear him talk as he was doing. She hoped that talking like this, along with two or three drinks, would slacken the tight, high pitch of his nerves.

"That's good," she said, shaking her round, sleek head.

"It's Carl," he said coming out of the washroom and picking up his tie. "Carl and Jeffrey Summer and Sheila Pearce. If anybody can get Henri away, they can. I'm just going along for the ride."

She had been rinsing the razor and brush as he spoke, and when he came to the door, dragging on his jacket, she cocked her head inquiringly; her thick straight hair had a deep, gun-metal glint in the soft light of the washroom.

"Sheila Pearce is like that, too?" she asked. "You didn't say much about her yesterday. Only that she'd given no trouble."

"Yes," he said in a judicious, neutral voice, "she's like that. She's just like Carl in that respect; and like Summer."

She said nothing, but she grinned at the towel as she dried the razor blade with her back to him. Roy, watching her closely, saw the slight swell of her cheeks as she smiled and he grinned too. He knew that she would lift the story of Sheila out of him with effortless, implacable curiosity. He didn't mind. He had intended to tell her, anyway, as soon as this was over; now he decided that he would give her the satisfaction of digging for it.

"Well," he said, turning from the door, going to his desk and picking up the briefcase. "That's it, then. I'll be off now."

She walked over and came close against him and rested one arm lightly around his shoulders. She smiled quickly and faintly.

"Be careful," she said.

"Of course," he replied, stroking his hand over the flat, burnished smoothness of her hair. "Don't worry any about me, for Christ's sake. Nothing can happen to me if anything goes wrong. It's Henri you have to worry about."

"I know," she said. "But just be careful all the same."

"I will," he said. "I'll be damned careful. See you tomorrow, eh, sweetheart?"

"You bet," she said, drawing him close to her in a hard quick hug and rubbing her cheek against his. "About eleven?"

"About that," he said, and turned to go down the stairs. She watched him steadily until, at the bend in the stairs, he turned and lifted his hand briefly. She smiled back and kissed her hand to him.

35

Driving fast, and with more conscious care than he normally used, he was well over halfway to the coast by middle afternoon. He had eaten at the Queenshaven Cricket Club where he was a member and where for years he had tried to climb from the Minor to the Senior Eleven. One year, before he became really busy, he had scored an average of fifty-seven point six in the Minor Cup matches and Morty Barrow, the Senior captain, had been keeping an eye on him. But he had fallen off the next season and he didn't think he would ever get enough practice in now to reach that standard again. He had shared a table with Morty Barrow at lunch, and afterwards he and Morty and an American who Morty was showing around, had drunk two rounds at the bar.

Now, he was driving on a flattish ten mile stretch beyond Mount Angeleno, but with a lower range to climb in front before reaching Castleville. Over in the east, behind Carl's place, that same range became suddenly steeper, forming the outskirts of the soaring conical peaks of Blue Range which filled the eastern tip of the island.

This stretch of the road was sugar country and he couldn't see over the tops of the high, tessellated, spear-like cane leaves as he pressed the Vauxhall along the gentle rise of the empty road. Two miles in from the road, among the tall canes, the long red column of a chimney soared against the profound, warm blue of the sky.

I'm glad it's June, he thought. Too early for the trades or the bad weather. I'm glad we're not taking him out when the sea might be really rough. Maybe I made it too difficult when I chose Columbus Head. Maybe I should have just taken him down to Jeffrey's place and shipped him out from the beach there. Or we could have chosen the bar beyond Castleville, or the mouth of Weeping Woman River. The water would have been easy there. Perhaps picking on Columbus Head was being too careful again. We'd look pretty silly if we got him this far and then drowned him.

The road had begun to climb a little as he thought. It was the first rise of the rolling country at the foot of the range. A car came over the crest in the road ahead and approached rapidly. As it came nearer he recognized the low, swept-back lines of Lloyd Pearce's green convertible. He put his arm out and waved, easing his foot on the accelerator and changing the gear as he did so. Lloyd was waving too.

The two cars came to a stop on opposite sides of the road and Roy got out of the Vauxhall and walked across the pleasantly hot, roughened macadam to where Lloyd was leaning over the door of his Cadillac. The convertible top was down and Lloyd was wearing a white, green-visored cap and heavy sunglasses with wash-leather blinds at their corners. He looked groomed and fresh and extremely handsome. Even when he smiled at Roy, the wrinkling of the skin had in it something chiselled and delicate.

"Hi," Roy said as they shook hands briefly. "What are you doing here? I'm just going over to your part of the world."

"Hullo, Roy." Lloyd raised his good-natured, richly brown face and smiled up at Roy. "Glad I met you. I thought we'd pass on the way. Carl told me you were coming over. He wanted us to play some tennis. I can't come, though. I'm off to Queenshaven on business."

"Business?" Roy said, remembering just in time not to sound surprised.

"Yes," Lloyd told him with casual, touching pride. "Part of our campaign for a cleaner Cayuna. Sheila suggested that I go over today and see Hewett about the advertisements. She has a new idea. She thought I ought to discuss it with Hewett."

"Oh, yes," Roy said. "I remember. She got the idea Sunday night up at Carl's. She's quite right, of course. In these things it's always better to discuss it personally. Ideas get lost in the post."

He could see the big cylinder of stiffly rolled poster-sheets lying on the back seat of the open car.

"You got my message about dinner on Thursday?" Lloyd asked. "I told Carl to tell you."

"Yes. Thanks. I'd like to come."

"Good. About eight. You'll like the Hamptons. They're thinking of buying a house out here, you know; for the winter months. They say it's better than the south of France."

"That's nice," Roy told him. "You'll be able to see a lot of each other, then."

"Yes," Lloyd said. "They want me to help them choose a site."

His face gleamed lightly with happiness and fulfilment.

"Good," Roy told him. "You'll be able to find them something really nice. You know the coast pretty well."

He smiled very gently at the face below him.

"Well," he said, "I must be getting on now. I have to be in Castleville soon after three. When will you be coming back?"

"Oh, later tonight," Lloyd said. "I'll see a few people after I've given Hewett his stuff. See you Thursday."

The engine of the convertible started with a low, smooth roar and Roy stepped back and waved as it rolled into the road and away. Then he walked across the road and got into his own car.

Nice, he told himself. Very, very nice. Lloyd was a problem and he was worrying me. He might have got curious about her taking the boat out so late. He might even have wanted to go. We couldn't depend on his being out social climbing. That Sheila. What a girl. I can just see her making him feel that Tolliver would collapse if he didn't see to those posters himself.

Then, as he changed down to second to take the short, sharp hill that would bring him to the pass leading down to the coast and Castleville, he began to think of Lloyd, not as a problem who had been circumvented, but as the man he had deceived and intended to deceive again. It was an uncomfortable feeling; not guilty or fearful, but heavy. He felt as if he had taken on the responsibility of protection to the stupid, kind, useless man he had just left.

The air was suddenly bright, now, as he came down to the coast. He turned the Vauxhall east at the crossroads for the two mile drive to Castleville. West of here, about four miles away, was Columbus Head.

He left Castleville in the sticky, weighted heat towards the end of middle afternoon. He was pleased with the work he had done at Harry Broome's office and he was sure, now, that in the dispute Broome was having with the Government about a cancelled contract, the court would have to find for his client.

He did not take the turning that led up into the hills and to Carl's place, but went straight past it along the road which would bring him to Tolliver.

The sweetish, rich smell of copra was heavy in the air as he drove up from the gates; and when he stopped under the poinsettia tree in the driveway he could hear, coming through the trees, quick, ripping sounds as they drove the coconuts down on planted iron stakes and tore away the husks.

One of the maids, one whose name he didn't know, came down the stairs as he crossed the lower verandah. He realised she must have seen him from the upper windows.

"Good afternoon," he said. "Is Mrs. Pearce in?"

"Good afternoon, Mistah McKenzie. Missis in de mornin' room, sah."

"Is she busy?"

"She figurin', sah. You want me call her fe' you?"

"No, I'll just go along there."

He looked quickly at her to see whether he could catch anything which might tell him that she knew of what had happened at Brandt's Pen on Sunday. The pleasantly smiling face was completely unreadable, but he didn't think she was ignorant of those hours.

He went along the passage and tapped once at the door and went into the light, wide cream and gold room he had entered only twice before. Sheila was at the end of it, at a table beside the tall shelves of unread, Victorian books. She was wearing big, horn-rimmed glasses and bent above a large ledger. There were two other ledgers before her, with their wavy-patterned leaf edges showing towards him.

"Yes?" she said, not looking up; and then as he came into the room without speaking, she turned from what she was doing, saw him, and got very quickly to her feet. Beneath the heavy, biscuit-brown tan, her face went suddenly bright with a leap of blood.

"Roy," she said. "I didn't expect you so early. I didn't think I'd see you until I went up to Carl's."

"I thought we could go up together," he said slowly.

He had stopped before he reached the table, remembering the open windows and the probable fact that they were being observed by expertly hidden watchers outside. Now he came forward and took her hand and pressed gently on its warm full palm and rubbed his fingers along the smooth hard back of it before taking his own hand away.

She gave a short, nervously delighted chuckle and took the spectacles from her face quickly. He watched her as she stood before him in her thin, starched, cotton shirt and yellow, embroidered dirndl; and as his stare went from her brushed-back, tightly banded hair to the large, broadly arched feet then back to the half-fearful, softly expectant face she lowered her short, thick lashes and shifted restlessly.

"Stop it," she muttered, hardly opening her lips.

He came up beside her, carefully not touching her.

"Were you busy?" he asked. "I hope I didn't interrupt anything."

"Silly," she said smiling. "I was doing the books, but they can wait. They don't have to be done before the end of the month."

He opened the ledger on which she had been working when he came in.

"Double entry!" he said. "You do things properly, don't you? Where did you learn this?"

"I took some lessons with old Trelawney down in Castleville. Do you know him?"

"Met him once, I think. He's an old soak, isn't he?"

"That's the one. He's always drunk by twelve o'clock but he's a marvellous teacher. I used to send for him early in the morning before he'd had time to get started."

She closed the ledger again, put it on the other two, picked them up and moved from the table. As she went past him he felt her long, slender yet heavily powerful hand rub briefly along his side in a quick caress. She went on into the middle of the room without turning her head and he followed her.

"I'll put these away," she said, "and then we'll go up to Carl's. O.K.?"

"Yes," he said, catching her up. "Let's do that. ...That was a good move of yours, by the way. I met him when I was coming across. I had been wondering how you'd get out tonight with him around."

"Who is that?" For an instant she seemed puzzled, then, "Oh, *him!* Yes. I nearly sent the posters off yesterday, until I realized Lloyd could take them today."

He held the door open and her tall body swayed lightly past him into the passage. She was not really slim when you looked at this long slope of her calves, the wide, full shield of her hips and the rounded length of her arms, but she had enough height to appear so, and the lightly nodding stoop added to that picture of awkwardly graceful slenderness.

"You'll have to drive up yourself," he said to her at the staircase. "I can't come back down with you."

"I know," she told him. "I'll drive the Morris."

"Good. I'll wait for you outside, eh?"

"Yes." She sounded strange, as if speaking were an effort she was doing mechanically from a dream. "Yes, you wait outside. I'll be right down."

He went out to his car and took off his jacket and tie, putting them folded neatly on the back seat next to his briefcase. Then he rolled up his shirtsleeves and got behind the wheel.

I never thought I'd feel this again, he thought as he looked across the brown grass of the wide field. Come on, girl. Hurry up.

The little grey Morris Minor hummed up behind the Vauxhall, coming round the corner of the house from the garage. It slowed when it drew abreast of his car and he smiled and nodded as he started the engine. When she heard him start up, Sheila drove on down to the gateway.

The Vauxhall caught up with her Morris just beyond Tolliver village and he accelerated, swerving out and pulling ahead before he cut in.

They went steadily and fast up beside the tilted, shining brown river and the brown-green checkers of the smallholdings and the big, yellow and crimson splashes in the thick bush of the hillsides. He led them past the place where they had stopped on Sunday to ask Sheila for help and when the road began to grow steeper and the bank of the hillside on his left became sheer and tangled he started to look for the place he wanted.

When he saw it he put his hand out and waved slowly, easing his foot on the accelerator as he did so. The Vauxhall creaked as it came to a halt.

He got out and stood aside as the Morris stopped behind his car. He bent down and put his head in the low window, reaching out to take her hand.

"Come along," he said. "I don't want to go up to the Pen just yet."

She only nodded as she rolled up the glass; and when she stepped into the road she slipped her hand under his elbow right away and drew his arm tightly against her.

"Darling," she said and lifted his hand and brushed her lips softly against his fingers.

It was empty on this stretch of the road. The hillside came steeply down to the tar, heavily grown with trees and bush. Below them were more trees and more wild, choked bush, growing on the valley wall down to the river they could just hear as it rushed through the steep, narrow bed to the flatter land they had just passed. The air was warm and the liquid motionless calm of a hill afternoon seemed to close round them like a transparent wall as they walked up the road in the golden, hot light.

"Where are we going?" she asked, quickly and happily.

"Just down here," he said and turned off the road, on to a grass grown, rough bridle track leading down to the hidden river.

"Where does it lead to?"

They were walking, knees bent, against the steep drop of the track and she put her arm around his waist now, hugging him hard, her wide flat hip moving closely against his.

"It goes down to a settlement by the river," he told her. "Carl and I used to go there when we were children, that's how I know this path. We're not going there, though. We'll stop soon."

"Stop soon," she said in a soft, thick voice.

He stopped and swung her round to face him on the stony, uneven track and kissed her.

It was a long, searching, never completely finding kiss and when they moved their lips and held each other, rubbing their cheeks together and breathing in shallow rapid gusts, he felt as though he had been on a long journey from this spot and come back.

"Jesus!" he said. "Come on. It isn't far."

He did not have to take her very much further. The place he was looking for was round the bend from where they stood, a small bluff, almost waist high in long grass, and overlooking a sheer, nearly perpendicular drop to the river.

When they reached the spot where the little bluff was, hidden from the track by a mesh of thorny raspberry canes, he jumped on to the bank, holding his hand down for her to take as he pulled her up beside him. He went before her and held the branches apart so that they would not catch on her skirt. The scratch of the prickles was sharply distinct and quite remote from any actual feeling. He seemed to sense the tiny scrapes along his flesh by sympathy and not because they were happening to him.

Sheila went past him, her eyes straight before her, her face proud-looking and bright. Only as she walked into the high, tassel-topped grass beyond the bushes did she turn and look back at him over her shoulder. Her eyes were hot and shining.

She knelt in the grass, sitting back on her heels, and when he sank down beside her the tops of the grass were above their heads and they were surrounded with the sunbaked, fragrant green smell. His throat had swelled and each breath he drew was making him dizzy. When he spoke he could hear the croaking, dull sound of his voice.

"Sheila," he said. "Sheila." Then he put his hands on her shoulders, pushing her back in the grass.

For the moment before he fell half on top, half beside her, as her long, powerful arms went round his back and the day became a darkening, sun-flashed confusion of earth smell, grass scent and the moist warm odour of her flesh, he saw the tremor of her wide, ripe mouth and heard the sound of his name murmured. And after that he saw nothing very clearly and heard only the roar of blood in his ears.

He lay on his back in the crushed grass, watching her as she slid the ribbon from her short tail of hair, clubbed the hair close to her neck with her fist, bit the knot in the ribbon loose and then deftly tied the ribbon back in place.

"You have grass stains on your skirt back," he murmured in a placidly interested voice.

She pushed the shirt tail into the waist band of her skirt and smoothed the skirt over her knees.

"That's all right." She smiled at him. "I have another skirt I brought along for tennis at Carl's. He thought we might have a game to make your visit seem just a social one."

"Fine," he said. "But if you and Carl want tennis you can play alone. McKenzie's out of that."

He reached up and took her hand and brought it to his lips. He kissed the fingers and nibbled gently at the firm mount under the thumb.

The corners of her mouth lifted faintly in a smile as she moved her hand along his jaw.

"Do you know that your jaw is too long for the rest of your face?" she said softly.

"Yes. Worrying about it keeps me awake at nights."

"But," she said, "you have a nice nose."

She ran her finger along the curve of the bridge.

"Good."

"And I love your eyes," she continued. "Even when they're bloodshot."

"That's to frighten my enemies."

She bent over and gently kissed him on each eyelid. "You fool," she said laughing softly, and: "Roy, I love you so."

He held her close against him and said against her ear: "I love you, too, Sheila."

She leaned up on her elbow, pulling away from his arm, and looked steadily at him.

"You don't have to say that, you know? I told you on Sunday that I never want you to pretend about it. This is good enough for me."

"I'm not pretending," he told her. "I felt it this morning when I thought of seeing you again today. And when I saw you this afternoon I knew for sure."

For the first time since this had begun between them she

looked really shy. She said nothing but buried her face in his neck and slowly tightened her arms about his shoulders.

"I'm almost afraid to believe it's happened," she whispered. "Roy. My dearest, I never thought it would happen like this."

"It's happened, though."

"I know." Her eyes, behind the close hedge of her lashes, had brown shadows on the green as she looked sidelong at him with shy, challenging enquiry. "Do you think I was too... too forward?" she asked. "Perhaps when you aren't feeling like this, you won't approve of the way I went on."

"Went on? What do you mean?"

"You know. I was a bit... brazen I suppose. Men don't like that, do they? I've never done it before. I wanted you so much, though."

He sat up and took both her hands in his. He was smiling.

"No," he told her, "you went on, as you call it, just right. I wouldn't have wanted it to happen any other way."

"I'm glad I did it like that, then," she said, putting her arm round his neck and leaning forward to kiss him softly on the mouth. Then she sat back and squeezed tightly on the hands that were holding hers.

The sun was behind him now, hot in the clean air of the hills and coating the bright grass in a shining, very pale yellow. The hard light beat against Sheila's face, making the skin of one cheek almost transparent and glinting on the copper wire streaks of red in her brown hair. There was a little pulse beating strongly and steadily in the hollow of her throat.

He leaned forward to meet her eager face, smelling, as their lips met, the warm, hay scent of her hair and her glowing, sun-hot cheek. For a minute he held her slender, longfulness against him, then he got to his feet. He glanced at the new, expensive Rolex watch he had bought yesterday.

"Come along," he said, looking down at her. 'We ought to be at Carl's by five."

Sheila sighed, made a grimace and put up her hand for him to take.

"Yes," she said, "I suppose we'd better. What a nice place this has been. How did you know of it?"

He pulled her to his feet.

"Carl and I brought our first loves here," he told her as they walked to the raspberry hedge. "Twenty years ago."

She stopped suddenly. Her face was interested and cautious. "Who were they?" she asked in a lightly edged voice.

"Two little girls from the settlement. Coolie royals. We used to go down there with Tom; you know, the one who's Carl's stable man now. He was about a year older than us and he used to take us down to watch the cockfights. I remember his uncle had a wonderful half-breed bantam which used to rip up everything they matched against it."

"How did the little girls come into it?"

"Oh, that was Tom again. He had a girlfriend down in the settlement and she had two friends. We all used to meet up here and scatter in the grass. I could show you to this day where my regular spot was, and Carl's, and Tom's."

"Don't bother," she said. She was trying not to smile at his broadly grinning, fatuously reminiscent face. "You must have been a wicked, wicked little boy."

He pulled back the canes for her to walk through and then came through after her, cautiously releasing the thorny branches.

"If it's any consolation to you," he said jumping down from the bank and joining her on the path, "we got what was coming to us. Not for that. For gambling at the cock fight. Some officious bastard saw us one day and told Carl's father."

"And what happened."

She was smiling now as they walked hand in hand up the path.

"Oh Lord!" he said. "When we got back, Arthur B. was waiting for us with a yard of tamarind switch in his hand. He looked fifteen feet tall and if he'd started to breathe smoke, I wouldn't have been surprised. First he chased Carl for about ten miles all over the property. Then when he'd finished with him, he tracked Tom and me down like a bloodhound. We'd hidden together for comfort, so that saved him the trouble of two searches. And after he was through, Delia stood us up and lectured us for about an hour on hell fire and the homes that gambling had wrecked. It was quite an evening."

They went up the last short steepness before reaching the road, their long shadows with joined hands before them, the loose stones tumbling back under their feet and clicking as they rolled down the path. The road was empty and still in the clear slanting light; and below them the sea was like grey, slightly rucked silk.

"It will be calm tonight," she said pressing his hand. "By the time we're going out the sea breeze will have dropped and the land breeze won't be enough to do more than stir the water."

"Good," he said. The tightness had come back to his stomach but his body felt calmer and more his own than it had done during the day. "You're quite sure what you have to do?"

"Quite sure, darling. Lie beyond the current until I see you give two long flashes on the torch; then come in and meet you coming out."

She went back to the Morris, and he switched on and fed power quickly to the engine.

He drove the few miles to Brandt's Pen at a steady forty miles per hour. Whenever he looked back, Sheila's car was hanging on his tail at about fifty yards' distance. Once, he wondered if she did everything as well as she made love.

This was about the time that Tiger Johnson, who had been out of town all afternoon in Saragossa, was coming back into Queenshaven on a truck which had given him a lift. He had been busy since two o'clock collecting a load of ganja in and around Saragossa, and the truck was one of the many that often brought the stuff from the country up to him concealed under the floorboards, taped under the mud-guards or stuffed up the end of an exhaust which had a hole further up the pipe to let out the fumes.

Johnson was anxious to reach Queenshaven and get the stuff distributed to the safe places. He hardly thought about Roy McKenzie or Etienne or Hector Slade.

Only once, as the big Bedford roared between the flat cane fields, jolting him where he sat on top of a load of ginger root, did he reflect that if he had time he would see Hector Slade this evening; and that if he didn't, tomorrow morning would do as well.

36

It was half-past six when Tiger Johnson, who had disposed of his ganja earlier than he had expected, went up the high, narrow, concrete steps of Police Headquarters, through the swing doors at the head of the steps, and into the orderly-room from the corridor beyond the doors.

He was a little disappointed to find that it was not Sergeant-major Flower behind the desk at the end of the room but another officer, a fat, black man he knew as Cowell. He had hoped to extend the business he had begun with Flower the night before. Not with any seriousness, but as a satisfactory preliminary to seeing Hector Slade.

As he came in and began his slow, deliberately provocative slouch up the room, one of the constables, the one who had reached for his baton on the previous night, came out from behind his broad, table-like desk and stood squarely in the path he would have to take. The constable's hands hung open loosely and comfortably at his sides, and under the white, close-fitting, high-necked tunic his body was held with the relaxed alertness of an expert wrestler.

"You come back?" he asked softly. "After what de sergeant-major tell you last night?"

Tiger Johnson came to a slow halt about a foot from the policeman. His smile was a coy, leering smirk, but he had quivered stiffly back on his heels like a snake reared tensely on its coils.

His dead, black eyes never left the constable's face as he said: "Yes, I want fe' see de chief."

"It's all right, Willoughby," an affable, mellow voice said behind the constable, "I'll see to this."

It was the fat Sergeant-major, Cowell, and he had come up so quietly that only Tiger Johnson had known when he left his desk, and that only because he had seen him over Willoughby's shoulder. Close up, you could see that Cowell's fat was not soft and flabby, but bulky and enduring like the earth on a mountain. It wasn't hard to see, either, the flat jawline under the fleshy rounds of his face.

"Well, Johnson, What you want, eh?"

Cowell's small, crumpled mouth smiled freely and the moon face beamed with genial tolerance and his big, muddy brown eyes, their whites made yellow by quinine, were steady and quite empty of any cheerfulness. Set in that laughter-seamed, kindly face they were like the eyes from another head, until you saw that between them and the tight, wrinkled lips there was much in common.

"I want see de chief," Tiger Johnson said. His arrogance was no longer casual; it was grim and thrusting now as he looked into Cowell's eyes. "I come yesterday fe' tell him somet'ing, but dem send me away."

"You come yesterday, eh? But, Tiger, man, you know dat you just can't see de commissioner like dat."

Cowell's voice was mild, filled with an affectionate, scolding fussiness which had nothing at all to do with what showed in his probing, muddily opaque, dangerous eyes. He lifted his plump hand and clapped it on Tiger Johnson's thin shoulder. When the pudgy fingers found the trapezius muscle they began to knead it with expert, paralysing viciousness. He did not appear to realize what he was doing as he twinkled another fat smile into Johnson's suddenly frozen face.

"I want see de chief," Tiger Johnson said in a thin, careful voice. He did not twitch under the exploration of Cowell's big hand, but after a few seconds his skin became grey beneath the black, and he began to look ill.

"All right, Johnson," Cowell's voice reached a new pitch of sunny friendliness. "You want see Commissioner Slade. Suppose you tell me an' I will tell him. If he t'ink it important him will call you in."

"No," Tiger Johnson's narrow, shapely, high forehead had thick sweat on it. "It's important. Is commissioner must hear it."

"You can't tell me?"

"No."

"Good, Johnson," Cowell told him soothingly. "If you must see de commissioner den wait here let me tell him."

He let go of Tiger Johnson's shoulder and began to walk away, moving with rolling, ponderous strides, making no more sound than a dancer in ballet shoes. He stopped and looked back.

"You really have somet'ing fe' say?" he asked, and now his voice sounded like the eyes looked.

"Yes."

"Good. I just want fe' know. 'Cause if you don't, den we will have fe' arrest you for somet'ing. I don't know what, but we will t'ink of a good charge."

He went out of the room, along to the end of the corridor, up the stairs there and to Hector Slade's office door on the landing. He knocked, and when he heard the piping bark from inside he opened the door.

Hector's Slade's big, dome-browed head raised from the papers he had before him. In the strong light from the reading lamp, his closely-trimmed, greying hair glinted like a cap made of spider web.

"Yes, Cowell. What is it?"

Cowell told him about Tiger Johnson's two visits. When he was finished, Hector Slade leaned back, his grey eyes thoughtful and interested.

"What do you think?" he asked.

"He has something, sir. I'd see him. He really wants to see you."

When Cowell spoke with people like Hector Slade his accent and diction were quite different from those he used speaking with people like Tiger Johnson.

"If you say so. Better ask Superintendent O'Malley to come, too. Bring Johnson up."

"Yes, sir."

Cowell turned to go to the door.

"Odd," Hector Slade said reflectively and Cowell paused and looked back. "Damned odd, eh? I never thought we'd see Johnson as a stool-pigeon. Did you?"

"No, sir. He either wants to fix someone very badly or there's money in it."

"Perhaps both," Hector Slade smiled. "Well, bring him up. My compliments to Mr. O'Malley and ask him if he would come along, too."

He picked up the papers he had been studying and read until O'Malley, a wide-shouldered, bow-legged Irishman, once a constable in Palestine, now a superintendent in Cayuna, came into the room.

"We're having a visit," Hector Slade said without looking up. "Tiger Johnson has something to tell us. Interested?"

"Johnson, sir? What did they pull him in for?" He came and stood beside Hector Slade's chair, a little behind it.

"They didn't, man. This is voluntary. Flower thought he was trying it on, but Cowell says it's genuine."

"If Cowell thinks so," O'Malley said, "then it's genuine. I wonder what it could be?"

Sergeant-major Cowell and Tiger Johnson appeared in the door, Cowell bulking behind the slight, harshly angular figure he pushed before him. When they were a yard from Hector Slade's desk, he stopped Johnson by suddenly clamping his hand on the shoulder he had squeezed.

Tiger Johnson looked round him once and then stood still. Even with nothing to lean on, he gave the impression that he was lounging. He had fixed his eyes on Hector Slade, and now a satisfied sneer lurked on the stiffly bearded, wild face and he was slowly moving his tongue between his red lips. Cowell stabbed him heavily in the back with a big, fleshy thumb and a look of bored, impenetrable arrogance replaced the sneer on Tiger's Johnson's face.

"Hurry up, Johnson," Hector Slade said. "I want to get home. What is it you want to tell me?"

"It important, Commissioner."

"Is it? Which one of your friends are you selling out?"

"Friends, Commissioner? What friends me have to sell? My friends is good people. Dem wouldn't interest you."

His tone was unconsciously wounded, and the savagely chiselled, ironic face bright with enjoyment. Behind their thick lenses, Hector Slade's eyes became two little holes, cold and grey.

"Johnson," O'Malley said.

"Yes, sah."

"Have you come here to play games?"

"No, sah."

"Because if you have, then Mr. Cowell and I have some nice games we could play out in the backyard with you. Understand?"

"Yes, sah."

"Good." O'Malley's voice was faintly regretful. "Now what is it you have to say?"

"I will get somet'ing for it, Commissioner?"

"If it's worth it," Hector Slade said, "and if you're not involved. If you're involved then voluntary Queen's evidence will mean less trouble for you, but not a penny."

"I not in it, Commissioner," Tiger Johnson said in a voice springy with laughter. "No, sah, I not in it."

Cowell had just taken Tiger Johnson downstairs and O'Malley was standing by the desk looking with embarrassed interest at Hector Slade's drawn, tightly-set face.

As soon as Johnson had left the room, Hector Slade had told O'Malley who it was that must have helped Roy McKenzie to meet and hide Etienne on Saturday night.

"Well," Hector Slade said stiffly. "Where is he? Where would you hide him if you were Roy McKenzie – or my nephew?"

His voice was crisp and dispassionate and he had taken the short-stemmed, black pipe from the breast pocket under the double line of faded, Great War, medal ribbons and was steadily filling it as he spoke. But his face had suddenly become the face of an old worried man and the eyes in the big, alertly cocked head were bleak.

"I think Etienne is at your nephew's place, sir," O'Malley said, and Hector Slade nodded. "I don't think McKenzie used him for any other reason," O'Malley continued. "It wouldn't have been worth the risk, bringing a non-party person into it. But he must have realized we'd be watching the houses of any known communists."

"Quite right." Hector Slade gave him the shy, tight smile which always lifted his face into handsomeness. "He's on the Pen, all right. That is if they haven't shipped him out already."

"Do you think they might have, sir?"

"Perhaps. It's always a possibility. But we'll assume that they haven't."

Sergeant-major Cowell came into the room and the two men looked inquiringly at him.

"I've checked on McKenzie, sir," he said. "He left his office at midday and didn't return. He isn't at home, either."

"Check with Castleville," Hector Slade said. "Ask them if he was there today and tell them to stand by for emergency orders. Marine Patrol to redouble search of waters off all landings and harbours."

"Yes, sir," Cowell said. He left the room.

"If McKenzie is over there now," Hector Slade said, "then they're probably going to get him away tonight. I don't think McKenzie would risk being seen where Etienne was unless he had to."

"Are we going in after him, sir?" O'Malley asked.

"No. We could arrest McKenzie and my nephew and all known communists on the coast, on suspicion, and then just hunt Etienne down. But we'd have to charge them on Scissors Clark's word. If they've shipped Etienne out already and we found nothing, we'd be in serious trouble. And if we did go in on a warrant, this would be a bad time. Etienne's not the sort to let himself be taken, at night, in that bush and mountain country. He's been a soldier and he's dodged police before. He might get away with it, alone. That's the sort of man he is."

"What are you going to do, sir?"

"If they don't bring him out tonight, we'll go after him just before daylight. I'm pretty sure just where he is on the Pen and with the dogs he can't get far, even if he hears us coming. I want the others, though. If it's tonight they've planned it for we can make a haul of the rest of them, too... Yes, Cowell, what did you find?"

"He was at Castleville today, sir," Cowell said coming into the room. "His car was outside an office during the afternoon. He left along the coast road."

"No more?"

"No, sir. He hasn't been seen coming back."

"He's up at the Pen," Hector Slade told O'Malley. "I think we'll get him tonight. We'll get him and the others."

He got out of the chair and crossed the room to where a huge framed map of Cayuna hung on the wall opposite his desk. His thin, creased face looked tired and woodenly sad, but his voice was brisk and steady when he spoke.

"Now, O'Malley," he said, and as the man joined him, "here's what we'll do. Get on to Castleville and tell them to have the patrol wagon stand by in the bush where the road comes down from Brandt's Pen. One plainclothes man to be sent immediately to Brandt's Pen village to telephone if any cars leave the property. My nephew's is a Humber, but they'll know that over there. The two launches from Manchester Bay and Port Christopher to join the two from Castleville and Resurrection Heights: they're to challenge all schooners and small craft within five miles of the coast. All stations along the coast with patrol wagons are to stand ready, and a watch on the houses of known communists, especially the fishermen. But don't let them know. If we handle this properly we'll get Etienne and perhaps five or six others. The patrol wagon is to tail them to wherever it is they hope to take him out from. Rifles, of course. I'll be leaving, myself, immediately, with thirty men and two dogs in case we have to go in for him tomorrow. Get Stevens, Massey and Donaldson and tell them to be down here in twenty minutes. Got it all?"

"Yes, sir," O'Malley said, "but the launches from Manchester Bay and Port Christopher won't reach the search area for two or three hours."

"I know. It can't be helped. If Andrews over at Castleville does his job with the wagon properly, we won't need them, though."

"Yes, sir. Is there anything else?"

"No. I'll get the Central, myself, for the men I'm taking. You carry on with the north coast signal."

O'Malley turned to leave the room. Halfway across the floor he paused and looked back at the lean, grey man who had gone to his desk and was picking up the telephone.

"Sir," O'Malley said. "Yes."

"I'm sorry your – Carl Brandt had to get mixed up with this, sir."

"So am I," Hector Slade told him. "But he knew what he was doing."

"Do you think if you got on to him – privately I mean – that we could settle it without waiting to catch them?"

"No, I don't," Hector Slade said heavily. "We would lose the chance of getting whoever's in it with them. Besides, my nephew's not that sort of man."

37

The plainclothes man who had been sent up by the Castleville police to the village of Brandt's Pen (driven up to within half a mile of the village in an innocuous goods van and let off, with his bicycle, at an empty corner) did not get there in time to see Sheila Pearce leave. She had left, in fact, before the signal from Hector Slade was sent through to Castleville.

It had been a good afternoon at the Pen. Roy McKenzie had sat watching while Sheila and Carl played three fast games of tennis. Then he had become stimulated by the sight of those two swift, disciplined bodies and gone into Carl's room to find and put on the pair of old canvas shoes he had once forgotten up here and never bothered to take back. He had taken off his shirt and vest and used one of Carl's sweat shirts, the hem coming down nearly to his knees and the elbows seeming to rest somewhere about his wrists. He had gone out to the lawn again, and he and Sheila played against Carl. They had beaten him for two games until he had selected the place on their court where they were both weak and driven volley after volley through this spot. After that, he had beaten them in three straight games and at the end he was taking them easily, even though they had been allowed the double court rules and he only the singles.

Then they had gone inside and mixed drinks and sat on the verandah, the three chairs drawn up to the parapet and facing inwards slightly so that they could see each other's faces, and had talked while the soft light took on grey tints in its yellow, and purple after grey, and suddenly became deep, brown dark before the black.

The first stain of night had seemed to come too quickly. One minute they were drinking and using each other's stories with complete understanding as a source for new ones, and then they had looked up and seen the first pale stars and Sheila was holding her arm above her upraised face to look at her watch on the wrist which even in this light was strong and shapely.

"It's time," she said. "I must be going now. I'll see you later."

"Are you taking Jackson with you?" Carl had asked as they went down the steps to her car.

"No," she had said. "It wouldn't be fair, would it? He didn't hire himself out for this."

At the car Roy had held the door open while she got in, her long legs in the brief, tight shorts looking powerful and heavy yet nice as any girl's legs he'd ever seen, and her body as she came close to him smelling clean and strong of the fine wool cardigan and her exercise-heated flesh.

When he closed the door, she had leaned out of the window and put her arm up to take the back of his neck in her firm hand. She had pulled his head down to her upturned face and kissed him hard with closed lips and nuzzled her cheek against his.

"See you soon, darling," she had whispered, and then in a voice of tranquil confidence, her lips still against his ear, "Don't worry, it's going to be all right."

Carl and he had stayed on the steps, watching the two red lights from her car jolt swiftly down the drive; and then they had gone in, showered, dressed and had supper.

Now, after supper, they were on the verandah again, waiting for when it would be time to go for Etienne.

"I wish you'd let me come out with you and Sheila," Carl said softly at the end of a long silence between them. They were both smoking cigars and the smoke was going up to the high ceiling, cloudy white at first then blue where it caught the light from the drawing-room, thin and tenuously grey in the shadows among the orchid boxes.

"No, boy," Roy said. "We went over that before. You'll have to drive the car away; besides, one man is enough for anything we might have to do out in open sea."

"O.K., then, you drive back and I'll go."

"No, Carl. I definitely ought to go. You know that."

Roy got up and stiffened nervously, stretching until he felt the muscles cramp. He looked at the luminous dial of his new watch. Because they had so recently come from strong light, the numbers and hands were dim, and he went to the door of the lit drawing-room to read the time.

"It's all right," Carl told him from behind, without looking round in his chair. "We've got a bit of time yet. I don't want to go for him too early and it wouldn't do to be hanging around the head too long, either."

Roy came back and stood by Carl's chair, his foot resting on the parapet. He smiled stiffly at the shadowed features of the blunt, square-cut face which he seemed to know more thoroughly every year without ever getting to the end of knowing and discovery.

"I'm sorry," he said. "I'm acting up a bit. I feel pretty tight inside."

"That's because you're really worried about someone else," Carl told him. "I want to get him out safely too; but not the way you want to."

"Thanks," Roy said. "You never miss saying the right thing, do you? It isn't only that, though."

"What's it? Having to go out with the boat?"

"Yes. Not the open sea, but that goddam stuff off the head. Not the drowning, either, but those bloody sharks and things."

"Not many sharks out there," Carl said, and Roy could feel more plainly than he could see the gentle, slight smile which went with the words. "It's not really shark water: more barracuda and congers."

They both chuckled and Carl lifted the bottle from the table by his elbow and poured two drinks, dashing the dregs from each glass over the verandah parapet before putting in fresh rum. He dropped ice and put water into the drinks and gave Roy his.

"Here," he said. "You just breathe in the face of any barracuda who comes for you and he'll be too damn drunk to bite you." He looked at the faint green glow of his watch dial. "Nearly time," he told Roy. "It's just after eight. I'll go for him in about five minutes and that will give us plenty of time to get him down to the head. Summer and his boys must be well on their way now."

"I hope they don't run into any trouble," Roy said. "It's a heavy order for a rowing boat."

"Who? Summer? My God, Roy, you don't know that man. If he has to get out and bring the boat in on his head, he'll do it. He'd row you up a waterfall."

There was a pause. Then Roy turned to Carl again.

"I didn't tell you," he said, "but Hector came to see me yesterday."

"Did he? Why? Was he trying to smell out something?"

"I thought so at first; and he probably was with one part of him. At least, if there'd been anything there he'd have spotted it; but he came to get that book from me; the one I told you about on Saturday."

"Oh, yes. I mentioned it to him."

"Also to invite me to share his lectures with him over at the university later this year."

"Good. Are you going to?"

"You don't think I'd let Hector have it all his own way over there, do you?"

Carl gave a delighted laugh.

"You and Hector," he said. "Until you two started to tell me about it, I hardly knew Cayuna had a history."

Roy looked at the face beside him which was half shadowed, half lit as Carl pulled on his cigar and the ash-covered tip burnt swiftly along the dry leaf.

Then Carl finished his drink and put it on the table beside his chair.

"I'm going up for him now," he said. "If I go now, we'll get him to the beach in good time."

Roy watched him go down the steps and get into the Humber which had been left at the end of the drive, under the lignum vitae tree, near to the corner where they were sitting. Carl drove it a little way down the drive and stopped in the heavy shadows of the ficus berry. When he brought Etienne in from across the pasture, they would get straight into the car. Nobody need see or hear them from the house.

When Carl got out of the car, Roy tried to listen for his footfalls crossing the drive as he went into the garden. But he could not hear anything. He could only see for an instant the big, dim shape of his friend's body as it moved in the open driveway.

Jeffrey Summer and his sons were coming in across the bad water off Columbus Head. They could feel the fast, clutching drag of the current and the boat heavy as she dipped and swayed, the gunwales close to the rushing surface.

Getting as far as this had not been hard. He had known that for several days, ever since the trouble in St. Pierre, the two police launches, from Castleville and Resurrection Heights, had been unusually busy along the coast; but he had realized also, that for two launches to patrol sixty miles of coast at night leaves a large territory of error open to the seekers and a larger territory of avoidance open to those who might not want to be seen.

To make sure, though, that he would not be surprised, Summer had taken the boat out to one of the fishing banks, joining up with several other boats on the way there. One of the police launches on the routine patrol which it had kept up for several days now, played its searchlight over the spread-out boats; then it had gone pushing down the coast towards Port Christopher. Summer had kept with the other boats until they began to separate in twos and ones. Not till then had he given the word to his sons, and in the dark they had swung in from the banks and made across the sea for Columbus Head. This was some time before the alert was radioed through from Castleville to the launches.

Now he was straining to see ahead of him on to the dull glitter of the swift water. The boys were only harder dark outlines against the soft spread of the night, but he could have known them by the sounds they were making even had he not positioned them himself. He could recognize George's sharp, heavy grunt as he dug deep to keep *Selina's* nose straight down the current; and Reuben's throaty groan; and Edward's exaggerated, smacking 'Ah' as the long-armed man supported on his side the power of George's pull; and lastly there was Aaron's tense, clean snarl as the air whistled into his lungs.

Jeffrey Summer leaned hard against the oar as a choppy shudder told him that they were getting too close to the rocks on which the sea was leaping in sudden, glassy explosions, the blossoming foam showing pale and bright against the soft dark and the running, dull sheen of the current.

"Pull hard, George, Aaron," he said. "Ease up, Edward an' Reuben."

He was forcing the blade deep in the water to help George and Aaron as they pulled against the swift, frightening dip and slide of the boat. And as he guided the blade he could feel the water around it clinging thick as molasses, almost forcing it from his flatly clenched hand. His wrist and muscles were trembling and stiff from the constant pressure and he could hear, now, the loud, broken chuckle of water against the rocks. The boat had begun to lift high and slap down hard in sharp, wild lurches, as the backwash got under her, and the spray was whipping over the bows into his face.

Jeffrey Summer had very few romantic or picturesque ideas about the sea. It was the place where he made a living, good some years, bad some years; it was unpredictable. That was all he felt about it. But as the stern skidded under him and *Selina* came broadside on to the current and began to rush towards the bright splashes of foam, he could almost believe that the sea was alive, that there was something monstrous in this brutal, sucking force which had twisted the steering oar in his helpless hand.

They were driving straight for the blurred lump of the headland now, pitching among broken choppy water which would catch *Selina* under her stern every few minutes and hurl her forward in a wild nose-dipping, stern-yawning swoop. When that happened, either the boys would lift their oars and let her ride it out, allowing Jeffrey Summer to bring her straight with a quickly bending wrist and flexibly tautened forearm, or one side of the four, alternately placed rowers would dig the blades in and heave back, dipping, heaving again quickly until the other two brought their oars into play to send the boat in on the clear passage between the rocks.

It was done with precise, almost silent co-ordination. Jeffrey Summer spoke three or four times and once he heard George call sharply, "Pappa!" and then the scrape of his son's oar-blade on the rock; but they were sweeping past it, then, and he kept *Selina* from striking by use of the stern oar.

Then they were in the big pool of calm water and what was between them and the beach was hard but nothing like what they had just come through; and here Jeffrey Summer slowly unclenched his numb fingers and held the long oar handle under his armpit as he massaged the muscles of his twitching forearm and stiffly aching wrist.

"All right, bwoys," he said. "Rest here little bit. We come early."

Their breaths hissed jerkily as they floated on the long heave of the ground-swell. Summer's body was wet with spray, and with sweat under the spray, as he stood looking at the dimly seen shapes of his sons' bent heads.

He was thinking that it had been a good thing to come in a little early. It had given the boys a chance to rest here where they would later meet the *Nisba,* and they would be able to rest again on the beach. It was going to be bad getting back out once they were past this point. He was aware that it was going to take everything he had ever learnt about the sea and everything he had ever taught to his sons.

And after they had got back out to sea they would spend the night fishing so as to have something to show when they came in tomorrow morning.

It was going to be a long hard night and Summer found himself wishing, for the first time in his life, that he were fifteen years younger.

38

Roy realized that he was waiting quite calmly for Carl to come back with Henri. This calm had come on him insensibly. He was only aware that for half an hour he had been sitting where Carl had left him and that the tight uneasiness was completely gone from his skin and stomach.

He got up and poured himself a very small drink and lifted the lid of the tall, cedar humidor to take a cigar. Slowly and reflectively he bit at the end, pierced the tobacco with a matchstick and lit the leaf-wrapped tip. Carrying his drink, he went to the steps and sat on the verandah edge, resting his feet on the steps below and leaning against the pillar. The stone was still warm from the day's sun. The cigar was drawing with crisp evenness and he decided that he would take a few for Henri before they left.

All the sounds that he knew well were coming from the

pastures around the house. Soft, contented sounds; not lazy, but replete and confident; each sound fitted to the others. The noise of animals, nightbirds, insects, a small wind moving across grass and in the trees; the activity shot with laughter and talk from the back of the great house; and, very faintly, the drifting murmurs from the yard behind the house itself.

He rose from the steps and walked to the corner where Carl and he had sat. From here he could better see the lights of Castleville and the village along the coast. He tried to see the water; and as he tried he thought of Summer who would be coming in about now with George and the others; and of Sheila, who would be coming in alone.

She came into his mind suddenly and completely: at first as he imagined she would be at the wheel of the *Nisba,* and then as she had been this afternoon when her face had been bright above her body.

He heard the soft explosion as Carl started the engine, then; and looking down the drive he saw the twin crimson dots of the Humber's rear lights glowing in the dark.

He went down the steps quickly and along the drive. He was quietly and serenely gay, with a hard, clear-headed confidence about what they were going to do and about what he could make with Sheila.

At the car he got into the front seat beside Carl and turned to smile at Etienne who sat well back among the shadows.

"Ça va camerade?" Roy said, speaking French the first time since Saturday night on the beach.

"Ça marche bien, camerade," Etienne said happily, and Roy felt the quick, nervously firm pressure of the small fingers on his shoulder.

Carl let out the clutch and the great, black car rolled out swiftly from under the tree.

They went out of the gate and into the road, slowing when they came to the village, but accelerating when they were on clear road again. Carl's hands on the wheel as he took the car steadily round the bends were huge, flatly hard and reassuring.

"I'm sorry, Henri," Roy said looking back again at the hard outline head in the back seat. "I meant to bring you a few cigars to smoke when you're out at sea. By way of celebration. But you came in so quietly that you startled me and I forgot."

"*De rien, Roy*," Etienne said. "Think nothing of it. You've had enough to think of these last few days."

They were going down the hill road fast now, the deep, powerful springs of the big Humber rocking them easily as Carl gently and surely touched the wheel to meet the curves. The high bank seemed to be leaping down on them as the hard light raced over the trees and bush and the cool, green smell was clean and pungent.

In the valley they could see the fuzzy, close-packed confusion of the trees and the long dull glitter of the river.

"That's the Weeping Woman River," Roy said, turning to Etienne and pointing into the valley. "It comes out down on the coast about three miles east from here. At one time I thought of taking you from there because it's a good channel; but it wouldn't have been safe to use it. Too many people."

"The Weeping Woman," Henri Etienne said. He sounded interested. "That is a strange name, Roy. Do you know why they call it that?"

Roy chuckled drily and tapped Carl lightly on the back. "Go on," he said. "You tell him, Carl. After all, your family's responsible for it."

"You tell it," Carl said. He turned his head briefly and nodded, smiling with the same dryness at Roy.

"It's one of Carl's ancestors," Roy explained, twisting round in the wide, deeply cushioned seat. "He didn't name it, but he was the direct cause of the name. He was chasing four of his slaves who had got away taking their women. He caught up with them as they were fording the river somewhere down there. They were making for the limestone country over in the west yonder." He gestured to the high, sharply piled mountains beyond the hills. "Anyway, they never made it. Johannes Brandt stood on the bank and shot them down as they were wading out on the other side. The men that is. He caught up with the women easily. He hadn't shot good enough, though. That evening, when he was coming back with the women, one of the men – they had been laid out on the bank till he returned – suddenly came to life as they were cutting off the heads to take back to the Pen. He sprang up, tore the cutlass from the hand of the man who was doing the cutting and chopped Brandt in two from his head to the breast bone. Then, to make sure they wouldn't take him alive, he went for the others. They had to shoot him eight times, and he had killed another man, before he dropped."

"And the name?" Etienne asked intently.

"I was coming to that. Well, that night at the Pen there were five women crying for their men. They cried all night. Johannes Brandt's wife, who was six months pregnant, and the four women who had seen their men shot down. And the name of the river changed after that. Nobody called it anything but the Weeping Woman after that night."

"It is extraordinary," Etienne said with calm thoughtfulness. "A less imaginative people would have called it Blood River, perhaps, or Dead Man River. Something like that. I prefer Weeping Woman."

The car was leaping over the flatter surface now and they were coming near to the crossroads on the coast.

"Not far now, Henri," Roy said. "Only about eight miles and you'll be on the boat."

"Good," Etienne said. "I have made three of these escapes in my life, four if you count coming here from St. Pierre; and each time I have found this part is the hardest to take calmly. I do not think I will do this again, Roy. This is the last time."

They reached the crossroads and Carl braked the car, leaving the engine to run in neutral while two cars passed them going east along the coast and a third car went by going west towards Castleville. Beyond the road, the sea was rolling softly on the beach and there were dull, hard glitters from the surface. The air was warm and salty.

Carl turned them west and when they were coming near to Castleville, Roy said, "You'd better duck down here, Henri; in case anyone sees you as we go through the town."

They went through the square, around the clock tower and out along the road to the head. Carl was going faster, now, than he usually drove and nobody was speaking. Two more cars passed them going east toward Port Christopher, and just before they reached the head, a long, massively sleek Jaguar came up from behind, silently, and was round them and away with one abrupt bellow of sound. Then they saw the dark solid bulk of the head lying on the sea and two minutes later the car slowed and they heard the sharp squeech of the tyres as Carl swung them across the road and the big car lurched heavily but smoothly as it went into the coarse grass and weeds which grew down to the roadside.

Columbus Head was shaped like a fist laid on a table. It was all rock, with a tight skin of poor, sour earth on which there was scrub and long grass and a few wind-bent, stunted trees. Even the coconut trees were short and thin. It was easy enough for the big Humber to drive up the slope to that point on the fist-shaped headland where the raised forefinger knuckle would have been. Below this, just where the thumb would lie under the other fingers as the fist lay clenched on the table, was the beach. A little path ran with steep treacherousness from the high, overlooking edge of the bluff sheerly down to the beach.

Jolting and swaying, the car went across the half mile of hard-baked, rutted ground between the edge of the head and the road. They could hear the continuous *whish-whish* of the grass against the tyre walls and the crack and scrunch of sticks and weeds under the hard rubber. When they pulled up near the path, Roy had already opened the door, and he jumped down before they had properly stopped.

"Come on, Henri," he said. "Let's go." He was pulling open the near door and reaching inside for Etienne's pack as he spoke. "I hope to God that Summer and Sheila got in all right. "

Etienne scrambled quickly from the deep, expensive-smelling compartment and went ahead of Roy round the back of the car to join Carl on the far side; and as they both came round from behind the Humber they heard Carl shout one disbelieving, furious expression of great filthiness and they looked and saw the white glare of headlights begin to bounce sharply as a car took the rough ground near the road.

They all knew what it was, in the same moment of instant recognition. Even without the purposeful, direct speed with which the light was coming to them across the headland, there could have been no question of the patly coincident timing. They knew this, and knew that long before they picked a way down to the beach on the little path, the huge police torches would be spotlighting their figures as the wooden-cased, Lee-Enfield, ·303 rifles were trained on them.

And in the split fraction of time that he stood there, his nerves and muscles suddenly stiffened by the cold, skin-prickling, stomach-contracting shock, Roy McKenzie realized what he would have to do.

He had sprung to the door of the driving seat and got behind the wheel without really being aware of the movement; and as he fired the still warm engine into life he heard himself shouting to Carl, "Get moving! Get him down to the beach!"

He had pulled the gear out of neutral and into first and was locking hard down on the wheel to bring the car round while the echo of his shout still hung on the air between the two men. Then they heard the savage grinding of the tyres, a fast thudding as the gears changed and the bellow from the exhaust as the huge black car bucked and went away in a tight, rapidly straightening curve.

Roy McKenzie thought of nothing during the twenty-five seconds that it took for the two cars to meet, except how to keep the Humber from stalling as he changed into high, getting up as much speed as he would be allowed in the time he had. He was trying not to fight the viciously flicking wheel and yet to keep the mass of the enormously powered car hurtling straight on the rutted ground.

Only at the last second, as the black and cream-painted wagon leapt into his headlights, and as he flung himself sideways in the seat so that the steering column would not be driven through his chest, did he have one piercing seizure of desolate regret and lonely protesting terror.

To Carl, who was stumbling down the path then, ahead of Etienne, the torch he carried lighting the loose-stoned, ankle-turning surface, it was as if the sound of the two cars meeting came out of the darkness and smashed into his chest like a huge fist: a single, ferocious cymbal clash of ripping metal which exploded unbelievably on the night and died away even as his stomach turned heavily with nausea.

To Roy McKenzie, who lay along the wide seat, his crossed arms before his eyes, the sound was a formless, crashing roar and it came with an incredibly sudden, unbearable force which wrenched and hurled him into a light-split, incomprehensible, rushing darkness.

Then he was lying on his back, looking up at the dull glints in a high, black wall and wondering what it could be. He did not know it was the roof of the overturned Humber resting on his legs. His mouth was full of grit and tasted salty, but he did not understand that either. There was something about himself which he felt he ought to remember but he was too tired and cold to bother. He wondered why where he was lying felt so hard and why he could not move. The high, black wall which he did not understand was going away from him; and as it went, he heard a man's voice behind it begin to cry out brokenly. He could hear the voice distinctly but he could not make out why it should be there.

"Jesus God!" the voice said. "Oh, Lawd Jesus God!"

And that was the last thing Roy heard.

39

Carl Brandt saw the green riding light of a ship about twenty minutes past twelve. He called down to Sheila from the raised deck of the wheelhouse where he was keeping watch and she opened the throttle and brought the *Nisba* in across the deep swell, running it up behind the stern of the rolling, stationary vessel.

As they passed under the towering, rust-and-salt-smelling plates, Carl flashed his torch along them and saw the name in big raised letters; and then as they came up alongside the sheer bank of the hull, a powerful light shone down on them and Sheila cut the engines.

Carl shielded his eyes against the dazzle of the searchlight and called up into the darkness.

"Are you the *Kosciuzko?*"

"Yes." A hard voice answered him. "What you want? Mind your boat against us in this swell."

The accent was heavily imperfect, but he could hear the cautious, unfriendly reservation in it.

"We have someone for you," Carl called again.

The light went out suddenly.

"Someone for us?" The voice was cold and unrevealing. "What you mean, you have someone for us?"

"Name of Etienne. Colonel Henri Etienne. You are supposed to pick him up. You got a message from Roy McKenzie."

"We get no message, but one of you better come aboard and explain. We have engine trouble, that's why we stop. We drop a ladder."

They heard the clang of wood against metal and Carl shone the torch along the hull as it swayed towards them and receded on the rock of the swell.

Carefully and slowly Sheila brought the *Nisba* up to where the ladder was swinging straight down then clanging back against the plates.

Etienne came out of the wheelhouse where he had been standing and Carl jumped from the roof into the well of the cockpit.

"It's all right," he said with tired impersonal bitterness to Etienne. "They know who you are but they're just making sure. You'd better go up and get them to fling a rope down to haul up your bundle."

As he went to the *Nisba's* side and grappled the ladder with the boat hook, he had no hatred for this man whose safety had been the cause of what Roy had done. He felt for Etienne only the same dazed, utterly remote neutrality that he had felt for everything since they left Columbus Head. When he heard Etienne saying goodbye inside the dimly lighted wheelhouse, and Sheila's voice replying, both voices were no more important or disturbing than the slap of water against the plates or the bump as the old motor car tyres which hung over the *Nisba's* side squashed against the hull. "Hurry, please," a new voice called above them. "We have stopped long enough."

"All right! All right!" Carl shouted up into the darkness where he could just see head shapes against the sky. "We're sending him up. Maybe he can fix your engines for you."

He heard an appreciative chuckle from above and the sound of voices and then someone who had not spoken before said in a burred accent but very fluently, "My compliments to whoever brought you out. It was fine navigation. We never expected you to find us."

"Thank you," Carl called back. "I'll tell her."

"It was a woman?" The strong, burred voice, which Carl knew belonged to the captain, inflected sharply with surprise.

"Yes," Carl said.

"Again, my compliments, and my deepest admiration."

Etienne came out carrying his bundle and dropped it on the deck beside Carl. There was just enough light from the binnacle lamp in the wheelhouse to break the darkness of the afterdeck and Carl could see the tight, heavy sadness on the slant-eyed face.

"Goodbye, Carl," Etienne said and put his hand on Carl's shoulder. His voice was grey, and the hand trembled like that of a tired man.

"Goodbye, Henri," Carl said. He was holding the boat-hook with both hands keeping the *Nisba* close against the swaying hull of the *Kosciuzko*. The little cruiser was rising and falling off on the swell which only rolled the big steamer, and it was hard to keep them together.

"Perhaps," Etienne said, but without any conviction, "perhaps he is still alive. There is always that chance."

"No," Carl said. "I don't think so, Henri. You better go up, eh?"

"Yes," Carl heard Henri Etienne's voice catch tiredly and harshly in his throat. "Goodbye, Carl."

"Goodbye, Henri."

The small, neat man brushed by him in the faint, cloudy yellow light, waited until the *Nisba* rode high on the heave of the swell, and seizing the ladder began to climb into the darkness. Carl could feel the jerk of his weight run down the ladder and along the boat-hook.

After a minute he no longer felt the staccato jerks. Then a few seconds later, while he still waited and held the hook on to the ladder, a rope's end was lowered from above. He let go of the handle with one hand and took the rope, passing it under the crossed lashing of Etienne's bundle, knotting it untidily but securely.

"O.K.," he shouted when he had finished. "Haul it up."

The bundle rose from the deck and he raised the hook from the ladder and stepped back. The *Nisba* began to fall away in the trough of the swell and as the hull went from them, they heard the slow thump of the *Kosciuzko's* engines begin. Sheila let in the clutch and opened the throttle and as they started to pitch on the sudden frothy wash from the steamer's side she took the *Nisba* away in a wide fast curve.

Carl fitted the boat-hook into the two brackets screwed on to the side-rail of the after-deck and went into the wheelhouse.

She turned as he came up beside her. Her face looked ill and frightened and her eyes had a dazed hard shine. That was how she had looked when he told her about Roy an hour ago.

"Go on," Carl said, and took the wheel. "Go and sit down. I can keep her straight for a bit."

She moved stiffly across the tiny cabin and sat on the bulkhead locker. Her hands were clenched tightly into her stomach and her eyes looked huge in the grey, waxy face.

"Maybe he only got hurt," she muttered. "You hear about people who get away with things like that. He might not have been killed, Carl."

"No," he said firmly. "You don't want to even consider that. They were both going too fast and he meant to smash them properly. If he's alive, it might even be worse than being dead."

"Stop, Carl," she said in a soft, agonized shout. "Stop."

The *Nisba* was lifting fast and clean across the deep sea swell; the water rising high by the bows in a broad, dappled glimmer and falling away darkly along the sides. When Carl looked back over the stern, he could not see the *Kosciuzko's* riding lights.

He switched off the engine, then, and left the boat to ride free as he went across and knelt before her at the locker.

"Sheila," he said putting his big hands on her arms and gently forcing her to look straight at him. "Don't fight it and don't pretend. There isn't anything either of us can say or do. Not now. We'll just have to go through with it."

Her face dropped on to his shoulder as if her neck had suddenly been broken and he felt her quick heavy breathing. Then she raised her head and looked at him from dry, shiny eyes.

"Why did it have to happen?" she asked wearily. "Why did it have to happen now, and to him?"

"I don't know," he told her. "I truly don't know. I only know that these things happen, sometimes, and that they generally happen to people like Roy."

It was then that they saw the wide beam of the police launch searchlight shine over the water on their port bow and that the big flood of white swept across the *Nisba* and shone on the water to starboard before it was brought back again and spread blindingly on the glass of the windshield.

Hector Slade was waiting for them on the police wharf at Castleville when they came in. Carl and Sheila were sitting on the locker in the *Nisba's* wheelhouse, a sailor-hatted policeman was steering, and a superintendent named Rogers was standing beside the policeman, leaning against the bulk-head with a sad, angry look on his sun-reddened face. Carl could see Hector Slade's figure on the wharf as they came in across the basin: he would have recognized that springy, tramping stride and crisply bobbing, big head at twice the distance.

The two boats, the *Nisba* first, and then the grey, rakish water police launch, came in steadily across the calm basin and up to the still, black water by the wharf. There were deeply set, golden splinters in the water, reflected from the lights burning on the wharf and in the shed.

Carl stepped up on to the tarred planks of the jetty and reached down to help Sheila up. Her hand in his was dry and cold. They both stood and watched Hector Slade walk across to them.

"Well," he said, stopping before them. "Where is he? What did you do with him?"

His face was cold and expressionless, and the creases in it looked as if they had been grooved in wet clay and baked hard. "Where is who?" Carl asked him. "What did we do with who?"

"Carl!" Hector Slade said. "Don't be silly, man. Etienne's fingerprints were all over your car. I've already cabled for them to send down the set they have in St. Pierre. We'll find more at your place, too. How did you get him away?"

"I'm sorry, Hector, but I can't tell you anything."

I hope they didn't catch Summer, he thought. If that bloody launch was too far down the coast it won't have got up in time to catch Summer coming out.

"You, Mrs. Pearce," Hector Slade said, turning to Sheila. "Are you prepared to tell us how you smuggled a wanted alien out of British territory?"

She shook her head, staring at him with wide, shining, profoundly disinterested eyes.

"No," she muttered and her voice was so low that Carl saw Hector Slade lean forward instinctively.

"Hector," Carl said.

"Yes?"

"I don't know how you found out," Carl told him, "and I don't much care, but stop questioning us, eh? We've already been charged and arrested. We'll talk to a lawyer. But for Christ's sake leave us alone."

"Very well, Carl," Hector Slade said. His voice sounded tired and sad suddenly, the way Etienne's had been. "If you want it like that. You'll have to make a statement, of course. Both of you."

"Can I post bail for us?" Carl asked.

"Yes, naturally."

They went out, then, through the shed and into the yard behind. Hector Slade's black Chrysler was there and what seemed like all the police wagons in Cayuna. They got into the back of the Chrysler and Hector sat in front beside the driver. Nobody spoke as they drove down to the police station in Castleville and Sheila's hand in his was clammy, now, being cold, and he could feel it quivering.

At the station he answered all the questions he had to answer, and then they led him out while they questioned Sheila. He sat on one of the worn benches against the wall in the outer office.

His mind was clearing now and the dazed, mechanically efficient numbness was beginning to seep from him. And as it went, he felt the first sick pain of grief and loss form inside and a tightly swollen, aching hardness in his throat. He swallowed and leaned back against the wall, closing his eyes. He had begun to think again of the policemen who had been in the wagon. Of them, and of the people close to them who would have had the news, now, for some hours. He did not think there was anything he could say about them that would not be an impertinence.

"Carl," Hector Slack said, "are you all right?"

He opened his eyes and saw his uncle's stooping pliant figure above him, looking down, and the angry, worried expression on his tight-mouthed face.

"Yes," Carl said, speaking with difficulty. "I'm O.K., Hector. I'm sorry about the policemen in that blasted wagon. How many?"

"You've remembered them, have you?" Hector Slade said harshly. "It's about time you remembered them. Four dead, including Wally Andrews, three badly hurt, one concussion and fractured femur. He did a thorough job, the fanatical little swine."

"Did he live anytime at all?" Carl asked. He knew he had to make himself ask these questions now.

"No. He was dead when we found him. I don't want his mother to see him as he is. I've phoned Mr. McKenzie to come over and authorize immediate burial."

"Can I bury him up at the Pen?"

"Yes; if Mr. McKenzie agrees."

"Thanks. Can I see him?"

"I wouldn't, Carl."

"I want to see him, Hector. Please let me see him."

This was something else he knew he had to do.

"Come along, then; I'll take you down."

Carl could remember several occasions on which this tall, grey man had spoken to him like this, but he did not think that there had ever been such gentleness and understanding in his voice as there was now.

They went outside and got into the Chrysler again and Hector Slade drove swiftly across the town to the morgue. Roy's body was no better than he had imagined, but no worse. Standing there in the damp air of the little room, with the sound of the ice blocks dripping into the zinc runnels around the table, Carl told himself that he had seen bodies as bad as this during the war. It said nothing to him, and he could feel nothing more than what he was feeling; but coming here was the last thing he had to do for Roy, except of course to see that he was buried at the Pen.

Back at the station, they found Sheila waiting for them in the outer office. Someone had given her a mug of coffee and she was holding it between her hands, in her lap, staring at it in a puzzled, absent way as if it was something utterly strange that had materialized while she was asleep. She looked up when they came in and they could see the weirdly bright, perfectly dry eyes. Her lips moved but no sound came from them and she looked down again on to the steaming brown surface of the coffee.

Hector Slade touched Carl's arm and went ahead of him into the superintendent's office where they had been questioned.

"What's up with her?" he asked Carl, jerking his head abruptly in the direction of the room where Sheila sat. "Has being caught scared her that much? She must have bargained for that when she went into this. Or is it the dead men that's horrified her?"

Carl told him.

"I should have known," Hector Slade said. "Roy McKenzie," he went on reflectively. "I thought I understood him. I didn't, though. I didn't think he would do a thing like this."

"Why not?" Carl asked him. "Would you have respected him if he hadn't?"

Hector Slade did not answer.

"Are you finished with us, Hector?" Carl continued. "Can we leave now?"

"Yes," Hector Slade said, and as they went to the door, "Would you have stopped him if you could?"

"I honestly don't know, Hector. Maybe. Maybe if I had got the chance I'd have forgotten what I'd promised to do for Etienne and stopped him. What would you have done if you'd been me?"

"You mean if I'd had a chance to stop him?"

"Yes."

"I don't know."

They went into the room where Sheila was sitting as they had left her. Carl took the mug from her hands and put it on the bench beside her.

"Come on," he said, and she rose obediently. "I'll take you home. Not Tolliver. My place. You can come down in the morning. Is that all right with you, Hector?"

"Yes," Hector Slade told him. "So long as I know where you are. You can go up in my car."

They went out and got into the black Chrysler for the last time. It was past four in the morning and it was very cool and Carl smelt rain on the mountains.

She leaned against him as they drove into the hills. Her body was stiff and yet she was trembling continuously and she would not look at him but stared out of the window at the heavy, pre-dawn blackness of the countryside. He did not try to say anything to her, and he was not sure that if he spoke he could hold the swollen pressure in his chest and throat.

They seemed to reach Brandt's Pen very quickly. The lights were on in the house, and Carl knew that the servants must have heard about it and that they would be awake and talking in the back. He did not want to see any of them now except Delia or Tom.

When they got out of the car, the policeman who had driven them up did not look at them or say good night. He stared before him and started the engine as soon as they had stepped into the drive. Carl had barely time to close the door.

He took Sheila by the arm and led her inside. She was walking with stiff, careful steps.

He left her in the big chair opposite the sofa and went over to the liquor cabinet. When he looked round, the bottle in his hand, he saw that she was crying. She was making no noise but her whole body has heaving in slow, agonized constrictions.

"I didn't want to cry before them," she panted as he came over and put his arm around her.

He said nothing, but held her lightly and firmly, trying to forget what he was feeling so that he could console her better.

When he looked up from the top of the glossy head which was rocking slowly against his chest, he saw Delia standing in the doorway. She was dressed in her housecoat but the iron-grey hair was pinned as neatly as ever. Tom was standing behind her, looking over her shoulder. They were both faces he was very glad to see just then.

"Is true, Mass' Carl?" Delia asked him. "Is true what dem say happen to Mass' Roy?"

He nodded slowly.

"At first we hear say was you in de car, too," she told him. Only her level eyes in the firm, still youthful face showed what her real age must be. "Den de police come up here, fe' ask question, an' we hear was not you get killed. We don't tell dem anyt'ing, though. Even if we did know what dem was asking, we wouldn't tell dem anyt'ing. Mass' Roy did go easy, sah? Him didn't suffer too long?"

"No," he said, speaking over the shaking body he held against him. "I don't think he felt much, Delia. I think he went pretty easy."

"T'ank God. You want anything now, Mass' Carl?"

He shook his head and gestured with his chin to where Sheila's head rested on his chest. Delia nodded and turned from the doorway and went back down the passage. Tom followed her.

Sheila did not cry for very long. She finished what she could not help doing and sat up, wiping her eyes and smoothing back her hair. Carl watched her as she deliberately and patiently put away the tears and became more like herself. It was not the least handsome thing he had seen another person do. He went and mixed two drinks at the cabinet, putting ginger ale in hers and taking soda water for himself. He brought them back to where she was sitting.

"Thanks," she said steadily, taking her drink and pressing his hand quickly. "I'll be all right now."

"Good," he said, sitting on the big leather ottoman beside the chair. "Just drink that and we'll have another. Talk if you want to."

"No," she told him, "I don't want to talk. And I don't want to cry any more."

Neither do I, he thought. I don't want to talk and I couldn't cry even if it would do any good. But, Jesus, we do get mixed up with other people's lives. We get mixed up in all sorts of ways. People don't seem able to leave each other alone.

The wind around the house was much stronger now, blowing in long steady gusts between the calm. As it moved among the leaves and across the grass, it sounded like the moaning of a river when you hear it coming from the mountains far away.

ABOUT THE AUTHOR

John Hearne was born in Canada of Jamaican parents in 1926. He lived and worked in Jamaica most of his life, teaching, lecturing at the university and working as a journalist. He was the author of six highly praised novels: *Voices under the Window* (1955), *Stranger at the Gate* (1956), *The Faces of Love* [*The Eye of the Storm* in the USA] (1957), *The Autumn Equinox* (1959), *Land of the Living* (1961) and *The Sure Salvation* (1981). A posthumous collection of his stories, *John Hearne's Short Fiction* was published in 2016. With Morris Cargill (writing as John Morris) he jointly authored three crime/ adventure novels: *Fever Grass* (1969), *The Candywine Development* (1970) and *The Checkerboard Caper* (1975).

His daughter, Shivaun Hearne, published an insightful and very honest account of his life, *John Hearne's Life and Fiction: A Critical Biographical Study* (2013).

He won the prestigious John Llewllyn Rhys Prize for *Voices under the Window*. He was an incisive critic and provocative commentator in the Jamaican press. He died in 1994.

ALSO AVAILABLE BY JOHN HEARNE

Voices Under the Window
ISBN: 9781845230319; pp. 145; pub. 1955, 2005; £7.99

Mark Lattimer is chopped by a stranger in the heat of a riot. He has been attacked because he looks white and middle class, though he is a politically committed lawyer working for the poor and the nationalist movement in Jamaica. Now he is trapped, brought to bleed his life away in a small, airless room, cut off from doctors, ambulances, police. As he dies, he talks to his companions, his black lover and a fellow party worker, and drifts into memories of his past: his privileged childhood, his time in London and the RAF, his affairs and marriage and the moment when he gives his allegiance to the poor. But now what meaning can be given to his life and death?

First published sixty-five years ago, *Voices Under the Window* was reissued in association with the Calabash International Literary Festival Trust in 2005 as a work that, in the words of Colin Channer, is a 'Molotov cocktail that ignites important questions of race and power ... questions still burning in Kingston today.' In his insightful introduction, Kwame Dawes finds in *Voices* a novel that is wholly contemporary in its treatment of the personal and the political, that lives because it is a 'deftly crafted work full of a sense of place and time, a work of psychological intensity and literary elegance.